THE TITANS

*Further Titles by Christopher Nicole
from Severn House*

OLD GLORY
THE SEA AND THE SAND
IRON SHIPS, IRON MEN
WIND OF DESTINY
RAGING SEA, SEARING SKY
THE PASSION AND THE GLORY

BLACK MAJESTY VOL. 1: THE SEEDS OF REBELLION
BLACK MAJESTY VOL. 2: WILD HARVEST

HEROES
THE FRIDAY SPY

THE SUN AND THE DRAGON
THE SUN ON FIRE
THE SHIP WITH NO NAME

CARIBEE

DAYS OF WINE AND ROSES?
THE TITANS

THE TITANS

A Novel

CHRISTOPHER NICOLE

This first world edition published in Great Britain 1992 by
SEVERN HOUSE PUBLISHERS LTD of
35 Manor Road, Wallington, Surrey SM6 0BW.
First published in the U.S.A. 1992 by
SEVERN HOUSE PUBLISHERS INC of
475 Fifth Avenue, New York, NY 10017

British Library Cataloguing-in-Publication Data
Nicole, Christopher, 1930–
  The Titans.
  I. Title
  823.914 [F]

  ISBN 0 – 7278 – 4319 – 2

Printed and bound in Great Britain by
Billing and Sons Ltd, Worcester

CONTENTS

This is a novel.

All the non-naval personnel and those under flag rank are invented, save in one or two identifiable cameos, and are not intended to portray real persons, living or dead.

Mr Winston Churchill and all officers in either the Royal or German Navy of flag rank are based upon actual characters, and are drawn as accurately as their letters, telegrams and the records of the time allow.

The historical background and battle scenes are also as accurate as the purposes of the novel will allow.

All the vessels depicted are real, with the following five exceptions:

HMS *Anson*, indicated as one of the St Vincent Dreadnought class.

HMS *Arrow*, a destroyer.

SMS *Roon*, indicated as one of the Moltke class battlecruisers.

The French pre-Dreadnought *Wagram*.

These fictional ships lead to an occasional minimal discrepancy in the number of ships involved in certain actions.

HM Submarine *C17*.

PART ONE

Wind and Water

CHAPTER 1

The Disaster

'First blood,' Harry Krantz said. 'I think we should drink a toast to the Battle of Heligoland Bight.'

Harry Krantz wore the insignia of a commander in the American Navy, and was thus, in the late summer of 1914, supposedly a neutral observer of the greatest war the world had yet known. But even had he not married into the British naval family of Dawsons, there would have been no doubt where his sympathies lay.

'Absolutely,' Captain Geoffrey Young agreed. 'Those lucky beggars.'

The pair were brothers-in-law, married to sisters. But Geoffrey was also captain of HMS *Anson*, a super-dread-nought of the Royal Navy's Home Fleet. That Harry had applied to serve as US Naval Attaché with the battle squadron, and specifically with *Anson*, had been at once partly because of the relationship, which had grown out of an old friendship – they had both served, as attachés, on board Admiral Togo's flagship at the Battle of Tsushima, nine years earlier – and partly because he, like most naval observers, believed that the decision at sea was going to be reached when the two greatest navies in the world, the British Grand Fleet and the German High Seas Fleet, met in combat.

But in this early stage of the war, the great ships' thunder had been stolen by the cruisers and destroyers, supported by the 'killer cats', the battlecruisers of Admiral Jackie Fisher's dream, in the first naval action of the conflict.

'Both the boys are all right, aren't they?' Harry was anxious. A large, somewhat gangling man even in his mid-thirties, he could look like a worried bloodhound. 'I haven't seen the casualty figures.'

3

He was referring to his two more immediate brothers-in-law, Peter Dawson and Giles Dawson. Peter was a watch-keeping lieutenant on board the battlecruiser *Invincible*, and Giles was sub-lieutenant on board HM Submarine *E4*. It was the Dawson tradition, inherited from their father and grandfather – admirals both – to enter the Navy, just as it was the Dawson tradition for their daughters to marry naval officers. Now it seemed to matter more than ever that the tradition be upheld and enhanced, because of the tragedies of this generation, which had led the eldest daughter, Georgina, and the eldest son, Jack, to involvement in the great spy scandal of 1906, and had resulted in Gina's suicide and Jack's lengthy term of imprisonment, following which he had disappeared, his social life, no less than his career, ruined.

'The boys are all right,' Geoffrey assured his friend. Altogether smaller, he was as precise in feature and manner as he was in dress and attitude. 'And the casualty figures are stupendous. Three German cruisers and a destroyer sunk, and some sixteen hundred casualties. We lost a hundred men and not a ship. Mind you, none of their heavy stuff got involved . . .'

'Probably wisely,' Harry grinned. 'There must be some sore heads in the Wilhelmstrasse tonight.'

'A win!' Harriet Dawson boomed, entering the bedroom and waving *The Times*. 'The German Navy has been absolutely routed. And *Invincible* was there. Peter was there. Oh, Geoffrey and Harry must be green with envy.'

Harriet, widow of Rear-Admiral Ralph Dawson, and mother of six children, was a large, loud woman who had only been temporarily crushed by the catastrophe of her eldest son and daughter.

Baby Mark wailed as Mary Young moved him from her right breast and settled him into the crook of her left arm.

'Hush, dearest,' she whispered as the baby whinged frantically for the second half of his feed. Tall and broad-shouldered, fair-haired and conventionally pretty, Mary had always seemed the strongest of the Dawsons. Her mother thoroughly enjoyed having her in residence 'for the duration,' as it was put, but there were times when she felt her daughter's priorities were confused.

'Aren't you pleased?' she demanded. 'We have beaten the German Navy. I am sure Geoffrey is pleased.'

'I am sure he is too. But it was a very small part of the German Navy, Ma. Is Peter all right? And Giles?'

'Well, they must be. We suffered hardly any casualties. Oh, I am so happy for them. If only we could get a letter from Lizzie, now, to say she's actually arrived, in this Connecticut place . . .'

For Harry Krantz had insisted that his wife, the youngest Dawson daughter, leave the War Zone and visit with his family in the States. Elizabeth had been reluctant to abandon the rest of *her* family, in all the circumstances, but she was too much in love with her American husband to argue.

'A brilliant action, don't you agree?' Winston Churchill asked the Commander-in-Chief in the Admiral's day cabin on board *Iron Duke*.

As First Lord to the Admiralty Churchill was fond of getting up to Scapa Flow to see his ships whenever possible.

Vice-Admiral Sir John Jellicoe did not look all that pleased; his face, always indicating the very precise mind that lay behind the tight features, was even more severe than usual. 'It could have been a most unmitigated disaster, First Lord.'

'Oh, come now, four ships sunk, to nil?'

'Four not very important ships,' Jellicoe pointed out. 'The fact is that Beatty hazarded the battlecruiser squadron for very little return. He calls it using a sledgehammer to crack a nut. And that is exactly what happened.'

'But the nut was cracked,' Churchill pointed out. 'In fact, it was crushed out of existence.'

'Yes,' Jellicoe said, drily. 'Have you studied the reports of the torpedo attack on the battlecruiser squadron?'

'It seems to have been a complete failure.'

'Because it was not pressed home. Oh, I'll agree the ships seem to have been handled quite splendidly. But

5

the fact remains there were only two or three torpedoes fired.'

'We caught them napping. And were going too fast for them to get into the best position.'

'Perhaps. But think of what might have happened, had a couple, or even one, of those torpedoes struck home. I am bound to say, First Lord, that every time I take the Grand Fleet to sea, looking for the enemy, I feel as if I am walking on very thin ice indeed.'

Churchill lit a cigar. Jellicoe had had a very distinguished career, both at sea and on land. He was also the protégé of the immortal Jackie Fisher, who only five years earlier had retired from the position of First Sea Lord. It had always been Fisher's intention that Jellicoe should command the Grand Fleet should, or rather, as everyone had known, *when*, hostilities with Germany become certain. He had now been commander-in-chief for just over a month, and the First Lord had been hoping for a more aggressive spirit.

'I think you are letting this torpedo thing worry you unnecessarily, Jellicoe,' he remarked. 'I do not believe that a fast-moving warship is ever at risk from a slow-moving submarine. Of course, if a ship has been crippled by gunfire, that is a different matter. Surely that was the lesson of Tsushima, and surely that is what happened off Heligoland?'

'I hope you're right, First Lord,' Jellicoe said unhappily.

'Besides,' Churchill added, 'if we are going to spend all our time worrying about torpedoes, we'd never take the fleet to sea at all.'

'His Majesty is not amused,' Vizeadmiral Franz von Hipper told his captains.

Neither were they, he judged, looking over the row of grim faces in front of him. Despite his efforts to encourage them in the aftermath of the fiasco – the failure of the German battlecruiser squadron to reach Heligoland until the battle was long over – now they had had time to think about it, and to read and listen to the British cries of triumph, he understood the work would have to be done all over again.

'Nor, frankly, is Grosseadmiral Tirpitz,' Hipper continued, stroking the short beard which dominated his otherwise cleanshaven face. 'He feels he has been placed in an invidious position. The Kaiser has always been a reluctant adherent of our greater Navy policy. He would far rather have spent the money on the Army. That he went along with our plans was because we were able to persuade him that our fleet would be able to take on the British with every hope of success. Now all he can see is that the British can with impunity raid into our coastal waters and go away again, having sunk four of our ships, with hardly any loss to themselves. He finds this intolerable.'

The captains made no comment; they found it pretty intolerable themselves.

'I have therefore called you here today,' Hipper said. 'To tell you again that this so-called battle in the Heligoland Bight was no more serious to us, and no more disruptive to our plans, than a pinprick. Let the British call it a great victory. We know better. It cannot be repeated; the area is now being sewn with mines. Now, obviously we have lessons to learn. One is that we must be quicker at raising steam and getting our ships to sea. This we are going to work on. But our overall strategic plan of whittling down the Royal Navy to a size where we can defeat it, is proceeding.'

'Is there news of Kapitan Baron von Eltz, Herr Vizeadmiral?'

'Yes. I am happy to assure you that Kapitan von Eltz is making a full recovery from his unfortunate *accident* . . .' he looked from face to face. 'And will soon resume command of SMS *Roon*. Thank you, gentlemen.'

Hipper considered Bruno von Eltz the most difficult officer he had ever had to handle. Not for any lack of discipline or dedication to duty. His purpose, to serve the Fatherland, was etched in those handsome features. But Bruno von Eltz, Hipper reflected, owing to his position in society, and the fact

7

that he was a baron and had inherited a vast newspaper and publishing chain and had yet elected to remain in the Navy, and even more, his involvement in the Dawson spy scandal and his sister's absurd decision to marry a Frenchman – who also happened to be a naval officer.

That he was very highly strung, Hipper had always known. That the crazy young fool would take the failure of the German battlecruiser squadron to engage the British so strongly as to attempt suicide . . . really, he should be cashiered.

But Bruno was such a talented man. And there were those mitigating circumstances.

But he would have to be watched, carefully, in the future.

'Ah, Herr Furrer.' Bruno von Eltz sat in armchair in his bedroom at Scholl Esjling, and held out his hand. He looked a trifle pale, but otherwise perfectly healthy; only the fact that he was wearing pyjamas and a smoking jacket, and that he was at the schloss instead of with the fleet, indicated that the rumours were true. 'I hope you did not mind my asking you to call?'

'I am flattered, Herr Baron,' said the Swiss correspondent, giving a little bow as he shook hands. 'May I inquire after the Baron's health?'

'It is mending,' Bruno said, staring at him.

'Am am happy to hear that, sir. Then you will soon be returning to your command?'

'Yes,' Bruno said. 'There is a war on.'

'Of course, Herr Baron. Of course.' Furrer was picking his words with great care. Everyone knew that von Eltz had attempted suicide; one does not consume a whole bottle of sleeping pills by accident, however determined the German Navy seemed to wish that to be accepted. But why? A man like Bruno von Eltz, rich, powerful, sophisticated . . . the man who discovered the truth would have a scoop on his hands. 'It would be a great privilege to visit you on board your vessel.' He gave a deprecating smile. 'My people know little about ships.'

'Why should they? Schnapps?'

'Why, thank you very much.'

'Carl?'

The valet, who had reluctantly donned uniform to be with his master even in wartime, and was wearing it now, hurried forward with two glasses. That despite his inheritance Bruno von Eltz insisted upon serving in the Navy, and taking orders from upstarts like Franz Hipper, remained a mystery to his servants and staff – they presumed it had something to do with his so-beautiful, so-profligate, sister.

And they were quite right.

'Sit down,' Bruno invited.

'Thank you.' Furrer seated himself, carefully folding the tails of his coat across his thighs. 'But you will understand, Herr Baron, that I will need some technical data to support anything I report.'

'Technical data?'

'About ships and sea battles. My readers have no understanding of these matters.'

'Ah, you are speaking of the action off Heligoland. I did not ask you here to talk about that.'

'Oh?' Furrer was clearly disappointed.

'I assure you, Herr Furrer, it was a very minor affair, no matter how the British have blown it up out of all proportion.'

'I see,' Furrer remarked, sceptically. He had read the English accounts of their 'great victory', and he had talked with some of the German sailors on their return to port, and had gathered the opinion that the sailors at least were bitterly disappointed that they should have missed what could have been the first big naval action of the war.

Bruno sat down and crossed his knees. 'I asked you to come down, Herr Furrer, because I believe you may be able to help me.'

'Anything, Herr Baron.' However disappointed that he was not going to be given some kind of exclusive on what had gone wrong at Heligoland, Furrer was genuinely pleased to be approached for help by a man such as the Baron von

Eltz – he had in his time received a lot of copy from the Eltz Newspapers . . . and given them quite a lot of news in return – suitably selected, of course: Hermann Furrer was not at all what he appeared, although Bruno did not know that.

He was also still hoping to learn the truth about that overdose of sleeping pills.

'The matter is of course confidential.'

'Of course, Herr Baron.'

'It concerns my sister,' Bruno said.

'Ah!' Furrer stayed carefully non-committal. He had never met the famous Helene, but what he had heard of her he did not like.

'You know she is married to a French naval officer?'

'Most regrettable,' Furrer murmured.

'Yes, in the present circumstances. I have had no contact whatsoever with her since the outbreak of war. My editor tells me she tried to telephone me on the very day war was declared, but naturally she did not get through; my ship was already halfway down the Kiel Canal. Since then, nothing.'

'I see,' Furrer said, thoughtfully. 'You would like me to see about getting her out of France?'

'Well, of course, if that were possible. But I am not sure she would be allowed to come; she rather foolishly accepted French citizenship on her marriage. That means she is obviously in a difficult position. I have written her a letter, and I would like her to get it. I would also like to receive a reply from her. Can you arrange this for me?'

'Well . . .'

'I will, of course, pay for your services,' Bruno said. 'Would a thousand marks cover all your expenses?'

'A thousand marks! Why, Herr Baron . . .'

'It is most important to me,' Bruno told him.

Most important. He had been relieved to have Helene well out of the way in Paris, so relieved that he had left her there when he might have had a chance to bring her home. Now she was forced to remain there, where her outspoken patriotism might well land her in trouble . . . He still did not want her at home – he knew now that their incestuous relationship had

10

been the prime cause of that deep depression that had driven him to attempt suicide – but he did wish to reassure himself that she was all right, and equally reassure her that he had not forgotten her: she was his only living relative.

'I shall be most happy to undertake such a mission, Herr Baron.'

'Good.' Bruno got up and took two envelopes from his desk. 'The one is addressed to Madame Tonnheur, the other to Herr Reuger, my managing editor. In it is the order for the thousand marks. If you will visit him first . . .'

'Of course, Herr Baron.' Furrer gathered that the interview was at an end. He had been summoned as an underling, given his instructions, and dismissed. For all his charm, Bruno von Eltz really had no feeling for those he supposed inferior to himself. The poor fool had no idea that he, Hermann Furrer, was doing far more to win the war for the Fatherland than all of his pretty ships put together.

Furrer drained his glass. 'May I wish the German Navy good fortune in its next encounter?'

Bruno, who had done no more than taste the schnapps, was oblivious to any intended sarcasm.

'The German Navy makes its own fortune, Furrer. Just wait, and read the newspapers.' He forced a smile. 'And count, as the British ships go down.'

On 5 September, HMS *Pathfinder*, a light cruiser, was sunk off St Abbs' Head. The survivors were unanimous in claiming that they had been torpedoed. The Admiralty was equally determined that they had struck a floating mine, and this was the official verdict. Just over a fortnight later, however, there could be no argument that the torpedo was, after all, a potent weapon.

Prince Louis of Battenburg, gazed at Churchill as the First Lord read the report.

Slowly Churchill raised his head.

'*Aboukir*, *Hogue* and *Cressy*, all sunk? Within half an hour? I'm afraid I just do not see how that could have happened,

11

Prince Louis. How many submarines were in the attacking force?'

Prince Louis gulped. 'As far as can be ascertained, First Lord, there was only one submarine involved.'

'One? For God's sake . . .'

'The trouble was, First Lord, that when *Aboukir* was hit, and she went down rather quickly, *Hogue* and *Cressy* stopped to pick up survivors.'

'They didn't look for the U-boat first?'

'Well, she had disappeared, and I imagine they supposed that having made a successful attack, she had gone away.'

'But she hadn't,' Churchill said grimly.

'No. She had dived below periscope depths in anticipation of counter-action, and when there was none, she returned to the attack. *Cressy* and *Hogue* were stopped by then, their boats down. They were sitting ducks.'

'When will these people learn that we are fighting a war?' Churchill demanded. 'Heroics are all very well, but the destruction of the enemy comes first. How many dead?'

'I'm afraid rather a lot, First Lord. The three cruisers had a total complement of two thousand two hundred. Only about eight hundred have been picked up.'

'Well, issue the sternest orders to all commanders that picking up survivors in future will have to wait until the attacking force, whether under or on the surface, has either been destroyed or has definitely withdrawn.'

Prince Louis nodded. 'What are you going to do?'

Churchill's shoulders sagged for a moment.

'What can I do, save put the best face on it? You too. But we need to get something back. What is the latest news of von Spee?'

Apart from a couple of isolated vessels, the only German naval strength at large at the outbreak of war had been the Pacific Squadron, based upon the Chinese port of Tsing-tao. This little fleet of fast commerce destroyers had not been taken too seriously, until after war had been declared, when it had been learned in London that it had been secretly reinforced by two very modern, powerful, heavy cruisers – *Scharnhorst* and *Gneisenau* – under the command of one of Germany's best known admirals, Graf von Spee.

'That's not very good either. The Japanese assumption that after leaving Tsing-tao Spee was making a westerly passage through the Indian Ocean and around the Cape of Good Hope was wrong. At least, he hasn't been sighted. He is at present lost somewhere in the Central Pacific, but he is accompanied by several colliers and we are now certain that he is making east, probably slowly both to conserve fuel and to escort them. But . . . he seems to have detached one of his cruisers to go west. This may have been a decoy. But there is at least a chance that she's out to destroy commerce. We've already had reports of Tahiti being bombarded by an enemy vessel. It has to be this one.'

'If an enemy raider gets loose in the Bay of Bengal with our transports still at sea . . . she must be tracked down and caught. Tell the Japanese we want all the assistance they can give in this matter. What big ships have we available out there?'

'The best we have on the spot is *Sydney*. She's five-and-a-half thousand tons and has eight six-inch guns. She also makes twenty-five knots. That makes her bigger, faster, and more heavily armed than any of Spee's light cruisers. She's also Australian manned, as you would expect . . . and the enemy will soon be in Australian waters, if he isn't already.'

'Good. Detail *Sydney* to find that raider and sink her. Send that request to Tokyo as well, however. Now, von Spee . . . if he were to get through and reach home we'd really be on the spot. But . . . he's crossing the Pacific. That means, even with colliers attached, he has to coal, and top them up, when he gets to the American side, because he knows he's not going to get the opportunity in the Atlantic. Where would be his best bet?'

'Assuming he must replenish before tackling the Atlantic, First Lord, I would say almost certainly Chile. Somewhere like Valparaiso.'

'How friendly are the Chileans to Germany?'

'A shade too much so, perhaps. But I'm sure they will abide by international law.'

'So von Spee will have three days to coal and then put to sea again. I assume we have a reliable man in Valparaiso?'

'Oh, indeed, First Lord.'

'So, at least for those three days we'll know where he is. When do you calculate he'll reach the South American coast?'

'That's an imponderable, because we don't actually know what he's doing now, where he is, or how fast he's travelling. He could get there at any time at all. By the end of the month, certainly.'

'And Sir Christopher Cradock is waiting for him.'

'Ah . . . with, at present, an inferior force, First Lord.'

'Which we are turning into a superior force as rapidly as possible,' Churchill reminded him. 'When will *Canopus* reach Port Stanley?'

'She should be there next week.'

'That doesn't give Cradock much time. I wish him told that he must seek out and destroy von Spee as soon as is possible. It is vitally important that he does this. You are quite certain that he will have the necessary force?'

'Once *Canopus* joins him, absolutely. She's a battleship. Her twelve-inch guns could sink those two armoured cruisers of Spee's on their own, quite apart from *Good Hope* and *Monmouth*.'

'Then let's sit back and hope for some good news,' Churchill said. 'What's this?' He gazed at the envelope Prince Louis had placed on his desk.

'My resignation, First Lord.'

'Your what? What on earth for? This disaster with the cruisers has nothing to do with you.'

'I'm not resigning because of any losses we may have suffered. But I'm afraid I have come to the conclusion that my presence here is not conducive to the best results.'

Churchill leaned back in his chair. 'That is nonsense, if you don't mind my saying so.'

'Do you read the papers?'

14

'As little as possible.'

'Well, I have been figuring very largely in them recently. A German in command of Royal Navy, etc, etc.'

'I have never heard such rubbish.'

'With respect, First Lord, my father is a general in the Kaiser's army.'

'Can a man be responsible for his own father?' Churchill demanded, with feeling. 'You have been a British naval officer all your life. For God's sake, your son is in the Navy. You want to ignore such claptrap.'

'I'm afraid I cannot. I am also afraid that it may be the attitude held by some of our people.'

'Name the officer.'

'I am not thinking of the officers, First Lord.'

The two men gazed at each other. Then Churchill snapped his fingers. 'Do you think I can replace you, just like that?'

'I am sure you can.'

'Well, I am not going to. Not at this juncture. We have too much on our plates. When this von Spee business is sorted out, perhaps. We'll talk about it then.'

'Three cruisers all in one morning. Gentlemen, Heligoland Bight is avenged. And I do assure you that is but the beginning. The race is not always to the strongest.' Hipper raised his glass. 'Gentlemen, I give you: Korvettenkapitan Weddingen. He is the first true naval hero of this War. I trust, I know, that you will all emulate him when the time comes.'

Alfred von Weddingen! Helene Tonnheur hummed happily as she cut the photograph from the newspaper and pasted it into her scrapbook.

He was a good-looking fellow, quite handsome, with clean-shaven, incisive features. A born latter-day pirate, or U-boat commander. The sort of man she should have married, she knew. He husband had clean-shaven, incisive features – but he was French.

And now he was far away. Helene was relieved about that. She had married with all the passion of her passionate nature.

Partly this had been because she wished to cock a snook at the Kaiser and the entire German establishment: they had been happy enough to make use of her beauty and her courage to obtain the specifications of the first *Dreadnought* battleship, but when she had completed her mission they had thought of her only as some kind of *femme fatale*, to be shunned by polite society.

Even Bruno had thought that, compounded by that unforgettable night when they had fallen into each other's arms, as lovers rather than brother and sister. The memory of that night had become a haunting nightmare to Bruno, made him obviously anxious to be rid of her.

Just as she had no doubt it had been a prime cause of his 'accident'. She had been so terrified at that news, had thought him dead. When she had learned that he was alive, her fear and grief had been replaced by anger, that he should attempt such a thing. Yet she still wished she could be with him.

It had been because of that night, and Bruno's guilt, she had set her cap at the French naval attaché, in the days when war had seemed remote. And when Helene von Eltz, five feet ten inches of utter beauty, her strong, handsome face cloaked in her flowing midnight hair, set her cap at anyone, resistance was useless. Only one man, that bastard Jack Dawson, had been able to resist her . . . and she had seen that he went to gaol.

Pierre Tonnheur had not wanted to resist her. But he had been no less of a bastard. Within a year of their marriage she had discovered he kept a mistress. A mistress . . . when he had Helene von Eltz, perhaps the most beautiful woman in Europe, as his wife!

She had wanted to end the marriage then, and he had refused. She had appealed to Bruno for help, and Bruno had merely laughed at her. They were all bastards. The coming of the War had sealed her imprisonment within France.

But the war had been a blessing in many ways. It had taken Pierre away from her side, to command a battleship in the French Navy. And it was being won by Germany. Nobody could argue that fact, on land, with the sound of the guns clearly audible in Paris. But everyone had said, at sea the British are supreme. Helene wondered what they would say now, as she gazed at Weddingen's face, smiling at her from the pages.

The door opened and Henri, her butler, brought in the tray of coffee.

Helene smiled at him. Even Frenchmen were acceptable today.

'Sad news, madame,' Henri remarked, as he set down the tray.

'Oh, yes,' Helene said happily. 'I am sure there will soon be more sad news. Much more.'

'Where the devil is she?' Rear-Admiral Sir Christopher Cradock growled, standing on the bridge of HMS *Good Hope* and staring out of the Port Stanley harbour mouth to sea. Most of his officers were doing the same.

As they had done every morning for the past week.

Even Cradock's personal servant Jack Smith had got hold of a pair of binoculars and clambered into the rigging, the better to see.

Canopus was overdue.

Everything seemed overdue. If the weather was at last warming up, it appeared that summer in the Falkland Islands was not going to be a matter of lounging in the sun. There was very seldom a sun at all, and the islands remained windswept and bleak.

When the squadron had first arrived, the islanders themselves had been delighted to have the three naval ships based at Port Stanley. Business had boomed for the few shops, and the equally scarce unattached young women had had the time of their lives. But there had not been sufficient of either women or goods to go round, and the men had soon become bored. Charges had multiplied, which had led to more discontent. There had been a rash of fights.

At least there was an end in sight. Cradock had his orders to go looking for the enemy as soon as *Canopus* arrived. But where was the battleship?

And then . . . smoke. Jack Smith checked again to make sure, then slid down to the deck, and hurried up the ladders to the bridge.

'Begging your pardon, sir,' he said.

Cradock turned his head to look at his orderly. Whenever he did this, a reflective expression crossed his face. The two men made a considerable contrast: the Admiral slim and smart, his neat, greying beard as much as the set of his lips indicating the essential confidence of the man; the seaman tall and heavy, yellow-haired and bearded – although this was also streaked with gray – and open-featured, even if the ready smile too often hid behind the habitual grimness of his expression. Smith had only joined the Navy a year before, but had served in the Merchant Navy before that – so he said. Yet every time Cradock looked at him he was certain he had seen him before. 'Yes, Smith. What is it?'

'Smoke to the north-east, sir.'

Cradock turned back again, and now the smoke was visible even from the lower position. 'Thank God for that.'

It was 18 October; the battleship was a fortnight overdue.

'Have you seen Cradock's telegram?' Prince Louis asked.

'Not a very happy one,' Churchill agreed. 'Just our luck that *Canopus* should arrive with engine trouble.'

'She was probably pushed too hard to get down there,' Battenberg said. 'Still, if she really can only make twelve knots, and she's only just arrived, this rather negates our plans to take von Spee on the Chilean coast.'

'I don't see why it should,' Churchill argued. 'I agree that it seems unlikely Cradock can reach Valparaiso before the Germans, but having crossed the Pacific, von Spee has to be heading for the Atlantic, and the only way he can get there is either round Cape Horn or through the Canal. I consider the latter most unlikely, as once he is in the Canal he is really pin-pointed. So, my bet is he will go for the Horn, after coaling. He will still need to do that by the most direct route, as there will be no more coaling – except if we suppose he can sneak in and out of the Falklands themselves – until

18

he gets home. That means coming straight down the coast. It seems to me that even if Cradock has to reduce his speed to twelve knots, he should be able to take up a position to cover the Horn, and force Spee to battle. With *Canopus* as his citadel, he can't lose. And if von Spee turns back, well, he'll be lost anyway; he'll either run out of fuel or run into the Japanese. Ascertain Cradock's intentions.'

'You mean to suggest to him that he should not wait for *Canopus* to be repaired?'

'Can she be, in Stanley?'

'Well . . . not very thoroughly.'

'Then she must fight as she is. Inform Cradock that is our wish. The important thing is, to fight.'

'Gentlemen.' Cradock looked over the faces of his five captains, for the armed merchant cruiser *Otranto* had also now joined the squadron. 'I have just cabled the Admiralty to inform them that tomorrow morning we leave Stanley for the West Coast of America. To find von Spee.'

The officers exchanged glances, while Jack Smith served tea.

'I understand,' Cradock went on, 'that this means I am not allowing time for *Canopus* to have her engines overhauled. I'm afraid you will have to bear with it, Wilcox. But the fact is, we simply have to stop Spee getting into the Atlantic, and our information indicates that he could be off the Chilean coast at any moment. I'm amazed he has not appeared yet. In any event, that is where I intend to stop him. He will have to coal, and that will give us our best chance. Now, he may try to fox us by dodging back and forth; we must be prepared for a long wait. I therefore intend to take our colliers with us, and if necessary coal at sea. They cannot make more than twelve knots, so *Canopus* will accompany them while the rest of us will press on and see what we can find.'

'With respect, Sir Christopher,' Captain Wilcox objected. 'As I understood my instructions before leaving England, no engagement was to be undertaken without *Canopus* in support. It was felt that *Good Hope* and *Monmouth* stood no chance against *Scharnhorst* and *Gneisenau*.'

The other captains nodded their heads in agreement, but Cradock bristled.

'No chance? There is always a chance, where ships are well and resolutely handled. In any event, I have not said I intend to engage Spee without the support of *Canopus*, Captain Wilcox. I have said that I intend to find out where the Germans are. Once we know that, we will make our tactical dispositions. We sail at dawn. Thank you, gentlemen.'

The captains filed out, and Cradock looked at Jack.

'I suppose you agree with them.'

'Sir?'

'That I'm taking a risk by not sticking close to the battleship.'

'I wouldn't know, sir.'

'Ever been in action, Smith?'

'Ah . . . no, sir.'

The hesitation had only been momentary, but yet again Cradock felt there was more to this man than met the eye.

'Well, neither have I, at sea. But neither have the Germans. In fact, there has never been a German fleet action, or even squadron action, in history. I think that's something people tend to forget. We have the background, the knowhow, the experience. They are still learning. That is going to mean a lot.'

'I read somewhere, sir, that *Scharnhorst* has the reputation of being the best gunnery ship in the German Navy,' Jack ventured.

'Target practice,' Cradock said scornfully. 'It's a different matter when it's the real thing.'

Rounding Cape Horn from east to west meant going into the prevailing weather. This had been quite good when the squadron left Port Stanley, but as it steamed south the clouds built, and off the Horn they encountered a full gale.

The waves were mountainous; they seemed higher than the bridge, as the ship went up and up and up, aiming, it

20

seemed, for the sky, and then slid down the trough on the far side with a sickening lurch. This was when the next wave looked at its biggest, looming above the ship and seeming about to swallow her.

Good Hope always came back up, of course, but often not quite far enough, and the foaming crests would break on the foredeck and race aft, surging around the forward turret before plunging into the scuppers.

While always to the north the bleak, empty cliffs of the Horn rose forbiddingly from the sea. There would be no mercy there for any shipwrecked sailor crawling ashore.

'This must be a nasty place in a storm,' the Admiral remarked.

He was not in the best of humours; the gale meant that even twelve knots was beyond the capability of the squadron; maintaining station and slowly forging ahead was all they could hope for, especially the colliers and the light cruiser *Glasgow*.

Yet he also brooded, well aware that his captains, although certain to support him loyally in whatever action he took, felt that his concept of sweeping far ahead of *Canopus* involved an unnecessary risk. When at last the Cape was rounded and they emerged into clearer skies, he had reached a decision, which he embodied in a telegram to the Admiralty:

'REAR-ADMIRAL CRADOCK TO ADMIRALTY
'GOOD HOPE 26 OCTOBER 7 PM AT SEA
'WITH REFERENCE TO ORDERS TO SEARCH FOR ENEMY AND OUR GREAT DESIRE FOR EARLY SUCCESS I CONSIDER THAT OWING TO SLOW SPEED OF *CANOPUS* IT IS IMPOSSIBLE TO FIND AND DESTROY ENEMY'S SQUADRON.

'HAVE THEREFORE ORDERED *DEFENCE* TO JOIN ME AFTER CALLING FOR ORDERS AT MONTEVIDEO.

'SHALL EMPLY *CANOPUS* IN NECESSARY WORK OF CONVOYING COLLIERS.'

'That should make everyone feel a lot happier,' he remarked.

21

'Yes, sir,' Jack agreed enthusiastically. *Defence*, with her four nine-point-twos and her ten seven-point-fives, was twice as powerful as *Good Hope*. She should have been there all along, in his opinion.

But the important fact was that they were going to fight, at last. Jack Smith did not suppose there was a single sailor or marine in the squadron who was not happy about that, but for him it held a peculiar significance.

The amusing thing was that when Cradock had asked him if he had ever been in action at sea, he had lied, as he had been forced to lie about so many things. As Lieutenant Jack Dawson he had stood on the bridge of *Mikasa*, with the other naval attaches like Geoffrey Young and Harry Krantz, and Bruno von Eltz, as the Japanese flagship had steamed into battle against the Russians in the Straits of Tsushima.

But that was a long time ago. Another era, another man. That man had been condemned as a traitor, and sent to prison. That man was dead.

Jack gave a grim smile. To everyone but Denise. Denise Robertson, who alone had maintained her faith in his innocence, who alone knew that he had sacrificed himself and his career to preserve the honour of his sister.

Well, that honour had to have been to a large extent avenged by Bruno von Eltz's attempted suicide. There was a peculiar satisfaction in that, but oddly, an even more profound satisfaction that Bruno had failed, and would live, and probably even return to service. Jack had every intention of one day facing his old enemy again, and calling him to account for all the tragedy he had brought upon the Dawson family.

Supposing they both survived whatever battles lay ahead of them. And for him, the battle promised to be sooner than later.

But Denise, who had unreservedly given him her love, also knew that the Navy was his life. Whatever was to happen over the next few days, she would be on his side, willing him on.

Willing him to come back to her.

'Read all about it! Read all about it!' The newsboys' cries echoed up from the street. '*Audacious* sunk! Super-dreadnought goes to the bottom with all hands! Read all about it!'

'For God's sake shut that window,' Churchill told his secretary. 'And ask the First Sea Lord to step in when he has a moment.'

'Yes, sir, First Lord.' The young officer closed the window and hurried from the room.

Leaving Churchill staring at the report on his desk. This was surely the worst moment of the war at sea. So far, at least.

Pathfinder had been a light cruiser. *Cressy, Hogue* and *Aboukir* had actually been due for scrapping, but had been kept on because of the War. He regretted the loss of fourteen hundred men, most of whom had been reservists with wives and families waiting for their safe return, but the ships themselves had been of no importance. Britain had entered the war with one hundred and eight cruisers, light and armoured, against Germany's forty-nine, and more were coming out of the yards every month.

But *Audacious*, only two years old, twenty-three thousand tons, ten thirteen-point-five-inch guns . . . sent to the bottom by a single mine!

The real catastrophe was that it should never have happened; *Audacious* should not have been within a hundred miles of that mine.

Some ten days previously, and in the teeth of all the First Lord's confident predictions, a German submarine had been reported inside Scapa Flow. In the flurry of activity which had followed, with shots being fired in every direction, it had been impossible to ascertain whether the report was accurate; the submarine had either been sunk or got away.

But this was Jellicoe's nightmare coming true, and added fuel to the Commander-in-Chief's continuing memoranda on the safety, or lack of it, of Scapa Flow. Jellicoe wanted to turn the anchorage into a fortress, and until that was done, to take the Grand Fleet across to the West Coast of Scotland, or to Northern Ireland, where it would be safe.

And several hundred miles away from the North Sea, should German High Seas Fleet come out.

There had been nothing for it but to agree; sceptical as he was about the chances of any U-boat surviving an attack on Scapa, Churchill recognised that if there is any place a sailor is entitled to feel safe, it is at anchor in his own harbour. Take away that security and morale would inevitably suffer. He had therefore sanctioned the removal of the Grand Fleet to Loch Swilly in Donegal . . . and it had arrived there just after a German submarine had laid a pattern of mines off the entrance!

It was a classic example of Murphy's Law. And it had cost a fine ship and five hundred men.

Battenberg entered the room without a word and placed an envelope on the First Lord's desk.

Churchill opened it, also without a word. He knew what it contained.

The date was 28 October 1914.

'Dear Mr Churchill,

'I have lately been driven to the painful conclusion that at this juncture my birth and parentage have the effect of impairing in some respects my usefulness on the Board of Admiralty. In these circumstances, I feel it to be my duty, as a loyal subject of His Majesty, to resign the office of First Sea Lord, hoping thereby to facilitate the task of the administration of the great Service, to which I have devoted my life, and to ease the burden laid on H.M. Ministers.

I am,
Yours very truly,
Louis Battenberg,
Admiral.'

Churchill raised his head.

'That was written before the news of *Audacious*,' Battenberg said. 'But that makes my going even more imperative, don't you think?'

Churchill sighed. 'I will write you a formal letter of acceptance.'

'Thank you. About those telegrams from Cradock and Stoddart . . .'

Rear-Admiral Stoddart's cable had been sent the moment he had heard from Cradock:

'I HAVE RECEIVED ORDERS FROM ADMIRAL CRADOCK TO SEND *DEFENCE* TO MONTEVIDEO TO COAL OBTAIN CHARTS AND TO AWAIT FURTHER ORDERS.

'SUBMIT I MAY BE GIVEN TWO FAST CRUISERS IN PLACE OF *DEFENCE* AS I DO NOT CONSIDER FORCE AT MY DISPOSAL SUFFICIENT.'

'I don't blame him,' Churchill said. 'Cradock really wants the moon. *Defence* as well as *Canopus*! I assume you refused Cradock's request?'

'I did, First Lord. But I am a little bit unhappy about his last sentence, using *Canopus* to escort colliers.'

'That is presumably until he locates Spee. Cradock is the last hope we have of restoring some balance to the situation. Thank you, Prince Louis.' Churchill stood up, and held out his hand.

Battenberg hesitated for several seconds; he would have preferred to pursue the matter, but he was no longer First Sea Lord, and Churchill obviously had a lot on his mind. Such as the name of his successor.

He shook hands and left the room.

Only a little while after Battenberg had left the office, another report arrived on the First Lord's desk: 'UNITS OF TURKISH FLEET INCLUDING GOEBEN AND BRESLAU TODAY BOMBARDED RUSSIAN PORTS OF SEVASTOPOL ODESSA FEODOSIA AND NOVOROSSISK . . .'

Troubles, Churchill thought, never come singly. Of course everyone had recognised that from the moment the German battlecruiser *Goeben* and her light cruiser consort *Breslau* had evaded the British Mediterranean squadron and reached Constantinople within a few days of the outbreak of war, and been taken into Turkish service, the odds on Turkey

25

entering the War on the side of the Central Powers had greatly increased. Since that fateful day there had been tremendous diplomatic activity from both sides to win the Porte . . . Germany had obviously offered more.

But Turkey's entry into the war added just one more burden to the Royal Navy.

A Navy which now desperately needed a service chief. His fingers drummed on the desk. Obviously he should pick up the telephone and call in Sir Henry Jackson, Chief of the War Staff. Jackson was experienced in every branch of Naval Administration, had been an enthusiastic supporter of the *Dreadnought* principal, was a man known and respected throughout the service as well as being just about the most senior active admiral . . . but did he have the flair to turnround this suddenly serious situation?

Not to send the ships to sea meant not to enforce the blockade, meant to admit, in effect, that Britain no longer ruled the oceans.

To send them to sea meant that they were going to be picked off, one by one, with apparently no chance of bringing the Germans to a fleet action.

It was an intolerable situation. It needed the application of a genius who was also a sailor . . . Churchill could think of only one man who filled that bill.

He brooded for some seconds longer, then picked up the telephone.

'Get me Lord Fisher,' he said.

'They'll squeal,' Jackie Fisher said, beaming across the First Lord's desk, his massive, white-domed face alight with excitement. 'For God's sake, dear boy, I'm seventy-three years old.'

'Have you any known illnesses?'

'I'm told I shouldn't try running up Ben Nevis.'

'Will you take the job?'

'They'll squeal,' Fisher said again. 'Everyone who ever hated my guts will be sharpening his knife.'

'You leave "them" to me,' Churchill said. 'Will you take the job?'

'Will I just.'

'Then you have it. There are all the recent telegrams.'

Fisher took the sheaf, began sifting through them. Churchill leaned back in his chair and watched him. He could almost feel the enormous intelligence emanating from this man's brain, the enormous knowledge too. And the enormous confidence.

It was catching.

Fisher raised his head.

'Have you requested Cradock to clarify his intentions in view of the fact that *Defence* will not now be joining him?'

'There didn't seem any necessity, with so much going on here. He's obeying orders.'

'In his own fashion. He's leaving *Canopus* behind.'

'I'm sure he's not,' Churchill argued. 'That would be a direct contravention of orders. We have always made it very clear that we do not expect him to engage Spee without the support of *Canopus*.'

'With respect, Winston, you are being very optimistic. How well do you know Cradock?'

'Well . . . I've only met him once or twice. He always struck me as being the very best sort of officer.'

'He is,' Fisher said. 'Given the right sort of supervision. He is the sort of man who is quite incapable of turning away from a fight. I wish we had more of them. That doesn't alter the fact that here he has been virtually told to fight, come what may. And he obviously means to do just that. As I read this telegram, Cradock is leaving *Canopus* to shepherd his colliers while he proceeds at his best speed with *Good Hope*, *Monmouth*, *Glasgow* and *Otranto*. My God, if Spee's big cruisers catch up with that little lot, you really will have a disaster on your hands. Anyway, I'm not at all sure that *Canopus* is going to be that effective. She's old, and I mean old.'

'She has four twelve-inch guns,' Churchill snapped. '*Good Hope* has two nine-point-twos. Spee has eight-inches at best.'

'Have you considered the age of those guns? They're virtually originals. *Canopus* can reach fourteen thousand

27

yards maximum, *Good Hope* not a fraction of that. Spee's eight-inches can go thirteen thousand, for God's sake. They're new.'

Churchill frowned at him. 'Do you wish Cradock recalled?'

'No. No, that would be disastrous for morale at this juncture. But he must be supported, just as rapidly as possible. What's the nearest powerful ship?'

'Well, *Defence*.'

'Which you have refused him. But she's ideal for the job, First Lord. Fifteen thousand tons, four nine-point-twos, why, she could take either *Scharnhorst* or *Gneisenau*. Where is she?'

'She's in the West Indies, with Stoddart. But surely a ship like *Defence* is needed in a vulnerable area like the West Indies?'

'Dear boy, a ship like *Defence* is needed where the enemy is. With your permission, we will change our minds and despatch her to Cradock immediately. And just pray she arrives in time. Meanwhile, let's get a telegram off to Cradock, instructing him under no circumstances to engage Spee without *Canopus* or until our reinforcements arrive. Better let Spee into the Atlantic than lose an entire squadron.'

Churchill pulled his nose.

'Fisher's back,' Geoffrey Young announced at dinner. 'That has got to be the best news we've had this war.'

The officers seated in *Anson*'s wardroom clapped their approval.

'He's kind of old, ain't he?' Harry asked, after the meal.

'Men like Fisher never grow old. You wait, things are going to start happening.'

'I sure hope so,' Harry said.

Heligoland Bight seemed a very long time ago.

'Fisher's back,' Harriet said, reading *The Times* at breakfast. 'Oh, isn't that just marvellous?'

'He's too old,' Mary objected.

'Of course he's not too old. He's a genius, and only seventy-three. You should be happy because he's a friend of Geoffrey's.'

'Well, I'm not. I just don't think Fisher is the best man for the job. Hello . . . there's the telegraph boy.'

Rawlston brought in the brown envelope on the silver salver.

Harriet took it somewhat gingerly, while Mary, trying to keep her nerves under control, fed Joan a piece of toast; Mark was mercifully asleep in his cot.

A telegram in wartime normally only meant one thing . . .

Slowly Harriet slit the envelope, took out the single sheet of paper inside. 'It's from America,' she said wonderingly, and then raised her head. 'It's from Lizzie. She's going to have a baby!'

The Horn behind them, the squadron steamed north along a coast no less formidable in appearance, but into steadily dwindling seas and steadily brightening sunlight. It was approaching the middle of spring.

Cradock now made his dispositions. *Canopus* was indeed left behind, while the two armoured cruisers and *Otranto* pushed on ahead. *Glasgow*, with her twenty-five knots of speed, was sent on even faster, to ascertain if the Germans had yet made the Chilean coast, and where they were.

No further signal had been received from England since leaving Port Stanley. Any signals would, in any event, now have to be relayed through Valparaiso as they were out of radio range of Stanley, but it appeared to all that the Admiralty was content with the Admiral's stated plans. Equally, no one on board any ship in the squadron had any doubt that it was Cradock's intention, once he had discovered Spee's whereabouts, to fall back on *Canopus* and bar the German entry to the Atlantic, forcing him either to fight at a disadvantage or run back into the vastnesses of the Pacific . . . and an eventual fuel crisis.

Jack thought that perhaps he alone properly understood the thoughts that were roaming through Cradock's mind as the squadron commander sat in his cabin, staring at the charts as if they held the secret of his future, or into space, as if communing with some intensely private god.

He was sure the Admiral was deeply troubled by the fate of Troubridge, who had been confounded by conflicting orders; it had been Rear-Admiral Troubridge's inability to act decisively, because of those orders, that had allowed *Goeben* and *Breslau* to escape in the Mediterranean – and had led to his own court-martial. Cradock's orders were hardly less conflicting. He must destroy the German squadron, which was in any event faster than his own, but he must not engage them without the support of *Canopus*, whose present speed was less than half that of the German ships.

Obviously he felt, correctly, that he was on a hiding to nothing.

The weather turned inclement again as the squadron forged north, and with the swell building all the time it was the night of Friday 30 October before the armoured cruisers and *Otranto* were abeam of the Archipeligo de Los, still some eight hundred miles south of Valparaiso. In the wardroom Jack and the other stewards served each officer a glass of port for the traditional 'wives and sweethearts' toast. No man took more than a single drink; although theoretically the wardroom mess was available at any hour of the day or night, very few officers actually drank while at sea . . . and especially with an enemy in the vicinity.

That night, however, there was an air of slightly forced macho convivialty because presumably the enemy was in the vicinity. The evening was topped by the arrival of the officer of the watch with a signal from *Glasgow*:

'OFF CORONEL STOP HAVE INTERCEPTED RADIO SIGNALS FROM GERMAN SHIP THOUGHT TO BE *DRESDEN* SPEAKING OUT OF VALPARAISO STOP PLEASE INSTRUCT.'

'*Dresden*,' Cradock said. 'One of the bastards, anyway. Valparaiso. Just as we expected.'

'*Glasgow* can handle *Dresden*,' said Captain Chapman. 'She has two six-inch and ten four-inch. *Dresden* has only a dozen four-point-ones.'

'The German may not be alone,' Cradock pointed out. He turned to the lieutenant. 'Make to *Glasgow*: remain on station, but retire if confronted with superior force. Am joining you with squadron.' He smiled at them. 'I think we should go to bed, gentlemen. Tomorrow may be a busy day.'

It was not until the morning of Sunday, 1 November, that the squadron sighted *Glasgow*, which had stood south looking for them. No further traffic had been heard from the German cruiser, but *Glasgow* had no doubt that she was still to the north of them.

'If she is coming south,' suggested Captain Brandt of *Monmouth* at the officers' conference which was called, 'I would say, stay where we are, and let her walk into our arms.'

'I think we should seek her out, and destroy her,' Cradock said. 'That is the object of this mission, gentlemen. We shall proceed to the north.'

The squadron got under way again in a brisk wind and heavy seas, the four ships spread in a broad line, some fifteen miles apart, to make sure the enemy cruiser did not sneak through, and in mid afternoon, when the British ships were roughly abeam of Coronel, *Glasgow* reported smoke to the north.

Jack was serving tea to the admiral on the bridge when this message arrived, and saw the gleam of battle in Cradock's eye.

'Signal squadron to alter course to starboard, and close *Glasgow*,' he said.

Another report came in a moment later. There was more than one ship coming over the horizon. *Glasgow* now counted four smoke issues.

Heads turned towards the Admiral. Four ships could only mean the main German squadron.

Cradock gazed at the horizon for several seconds.

'Make to *Canopus*, inquiring exact position,' he said.

The signal lieutenant hurried from the bridge to the wireless room.

'And ourselves, sir?' Captain Chapman asked, in a low voice.

'Alter course to starboard.' Cradock glanced to the west. It was nearly five in the afternoon, and the sun was beginning to droop into the windswept clouds that masked the horizon. 'Instruct all others to do the same. We must stop them putting into Coronel.'

Chapman looked astonished, as well he might, Jack thought. If either of the squadrons needed to seek shelter in a neutral port, it was their own. But the Captain gave the orders, and the British ships altered course to close the coast, which was some fifty miles distant.

Canopus now replied that she was two hundred and fifty miles astern.

'Twenty-four hours,' Cradock said, biting his lip.

'The Germans don't know she is there. They'll follow if we fall back,' Chapman argued. 'And that will shorten the time.'

'Signal from *Glasgow*, sir,' said the signal lieutenant. 'Enemy squadron altering course to port.'

'They're making for Coronel,' Cradock said.

'Well, sir, why not let them?' Chapman asked. 'They'll have no more than three days, by which time we will have *Canopus*.'

'They will know that,' Cradock said. 'It is a ruse to sneak by in territorial waters. Well, we'll see about that. Inform all commanders to clear for action, but to alter course north by east, and form line: *Good Hope*, *Monmouth* and *Glasgow*.'

Chapman gulped. 'You intend to engage, sir?'

'That's what we're here for. On the new course, the sun will be to our advantage, as it will shine in the eyes of the Germans.'

Chapman wasn't interested in the sun; it was now setting fast and the advantage would be a very brief one. 'With

32

respect, sir . . .' the Captain searched for words which could indicate his concern without suggesting he considered they were committing suicide. '*Otranto* is quite incapable of taking part in a fleet action.'

'You are absolutely right,' Cradock agreed. 'That is why I am not calling her into the line. Signal *Otranto* to withdraw to the south as rapidly as possible. Tell her to rendezvous with *Canopus*.'

'Yes, sir. That will leave us with three ships to the enemy's four, sir.'

'I am aware of that, Captain. But numbers alone do not signify victory, or defeat. If our ships are damaged, we can withdraw to the Falklands, and succour. If Spee's are damaged, he has nowhere to turn. That is the difference in our positions. That must be our objective. Damage the enemy, and then withdraw, and await his destruction. Understood?'

Chapman looked as if he would have argued further, but instead nodded. 'Aye-aye, sir.'

The ship hummed as it was cleared for action. On their beam *Monmouth* was also a hive of activity, and *Glasgow* was closing fast.

Reluctantly *Otranto* was turning away.

And now the enemy ships could be seen by the naked eye, from time to time, as they rose to the tops of the swell, before sinking back out of sight again; at this distance, something like nine miles, they looked like toys.

'Accurate shooting isn't going to be easy in this sea,' Chapman commented.

'It will be difficult for them as well,' Cradock said.

The Germans had also formed into line.

'Two large in front, two small behind,' Cradock said, peering through his glasses. 'He must've detached two. Range?'

'Eighteen thousand yards, sir.'

'He's keeping his distance,' Chapman commented.

Cradock looked at his watch. It was six o'clock, and there was at most only just over an hour of daylight left.

'We'll have to close,' he said. 'We would have to, anyway, we can't hit him at this distance. Make to

33

Canopus that we're going into action. and steer east by south.'

'Aye-aye, sir.'

Jack stood to attention. 'Permission to serve a gun, sir?'

Cradock glanced at him. 'You, Smith? What do you know about gunnery?'

'Ah . . . I have some experience, sir.'

Cradock looked at him even harder. 'There are a lot of things about you I do not understand, Smith. No, you cannot serve a gun. But I will tell you what I wish you to do: shave off that beard.'

'Now, sir?'

'Yes, now. Or tell me who you really are.'

Jack hesitated. But obviously there were several men capable of recognising him once the beard was shaven.

'Jack Dawson, sir.'

'Dawson? Good God! I thought there was something about you . . . Captain Chapman, place this man under arrest.'

'Now, sir?' Chapman was equally astonished.

'With respect, sir, I do know about guns,' Jack said. 'Why not arrest me after the battle?'

Cradock glanced at him, then gave a grim smile. 'Very well, Mr Dawson, you may serve with the secondary armament. And as you say, we'll talk again, after the battle.'

'Aye-aye, sir.'

Jack's brain was tumbling as he went down the ladders. Of all the careless things to have done . . . yet, as Cradock had obviously been suspicious of him for some time, the truth would have come out sooner or later . . . probably sooner. And he was being given a chance to fight, for the first time.

And, no doubt, the last.

The British squadron had now turned east to close on the enemy, with the result that they were steaming away from the weather, and the motion had considerably eased. But even so the six-inch battery to which Jack was directed, on the port side, was ankle deep in water from each surge.

34

'These goddamed things are too low to be effective in heavy weather,' growled Petty Officer Mitchell, who was gun captain. 'We'll only be able to fire on the up.'

'If we ever get within range of the bastards,' growled one of his crew.

'We're altering course,' said another, as *Good Hope* came round again, now steering virtually south. That was at least the direction Jack felt they should have been steering all along, but of course Cradock was not attempting to get away; he was concentrating only on engaging.

But the Germans were keeping their distance, aware not only that they outranged the British ships, but that the sun was sinking fast. The men waited for the orders to fire, but none came.

Jack cast a hasty glance around him. Because of the clouds to windward it was growing dark very rapidly, but *Monmouth* and *Glasgow* were still in line astern – *Otranto* was lost in the dusk, presumably some miles to the south by now.

He tried to make out the enemy, but could not see them against the high land behind them, already lost in shadow. Then he saw flashes of light, and the lower deck, already half lost in knee-deep water with every roll, was totally obliterated by flying spray.

'Shit, that's good shooting,' shouted Petty Officer Mitchell. 'When do we get to fire this fucking thing, you bastards?'

Above them, the after nine-point-two exploded. What it was firing at, Jack could not imagine. Except when they were actually firing, the German ships were invisible, while the British squadron were bathed in the eerie afterglow of the sunset; the sun itself was gone, but the clouds were sufficiently high to leave a bright red backdrop, against which *Good Hope* was silhouetted like a beacon.

The sooner that was gone the better, he thought, as the ship rolled again, and water flooded the deck.

Before she came back up, there was a shuddering explosion, which made the cruiser tremble from stem to stern. Jack found himself on his hands and knees, looking up at the bridge, which was enveloped in flame and smoke.

'Holy Jesus Christ!' Mitchell muttered.

Jack had no sooner regained his feet than he was thrown down again, this time by an explosion from aft, where the turret had been blown away – having hardly fired more than a couple of shots; the forward gun had not fired at all.

'She's going,' Mitchell snapped.

Suddenly the water looked much closer than before, and it had been close enough then.

'Life jackets!'

But there weren't any to hand. Nor were there any officers to order abandon ship, as the bridge continued to blaze merrily.

The next German salvo actually missed, whining overhead. Jack looked astern, at *Monmouth*, also on fire from several hits. He could not see *Glasgow*.

I am going to die, he thought. After all my dreams of facing Bruno von Eltz, of rehabilitation, of getting home to Denise, I am going to die, here in an unknown sea, as far away from England as it is possible to be.

Yet the urge to survive was still strong in him. As the water rose to the deck, and *Good Hope* uttered the great sighs and terrifying groans of a ship about to sink, he threw himself away from the rail and into the sea, striking out with the clean strokes of a good swimmer.

No one immediately followed him, although he heard shouts behind him. He would not look back, nor would he admit to himself how cold the water was; it was well above freezing, but was yet icy to his overheated body.

He swam for several minutes, as hard as he could, rising on the swell and then plunging down into the troughs again. When he had to pause for breath, he turned on his back, and was surprised, and a little dismayed, to see *Good Hope* still floating, ablaze amidships and aft. But as he stared through the gloom, he could just make out the shapes of men hurling themselves into the sea behind him. As they did so, the cruiser sank beneath the waves.

Within seconds the undertow was reaching for him, and he was sucked down. But he had put enough distance between himself and the maelstrom to regain the surface with a few powerful strokes.

Then he was alone, listening to the sound of distant gunfire, the whine of the wind and hiss of the swell . . . with the cold biting into his bones.

He made himself swim, east. That way was land. Thirty miles at least, but still land. He would not give up.

But perhaps it was closer than that. He had no idea how long he had been swimming, fighting the urgent desire to stop and rest, and close his eyes just for a moment, making himself thrust one arm in front of the other, when he became aware that there was something huge and black immediately in front of him, rising out of the water.

And people, shouting, and then a bright light, being played over the surface of the sea.

'Help!' he shouted, summoning all of his remaining strength. 'Help me!'

CHAPTER 2

The Reckoning

The great ships slipped out of the November mist; before them lay the low coast of the eastern bulge of England, the dawn lights of the seaport of Great Yarmouth. In line ahead, the five battlecruisers swung northward to lie broadside to the land, and the port; they were about seven miles off.

Peering through his binoculars, Bruno von Eltz wondered if they had yet been noticed, and if they had, what were the feelings of those on shore.

Certainly they would not yet believe the battlecruiser squadron was not their own.

'Message from flagship, Herr Kapitan.' Signal Ober-leutnant- zur-See Walter stood to attention. 'Open fire.'

Bruno nodded. 'Open fire, Herr Korvettenkapitan.'

The order went down to the turrets. The eleven-inch guns had already begun their swing to port, and a second later *Roon* heeled to starboard as they exploded together, an enormous burst of sound, whining away into the distance.

A few moment's wait, while all eyes were turned on the shore.

'Hits,' said Korvettenkapitan Kroess. 'Many hits.'

'Reload.'

Bruno kept his binoculars levelled, marking the bursts, the sudden upsurges of flame. There were people dying over there. Helpless civilians, probably still in their beds, certainly totally surprised by the sudden rain of shells descending on their hitherto peaceful lives.

He felt quite sick.

He knew, of course, that this was all part of the master plan; he had had it drummed into him often enough. The aim was not to murder innocent men and women and children –

38

not to mention dogs and cats and horses and cattle; they were the incidentals to the business of fighting a war.

The true aim was to force the British to patrol their coasts, with heavy ships, thus leaving them vulnerable to attack by torpedo and mine. There were no British ships to be seen today. No doubt it had never crossed the minds of those at the Admiralty that the Germans would dream of bombarding undefended and unimportant coastal towns.

It would cross their minds now.

'Guns are ready, Herr Kapitan.'

'Fire, Herr Korvettenkapitan.'

Once again the ship rocked to the explosions.

Walter was back. 'Signal from flagship, Herr Kapitan. Mission accomplished, squadron will return to base. Well done.'

'Gentlemen, I have called you together so quickly, not only to congratulate you on the entire success of today's operation, but also . . .' Hipper looked from face to face. 'To tell you that on my return I found the most stupendous news awaiting me. Gentlemen, the German Navy has gained its first great victory. Two days ago, on Sunday 1 November, the British South American Squadron was annihilated by the German Pacific Squadron, commanded by Konteradmiral Graf von Spee.'

His officers stared at him in disbelief.

As Hipper saw. 'The news arrived in a telegram from our Consul in Valparaiso, and has been confirmed by Spee himself on his return to that port. At seven o'clock on Sunday evening he was engaged by three British ships. Of these the two larger ones, identified as *Good Hope*, the flagship, and *Monmouth*, both armoured cruisers, were sunk, *Good Hope* by gunfire and *Monmouth* by torpedo after being badly damaged and refusing to surrender. There were no survivors from either ship. The smaller vessel, understood to be the light cruiser *Glasgow*, escaped into the darkness. Admiral von Spee reports that his squadron suffered no damage, and sustained no casualties.'

39

There was a moment's silence, then a chorus of cheers and hand-clapping swept the wardroom.

Stewards hurried forward with trays bearing glasses of champagne.

'Gentlemen!' Hipper called. 'I give you: the German Navy. What price Heligoland now, eh?'

The meeting became very noisy. It was several minutes before Bruno could find himself beside the Admiral.

'Well, Bruno,' Hipper said. 'What did it feel like to be at sea again, eh, after hospital?'

'It felt very good indeed, Herr Konteradmiral.'

Hipper wagged his finger. 'Well, we must make sure that there are no more accidents, eh? We have a war to win.'

'There will be no more accidents, Herr Konteradmiral,' Bruno promised. 'May I ask, did Spee have his entire squadron, Herr Konteradmiral?'

'Yes, indeed. Well, less *Emden*, which he had detached for commerce-destroying in the Indian Ocean. Actually, only four of his ships were involved in the battle itself. *Nurnberg* was some way behind. But all played their parts. It was a torpedo from *Nurnberg* that sank *Monmouth*.'

'But . . . if that is right,' Bruno said slowly, 'it means that three inferior British ships attacked four German. That was suicide.'

'It was an odd thing to do, I agree,' Hipper said. 'But we must not concern ourselves with what heroics the British wish to indulge in. They can attack us any time they choose, when the odds are in our favour. Would you not agree, Bruno?'

Bruno muttered that he did. But however he might have tried to destroy himself, he just could not conceive of a man wilfully destroying his entire squadron.

Bruno returned to his ship feeling very depressed – which was something the doctors had warned he must not allow to happen – and found Herr Furrer waiting for him.

'Ah, Furrer. At last. You have news of my sister?'

'I have a letter from her, Herr Kapitan.'

'That is very good.' Bruno took the envelope, frowned.

'This has been opened.'

'I am sorry, Herr Kapitan. I was stopped at the French border, and searched. They examined all my mail.'

'Have they the right to do this? You are a neutral citizen.'

'I am known to travel between Switzerland and Germany as well as Switzerland and France, Herr Kapitan. I thought it best not to protest, otherwise in the future I might merely be prevented from entering France, and that would be of no advantage to anyone. Besides, while I know it is annoying, I am sure there is nothing Madame Tonnheur would have written which can possibly embarrass her. Or you.'

As if the little toad wouldn't have read it, once it had been opened, Bruno thought angrily.

He slit the poorly re-sealed envelope.

'My darling,

'What a dear little man you have acting as your courier. I received the shock of my life when he announced himself.

'And how angry I became when he told me that you have received none of my letters since this ghastly war started. When I think what you have been through! How I wished to be at your side, but this tyrannical government under which I am forced to exist would have none of it. What barbarians these people are!!! My darling, I wish I could remember everything I said to you. Some of it was quite important, I know. I will try to remember, and tell you, soon.

'Pierre writes mysterious notes from mysterious places. But from his last I understand that he and his ship, *Wagram*, are off to Constantinople to fight the Turks. I do not know whether I wish him to come back or not. Surely if he were killed or something I would be allowed to return home, and end this purgatory of sitting here, listening to people I do not like – and who do not like me – dreaming only of my next letter to you.

'And now, from you.

'My darling, our secret makes me feel that I am with you even when we are so separated. I had hoped to be home again

41

by now. I wept when that idiot Kluck began to retreat. The French are of course calling it the Miracle of the Marne. I do believe that if Joffre were to stand for emperor he would be elected without a dissentient vote, save amongst those of his generals who recognise him for what he is, a total dolt who has been saved by the incompetence of our own generals.

'But my darling, when will it end, now that there seems no hope of our taking Paris, this year at least? Christmas seems so close, and I had meant to be home for Christmas.

'Write me again soon, and tell me what you wish of me. You shall have it.

'All my love,

'Helene.'

Bruno stared at the words. What memories they brought back. What memories Helene was deliberately trying to invoke. All shameful. It had been Helene who had determined to seduce Jack Dawson in the hopes of gaining the specifications for the first *Dreadnought*. She had failed, but her criminal plan had brought him together with Jack's sister Georgina, a girl so anxious to be a rebel against what she considered the comfortable arrogance of the English ruling classes that she would betray her country, and so innocent that she could not cope with the consequences.

And when it was done, with Gina dead and Jack in prison, and the von Eltz's had returned in triumph and, at least in his case, secret shame, to Germany, it had been Helene, on that unforgettable night at Schloss Elsjing, who had lured her helpless, drunken brother to her bed.

The weight of guilt on his shoulders was sometimes quite unbearable, even now, when he had sworn never again to consider self-destruction. Hipper supposed he had swallowed those pills because of frustrated zeal. If the Konteradmiral were ever to find out the truth . . . As for having her return . . . he did not dare consider it. Perhaps, being forced to exist in the purgatory that was France – at least for a German – was what she most deserved.

'Is all well, Herr Kapitan?' Furrer asked.

It was probably best to believe the rat had not read the letter, Bruno thought, else would he be forced to strangle him.

'Yes,' he said. 'All is well, Herr Furrer.'

'And will there be a reply?'

'Yes,' Bruno said. 'Call here in two days' time.'

Furrer got up and bowed.

'A whole squadron destroyed!' Harriet shrieked, dropping *The Times* on to the floor. 'A whole squadron! My God! How could it happen?'

'We don't know the report is true,' Mary pointed out. 'Anyway, a whole squadron? Even the Germans are only claiming two ships.'

'Two ships. Do you know how many ships that makes it we have lost since the war began?' Harriet had a statistical mind, and had been keeping a careful tally. 'Six, cruisers or better. And they've only lost three. It's ridiculous. And now they've gone and blown up Great Yarmouth. Who says Britannia rules the waves? Churchill should be fired.' She stamped off to the kitchen in a fury. Cook was going to have a hard morning.

'Did you know any of the guys on board *Good Hope* or *Monmouth*?' Harry asked as he and Geoffrey breakfasted together.

'Frank Brandt and I were at Dartmouth together,' Geoffrey said.

'Tough.'

'It's a bloody mystery,' Geoffrey said. 'They're supposed to have had a battleship down there with them. How the devil can the Germans claim to have got away without a scratch?'

'Maybe they're not telling the whole story,' Harry opined. 'Still . . . it sure gives them something to play with. What do you reckon your brass is going to do about it?'

'They had better do something,' Geoffrey growled. 'All we are doing is sitting around here waiting to be hit somewhere else. We can't even protect our own seaports, it seems. Christ, why don't we just get all of our ships together and steam right down into Wilhelmshaven and blow the bastards apart?'

'Because you'd never get there, through all those minefields.'

Geoffrey gave him a dirty look. But he knew he was right.

Harry wished there was something he could do to help. He almost wished he could feel as miserable as everyone else around him. But he couldn't manage that. In fact, he was hard put to it to stop himself from smiling every time he saw himself in a mirror.

He was going to be a father, and by the most adorable girl, who would be coming back to England in a few weeks, for Christmas. He was the happiest man in the world.

But he still hoped the Brits managed to do something about this fellow Spee.

'Good morning, First Lord.' Lord Fisher seated himself before Churchill's desk. 'I have received a signal from Admiral Carden that he, in conjunction with the French squadron, yesterday bombarded the Dardanelles. This was on instructions from me. We can't let the Turks have it all their own way.'

Churchill raised a weary head.

'That's the good news, is it?'

'At the moment, yes.' Fisher frowned. 'Did you sleep?'

'Oh, I always sleep. But I went down to Yarmouth to see for myself. Actually, it is amazing how five battlecruisers can bombard a town and do so little damage. But all things are relative. They did enough damage, killed enough people, to upset everyone. What are we going to do about it, John?'

'Time enough for that. We can't cope with hit and run raids. We never claimed we could. It's Spee we have to settle.'

'There's no doubt about the report?'

'I'm afraid not. We've received a signal from *Glasgow*.'

'Where is she now?'

'On her way back to the Falklands. With *Canopus* and *Otranto*. I've told them to get the hell out of there. Unfortunately, *Canopus* will probably have to stay; I gather her engines are just about done. But I'm sending *Glasgow* and *Otranto* to the River Plate for the time being.'

'Until we catch Spee. We will, you know.'

'Oh, I have no doubt about that, First Lord.'

'I've made some rough combinations up, having regard to Spee's options, and what we have available. Tell me what you think of these.

'Option Number One, to remain on the western South American coast, perhaps move a little further north, and rely upon being able to coal again, while he destroys shipping. As far as I see, to deal with that one, we have *Australia*, three Japanese ships, one of them a battleship, and *Newcastle*. That's the force which has been tracking Spee since Tsing-tao. That should be sufficient, don't you think? *Australia* is a battlecruiser, nineteen thousand tons, eight twelve-inch, twenty-five knots. *Newcastle* is a sister to *Glasgow*, and the Japs have got to be worth something.'

'Oh, *Australia* alone would settle Spee's hash,' Fisher said. 'If he goes that way. But he won't.'

'Well, then, suppose he turns back into the Pacific? If he heads north-west, there's a Japanese squadron in the Carolines which should stop him. If he heads due west, there's a Japanese squadron in the Tonga group, together with the French cruiser *Montcalm* and the Australian light cruiser *Encounter*. She's a powerful little ship, six thousand tons, eleven six-inch. That lot should also be able to stop him.'

'Of course, but Spee isn't going to turn back into the Pacific either, First Lord. I don't know where he thinks he may be able to coal, apart from South America, and even if Peru and Equador are as friendly as Chile, he'll soon exhaust his available time in neutral ports. More important, he seems to have fired quite a lot of shells to sink our two. He can't replace those anywhere but Germany.'

'Right, so he comes round the Horn,' Churchill said. 'I don't think he'll try the Canal, because he knows we have a powerful squadron concentrated there. We can't do anything about him out of the Falklands right this minute, with only *Canopus* and *Glasgow* available. But *Defence* will be there any day now. Obviously she can't take on the Germans by herself, but we should be able to raise some sizeable forces as he moves north. I think, once we know he's headed for the Horn, we could move *Albion* and *Minotaur* from the West Indies to join *Defence*, all good armoured cruisers, plus some light cruisers, and concentrate them off Montevideo. That should stop Spee breaking into the Atlantic. But just to cover, we could have *Warrior*, *Black Prince*, *Donegal*, *Cumberland* and *Vengeance* off the bulge of Africa, say in the Cape Verdes.'

Fisher was showing signs of impatience.

'With respect, First Lord, none of those combinations can *guarantee* Spee's destruction. So we'll put up three armoured cruisers instead of two. He disposed of two without too much trouble, didn't he?'

Churchill sighed. 'I wish I could understand what was in Cradock's mind.'

'I know what was in his mind. A whole lot of things. Troubridge. His overwhelming desire to fight. And, hopefully, and more rationally, the feeling that if he could just damage Spee's ships, so far from any repair base, it would be worth losing his own. Had he managed to hit them once or twice, he might have been proved right. But he was a brave man, and we must respect both his courage and his intentions. The question, now, First Lord, is how we avenge him, and put the Royal Navy back where it belongs, on top of the world. That is only going to happen by the utter destruction of Spee and his entire squadron. And that is not going to be accomplished by any combination of armoured cruisers.'

Churchill gazed at him.

'You want to detach a battleship from the Home Fleet? With the Germans already bombarding our coasts? Suppose that raid on Great Yarmouth was just a reconnaissance in force for the High Seas Fleet?'

'I doubt that very much, First Lord. But even so, I believe we have enough to stop them. Yes, I would like to detach a capital ship to deal with Spee. Not one. Two.'

'Two?'

'Yes. Two battlecruisers. Send them with adequate support, at full speed, to the Falklands. If we enforce total secrecy, they'll be there and have done the job before anyone in Germany, or in this country if we play it right, even knows they've gone.'

'You are asking me to authorise the despatch of two battlecruisers from Beatty's squadron, and send them to the Falklands, without any certainty that Spee is going to try that way? That could be the wildest goose chase in history.'

'That is where they'll find Spee, First Lord. He'll need to coal, and there's nowhere south of Valparaiso, that he knows of, save the Falklands. Also, it's a coaling station for British ships, and an important cable and wireless station. Also, it's where *Canopus* has gone to, and he'll know that, because he'll be picking up our signals. He'll also know, or soon find out, that *Canopus* is now virtually a hulk.

'But there's another point. He knows he can't get home. No one can seriously expect to steam through the North Sea, with all the tonnage we have up there, without being brought to action. But he's a good officer. He'll now be brooding on how he can best use his ships before, inevitably, they run out of both shells and coal. For all those reasons, he'll make for Stanley, firstly to coal, then to destroy the bunkers and the wireless station, and lastly, he will also mean to destroy *Canopus*. I'll give him an even better reason. The battlecruisers will need scouts. Let us order, openly, *Glasgow* to return, along with, say, *Kent* and *Caernavon*, all to concentrate on the Falklands. That is the same sort of force Spee defeated off Coronel. He's a fighting seaman. He'll go for it. The odds on his getting back to Germany are remote, but if he could destroy yet another

47

British squadron, he could then lose his ships with pride. He has no better plan. But . . . he won't know that our squadron also includes two battlecruisers.'

'Can we possibly have them there in time? It's eight thousand miles from here to Stanley.'

'And a ship like, say, *Invincible* can steam at twenty-five knots. I'm not suggesting she try to maintain that speed the whole way. But she can certainly be there in three weeks.'

'She'll need a refit first.'

'Two days will do it.'

'And she only has a three-thousand-mile range at full speed,' Churchill continued to object. 'Maybe four at reduced.'

'So, we'll have to arrange for colliers to meet her at sea at a selected point, and then she can fuel again at our secret station in the Abrolhos Islands off northern Brazil. Only the result matters here, First Lord.'

'And if Spee has done the Falklands and gone on?'

'They'll still catch him. But I'm not sure he will have done the Falklands and gone on. We know he's in Valparaiso at the moment, coaling. He still has to decide what happens next. We'll get him, First Lord. We'll get him.'

'All right,' Churchill said. 'You want *Invincible* and another.'

'*Inflexible*.'

'And the commander? You're not thinking of Beatty, I hope.'

'I would very much like to send Beatty, First Lord. He is the ideal man for a job like this. But I accept that were the German High Seas Fleet to come out and it be discovered that Beatty was in the South Atlantic you and I would probably both be sent to the Tower. No. I would say . . . Sturdee. There's your man.'

Churchill's head jerked. Not only was Vice-Admiral Sir Doveton Sturdee seated at his desk in this very building, as Deputy Chief of the newly formed Naval War Staff, but as a supporter of Sir Charles Beresford, Fisher's lifelong rival, he and Fisher had loathed each other for years.

For just a moment the First Lord wondered if Fisher was still fighting past battles, believing that Sturdee would not be able to catch Spee and would thus suffer an irretrievable loss of reputation.

But that was an unworthy thought.

And, as if Fisher suspected something like that was passing through Churchill's mind, he added, 'He'll do it, First Lord. He's the man for the job.'

'What the devil is happening, do you suppose?' Peter Dawson asked Mark Croom, as the two lieutenants stood on the quarterdeck, having just been part of a guard of honour to receive the Deputy Chief of the Naval War Staff.

Like his brothers, Peter was tall, fair, and heavily built. Unlike the other members of his family, he was somewhat sombre, both of expression and mind. The calamity which had overtaken his elder brother and sister weighed heavily upon him, and he was very aware of having become the senior member of his generation – he was a year older than Mary.

But he, more than everyone else, wanted action to expiate unpleasant memories, and the sudden appearance of a Vice-Admiral . . .

Admiral Sturdee had first of all called on Admiral Beatty on *Lion*, and had then been rowed across, to a chorus of boatswain's whistles, to *Invincible*.

'Some kind of inspection,' Croom suggested.

But an hour later *Invincible* was at sea, followed by *Inflexible* – with Sturdee still on board.

'Well, I imagine we've been detailed to patrol the East Coast, against another hit and run raid by Jerry,' Croom said. 'We're probably going to drop the old boy off at Harwich.'

'That would make sense,' Peter agreed. 'Save that we're steaming north, not south.'

The battlecuisers steamed round the north of Scotland, and then down the west coast, for Devonport, where they would refit. They reached the port on 8 November, and next day Churchill received the following telegram from the squadron commander:

'THE ADMIRAL SUPERINTENDENT DEVONPORT REPORTS THAT THE EARLIEST POSSIBLE DATE FOR COMPLETION OF *INVINCIBLE* AND *INFLEX-IBLE* IS MIDNIGHT 13 NOVEMBER.'

'Four days? That is preposterous,' the First Lord exploded.

The First Sea Lord read the message.

'And he proposes to send them to sea on Friday the Thirteenth. Has the man no decent superstition? I think this is an occasion for pulling rank, First Lord. In every possible way. Every day matters.'

Churchill immediately wrote a reply:

'SHIPS ARE TO SAIL WEDNESDAY 11 STOP THEY ARE NEEDED FOR WAR SERVICE AND DOCKYARD ARRANGEMENTS MUST BE MADE TO CONFORM STOP IF NECESSARY DOCKYARD MEN SHOULD BE SENT AWAY IN THE SHIPS TO RETURN AS OPPORTUNITY MAY OFFER STOP YOU ARE HELD RESPONSIBLE FOR THE SPEEDY DESPATCH OF THESE SHIPS IN A THOROUGHLY EFFICIENT CONDITION ACKNOWLEDGE'

Invincible and *Inflexible* sailed on 11 November, slipping out into the vastness of the Atlantic Ocean, and disappearing.

It had been an enormously busy two days, and the crews were exhausted. Re-fitting a capital ship for service was not merely a business of loading munitions and checking over the engines; there was the matter of feeding the crew. Peter, as assistant to the Executive Officer in this task, gaped at a shopping list which left him breathless. It consisted of:

Sixty tons of potatoes
Thirty tons of fresh beef
One thousand boxes of cigarettes
Six cases of table salt
Two hundredweight of butter beans

Seventy-two tins of biscuits
One and a half hundredweight of macaroni
Four cases of preserved parsnips
Five hundredweight of soda
Twelve dozen bottles of curry powder
Eight dozen cases of tinned peas
Two hundredweight of German sausage
Fifty twenty-eight- pound buckets of lard
One hundred and eighty sides of bacon
Two thousand, four hundred pounds of margarine
One hundred and fifty boxes of chocolate
Six cases of tinned apples
Four cases of apple rings
Eight cases of herrings in tomato sauce
Twenty-four dozen bottles of sauce
Eight dozen tins of pineapple
Twelve dozen tins of pears
Twenty-four dozen tins of peaches
Two hundredweight of currants
Two hundredweight of sultanas
Two hundredweight of tapioca
Two hundredweight of prunes
Thirty whole cheeses
Thirty-six cooked hams
One hundred and twenty pounds of cake
Six cases of sardines
Half-a-hundredweight of pearl barley
Twelve cases of tinned brawn
Eight cases of tongue
Eight cases kidneys
Fifteen hundredweight of salt fish
Twenty-four boxes of kippers
Twelve boxes of haddock
Fifteen boxes of bloaters
Seven hundred and twenty dozen fresh eggs
Seventy cases of tomatoes
Half-a-ton of onions
Two hundred boxes of fresh tomatoes

At least, he reckoned, one got a pretty good idea of what the British sailor liked to eat.

Speculation as to their destination was rife, but it was not until they had been at sea three days that Vice-Admiral Sturdee addressed all hands.

It occurred to Peter that the only way to describe the Admiral was 'foursquare'. Square chin, flat mouth, big nose, wideset eyes, high forehead: he looked formidable. And traditional. Not for him the turned-down collar which was becoming so popular since first indulged by Beatty; Sturdee still wore the wing collar, and his hat was foursquare on his head to match – again in the strongest possible contrast to Beatty, who habitually wore his cap at a rakish angle.

'I have first of all some good news to give you,' he said. '*Karlsruhe*, the five-thousand-ton German cruiser which has been loose on the West Coast of Africa, has been forced to take refuge up a river in Tanganyika, and has been blockaded there. She will not come out again.' He paused to let that sink in. 'Now for some even better news. *Emden*, the other commerce raider, has been brought to battle by HMAS *Sydney* off the Cocos Islands, and sunk.' Another pause. 'And now for the best news of all. The destruction of those two raiders means that the only German warships at sea anywhere in the world, except for the Baltic and limited areas of the North Sea, are those of Admiral Graf von Spee's squadron. I can now tell you that our orders are to find and destroy Graf Spee and his ships. That is our mission, and that is what we are going to do.'

The ship burst into wild cheering.

The question is, Peter thought, does such a traditionalist have the verve to take Spee?

A fortnight after leaving Devonport, the battlecruisers reached the Abrolhos Rocks, where the British Government had set up a secret coaling station well before the outbreak of war. Here they found waiting for them Admiral Stoddart and his squadron: *Caernarvon*, a somewhat old eleven-thousand-ton armoured cruiser, which carried four seven-point-five-inch as well as a six-inch battery; *Cornwall* and *Kent*, both, like the ill-fated *Monmouth*, ten-thousand tonners armed only with six-inch guns; *Glasgow* and her sister ship *Bristol*; *Orama*, an armed merchant cruiser, and *Defence*.

Defence was detached to cover the Cape of Good Hope, just in case Spee, in line with Fisher's concept that he knew he was on a suicide mission, decided to raid the Indian Ocean. She would be joined off the Cape by several other ships. The rest of the squadron, having coaled, steamed south, for the Falklands.

'Will we be in time, do you suppose?' Peter wondered.

Jack Dawson opened his eyes and blinked blearily at the deckhead above him.

He knew immediately that he was on board a ship. But a ship that was at anchor. There was no roar of engines or swish of the sea; only the hum of the diesel-powered generator, the clicking of feet, the cry of the sea-birds.

Memory ended with the water, so cold and dark. And a huge shape looming above him.

He turned his head with a great effort. His throat was parched, and he was very weak.

Instantly two orderlies came up to the bunk and peered at him. They muttered at each other in German, and one hurried off while the other fed Jack some water, which tasted like nectar.

'Where am I?' he muttered. 'What ship is this?'

The orderly merely smiled.

Some time later an officer came in. He was obviously the surgeon-commander. He examined Jack thoroughly, and then gave orders. A meal was brought, mainly hot soup, but with some pieces of meat in it.

Jack chewed, slowly and carefully.

'Will you not tell me where I am?' he asked.

'You are on board SMS *Scharnhorst*, Mr Dawson,' said a voice from the doorway, in good English.

Again Jack twisted his head with an effort, and watched a tall, very handsome man, with a carefully pointed beard and lively eyes, enter the sick bay. He took off his cocked hat as he did so, while Jack recognised the insignia of a Rear Admiral in the German Navy.

He tried to push himself up the bed to assume an attitude of attention. But . . . Dawson?

Maximilian Graf von Spee stood above the bunk and smiled at him. 'Do not attempt to move, Mr Dawson, until the surgeon tells you to. You are very fortunate to be alive. In fact, you are the only survivor from your two ships. That is, if you wish to be a survivor.'

Jack frowned at him, and an orderly hurried forward with a chair. The admiral sat down next to the bunk.

'Where are we, sir?' Jack asked.

'In Valparaiso, coaling.'

'The date?'

'The sixth of November.'

Jack sank back on to the pillows.

'Your last memory will be the night of last Sunday,' Spee suggested.

'Yes, sir. I was in the water . . .'

'Shouting at the top of your lungs, and as I had stopped engines momentarily, you were heard by one of my people. He has very good ears, because we were blowing off steam, and *Gneisenau* was still firing.'

'*Monmouth* . . .'

'Went down with all hands. Just as did *Good Hope*, but for you. *Monmouth* became separated from your other ships, because, as I believe from a radio message we intercepted, she was taking so much water forward she had to keep her stern to the seas. She therefore made north, out of the battle. It was her misfortune to encounter *Nurnberg*, which was some distance behind my main squadron. *Nurnberg* called upon her to surrender, and she opened fire. With one gun. Presumably that is all she had left. So *Nurnberg* fired a torpedo, which sank her.'

'My God,' Jack muttered.

'Brave men, if perhaps foolish. However, you will be pleased to know that your light cruiser escaped, as did the armed merchantman. Now, I have told you what happened in the battle. Perhaps you will tell me what led your admiral to attack me with such an inferior force?'

'I have no idea,' Jack said. 'Save that he thought he might damage you too far from a support base for adequate repair.'

'A theory. Did he have no support himself?'

Jack did a hasty calculation. Cradock and the South Atlantic squadron was destroyed. Obviously the Admiralty would launch another, and hopefully stronger, squadron to deal with the situation, but they had to have the time to concentrate. Therefore telling Spee about *Canopus*, which might well limit his scope of action, would hardly be a betrayal of his country.

'Oh, yes,' Jack said. 'There was a battleship not three hundred miles away.'

'A battleship?' Spee's eyes narrowed.

'HMS *Canopus*. Armed with twelve-inch guns. She's not very fast, so Admiral Cradock left her behind while he came looking for you. But as I understood, his orders were to fall back on *Canopus* when you were sighted, and bar you access to the Atlantic.' He spoke slowly, with considerable effort. 'Only he didn't fall back.'

Spee gazed at him for some seconds.

'You would not be lying to me, Mr Dawson?'

'I give you my word of honour as an officer and a gentlemen, sir, that HMS *Canopus* is, or was, some three hundred miles south of Coronel last Sunday afternoon. I imagine she has been joined by *Glasgow* and *Otranto* by now.'

'That is an interesting piece of news. One I shall have to consider. As you say, it makes the actions of your admiral even more inexplicable. But now I would like to speak about you. You see, I am the only member of my crew who is the least fluent in English, and so, when a man dressed in seaman's clothing was dragged from the sea, wearing the insignia of *Good Hope*, and began to ramble deliriously, I came down to hear what you had to say. You spoke of a man called Jack Smith. Who is Jack Smith?'

Jack licked his lips.

Spee smiled. 'As I suspected, you are Jack Smith. But you also spoke of Jack Dawson, and Bruno von Eltz, and the fair Helene.' His mouth twisted in a grimace of distaste. 'So, you were released from prison, and rejoined the Navy as a common seaman under an alias. That was a bold thing to do. But why the alias?'

'I was not released from prison,' Jack said. 'I was paroled, and broke my parole to join up. If I am identified, I will be sent back to prison for four years.'

'Ah. I thought there was something like that at the back of it. That is why I reported that there were no survivors from either of your sunk ships.'

'I do not understand.'

'Well, you see, I am afraid that instead of going back to Dartmoor for four years, you are going to a German prison camp . . . for as long as this war lasts.' He gave a somewhat sombre smile. 'Supposing I can get you there. If I *can* get you there, however, do you not think it would be a good idea for you to clear your name?'

'Can I do that?'

'I think you can. The case aroused some interest in Germany, as you may imagine. Especially in the Navy. And of one thing we are all absolutely certain: you did not give the secrets of *Dreadnought* to Helene von Eltz.'

'How can you be sure?'

'Because Bruno swore it on his honour as a German officer. Now . . .' he held up his finger as Jack would have spoken. 'I do not know why you pleaded guilty, who you were sheltering, and I am not going to ask, but surely a signed affidavit from Helene that you are not the guilty party would force a revision of your sentence. Add to that your patriotism in returning to sea . . . I think we could have your sentence quashed. After the War, of course.'

'Supposing Helene would provide me with such an affidavit, sir.'

'I think she should be pleased to. Especially now that she is a respectable married woman. Did you not know that?'

'No, sir, I did not.'

'She married a French officer by name of Tonnheur. A remarkable thing to do.'

'Tonnheur?' Jack's eyes widened in surprise. 'But I know him. We were at Tsushima together.'

'Well, you see, it is a small world.'

Jack allowed his eyes to close for a few moments. Opening them again, he asked, 'Why do you wish to help me, sir? We are at war.'

'We are both naval officers, Lieutenant Dawson,' Spee pointed out. 'We share a common code, of behaviour, of ideals, if you like. Do you know, I was in the German naval contingent which marched on Peking in 1990 to relieve the legations? Fighting, if not alongside me, very close and in the same cause were Callaghan, Jellicoe, Beatty, and, believe it or not, Cradock himself. Brave men. How can I hate such men? Our respective governments may have decreed that we should fight each other, but when the fighting is over, as it is now for you, then we revert to being officers and gentlemen, with a common bond, the sea and our honour, and therefore with a duty towards ourselves and our fellows. I believe you were unjustly imprisoned. I would like to see that tarnish on your career removed.'

Jack simply didn't know what to say.

Over the next few days Jack rapidly regained his strength. By then the German squadron was again at sea, but travelling very slowly south.

A species of uniform – very ill-fitting – was found for him, and he was invited to the Admiral's cabin. There he found himself sitting down with two very young men who each bore a startling resemblance to Spee.

'My sons,' Spee said. 'Heinrich serves on *Gneisenau*, Otto on *Nurnberg*. But they are allowed to visit me from time to time. I have explained to them your situation, Lieutenant. But no one else is aware of it.'

Jack shook hands with both the young men.

'Yours is a most fascinating story,' Otto observed in stilted English.

'I suppose it is, regarded from a distance.'

'It has surely been very bad hell for you,' Heinrich smiled sympathetically.

'So bad, I imagine, that only you can know just what hell it has been.' The Admiral nodded to the rating, who entered with a tray of coffee, to pour it out.

'I can only express my gratitude for your interest, sir,' Jack said.

'I hope you will continue to feel like that.' When the coffee had been served and the seaman had retired, the Admiral continued. 'As I said when last we spoke, I cannot guarantee you a safe voyage to Germany. I would imagine that the Royal Navy would very much like to catch us, and the more I consider the situation, the less do I see how I can avoid being caught. You have so many ships . . .' he mused for a moment, and then smiled. 'Do you know that on my return to Germany I was to be appointed admiral in command of the High Seas Fleet? How I looked forward to that. But as I cannot get there . . . you understand that it must be my duty to do all the damage I can before attempting to return home.'

'I understand that, sir.'

'There are so many imponderables. One is that this ship alone fired thirty-five eight-inch shells at *Good Hope*. I think perhaps too many. I would have expected this ship, certainly, to have done better, although I must confess conditions for accurate shooting were nearly impossible. However, there it is, we have only just over forty left per gun. Enough for perhaps one engagement. You see my dilemma, Lieutenant. Rush for home, keeping my shot for a last engagement with your ships, or expend them on some worthwhile target closer to hand? So then, I must define a worthwhile target.'

Jack sipped his coffee. He was beginning to understand why the German was not cock-a-hoop over his victory.

'I have dispatched *Leipzig* scouting down the coast,' Spee went on. 'She has found nothing, but you will be pleased to know that, sending a boat ashore in search of information, she was told that a large British warship had been in these waters only a few days previously, steaming south at a low speed. I presume that to be *Canopus*. I am very relieved to have confirmation of your story.'

Jack inclined his head, and glanced at Spee's sons. The two young men were turning their heads to and fro, as though watching a tennis match, as they tried desperately to follow the English conversation.

'Now the question is, Lieutenant, what are the intentions of the captain of *Canopus*?'

'I would say to block your entry into the Atlantic, sir.'

'I wonder. As I say, no sighting has been made of the battleship. Therefore it is reasonable to suppose that she has no intention of engaging us, but is getting away as best she can. Now, as you say, she may be meaning to lie in wait for us at Cape Horn, but that would be a remarkable place to fight a battle. In those seas I doubt we would be capable of hitting each other. Besides, I have received an interesting message from our Consul in Valparaiso. Our Navy has intercepted various messages being put out by your Admiralty.

'As I imagined would be the case, the Royal Navy is assembling squadrons all over the place, trying to anticipate my every move. Your Mr Churchill, and his admiral, Lord Fisher, appear to be handicapped, however, by a refusal to detach any worthwhile capital ships from their Grand Fleet, which glares at our High Seas Fleet across the North Sea. The result is that I do not think there are any of these new combinations I cannot fight on at least even terms.

'Most interesting of all, however, is the combination they are setting up for the South Atlantic. It consists of three armoured cruisers, but none of them is any stronger than *Good Hope*. Yet they are being ordered to concentrate on the Falklands. There can be only one reason for that. Were those ships to encounter my squadron at sea they would be destroyed. Thus *Canopus* has also been ordered to return to the Falklands to give these ships support.'

'That seems likely, sir,' Jack agreed. If the Germans could

be dissuaded from attacking the islands, and steamed on into the Atlantic short of fuel and shot, surely that would be to Britain's advantage.

But this man wanted to help him, across the gulf of warfare. Where his own country had rejected him, a German naval officer wished to help him clear his name. Yet it was his duty to humbug him in every way – or he would indeed be betraying his country.

Spee was smiling. 'I know how your mind is working, Lieutenant. Permit my brain to work as well. Your Admiralty hopes that I will conclude that attacking the Falklands is now too dangerous. And the Falklands is my only source of coal, unless I apply to Brazil or Argentina. Thus they feel I must do this last, and they will again know where I am. They are overlooking one vital point. Do you play chess, Lieutenant Dawson?'

'I know the moves, sir.'

'Well, it is a fascinating game. And it can so happen that at certain times during a game of chess, a piece may find itself in a position, perhaps behind the enemy ranks, where it is certain to be taken. Now, the player who commands the piece may just say to himself, well, that is that, and turn his attention elsewhere. But, instead, he may consider the piece to be what is called, by chessplayers, 'desperado'. It has got to fall, therefore why not work out how it can do the maximum damage to the enemy first?'

Jack nodded. 'And you consider yourself desperado, Admiral?'

'I'm afraid that is what I am. I have almost no hope of getting this squadron back to Germany. As I have said, it would mean fighting my way through the entire Royal Navy, and I have only enough shot for one more engagement. So you see, I have decided my worthwhile target. We shall do what your Navy thinks we cannot, and attack the Falklands. Your ships will have to coal when they arrive. If we can catch them all in Port Stanley, we will be able to attack them one by one as they come out. We will hopefully sink several of them, we will certainly destroy the coal supplies, and also the wireless station. Perhaps we will destroy *Canopus* as well. She is an old ship, and I do not think she is as powerful as the Royal Navy pretends.'

'And afterwards, sir?'

'Supposing we survive, you mean? Well, that must be in the lap of the gods. But we will have done our best. That is what I meant when I said I cannot guarantee you a safe return to Germany.'

'I understand, sir.'

'Are you unhappy about that? You do not think I am doing a Cradock?'

Jack considered.

'I think it is what I would do myself, in the circumstances, sir.'

Spee smiled. 'Well, then, now it is only necessary to take our time over getting to the Falklands, to be sure your cruisers reach there first. Let me see . . . today is the twelfth of November, and the message ordering the concentration was received yesterday. How soon do you suppose this new squadron can reach the Falklands, Mr Dawson?'

'That would depend where they were starting from, sir. Do you have the names of the ships?'

'Oh, indeed.' Spee picked up the slip of paper from beside his plate. 'They are *Caernarvon, Cornwall* and *Kent*.'

'Admiral Stoddart's squadron in the West Indies.' Jack frowned. 'There should be a fourth ship, *Defence*.'

'She has probably been left behind to guard the mouth of the Panama Canal,' Spee said.

'Very likely, sir. Well, the ships will probably have to do a brief refit, and then they will have to coal . . . hardly less than three weeks.'

'My own estimation, At this speed, we will get to the Falklands in about twenty-six days. Shall we say, the eighth of December, Mr Dawson? On that day there will be a battle.'

Otto and Heinrich had followed their father's words.

'Ja, December eight,' the elder nodded.

'Ja, is good,' his brother agreed.

They shook Jack's hand again before he left the cabin.

61

Peter Dawson was on watch when the radio message was received from *Glasgow*, which was some way in front of the main squadron.

'Islands in sight.'

It was the afternoon of 7 December.

Following his standing orders, Peter immediately called both the Captain and the Admiral, then focused his binoculars.

Cay and Sturdee arrived together.

'Report,' said the Admiral.

'I can make out *Canopus*, sir.'

Sturdee also had a look.

'Undamaged.' He swept the horizon. 'Damn. Spee's passed them by.'

'Isn't it possible he might not have arrived yet, sir?'

'From Valparaiso? He should have been here a week ago. I felt sure he'd have to take the Falklands, for the sake of the coal. Damn, damn, damn. He must have arranged another supply port. But where?' He drummed his fingers on the bridge rail.

'Well, sir, we have no choice,' Captain Cay pointed out.

The squadron had steamed at full speed from Abrolhos.

Sturdee nodded.

'You'll prepare all ships for bunkering immediately, Captain. I want to be out of Stanley by tomorrow afternoon, looking for von Spee. Understood?'

The harbour was reached by dusk, and coaling began immediately, to go on all night.

The captain of *Canopus* came on board for dinner, and reported neither sight nor sound of the German squadron.

Captain Wilcox did point out, however, that as it was some four thousand miles from Valparaiso to Stanley, which was close to the limit for the German cruisers, Spee would need to cut his speed to conserve fuel. And if, as seemed likely, he was bringing his colliers with him to give him the range to return to Germany, he would hardly be making more than twelve knots.

'So he could still be coming,' Sturdee said. 'But we don't know that, unfortunately. We are going to have to make a sweep, Wilcox. How are your engines?'

'They've just about had it, sir. I crawled back here at eight knots. Now they've entirely given up, so much so that after conferring with the Governor, I have run my ship aground so that she cannot be sunk but can be used as a fortress until engineers are brought out here from England. That's what makes me think Spee is still south of us. I expected to be overtaken by him, but never was.'

It was three in the morning before Peter at last managed to fall into his bunk; in the next cabin Croom was snoring lustily. The ship hummed with noise, and was yet strangely quiet after the three furious weeks at sea.

Which were going to begin all over again tomorrow. Or rather, today.

He fell into a deep sleep, and was awakened by the jangling of alarm bells.

'Smoke, on the southern horizon.'

Peter dragged on his clothes and raced up to the bridge. The ship coaling had not yet finished, and black dust was clinging to the paintwork, even hanging in the still air, for it was a totally calm morning.

Officers were appearing from everywhere.

'Identification!' Sturdee snapped.

It came a few minutes later, at ten to eight.

'Ships identified as *Gneisenau* and *Nurnberg*, sir.'

'Only two? Where the devil are the others?' Captain Cay demanded.

'Two will have to do for the time being,' Sturdee said. 'God, what a mess,' he added, looking at the coal dust coating the palm of his hand. 'You will have to terminate coaling immediately, Captain. Command all other ships to do the same. And commence raising steam.'

'Yes, sir.' Cay hesitated. 'I'm afraid that will take not less than two hours, sir.'

'Two hours.' Sturdee snapped his fingers, but showed no other sign of irritation.

'Shall I have the men clean ship, sir?'

'Why not? But first, pipe all hands to breakfast, Captain. The Royal Navy always fights on a full stomach.'

'Ah, Lieutenant Dawson.' Admiral Von Spee was all smiles as Jack emerged through the doorway, surprised and gratified to be invited on to the bridge of SMS *Scharnhorst*. 'We have just received a signal from *Gneisenau* that the islands are in sight. She is returning to us now.'

Jack looked through the screen at the smoke on the horizon. The hulls of the two ships rapidly came into view.

'I wonder what we shall find,' Spee said. 'In Stanley.'

The ship was being cleared for action, everything inflammable in the officers' cabins being carried below out of harm's way. Shells were being fed into the hoists, and the sailors, their cap ribbons fluttering in the breeze caused by the ship's speed across the calm sea, were hurrying to and fro, laying out hoses, placing buckets . . . in the sick bay the surgeon would be sterilising his instruments.

Everyone was very calm, and very purposeful. And very confident.

Jack wondered if he was about to watch the destruction of another inadequate British squadron. And wondered too what the world would say if it could know that Lieutenant Jack Dawson, RN, was standing on the bridge of the German flagship as it went into action. But the world would never know that.

And of all the world, only Denise mattered. But Denise would suppose him dead – as far as the world knew, there had been no survivors from *Good Hope*. That was the thought that haunted him more than anything else.

And there was nothing he could do about it.

'There,' said Oberleutenant-zur-See Helfrich. 'A perfect landfall, Herr Konteradmiral.'

Binoculars were levelled as the low green hills rose out of the sea.

'They will know who we are by now,' Spee said. 'Will they come out, do you suppose, Lieutenant Dawson?'

'They will certainly try to, sir,' Jack said.

'Then we must prepare for them. Make to fleet, Oberleutnant: line will be formed ahead to bring maximum guns to bear; *Scharnhorst* will lead, *Dresden* will follow, *Gneisenau* will be third, *Leipzig* fourth and *Nurnberg* will bring up the rear. Fire will be held until the British ships come out; I do not wish to risk bombarding the town itself. Colliers will maintain a good offing until after the engagement.'

The lieutenant hurried off to the wireless room.

'Ship is ready for action, Herr Konteradmiral,' reported Captain Schmidt.

'That you, Herr Kapitan.'

Jack gazed at the now rapidly approaching shore, and at a ship starting to emerge from the arms of land which enclosed the splendid natural outer harbour, and which in turn left the inner harbour, on the shores of which was Port Stanley, one of the most sheltered in the world.

'Identify her for me, Mr Dawson,' Spee requested.

Jack peered through his borrowed glasses.

'She is an armed merchant cruiser, sir. Probably *Macedonia*.'

'Well, I hope she is trying to escape. For her to engage would be suicide.'

'There is another one,' said Kapitan Schmidt.

'Mr Dawson?'

'That is a County Class cruiser, sir. Either *Kent* or *Cornwall*.'

'Prepare to open fire, Herr Kapitan.'

The orders were transmitted to the turrets.

Then there was a roar from in front of them, and a burst of white water.

'Those were big shells,' Spee commented. 'Gentlemen, I think *Canopus* is firing at us.'

'Shall we reply, Herr Konteradmiral?'

'Keep your fire for the ships coming out. We will deal with

Canopus afterwards. Now then, what is that ship astern of the cruiser, Mr Dawson? She looks somewhat larger.'

'Ah . . .' Jack stared at the tripod mast which was slowly emerging from behind the bluffs guarding the harbour. He could not believe his eyes, even as his heart seemed to be leaping about his chest.

Schmidt had seen the telltale mast as well.

'Herr Konteradmiral,' he gasped. 'That is a dreadnought.'

Spee shot him a glance, then levelled his own glasses.

'A battlecruiser, sir,' Jack said. 'Of the Invincible class.'

Spee slowly lowered his binoculars. Jack could imagine what was going through his mind. Because he had, inadvertently, done a Cradock. A battlecruiser, eight twelve-inch guns and twenty-seven knots, was even more superior to *Scharnhorst* than *Scharnhorst* had been to *Good Hope*.

'Herr Konteradmiral . . .' Schmidt could scarcely speak. 'There is another . . .'

Once again the glasses came up, and they watched the second huge grey shape emerging from the harbour.

Spee sighed.

'Well, gentlemen,' he said. 'I seem to have led us into a trap.' He gave Jack one of his sad smiles. 'Your Mr Churchill and Lord Fisher are smarter than I thought, Mr Dawson. I am afraid that I will not now be able to return you to Germany, even via a neutral port.'

'What will you do, sir?'

Spee looked at the battlecruisers, still not quite clear of the land.

'The only thing I can do, Mr Dawson. Run like hell. And pray.'

The time was 0920, 8 December, 1914

'Hurrah for old *Canopus*,' Mark Croom shouted, as *Invincible*'s anchor at last came up, steam belching from her funnels.

The hour since finishing breakfast had been the longest of Peter's life – and he suspected that went for everyone. This was more than merely avenging Cradock; it would be the first time a dreadnought had ever gone into full action –

Heligoland Bight had really been just target practice against an enemy unable to hit back with any effect.

Now the ship was beginning to surge through the water, and now too the German squadron could be seen, having turned to the south-east, at a distance of perhaps eight miles, but drawing away every moment, as they were already at full speed. Further to the south, the colliers were just visible, also having reversed their courses.

Still no order to open fire was given, as the entire British squadron slowly came out of harbour; Sturdee was confident of overtaking his prey. *Invincible*, *Inflexible* and *Caernarvon* fell into line, with *Kent*, *Glasgow* and *Cornwall* forming another. *Bristol* was still coaling; she had been the last to commence. *Macedonia* remained waiting just outside the harbour; her orders were to accompany *Bristol* to capture or sink the colliers, when the light cruiser was finally ready.

There was some jockeying for position, as the light cruisers could not match the battlecruisers for speed, and Peter watched with dismay the German squadron appearing to draw still further away. But this was apparent to the bridge as well, because now the engine throbs became faster, and leaving the light cruisers behind, *Inflexible* and *Invincible* surged forward.

Now the gap began to narrow. The German ships could clearly be seen beneath the pall of smoke left by their funnels as they steamed flat out. But they were not fast enough, and with every second the battlecruisers were drawing closer.

But they were very long seconds as the morning ticked away. Men's throats became parched and they licked their lips as the sun rose into a cloudless sky. It was the most perfect summer morning imaginable. Peter found himself wondering what the Germans must be feeling, watching death approaching them with every moment, in such marvellous conditions.

Again the contrast to the mist of Heligoland was startling.

It was twelve-thirty when the order came, and it took him by surprise.

'Range nineteen thousand yards.'

That was extreme. But the battle was about to commence.

He made the necessary adjustments, grinned at his gun crew, adjusted his ear flaps.

'Stand by!'

A moment later the gun exploded with a huge burst of sound. The breech came scything back, and crashed forward again. As it opened the mechanical loader forced the next twelve-inch shell into the space, and the breech clanged shut.

'Range eighteen thousand yards.'

Closing all the time.

Peter cast a quick glance out of the turret. The British squadron had opened up, *Caernarvon* having gone off to starboard and *Glasgow* to port, obviously in case any of the German light cruisers should attempt an individual escape. *Cornwall* and *Kent* continued to steam in line behind the battlecruisers, but the range was still far too great for them.

'Range fourteen thousand yards.'

Now it was closing even faster. The guns fired almost continuously, so that the head, the ears, even the heart and lungs, seemed to be swirling through noise. While the voice remained calm and thoughtful, even when relaying good news.

'We have a hit on *Scharnhorst*. Range thirteen thousand yards.'

There was a giant whoosh, and water flew across the foredeck. Instantly *Invincible* heeled.

'We're turning away,' said Petty Officer Worthington, incredulously.

That was instantly confirmed.

'Range fifteen thousand yards.'

'Makes sense,' Peter shouted back. 'At long range their guns can't reach us. The Admiral doesn't intend to take any risks.'

The course was altered even further to port, and Peter took another quick look. Spee had apparently realised that he couldn't escape, and had turned towards the battlecruisers, desperately trying to close the distance to where his guns might be able to inflict some damage. At the same time he had told his light cruisers to continue to run for it, and they were rapidly disappearing, followed by *Kent*, *Cornwall* and *Glasgow*; *Carnarvon* remained with the big ships.

How *Glasgow* must be relishing this about turn, Peter thought.

And then suddenly everything went black.

'A hit, at last,' Oberleutnant Helfrich said. 'On one of the forward turrets.'

'But they are turning away again. Damn,' Spee said, and glanced at Jack. 'Your admiral is a cunning fellow. Well, I did the same to poor Cradock.'

'Shall we bear off too, sir?' asked Kapitan Schmidt.

Spee moved to the back of the bridge to look down on the fire raging amidships, the men desperately flooding the deck with their hoses. There was another fire further aft, although this was under control. But his beautiful ship was badly wounded. She was never going to get back to Germany, no matter what he now did.

'No,' he said. 'Close the enemy. If we can use our torpedoes . . .'

Just as Cradock had wanted to do, Jack thought. He watched in fascination as the Germans once again altered course towards the British, and the British once again kept away, their guns blazing, and found himself on his hands and knees. A shell had burst very close to the bridge, shattering the screens and wounding several men.

Spee too had been thrown to his knees. Now he scrambled back up and looked to where *Gneisenau* was also on fire, but still kept shooting.

'Herr Konteradmiral.' Oberleutnant Helfrich had a sheet of paper in his hand. 'Message from Vice-Admiral Sturdee. He requests you to surrender to stop this useless bloodshed.'

Spee looked at the paper, then at *Invincible*, still wreathed in smoke as she loosed another broadside. Then he looked at Jack, also slowly getting to his feet.

'Herr Konteradmiral.' Kapitan Schmidt's voice was excited. 'Look there, Herr Konteradmiral.'

He was pointing to the south, and Jack saw what he meant: looming up over the horizon was a huge dark cloud, and beneath it there was clearly rain – and poor visibility.

'Reply to Admiral Sturdee that I will continue to fight my ship,' Spee said. 'Alter course, Herr Kapitan. Make to *Gneisenau* to do the same.'

Scharnhorst slewed round, away from the British. But *Invincible* followed, and immediately the German ship was struck again, a fearful blow on the stern which sent a turret flying into the air as if it had been matchwood, opened up the deck, and left the engines roaring impotently as the ship lost way.

'My God! That is a mortal blow,' Schmidt wailed.

'Bring her round. We have still the forward guns,' Spee snapped.

The helmsman spun the wheel, but to no effect.

'We have lost steerage, Herr Konteradmiral.'

The stern was already perceptibly lower in the water as the bows came up.

Spee seized the communications microphone.

'This is the fleet commander speaking,' he said. '*Scharnhorst* is sinking. You are permitted to leave your stations and abandon ship. I thank you, in the name of the Kaiser, for your loyal and devoted service.'

He replaced the mike.

Jack found he was holding on to an upright, as the bridge deck was already beginning to slope. And also realised that there had been no explosions for several seconds, save for the small ones where the spreading fires came across a live shell. But the flames would soon be doused; water was lapping at the quarterdeck.

He stared across the ocean, saw *Invincible* steaming on to aid *Inflexible* in dealing with *Gneisenau*, which was still firing as she retreated towards that saving rainstorm.

'They have no time for us,' Spee said. 'I wonder if she will get away.'

Jack knew he was thinking of Heinrich.

'Well, Mr Dawson,' the Admiral said. 'It is your fate to

have to swim for it twice in six weeks. I think you should go now. The British will come back, eventually.'

Jack swallowed.

'And you, sir?'

'I think I will stay here. I have spent a great deal of time on this bridge. I have no real desire to leave it. In any event, I am not a very good swimmer.' He held out his hand. 'It has been a pleasure knowing you. Who knows, perhaps we would have cleared your name. Good fortune, Mr Dawson.'

Jack hesitated, then squeezed the fingers. He stood to attention, saluted, and hurried outside.

The stern was now well down, and water was pouring into the great hole left by the exploding turret. Yet none of the crew had so far left the ship. Instead, they were crowding forward, into the bows. But that promised disaster, when she went, and *Scharnhorst* very clearly only had a few minutes left.

Jack looked for the British. But the battlecruisers, followed by *Caernarvon*, were already several miles away, pounding *Gneisenau*. Very correctly, they were leaving any thoughts about survivors until after the battle was won.

When it might be too late.

But he had no intention of dying if he could possibly avoid it. He went down the sloping ladder, reached the deck, felt the scorching heat of the now abandoned blaze, which was consuming the funnels; even as he watched one of them came down with a splintering crash – the blast of exploding engine room air knocked him down. But the explosion had torn up a section of deck.

Jack reached his knees, and saw a length of wooden planking which had been shattered, one end thrust upwards by the explosion. It was perhaps eight feet long, and it would float. Its inner end was still attached, the wood splintered in several places. It was the work of a second, with his great strength, to tear it free.

He threw the wood over the side, then dived behind it, surfaced and, without looking back, swam away from the sinking ship, pushing the length of wood in front of him.

CHAPTER 3

Dogger

Jack was some fifty yards away from *Scharnhorst* when she sank. He heard the 'whumpff' from behind him, and threw both arms round the deck board, bracing himself for what would follow.

Down he went, lungs full of air, his legs kicking as he tried to counteract the pull, hanging on to the board with all his strength as it sought to slip away from him. Then he was shooting upwards again, and taking great gulps as his head broke the surface, swallowing the oil which had come bubbling up from the bowels of the sinking ship, and vomiting.

But the oil slick, which was spreading all the time, made the already calm sea into a millpond; it was the strongest possible contrast to the cold and surging waves off Coronel.

For a moment he could hear nothing; his ears were filled with water. He gasped, swallowed, and they popped. He looked up at the afternoon sky – it was about 1630 – and then twisted his head to and fro. He heard the sounds of gunfire in the distance, saw smoke. Nearer at hand there were men shouting, but very few.

He could make out some heads, swimming. They were a good distance away, and he had no intention of closing with them, or of using his strength in any way, save to keep afloat for as long as was necessary to be picked up; the water was not warm, but with midsummer's day due in a fortnight it was not very cold, either, and by using his legs he kept circulation going.

But was he going to be picked up? The sky was slowly growing darker, and though the rain cloud did not seem to be approaching any more, he was soon going to be quite invisible. The shouts behind him were dwindling as the exhausted men gave up trying to keep afloat. They did not have the same faith in the Navy as he did. He knew those battlecruisers would be back as soon as *Gneisenau* was sunk.

And the shooting had stopped. *Gneisenau* was either down or surrendered. They'd be on their way.

He wondered if there were any sharks in the South Atlantic.

Even his legs were numbed; his hands had already lost feeling. And it was dark. He was not going to be picked up, after all. And yet . . . he heard the grind of very powerful engines. He could see nothing in the darkness until a searchlight beam cut through the water, playing over the oil that still covered the surface, and which marked the tomb of *Scharnhorst*.

He watched the beam, moving to and fro. It came from high up, so it was mounted on a big ship. Slowly it flooded each patch of sea, coming closer, ever closer. He tensed his muscles, prepared. It bathed him for a moment, and he raised himself on the plank and waved desperately. The plank went under, and he went with it. When he surfaced, the searchlight beam was several yards to his left. They hadn't seen him. They . . . but it was coming back. Someone had seen something.

It played on him, and again he waved. This time the searchlight stayed on him.

Jack sat on a bunk in *Invincible*'s sick bay, and realised he was looking at his own brother.

Peter was unconscious, and his head was bandaged. There were other bandages as well.

How he wanted to go across and touch him.

He hugged the blanket more closely around him, but still shivered. They had given him a hot bath, as much to wash off the oil coating him as to warm him up, and then half a tumbler of rum, and still he shivered.

'How do you feel?' asked the surgeon-lieutenant, taking his temperature for the fourth time. 'Hm. Improving. You were in the water the devil of a long time.'

'Yes, sir. I feel fine, sir. Or I will when I stop shivering.'

'Hm. Rum do, picking up an Englishman from a German ship. You were the only survivor, you know.'

'Yes, sir. Anyone from *Gneisenau*?'

'Oh, yes, a couple of hundred there. Well, I've reported to the Captain, of course. I imagine he'll want a word.'

'Yes, sir.' Jack looked at Peter. 'Is the officer bad, sir?'

'He'll pull through. His turret took a hit. One of the very few Jerry shells to reach us. Ah . . .' An orderly was standing to attention.

'The Captain will see the prisoner now, sir.'

Jack raised his eyebrows.

'Am I a prisoner, sir?'

'That's up to the Captain. Or the Admiral.'

Both Captain Cay and Vice-Admiral Sturdee were waiting to interview him, in the Admiral's day cabin – although it was nearly midnight. Jack felt very incongruous, wearing only a blanket and a pair of outsize woollen socks provided to keep his feet warm – and standing between two marine privates.

The ship was underway again, and making back for Port Stanley.

'You gave your name as Jack Smith,' Captain Cay said. His voice matched his face, lean and incisive. 'Explain.'

Exhausted and groggy as he was, Jack had already done some thinking. The idea that Spee might help him clear his name had clearly only been a dream. To reveal his true identity to these officers would most certainly land him back in gaol. It was sheer bad luck that he happened to be picked up by a ship on which his own brother was serving . . . but he doubted even Peter would recognise him now – and they were not likely to come into a lot of contact.

So . . . back to square one.

'Jack Smith is my name, sir. Ordinary Seaman. I was off *Good Hope*, sir.'

Sturdee frowned. 'There were no survivors of *Good Hope*.'

'I was a survivor, sir. I know the Germans reported there were none. That was an error.'

'You understand we will check that out, sailor?'

74

'Yes, sir.' He knew they'd find the name of Jack Smith on the roster. 'I was Rear-Admiral Cradock's orderly, sir.'

'Hm. How did the Germans treat you?'

'Very well, sir. Rear-Admiral von Spee was a proper gentleman.'

'So I understand. Very good, Smith. Return to sick bay. We'll see about getting you another ship, when we get home.'

'Thank you, sir. If I may ask, sir . . .?'

'Yes?'

'I understood that one of Rear-Admiral von Spee's sons was serving on board *Gneisenau*. Did he survive?'

'No officer named Spee was picked up, from any of the German vessels, Smith. Dismissed.'

So the other brother had also died. His secret was back to just Denise and himself. In many ways, that was a relief.

Churchill leaned back in his chair and smoked a cigar.

'I feel about ten years younger,' he remarked.

'You deserve to,' Fisher agreed. 'When you think . . . if you hadn't put a rocket under that dockyard superintendent, Sturdee would have arrived too late.'

'Yes,' Churchill said happily. 'As it is . . . *Scharnhorst, Gneisenau, Nurnberg, Leipzig*, all gone . . . I think we can say Cradock has been avenged. Sturdee deserves a medal.'

'He let *Dresden* get away,' Fisher growled, old animosities suddenly resurfacing.

'We'll get her. She has nowhere to go. Well, I'm for the House. They'll enjoy this.' He got up. 'Pity about Spee and both his sons.'

'His fault for having them in the same squadron,' Fisher remarked. 'What do you make of this remarkable Smith character, who claims to have survived both *Good Hope* and *Scharnhorst*?'

Churchill put out his cigar. 'It seems that he did survive them. There certainly was a Jack Smith listed on *Good Hope*. He must have more lives than a cat.'

'I would say he's pretty well used them up by now, First Lord. Still, when he gets home, we'll give him some publicity. Staying power of the British sailor, eh? The press will like that. Now, First Lord, there is this report from Room Forty.'

Churchill sat down again. This was a subject in which he took a deep personal interest.

The war had only been a few weeks old when the Russian Ambassador had called to see him, to tell him that the Russians might, entirely by chance, have pulled off a most remarkable naval coup. A German light cruiser, *Magdeburg*, had struck a mine in the Baltic, and washed ashore from her had been the body of an officer with, concealed in his uniform, the entire German naval Code.

This the Russians had been prepared to offer to the British Admiralty.

Churchill had of course jumped at the opportunity, and under the Director of Naval Intelligence, Admiral Sir William Hall, had set up a special department, called Room Forty O.B., purely for deciphering the German messages as heard over the air.

The initial results had been disappointing as nothing of any importance had been picked up. But now for the first time Room Forty thought they had something.

'Can we trust it?' he asked.

'I think we have to,' Fisher said. 'If only because it is the first positive product of that Russian coup; we have to give it a go. Room Forty says that the German battlecruisers will be raiding the East Coast on the sixteenth of December. I would like to detach a battleship squadron to co-operate with Beatty and see if we can't do the bastards.'

'And if Room Forty have got it wrong?'

'It'll be a training exercise; Jellicoe's lot aren't doing much over in Loch Swilly.'

'Well . . . go ahead. And just let's pray none of our super-dreadnoughts hits a mine.'

The German battlecruiser squadron duly bombarded Hartle-
pool, Whitby, and Scarborough in the early hours of 16
December, and then returned to port.

No British dreadnought was seen because, although Beatty
put to sea, there was thick fog for most of the day.

Admiral von Ingenohl, who had replaced Holtzendorf
as Commander-in-Chief of the High Seas Fleet, sent the
battlecruisers a message of congratulations, which Hipper
duly passed on. 'Now we have avenged Von Spee and his
gallant men.'

Bruno von Eltz was not amused. If killing civilians –
according to the British, seventy-eight had died in the
three coastal resorts, with over two hundred wounded –
was truly what the High Command considered avenging
their shattering defeat at the Falklands, they were reverting
to the Dark Ages.

He sat down to write to Helene. It was a duty he
set himself, a penance for his part in their joint sin
– though she was his only relative, it afforded him
no pleasure. There was little to say – the French
were apparently reading most of the letters carried by
Furrer.

Invincible and *Inflexible* returned to England somewhat more
slowly than they had steamed out to the Falklands. Both
Christmas and New Year were spent at sea, but they were
happy occasions; there was much to celebrate.

Jack was pleased to see that within a fortnight Peter was
up and about, although still excused duty; his wounds were
more serious than had at first been supposed. He remained
very weak and it was clear he would need several months
of convalescense before being fit for service again. Jack
had himself rapidly been absorbed into the starboard
watch, where he found himself the centre of attention,
everyone wanting to hear what life on board a German
warship was like even more than the last moments of *Good
Hope* . . . or endless speculation on what Cradock had had
in mind.

Lost amongst a complement of seven hundred and eighty-four officers and men, Jack and Peter never came into contact at all.

When they finally steamed up the Channel Jack was again summoned to the Admiral's cabin.

'As you can imagine, Smith,' Sturdee said. 'There is a good deal of satisfaction being felt at our success. It has therefore been decided by the Admiralty that reporters will be allowed on board *Invincible* when we dock, with their, er, photographic equipment. It has also been decided that they shall be allowed to interview you.'

'Me, sir?'

'Well, you have had two remarkable escapes. You must also be the only British naval seaman who has actually been on a German man-of-war throughout a battle and returned, as it were, to tell the tale. You are newsworthy, Smith, and news is important.'

'Yes, sir,' Jack said uneasily. 'Will they wish a photograph, sir?'

'Oh, undoubtedly. Now, Smith, I wish you to be very careful what you say to these reporters. I know that you feel you were very well treated by the Germans, but they are our enemies, and as you may know, they have been engaging in all manner of frightfulness, such as bombarding our East Coast towns and thereby murdering innocent women and children. It would not go down very well were you to tell the press that they are good fellows. Understood?'

'Yes, sir.'

'And, of course, you will give away nothing that could conceivably be regarded as secret about either their ships or ours. Understood?'

'Yes, sir.'

'Well, then . . .' Sturdee gave one of his very rare smiles. 'I'm not sure there may not be a medal in all this for you, Smith. Dismissed.'

'Some show,' Harry Krantz remarked. 'I guess the old Royal Navy really does rule the waves, eh, Geoff?'

'Some people have all the luck,' Geoffrey growled. He peered through the port of his day cabin at the low hills of Ireland. 'While we are stuck as far away from the battle zone as is possible.'

For Jellicoe was steadfastly refusing to permit the return of his fleet to Scapa Flow until it had been fortified to his satisfaction, despite mutterings from the Admiralty.

'And when we do get to sea,' he continued, 'we spend an entire week drifting about in the fog, seeing not a damned thing.'

Anson had been one of the battleships detailed to engage the German battlecruiser squadron, without success, before Christmas.

'Your day will come,' Harry said. He had been as frustrated as anyone at not seeing action. 'You reckon Peter is all right?'

He had been listed amongst the severely wounded.

'The lucky beggar's probably down in Dorset right this minute,' Geoffrey said. 'Living off the fat of the land.'

'Talking about luck,' Harry said. 'What about this guy Ordinary Seaman Smith, eh? Or maybe I should say Able Seaman Smith. He's been promoted.'

'The great survivor,' Geoffrey commented,

'Say, you read the article?'

'I never read newspaper articles,' Geoffrey said.

He was in a distinctly grouchy mood as, quite apart from the 16 December fiasco, there had been no Christmas leave for the fleet, and it was now six months since he had last seen Mary or Joanna . . . and he had not seen his son at all, as yet.

'Well, you know, I would swear I've seen this guy before,' Harry said.

'All men with beards look alike,' Geoffrey pointed out.

'Still . . . hey, is that a mail call I hear?'

Geoffrey's orderly appeared in the cabin a few minutes later.

'Two for you, sir. One for Commander Krantz.'

Both men rather grabbed at their letters. One of Geoffrey's was from his mother, the other from Mary. All was well at home, at least.

He raised his head to look at Harry, who was frowning.

'Nothing wrong with Liz, is there?'

'She's got some kind of bug.'

'Oh, no. Is it serious?'

'Well . . . I guess not. But the doc says she can't travel in her condition until it's cleared up. So she won't be here for Christmas, like we planned. Damnation.'

'Better safe than sorry,' Geoffrey said.

Peter was indeed down in Dorset; *Invincible* was going to be in dock for some weeks, being both repaired and refitted after her exertions, but in any event he had been given extended leave to regain his health after his shattering experience.

Harriet and Mary were delighted to have one of the family home, once they were reassured that the bandages on his head and arm were really only for safety and would soon be coming off. He was able to play on the floor with Joan and little Mark while he told the story of the battle, and in turn, Mary and Harriet passed on the latest news of Geoffrey, Harry Krantz and Lizzie.

'Harry has now decided that in view of everything, Lizzie should stay with his parents until the baby is born,' Harriet explained.

'And Lizzie agreed?'

'Of course. Lizzie,' Mary said, 'does everything Harry tells her to. As a good wife should.'

Peter raised his eyebrows.

'He really is quite a forceful character,' Harriet agreed.

'It still feels damned strange to have a brother-in-law I've never even seen,' Peter confessed. 'Now, what's the news about Giles?'

'We think he is in the Mediterranean,' Harriet boomed.

'In a British submarine? What on earth is he going to find to torpedo down there?' Peter wondered.

He was sitting in the drawing room with a newspaper the next morning when Rawlston appeared.

'Excuse me, Mr Peter, but we have a visitor.'

80

'Mrs Dawson's upstairs,' Peter said, hastily straightening his tie.

'The young lady has come to see you, sir.'

'Me?' Peter got up, gazed at the young woman in the doorway. There was something vaguely familiar about her.

'Lieutenant Dawson? Oh, you look terrible.'

'Do I? I do apologise. Ah . . .' His fingers strayed to the shaved patch on the side of his head, where stitches had just been removed, and the mass of small cuts just healing on his face.

She came into the room, held out a gloved hand. 'Mavis Trenchard.'

'Trenchard,' he said. 'Not the vicar's . . .?'

'Daughter,' Mavis Trenchard said. 'I don't suppose you remember me, Mr Dawson.'

'Ah . . . of course I do.'

He remembered a scrawny little girl with pigtails, who had occasionally come over to play with Lizzie; they were about the same age. But that had been years ago. Since Lizzie had left school they had not seen much of each other.

And this was no scrawny little girl. Mavis Trenchard was a buxom young lady with auburn hair, freckles, and a deliciously upturned nose.

'Won't you please sit down,' he said. 'Rawlston, I think we could have some tea, or would you prefer coffee, Miss Trenchard?'

'Oh, tea will be fine, thank you.'

Mavis sat down and crossed her knees. She was also, it occurred to Peter, singularly self-possessed.

'It's awfully good of you to visit,' he said. 'I suppose it goes with the job.'

'What job?'

'Ah . . .' he realised he had made a gaffe. 'Well, being the vicar's daughter.'

'No, Mr Dawson,' Mavis said. 'It does not go with the job. I came because I wanted to be sure you were all right.'

They gazed at each other. It really was the most attractive nose he had ever seen.

'Well . . . as you see, I'm perfectly all right. These cuts were all superficial. I'm only waiting for my right arm to heal now. Jerry tried to blow it off, you see.'

'I'm amazed you can be so cheerful about it.'

'I was one of the lucky ones.'

'I know. It's terrible to read of the great loss of lives, ours at Coronel and the Germans at the Falklands.'

Rawlston appeared with a tray of tea and biscuits and placed it on the table between them.

'Shall I pour?' Mavis asked.

'Please. I shall only make a mess if I attempt to hold the pot with my left hand.'

'I'm sorry I said you looked terrible when I came in,' Mavis said. 'You actually look very good, considering.'

'Oh!' Peter flushed. 'Thank you. It's awfully good of you to say so. Won't you stay to lunch?'

'Ah, AB Smith,' said the Duty Lieutenant. 'Bang on time, eh? That's the spirit. Well, I have some tremendous news for you. You have been assigned to HMS *Queen Elizabeth*.'

'Aye-aye, sir!'

Jack stood to attention, unable to suppress a grin of delight. *Queen Elizabeth* was the first of the new oil-burning battleships to be completed; there were only going to be five, now, *Agincourt*, which had not yet been laid down when the War had started, had been scrapped, the Admiralty idea being to concentrate on ships already in the process of being built before worrying about entirely new ones. But no one in the Royal Navy had any doubts that the Queens, as they were affectionately called, were the most powerful warships ever designed . . . and the cleanest.

'Very good,' said the Lieutenant. 'You will report for duty on Monday, the twenty-fifth of January. Understood?'

'Aye-aye, sir.'

'Well, that gives you a week's leave, starting now. Enjoy yourself, Smith.'

As with the last time Jack had been given leave, the temptation to go down to Silver Streams was enormous. But Jack Dawson was gone forever. Had to be gone forever.

Besides, there was Denise.

His heart was pounding as he telephoned the number she had given him, desperately afraid that it might be the wrong one; all of his gear had been lost with *Good Hope*, and he was relying entirely on his memory.

The time was seven o'clock. He knew she had quarrelled with her parents over her refusal to marry the man they had chosen for her, lived on her own, and had a job. Thus he had waited; he wanted to be absolutely sure she would be home.

The phone rang and rang, and his heart slowly sank into his boots. No doubt, on learning of his death, she had gone home to Northampton after all.

He was about to replace the receiver, when a quiet voice said, 'Hello.'

'Hello,' he said.

There was a moment's silence. Then she asked, 'Who is this?'

'Jack.'

Another brief silence. 'Jack? Jack Daw . . . Jack Smith? Jack Smith is dead.'

'Don't you read the newspapers?' But of course, the story hadn't made the papers yet. 'I'm alive. You're not . . . I mean, do you still want to see me?'

'Oh, Jack!'

'I thought maybe you'd got married.'

'No,' she said. 'I haven't got married.'

'Can you get some time off?'

'I'll get it.'

'Well . . . perhaps we could go back to the same little hotel off Northumberland Avenue? There'll be no questions asked.'

'I should like that,' she said. 'When?'

'How about now?'

'Is there a room?'

'We'll find somewhere,' he promised her.

There was a room, and indeed Able Seaman Jack Smith was welcomed with open arms by the proprietor, who remembered him from 1913. The welcome was greatly extended the next day, when the news of his two miraculous escapes from death made headlines in the newspapers, along with photographs and suitably modest remarks.

'The German Navy is a force against which we can fight with honour,' Jack had said, and been quoted. 'They fought like men, and they died like men.' Hastening to add that these were clearly men uncontaminated by Kaiserism, and such frightfulness as the bombardment of unprotected coastal towns.

'They're still a lot of Huns,' the landlord opined, quoting.

Denise made no comment on that.

'I thought you were dead,' she whispered, as she huddled in his arms.

'Well, to tell the truth, I thought I was too, from time to time. But I'm here. There has to be something to believe, in that.'

It was something they both wanted to believe. For Denise Robertson there was the sheer joy of having the man she had loved since she had been a girl back in her arms. For Jack there was the still unbelievable proof that this girl, whom he had first noticed, and flirted with, ten years before when she had been no more than a schoolgirl friend of his sister Mary's, and his future had seemed so certain, and certainly successful as well, actually loved him, and believed in him, and was willing to share her all with him, regardless of society or convention, family or friends . . . or the impossibility of ever acknowledgng him as who he really was.

And thus, the impossibility of ever marrying him? How could Denise Robertson ever marry an Able Seaman? It was not something she wanted to discuss, in wartime. He realised that she had been forced to consider herself a widow, if an unmarried one, when the news of Coronel had been received in England. It was not an experience she was anxious to undergo again.

As during that week they had shared in 1913, before he had left with the South Atlantic squadron, they wanted only to lie in each other's arms, share each other's bodies, begrudged the time wasted when they had to eat. But as before, they went out to dinner together on the last night before he was due to join his new ship, and with all of London were electrified by the news shouted from the stands. 'Read all about it! Read all about it! Great British victory in the North Sea! German battlecruiser squadron destroyed! Read all about it!'

'We could not have chosen a better day for it,' remarked Korvettenkapitan Kroess, peering out through the bridge screens of the battlecruiser *Roon*. 'This must be the best visibility we have had, this war.'

As if we have had a few wars previously, at sea, Bruno von Eltz thought.

But a brisk north-easterly wind was certainly keeping the mist away, and as the winter darkness began to fade he could make out the shape of *Derfflinger*, two cables' lengths ahead of *Roon*, dipping into the swell and leaving a bubbling white wake astern. The wind was also pushing up the sea against the German battlecruisers, which were steaming in line ahead to the north-west.

They had left the Jade estuary at two that morning, and this time were making for Scotland itself.

All their earlier efforts to manoeuvre the British into battle at a disadvantage had failed. Hipper had been quite unable to understand how the brutal bombardment of the north-east coastal resorts of England just before Christmas had not been responded to, with violent anger, by the Royal Navy. True, there had been rumours that a British squadron had been at sea, but if they had, it had been to no purpose.

The failure of the two fleets to meet had started the usual question-asking in Berlin. Von Ingenohl had been accused of behaving too passively, especially, as was now known, the Grand Fleet had been withdrawn to the north coast of Ireland, far away from being able to take part in anything less than a set-piece battle.

So the strategy had been put into force yet again, only this time Hipper had been ordered to take his ships to the very edge of the Firth of Forth itself, and see what happened. Surely Beatty would come out, and then would be led into the arms of the High Seas Fleet which would just about now – Bruno looked at his watch; the time was 0715 – be emerging from the Jade.

Certainly something had to be done. The German Navy, perhaps the entire nation, had been profoundly shocked by the destruction of Spee and his squadron. No one had expected the Admiral actually to be able to bring his ships back to Europe; the difficulties were too immense. Opinions on what might happen had varied from internment to eventual piecemeal destruction, after doing an enormous amount of damage to the Allied Atlantic shipping.

Instead of which they had been seized and destroyed as an elephant might have stepped on an ant.

It was the secret ruthlessness with which the British had sent two dreadnoughts to do the job that had sent a shiver down the spine of the German Navy. It had created an impression that whenever the British chose, they would destroy whichever German ships got in their way. Morale had suffered, and only a successful action could restore it.

Thus today . . .

'Signal from light cruiser squadron, Herr Kapitan.' Becker was at his shoulder. 'Enemy cruiser sighted.'

A moment later, drifting across the morning, came the sound of gunfire.

Bruno and Kroess levelled their glasses, and made out the smoke from the funnels of the cruisers; visibility was at least twenty miles.

British cruisers . . . the two men looked at each other.

Becker had returned to the wireless room. Now he was back.

'Signal from fleet commander, Herr Kapitan. Squadron will reverse course and steer south-east. Immediately.'

Moltke was already turning; she flew the flag of Konter-admiral Funke. *Seydlitz* was behind her, flying Hipper's flag. *Derfflinger* followed, and then *Roon*. The armoured cruiser

Bluecher brought up the rear of the main squadron, while the light cruisers and destroyers came scurrying back.

'Something's up,' Kroess muttered.

'There!' Bruno said.

Emerging over the horizon were five huge ships. The British battlecruiser squadron, at last! Clearly Hipper must have overheard the British light cruisers reporting back to Beatty.

'What the devil are they doing out here?' Kroess asked at large. 'Almost as if they knew we were coming.'

'They are making a routine sweep. We had to meet them one day,' Bruno said with satisfaction. 'All guns prepare to fire, Herr Korvettenkapitan.'

The orders were sent down to the turrets and the shell hoists went into action.

'Orders from fleet commander, sir,' Becker said. 'Rearmost vessels will drop contact mines.'

'Understood.'

Korvettenkapitan Kroess was already barking into the telephone, and the squadron slightly altered course, steering diagonally instead of in line ahead, so that the mines being strewn from the stern of *Roon* and *Bluecher* would not hit any other German ship.

'The swines know what we are about,' Kroess said.

For the British had also altered course, to port, taking them out of the line of the drifting mines. And yet they were closing; they had the superior speed. They made a splendidly dramatic sight, clearly etched against the brightness of the morning, smoke streaming from their funnels, white bones racing away from their bows, grey shapes, sleek and beautiful – and deadly.

'Range twenty-six thousand yards,' intoned Oberleutnant-zur-See Martinsen, the Gunnery Control Officer.

Bruno drummed his fingers on the rail as he went outside on to the bridge wing for a better look at the enemy, plunging through the sea, their great bows burying themselves in the backs of the waves, and then rising again, tossing spray aft.

The Germans were doing the same.

He wondered where the German High Seas Fleet was at this moment. But they had not anticipated meeting the British so soon. Almost as if they had known what was coming, Kroess had said.

'Range twenty-four thousand yards.'

Bruno looked at his watch: 0830. He went inside. 'Take another reading, Herr Oberleutnant.'

There was a moment's wait, then the voice came down the tube again, 'Twenty-four thousand yards, sir.'

Bruno looked at Kroess. 'What is our speed?'

'Twenty-six knots, Herr Kapitan.'

'And they are closing the range at a mile in half an hour? I want more speed, Herr Korvettenkapitan.'

'Yes, sir, Herr Kapitan.'

The order went down to the engine room, and more black smoke belched from the funnels while the vibration increased. The rest of the German squadron had also increased speed, but *Bluecher*, a slower ship than the battlecruisers, began to drop behind.

Bruno chewed his lip as he watched her. But the decision was Hipper's.

'Range twenty-one thousand yards.'

It was 0900.

'Order from fleet commander,' Becker reported. 'Speed will be reduced. Contact must be maintained with *Bluecher*.'

Bruno gave a sigh of relief, even if it meant that at least an exchange of fire was certain.

Where, oh where, were the battleships of the High Seas Fleet?

'Range twenty thousand yards.'

0930.

There was still a long way to go.

'The British are having trouble as well,' Kroess remarked.

The three leading British ships were pulling away from the two rear ones.

'Those last are the old ones,' Bruno commented. 'Probably two of the Invincible Class.'

But there could be no question as to the identity of the leading ship: she was *Lion*, the pennant of Sir David Beatty streaming in the wind. Or the ship immediately behind her,

88

the biggest battlecruiser in the world: *Tiger*. And the most powerfully armed.

'Range eighteen thousand yards.'

1000. Bruno watched black smoke wreathing above the leading British ships, and watched, too, plumes of water surrounding *Bluecher*.

'Good shooting,' Kroess growled.

'Orders from fleet commander,' Becker said. 'All vessels will engage whenever possible, but course must be maintained.'

'Understood.'

Bruno returned to the bridge wing. Eighteen thousand yards was an immense distance to fire and hope to hit something. It would be better wait, until . . .

He gasped in horror as one of the next British salvo struck *Bluecher*. There was a flash of blue light as the steel of the shell hit the six-inch armour plating protecting the cruiser's deck, then there was a gush of red-tinged flame as the lyddite exploded.

Bluecher could be seen to tremble from stem to stern, and for a moment fell away from her course.

Bruno stepped back inside.

'Open fire with stern guns,' he snapped into the telephone.

'Range seventeen thousand yards,' Martinsen said doubtfully.

'Open fire,' Bruno repeated.

A moment later *Roon* trembled as her stern turrets exploded. *Derfflinger* was also firing now.

But nothing was going to save *Bluecher*. Even as Bruno was giving his orders she had been struck again. One of her after turrets was a shambles, and she was on fire amidships.

The leading British ships now transferred their fire to the rest of the German line, leaving *Bluecher* to be dealt with by the two rearmost ships and the light cruisers. Waterspouts began bursting all around *Roon*, and a few minutes later the inevitable happened; there was a burst of smoke and flame from aft as the ship shuddered.

'Fire control!' Kroess was shouting into the telephone.

'Get down there!' Bruno snapped.

Eleven-inch against thirteen-point-five, he thought bitterly, as he looked down on the shambles of his afterdeck. That is no way to fight a war.

But D turret was still firing.

He looked ahead as *Derfflinger* also exploded in smoke, but she had been hit as well and, in front of her, he could see that *Seydlitz* was also on fire in at least two places. Only *Moltke*, leading the line, had so far escaped damage.

My God, he thought, I am witnessing the destruction of the German Battlecruiser Squadron.

'Fire under control, Herr Kapitan,' panted Kroess up the telephone. 'But C turret is definitely out of action.'

'Keep firing,' Bruno said, and gazed at *Bluecher*. Some miles astern now, she was a mass of flame from stem to stern, surrounded by British cruisers, and as he watched there was another huge gush of smoke and flame and metal where she had been struck by a torpedo. Now she was slowly heeling over, her decks crowded with men, about to die.

Bruno swallowed. His throat was dry.

'There go the destroyers,' Becker remarked.

The little ships surged past the battlecruisers. Hipper had realised his danger of annihilation, and was sacrificing his destroyers. They raced straight at the steadily closing British ships, while everyone held their breaths, praying that a torpedo, or better yet, two, would strike home.

It was a forlorn hope. Had it been night now, or fog . . . but the day remained beautifully clear and bright, and the destroyers were sitting targets. As they came within range, and while they were still outside torpedo range, the six-inch secondary batteries of both *Lion* and *Tiger* came into action. The shells tore the destroyers apart, left several sinking, and sent the others reeling from the fight.

'This is a serious situation, Herr Kapitan,' Kroess observed, having regained the bridge, capless and smoke-stained.

'It is a lost situation,' Bruno told him. 'We need a miracle.'

And then there was a miracle. *Lion* was forging closer and closer, her guns blazing, her bows rising right out of the still big waves before crashing down again. And on those bows there was now an explosion. It did not seem very big, and none of the Germans knew which ship had fired the shot . . . but immediately the British flagship slewed out of the line, momentarily out of control. By an unlucky, or lucky, chance, the shot had severed the feed line to the port engine, which had promptly failed.

The Germans watched in amazed relief as the entire British squadron now turned away; it was only later they learned that *Lion* had also had her wireless aerials shot away, and was unable to communicate with the rest of the squadron, which had merely been following her, save by flag or lamp.

Now they watched a destroyer hastily going alongside to transfer the Admiral to another ship, while the last of the battlecruisers came up to take the stricken flagship in tow.

But while that was happening the Germans were pulling away.

'Range eighteen thousand yards,' said Oberleutnant Martinsen, with some relief.

'Cease firing,' Bruno said.

The distance between the German and British squadrons was increasing with every minute, and there was little chance of the British renewing the action; Heligoland, with its minefields, was only seventy miles distant.

It was time to count the cost. *Seydlitz* was still on fire, although her speed seemed unaffected. *Derfflinger* had had two turrets put of out action, but her fires were under control. *Roon* had had one turret knocked out, but she also was no longer burning.

And far, far astern, *Bluecher* was slowly turning over to plunge to the bottom of the North Sea.

'Schnapps, Herr Kapitan.'

Kroess thought of everything. Now he raised his glass. 'To the next time. The next time we will do better.'

He was also an incurable optimist, Bruno thought.

But again he thought, where, oh where, had been the High Sea Fleet?

CHAPTER 4

Death From Below

'What went wrong?' Grand Admiral von Tirpitz stood at his desk and faced his fleet commanders. 'That is what His Majesty wishes to know. That is what I *have* to know. What went wrong.'

He glared from face to face.

'Firstly,' Hipper said. 'My squadron was badly composed for such an encounter, such a plan. You will know, Herr Grosseadmiral, that I protested against the inclusion of *Bluecher* in the first place. She was not sufficiently heavily gunned, she was not sufficiently heavily armoured, and above all, she lacked the requisite speed. Result? She was sunk, and three of my ships were badly damaged because we had to reduce our own speed to keep company with her.'

'Without her, you would only have had four capital ships to the British five,' Vizeradmiral Scheer pointed out.

'A weak ship is a liability, Herr Vizeradmiral. She does not increase strength.'

'On the other hand,' put in Admiral von Ingenohl, 'It could be said that by the British concentrating on *Bluecher*, the rest of your squadron was enabled to escape.'

'Had we been able to steam at our full speed, Herr Admiral I believe we would have escaped with less damage. But that brings me to the second point: there was a complete lack of support from the High Seas Fleet. Even steaming two or three knots below our maximum, when the action was broken off we were within seventy miles of Heligoland. Yet not a single battleship was there to support us.'

Tirpitz looked at Ingenohl.

Who looked, hopefully, at Scheer.

Scheer cleared his throat.

'There were technical difficulties in getting the High Seas Fleet out of port. The action took place much earlier than anticipated. Had it been delayed another few hours, the entire High Seas Fleet would have been available.'

'Some of them must have got out,' Hipper snapped. 'Five dreadnoughts, and we would have utterly destroyed Beatty.'

'It was my decision to keep the fleet together,' Ingenohl said stiffly. 'How was I to know you would encounter Beatty so far from his base?'

'That is my third point, Herr Grosseadmiral,' Hipper said. 'What was Beatty doing there, closer to Germany than to England? Do you realise what that means, gentlemen? It means that he left Rosyth on the evening of Saturday 23 January, at about seven o'clock. We did not leave port until two on Sunday morning. What was he doing at sea?'

'Perhaps he was on his way to make another raid on Heligoland,' Tirpitz suggested.

'In which case it was a fortuitous encounter for us,' Scheer remarked. 'You stopped his plan, and inflicted serious damage upon his flagship.'

Hipper did not look the least reassured.

'You have presented your case very ably, Herr Vizeradmiral,' Tirpitz said. 'And your points will be noted. It is now my duty to decide where the War at sea goes next. It is obvious that with all of our battlecruisers except *Moltke* and *Von der Tann* under repair, dreadnought activity must cease for the next few months. And as you have pointed out, Herr Vizeradmiral, before it is resumed we must have a better and more co-ordinated system.

'Does that mean we do nothing at sea for that time? That would be fatal, both to the war effort, and to the German Navy. If I am to persuade His Majesty to keep building dreadnoughts for us, we have to show some continuing returns.

'Now, it seems to me that we have a field which has so far been untouched. I am speaking, of course, of the British Merchant Marine.'

The admirals exchanged glances.

'Do not think we would be engaging in some kind of latterday piracy, gentlemen,' Tirpitz said. 'It is beyond any doubt that a very large number of British so-called merchantmen have been armed with at least one and, in some cases, two guns. This arming of these ships was carried out in great secrecy some years ago, for just such a situation as this. There is also no doubt, according to the reports from our agents in the United States and Canada, that these ships, even the big passenger liners, are secretly transporting vast quantities of arms and ammunition for the use of the British armies. On both of these counts, I regard them as obvious targets for our U-boats.'

'With respect, Herr Grosseadmiral,' Scheer said. 'Our U-boats have already tried to stop one or two of these ships, and had a hard time of it.'

'Because of the guns. That proves my point.'

'Anyway, Herr Grosseadmiral,' Hipper said, 'surely the idea of a submarine trying to stop a ship like *Lusitania* is a joke. She steams at twenty-three knots.'

'Agreed. And she is armed with at least two six-inch guns. Would you not say, Herr Vizeradmiral, that she is actually a warship?'

His admirals stared at him, none of them daring to believe his ears.

'We shall, of course, go about this in an orderly manner,' Tirpitz told them. 'To begin with, I intend to propose to the Kaiser that we announce that from a certain date, the British Isles and its adjacent waters shall be designated part of the War Zone, and that any vessels . . .' he paused, to emphasise the words . . . '*any* vessels found in those waters will be liable to be sunk without warning. If civilians choose to travel after we have made such an announcement, it will be at their own risk. It will be the same thing as if a trainload of sightseers were to travel up to the front line in Flanders during a battle. No one would be so crazy. Well, then, we must expect the British and American businessmen and holidaymakers who travel so carelessly to and fro across the Atlantic not to be crazy either.' He looked from face to face. 'If anyone has any objections, I would like to hear them now.'

There was a brief silence.

Then Hipper said, 'If a big British merchantman with women and children on board is sunk, Herr Grosseadmiral, and lives are thereby lost . . . well, it is a good thing that Germany is going to win this war, isn't it?'

'Signal failures,' Lord Fisher growled, throwing the detailed report of the Battle of the Dogger Bank on to the First Lord's desk. 'God knows there weren't signal failures in the old days, when the only signalling was done by flags or commonsense. What in the name of God was Moore doing? He was second in command. He should have taken over the moment he realised *Lion* was crippled.'

'But Beatty was already trying to transfer his flag,' Churchill pointed out. 'And the fact is, John, we gained a victory. They lost a ship, and most of the others were pretty cut up. Better yet, we now know that Room Forty can deliver the goods.'

'Maybe, but next time we have to be more ready to take advantage of them,' Fisher said. 'Now, First Lord, what are we going to do about this pronunciamento of Tirpitz's?'

'Do you suppose he means it? Is the man a criminal?'

'In the eyes of some, any man who fights a war is a criminal, Winston. That includes you and me. If you adopt a win at all costs policy, what is the difference between bombarding a coastal resort and indiscriminately killing a hundred people, and sinking a ship without warning with the same result?'

'That takes us back to the days of piracy,' Churchill said.

'Our point of view. Not necessarily Germany's. And whether we like it or not, you have to admit that for us to lose a big liner like *Lusitania* or *Mauretania* would be a bit of a blow.'

'Is there a submarine in the world could possibly hit one of those?'

'The odds are against it, I agree, if there is the least proper look-out maintained, and if the captains follow proper procedure, like continuous zig-zagging and alterations of speed. However, I think we should be safe rather than

95

sorry. I think we should put an embargo on big passenger liners sailing until we see whether Tirpitz really means it or not.'

'Won't that rather be like surrendering without firing a shot? Anyway, have we the legal right to do that? What will Cunard say?'

'I think if you put it to them, First Lord, Cunard will see our point. I imagine Tirpitz will have second thoughts about this War Zone nonsense in a few weeks . . . and anyway, if this Dardanelles operation comes off, he'll have too many other things to think about.'

'The Dardanelles,' Churchill breathed, his eyes glowing. The whole concept of a Franco-British fleet steaming up the Narrows and blasting the Turkish forts out of existence, before putting an end to the Sultan's regime at gun point in Constantinople, had fired his imagination. 'Can they do it, John?'

Fisher tapped his nose. 'If Carden says he can do it, then I believe he can. And he'd better do it quick. I want *Queen Elizabeth* back with the Grand Fleet just as soon as possible.'

'Shit!' remarked Harry Krantz. 'Of all the goddamned luck.'

'Problems?' Geoffrey raised his eyes from his own letter.

'You won't believe this, but now that Lizzie is perfectly fit again, she can't get a berth.' He grinned even through his annoyance. 'I mean on a ship. Seems all the liners are embargoed while this submarine scare is going on.'

'Hm. But really, old man, isn't she six months pregnant?'

'That's absolutely right.'

'Then maybe she shouldn't be taking a sea voyage in any event. The Atlantic in February can be hellishly rough.'

'Yeah.' Harry brooded for several minutes. 'I guess you could be right. I'm going to have to run out on you, Geoffrey. I'm due some leave, and maybe a new posting. But I want to be with Lizzie when it happens.'

'Of course,' Geoffrey agreed, thinking back to the birth of young Mark, whom he had still had not yet seen. But perhaps it might be possible soon . . . over the past six months he had been aware of a tightness in the chest, a breathlessness, which had suggested something might be wrong in there.

The temptation to put in for sick leave was enormous. But that he might be seriously ill was not something he wanted to admit, even to himself. He had always been perfectly fit . . . and the complaint had come on within a few weeks of the outbreak of war. He could not possibly admit that a man who had spent his entire life in the Navy, preparing for just such a war, could be so stressed by the fact of it that his heart was giving out.

That was certainly something he could never admit to Mary, either.

And to put in for sick leave might involve him being relieved of his command. He could not risk that.

And surely the condition would improve, as the war settled down. He had to believe that.

So . . . he would wait until he could legitimately ask for leave. Some time later on this year. Young Mark would wait until then.

'You won't be missing anything over here for awhile, after the pasting we gave them at Dogger,' he told Harry. 'What you want to do is get a posting to the Med. That's where all the action is going to be, this year.'

Jack had cruised in the Mediterranean as a midshipman, and had always had pleasant memories of its blazing sun and sparkling blue water. But he had never cruised in a ship quite like *Queen Elizabeth*.

Neither had anyone else.

With her thirty-thousand-plus-ton displacement, her speed of twenty-five knots, and her eight fifteen-inch guns, she was simply the most powerful ship ever commissioned.

And there were three sisters already in the water, and a fourth about to be launched.

But it was not merely the power of her that attracted; her oil-fired turbines were the smoothest Jack had ever sailed with; she seemed to glide through even the roughest sea.

She was, of course, brand new. She had only been launched the previous month, and this jaunt to the Mediterranean was in the nature of a shake-down cruise, with some gunnery practice intended at the end of it. Thus there were little problems to be coped with, but this merely added to the interest of getting such a magnificent piece of sea-going hardware into fighting trim.

Jack felt happier than at any time since the treason trial. Of course he would have liked to be on the bridge – he might well have been Gunnery Officer on this ship, with the rank of Commander, had things turned out differently. But he was on the ship, and he was now a respected veteran of two naval battles . . . and he had held Denise Robertson naked in his arms.

He couldn't blame her for continuing to be a little bit reticent about marriage; socially, in their current positions, they were light years apart. But she had bridged that span, and she would do so again.

And they would eventually get married.

Perhaps when the Navy had blown a few chunks out of Constantinople, although everyone was sure it would never come to that; the mere appearance of the fleet would cow the Turks into surrender, it was agreed.

There had been a brief stoppage at both Gibraltar and Valetta, for fuel and mail, but now the huge ship was approaching her destination. For the last twenty-four hours she had steamed past the beautiful islands of the Aegean Sea, gleaming white in the February sunshine, so remote from the grey skies which had hung above them when they had left Portsmouth the previous week. And now ahead of them could be made out the hills of the Dardanelles, and the mainland opposite, seeming to merge as *Queen Elizabeth* approached from the south-west.

The far hills, Jack remembered, were where Troy had been situated. They were at the one of the oldest recorded battlefields in the world.

He counted some eighteen other capital ships waiting for them. None of them were dreadnought battleships, of course; this was to be a bombardment, not a naval battle in which speed and armour plating would matter – the Turks only had *Goeben* and a couple of very ancient battleships with which to oppose them. But there was one other modern ship, the battlecruiser *Inflexible*, ready again for action after the Falklands.

They all looked like toys beside *Queen Elizabeth*, and as she steamed up to take her allotted place the crews, both French and British, dipped their ensigns and lined their rails to give three rousing cheers.

Then it was time to fraternise, the British and French sailors being encouraged to visit each other's ships, and splutter at each other in languages they could not understand.

'Let's see,' said Midshipman Barber, looking down his list. 'We want one lot to visit *Bouvet*, Captain Dubois. You, you, you, you and you. You will command, Petty Officer Martin. The next lot will visit *Wagram*, Captain Tonnheur. You, you, you, you and you. Petty Officer Hill will command.'

Jack realised that the boy's finger had included him. Tonnheur? There could hardly be more than one officer in the French Navy with that name, and if there was, certainly not one who would, by the normal process of seniority, have arrived at the rank of Capitaine de Vaisseau.

Pierre! Who was now married to Helene. They were about to come face to face. And there was nothing he could do about it.

But if his own brother hadn't recognised him, there was little chance of Pierre doing so. Why, he hardly expected to recognise the Captain, after ten years.

They weren't in love with each other.

It was, nonetheless, a somewhat traumatic experience to have his hand shaken by the French captain; for a moment Jack thought he was also going to have his cheeks kissed, but Pierre decided against it, perhaps because of the beard, perhaps because he had been told that sort of thing wasn't done in

England. Jack had been the first in line, and he didn't kiss any of the others, either.

Pierre himself was actually perfectly recognisable, even if he had put on a little weight, and there were lines of disappointment and worry in his face.

Jack breathed a sigh of relief when, after consuming a large quantity of Ricard, he regained *Queen Elizabeth*. He was not likely to have to face Pierre again.

But then he came up against another problem: several British submarines had been sent to the area, and on one of them, *C17*, he learned there was a certain Lieutenant Giles Dawson.

Fortunately, the submariners and the battleship crews weren't required to come into contact with each other at all.

Commander Manly faced looked at his officers across the tiny wardroom table in HMS *C17*.

'Admiral Carden has no real idea what lies between the fleet and Constantinople,' he told them. 'We have interrogated certain of the local people, of course, but what they have to say is mostly rumour. However, it is hardly credible that the entire straits, and the Sea of Marmara, are *not* defended. It is our business to discover what those defences are.' He grinned at them. 'We move out at dawn, tomorrow. Giles I'd like a word with you.'

Lieutenant Giles Dawson waited as the other three officers filed out; *C17* had a complement of forty-seven ratings and five officers. Giles himself was in the typical Dawson mould, tall and fair and powerfully built – quite the wrong shape for a submariner, as he had early found out. But he was now more experienced than his commanding officer. Giles Dawson had served in *E4* at the Battle of Heligoland Bight, just after the start of the war, and since then on innumerable North Sea patrols. Manly, but recently promoted to command of *C17*, was glad to have such a man as his executive officer, even if he was well aware – and had warned his sub-lieutenants – that Giles Dawson was not a man to be in any way ragged: everyone in the Navy knew how his eldest brother had been sent to prison for betraying secrets to the Germans.

Now he grinned as he knocked out his pipe; *C17* was alongside on the surface, in Mudros Harbour, with all hatches open. 'At least the sea will be warm.'

'What are we looking for?'

Manly shrugged. 'Minefields, torpedo boats and shore batteries, of course.'

'Have the Turks that kind of knowhow?'

'Nobody knows, for sure. It's up to us to find out. Any news of Peter?'

'He seems to be on the mend,' Giles said. 'But I have no idea when he will be ready to return to service.'

'Hard to say whether he's lucky or not,' Manly remarked. 'Supposing he is on the mend. Well, I'm for an early night. We could have an interesting couple of days coming up.'

'I'll say amen to that,' Giles agreed.

But sleep was hard to come by. This was not in any sense an apprehension of what the morrow might bring; six months of war had taught Giles Dawson that that was a waste of time. Rather was it a reflection of things past, and what might have been. No doubt he was *too* reflective. Peter was able to take things more in his stride. But then Peter had already been home some weeks when Giles had arrived at Silver Streams for his furlough before departing for the Mediterranean.

It had been his first furlough since before the outbreak of war, and there had been a great deal of celebrating, pointed up by the fact that Peter was also at home. Peter, however badly wounded, even seemed to have accumulated a girl friend – the vicar's daughter, of all people!

Superficially, in fact, the family seemed to have weathered all of the storms of the past few years, and emerged, if not triumphant, at least as a cohesive whole.

Mary was married to Geoffrey Young, an old family friend, and, indeed, hero, and was twice a mother; even though she had not seen her husband for several months, she seemed happy enough.

101

Liz was married to the apparently ebullient American, Harry Krantz – Giles had never met him – and was now safely on the far side of the Atlantic, and also about to become a mother, it seemed.

And Peter had covered himself with glory in the battle off the Falklands, even if he had been severely wounded.

Even baby Giles, Giles reflected, had not done too badly.

While Mother had recovered all of her old bounce and boom.

Yet Giles, returning home after so long, had been aware of tensions, uncertainties, and certainly apprehensions, which were strange to such a fun-loving, happy group as he remembered from the old days. Obviously it made sense for them all to understand that amongst the men, at the least, there was no guarantee of survival; this applied even to the neutral, Krantz, who was an attache with the Grand Fleet – if Geoffrey and his ship went down, Krantz would go with it.

But there was more to it than that, Giles knew. Britain had not fought a naval war since 1815; that was a hundred years ago. Even the Crimea, at sea, had been nothing more than some bombardments of Russian shore positions. Three generations of Dawsons had served in the Navy, and dreamed of sailing, and then steaming, into battle against a worthy opponent. Now that moment had come.

How Jack would have loved it, he thought, as his eyes finally closed.

C17 cast off at dawn the following morning, using her diesel engines to slip across the surface of the calm sea towards the waiting battleships. Even if the officers on the conning tower knew that there were only two dreadnoughts present, and that this was, therefore, a second eleven, the great ships made an impressive sight. But all eyes were on *Queen Elizabeth*, so much larger than the rest. That she was also so much more heavily armed and armoured, and yet could steam so much faster, than any other ship in the fleet, made the heart swell.

Giles thought it must be the greatest feeling on earth, actually to sail in her.

The fleet behind them, they watched the hills of Turkey rising out of the sea in front of them. At this distance it was impossible to make out the strait itself – the land looked solid – but Manly was keen on history. 'You are looking at Troy, gentlemen,' he said. 'This is the same sight Agamemnon and Ulysses saw three thousand years ago.'

'Let's hope we're not here for ten years as well, sir,' remarked Sub-Lieutenant Ganning, the wardroom's wit.

'That's close enough,' Manly decided. 'Dive, dive, dive.'

The officers slid down the ladder, Manly closed the hatch; *C17* was already sliding beneath the waves.

'Periscope depths.'

The tube went up, and Manly started inspecting the shore to either side as the submarine glided into the very centre of the channel. Giles stood at his side with his noteboook.

'Nothing to starboard that I can see. Forts to port. One, two, three . . .' he called them off; there were more than thirty of them. When he raised his head, he grinned at Giles' expression. 'Just earthworks and a single gun; hardly more than a ten-inch at best. Nothing our chaps can't deal with.' He put his face back to the eye-piece. 'Patrol boat. Prepare to dive. No, he hasn't seen us. Hello . . . add to that report, Number One; several howitzers on movable platforms, mounted behind trucks. Those might need watching. Now, coming up to the Narrows. Byron swam across here once, chaps. Just to prove it could be done. Oh, oh, guess what I see.'

Giles could guess, and wrote down, mines.

'Take her down,' Manly commanded, and *C17* sank into the depths, while the periscope also came down.

Giles looked at him.

'We have to see how far in it stretches,' the Captain explained.

C17 seeped forward. Now they heard the scraping of a wire along the hull, slowly slipping astern. The wires could do no damage, and the mines were of the contact variety; the only risk was of a wire catching in the propellors, and the mines thereby being sucked down.

They emerged from that row of mines, but only a mile further on there was another, and then another; *C17* penetrated six in all, each penetration a period of nerve-racking suspense, until the narrow channel at last opened in front of them.

'Marmara,' Manly said, with some satisfaction.

By now it was late afternoon, the winter sun drooping rapidly towards the hills behind the ferry port of Gallipoli. *C17* surfaced, and lay still on the water, her generators using fresh air to recharge the batteries, her men equally taking great breaths after their long hours submerged.

'Carden isn't going to like what we have to tell him,' Manly remarked, smoking his pipe.

'He must have known there would be mines,' Giles argued. 'It's just a matter of giving the sweepers cover; we've enough firepower for that.'

'I imagine you're right.' The Captain stared to the north. 'Do you realise there's nothing between us and Constantinople?'

Giles grinned. 'Feel like taking a look?'

'Well . . . perhaps we should. After all, there *is* a Turkish Navy.'

'If we show ourselves, will it not warn the Turks that an attack is imminent?'

'If they don't know that, they're blind. But if we could take out *Goeben*, just for example, it wouldn't do their morale much good.'

C17 motored north, on the surface, into a clear winter's night. The breeze was light, and the sea calm. From time to time they saw lights, but none approached; the Turks obviously felt utterly secure in their inland sea. And before dawn they saw the glow of Constantinople on the horizon.

There were several large vessels anchored south of the city, but these were impossible to identify in the darkness. Manly stopped engines, and remained on the surface until the last possible moment; once their presence was discovered, they would probably have to spend several hours under water.

Giles stood beside him on the bridge, both men peering through their binoculars. It was distinctly chill, and they wore gloves as well as greatcoats.

'No *Goeben*,' Giles commented.

'Maybe not. But that's a large warship.'

'Pre-dreadnought.'

'But worth sinking, wouldn't you say?'

'Looks good to me.'

'Action stations,' Manly said. 'Dive, dive, dive.'

C17 sank beneath the waves, to periscope depths.

'Slow ahead,' Manly said, peering through the eyepiece.

The submarine slipped silently forward.

'Sitting ducks,' Manly remarked. 'Take a look, Number One.'

Giles positioned himself. The Turkish ships were now hardly more than three miles away. The battleship was surrounded by several destroyers and smaller craft; it would be a matter of finding their way through. But certainly the Turks were utterly defenceless; there were not even any nets down around the big ship, while shore boats moved to and fro.

'Lay our course back for the Dardanelles, Number One,' Manly said.

Giles sat at the chart table with his compass and dividers, made a note of the course they would require.

'Stand by,' Manly said, eyes glued to the periscope.

Still *C17* was travelling Slow Ahead, her periscope leaving only the smallest telltale ripple on the surface, while the captain waited for a clear shot.

'Damn,' he commented. 'We're spotted. Fire bow tubes.'

There was a huge hiss as the torpedoes were released.

'Take her down,' Manly told the quartermaster. 'Course, Number One?'

'South a quarter East.'

'South a quarter East,' the helmsman repeated and the submarine came down. As she did so, she trembled from a distant explosion.

'A hit,' Manly said. 'Well done, lads.'

'The big one, sir?' asked one of the ratings.

'That we shall have to see, in due course,' Manly told him.

Above them now they could hear the whirring of propellers, but the Turks had no adequate means of either detecting or attacking underwater craft; their only hope had to be that the submarine might show itself.

But Manly held his course for half an hour before coming up to periscope depths. 'She's listing,' he told his crew. 'I would say she's going. Certainly she's out of action for several months.'

'Hurrah!' Giles called, and the crew responded with a will.

But they were not home yet. Fast patrol boats raced overhead to warn the Dardanelles that an enemy submarine was loose on Marmara. *C17* had to remain submerged all day, and the air was foul when at dusk Manly at last felt able to surface.

They gazed at the lights of Gallipoli on the starboard bow, while ahead of them the strait itself was criss-crossed with searchlights.

There was no hope of navigating the strait, with its several dogleg bends, fully submerged.

'Take her down to periscope depths,' Manly commanded. 'And slow ahead.'

It was the longest night of Giles' life, as in addition to the scraping wires of the anchored mines, they could hear the whirr of propellers above them. Yet the submarine forged steadily to the south, past one field and then the next; from time to time, when Manly could see ahead for more than a couple of miles, sinking below periscope depths, then cautiously re-emerging when another bend had to be negotiated.

The minutes and the hours ticked away, every second taking them closer to safety.

'Only one left,' Manly announced, at four in the morning. 'Then . . .'

There came a grating sound from beneath the hull.

Every man looked at every other. A mine? But Giles knew differently. 'We're aground.'

'Damnation,' Manly commented.

Helming blind so much of the time, they had drifted too far to the left of the channel.

'We'll have to take her up,' the Captain decided. 'Can't wait until daybreak. Gun crew stand by.'

C17 carried a three-pounder gun on her foredeck.

Manly took a last look through the periscope, then snapped, 'Surface. Down periscope. Gun crew to deck.'

C17 broke the surface with a whoosh, and instantly men leapt to the gun, which rose through a flap in the deck. For the moment they were unseen, and Manly gave the orders for full speed ahead; they needed only a few seconds to regain deeper water. But as the submarine surged forward, they were picked up by a searchlight, and then crossed with another, and in the same instant the guns began to boom, while the various patrol boats also opened up with machine guns.

'Return fire,' Manly bellowed, and the three-pounder barked, but ineffectually.

'Should be far enough,' Giles suggested, standing beside the captain on the conning tower and watching the splashes not fifty feet away; it needed only one of those to slice into the hull and they were done.

'Agreed.' Manly lifted the cap of the voice tube. 'Dive, dive, dive. Gun crew be . . .' he gave a gasp and fell to his knees.

Giles realised he had also been hit; although he felt no pain his entire right side had gone numb. And *C17* was already sinking beneath the surface. Desperately he pushed Manly's body down the ladder and tumbled behind it, dragging the hatch cover shut and shooting the bolts only seconds before the submarine disappeared.

Manly lay in a heap at the foot of the ladder.

'Is he . . .?' asked Ganning.

'I'm afraid so.'

107

'But you . . .' Ganning gazed at the blood dripping from Giles' sleeve.

'I'll get you home,' Giles promised.

'Good work,' Admiral Carden said. 'Oh, good work. How are you feeling?'

'A little peaky, sir.'

'Well, it's home for you. And a medal.' He sighed. 'It's home for me, as well.'

Giles could see that the Admiral was yellow and trembling with a malarial ague.

'It was Commander Manly took us in, and brought us out, sir.'

Carden nodded. 'I don't intend to forget that, Lieutenant. But you are both to be congratulated.'

'And the minefields, sir?'

Carden gave a weary but confident smile. 'Now at least we know where they are, Lieutenant. Thanks to you.'

The next day, 19 February, the bombardment began. It was a quite awe-inspiring spectacle. The fleet was in any event elated by the triumphant entry of *C17* into the Sea of Marmara, and if it grieved the loss of the submarine's gallant commander, it was determined to avenge him. The battleships and battlecruiser formed an arc around the promontory, and as they immediately found the range, the huge shells quickly began striking home; the Asiatic side was ignored as it was apparently undefended.

Jack was more elated than most. The name of Lieutenant Giles Dawson was on everyone's lips, and if the boy had been wounded, he was at least in no danger; it had in fact been decided that instead of going home, he should remain at the hospital camp in Mudros until ready to resume service. This was no doubt a disappointment to Giles, but on the other hand, it was rumoured that he was to replace Commander Manly as captain of *C17* as soon as she was repaired and refitted, and he himself was well again. This would almost certainly mean a third, thin, stripe and he was also clearly in the running for a medal.

But today was to be an even greater triumph for the Navy, surely.

Jack of course had no binoculars, but even with the naked eye he could make out the pillars of earth and rock rising into the air as each shell landed. Presumably there were men in that mixture as well.

There was absolutely no reply. It was like target practice, save that there were living people on the end of it.

Everyone became rather hysterical. There was something clearly immoral about shooting and not being shot at in turn, and this had its effect. So did the noise. The bombardment went on from dawn until dusk, for a month. It really was impossible to suppose that a single soul remained alive on the peninsular.

To make it even more surrealistic, a seaplane carrier had been attached to the fleet, and its machines daily circled over the land, returning to report how accurate the shooting had been. It was the first time Jack had ever seen airplanes in action, or close to, as they came down on to the calm seas for recovery by their parent vessel.

'Why don't they give them some light shells to drop from their aircraft?' Petty Officer Martin asked. 'They'd be able to see exactly where to place them.'

'Save that they couldn't, Petty Officer,' Midshipman Barber argued. 'How could they hope to hit anything while flying over it at a hundred miles an hour?'

As an erstwhile gunnery officer, Jack was more interested in what damage the continuous firing was doing to the gun-barrels. *Queen Elizabeth*'s armament was as new and specially designed as everything else about her, and her endurance per gun was supposed to be far greater than the hundred rounds accepted as normal for most big guns . . . but they had fired close to a hundred rounds already, with no apparent end in sight.

By the time the first month was up, it became apparent that this was to be a bigger show than had first been imagined.

109

There was of course a constant flow of transports from Malta. In the beginning these had been bringing fresh supplies of shells and cordite, but as February wore into March, the transports began bringing troops. These were disembarked on the nearby Greek island of Lemnos, the port of which, Mudros, was being developed from a hospital into a huge advanced base for the Allies. But their officers, including General Hamilton, the commander, came on to the Dardanelles to see things for themselves.

'They're thinking of an occupation,' Petty Officer Martin remarked. 'What do you think of that, Jack me boy?'

They had become quite friends.

'Better them than us,' Jack commented. 'Can you imagine the stink over there?'

Sometimes, when the breeze was off the shore, he thought he could smell it. No bodies had been buried, save under rubble, for four weeks . . . and even in February the sun was warm.

Soon naval landing parties were sent ashore to ascertain the situation. Jack was with one of those from *Queen Elizabeth*. They had been armed with rifles and bayonets, and had marine support, as the steam pinnace nosed into the little bay to which they had been directed. Above them was one of the Turkish forts, and they went at it on the double, uncertain whether some desperate defenders might have been left behind.

They saw no defenders, alive or dead, oddly enough, although there were the sickening, fly-strewn, stinking remains of some sheep. The fort itself had been reduced to powder, and its one gun, a ten-inch, was just shattered metal.

'I suppose they got their people out in time,' Midshipman Barber said. 'Still, we were sent to make sure the fort was destroyed, and I think we can say that.'

But some of the other landing parties were fired upon, and one or two had regular skirmishes with still active Turkish troops.

Next day, 17 March, an order from Vice-Admiral Carden was sent round the fleet, and read to all hands.

'You have carried out your duties with exemplary devotion, and we have accomplished the first part of our campaign. I thank you all.

'I now have to tell you that as of today I am relinquishing my command. Sadly, this has been forced upon me by my health, which I am informed will no longer support this climate.

'Your new commander will be Sir John De Robeck, whom you all know and appreciate, and whom I know you will serve with the devotion you have given me.

'I will now wish you goodbye and good luck.'

Martin and Jack looked at each other in consternation.

'The day before we force the Narrows?' the Petty Officer demanded.

'De Robeck's a good man,' Jack said.

Indeed, there was hardly a more popular officer in the Navy than Sir John Michael De Robeck. Tall, broad-shouldered, fair-haired, he was a picture of how Jack had always imagined he would like to look himself, when he attained flag rank. And of his professional skill there could be no doubt, while, as he had been Carden's second-in-command throughout the operation, and had himself bombarded the shore batteries from his ship *Vengeance*, he knew all about what was involved.

It was surely just a matter of getting at the Turks.

Next morning, the fleet moved into action.

The outer forts had been completely silenced, but not those guarding the Narrows between Khalid Bahr and Cannakkale. These had been reconnoitered by both British destroyers and submarines, since *C17*'s daring venture, and the minefields had been carefully pin-pointed on the charts. But shots had been fired from the forts, as well as what were called the Intermediate Defences – the movable batteries first reported by *C17* – and it was evident that these too would have to be blasted out of existence before the minefields could be swept and the fleet proceed to the Sea of Marmara and thence the Turkish capital.

111

Still, this was regarded as a less onerous duty than the original bombardment, as it would be at almost point-blank range: there was even a chance the Turks might fire back.

The fleet was divided into three groups.

Line A consisted of *Queen Elizabeth*, *Agamemnon* and *Lord Nelson*, both pre-dreadnoughts, and *Inflexible*; this group was to fire at the forts from a range of fourteen thousand yards. With this group were two other pre-dreadnoughts, *Triumph* and *Prince George*, which were to blast the Intermediate Defences.

Line B consisted entirely of pre-dreadnoughts, five French ships and the British vessels *Cornwallis* and *Canopus*, this last happily repaired and home from the Falklands. The French squadron was to close in on the forts at the Narrows, and hit them from a range of only eight thousand yards; the two British ships were to cover the mine-sweeping during the night.

The third group was the reserve squadron of six British pre-dreadnoughts; these were intended to move up after four hours and replace some of the bombarding vessels.

The action began at 1130, when *Queen Elizabeth* led her squadron to the attack, and opened fire from her allotted range. Immediately the Turks did reply, not from the forts themselves, which found the distance too great, but from howitzers of the Intermediate Defence zone, which of course could be moved as required. Indeed they made quite good practice, and soon a regular ding-dong was in progress, with all the warships being hit several times – but their armour-plating was never penetrated, and the only casualties were caused by flying splinters.

Working in A-turret Jack was hardly aware of the enemy shot at all.

Their own shooting was perfection. After only about twenty minutes one of *Queen Elizabeth*'s fifteen-inch shells struck Fort No 20, and there was a tremendous explosion which suggested that a magazine had gone up; certainly there was no further firing from that fort. Shells were also seen exploding in Forts 13 and 17.

Now that the initial softening-up process had begun, the French squadron, led by Admiral Guepratte, steamed through the British ships to take up their close order position. Jack looked out of his turret long enough to see *Wagram* going by, quite near. He could not identify any of the officers on the bridge, but he knew Pierre was there.

He wondered if this was the first time the Frenchman had been under fire since Tsushima.

The French ships reached their positions, and opened fire.

The forts were still replying with the utmost vigour, and the afternoon took on an aspect of terrible violence, for the ships did not keep still, but wheeled to and fro while delivering their broadsides in order to confuse the Turkish gunners – these were good enough to leave the fleet continually shrouded in huge plumes of white water. While on the land the red flashes, both of Turkish gunfire and exploding shells, and the equally dramatic plumes of dust and rock which rose into the air whenever a shell struck home, painted an unforgettable picture.

The noise of course was tremendous, and through it all the destroyers and picket boats darted back and forth, miraculously unscathed.

But there was only one possible end to such an uneven contest. Just before 1300 Fort No 13 was destroyed by the same sort of explosion as had done for No 20. No 8 now stopped firing. And the French were seen to be hitting Fort 15 almost at will. By half past one the Turks were hardly replying at all, and ten minutes later their firing had entirely ceased; none of their gunners could stand the bombardment.

This initial battle being won, the tactical plan went into effect, and the minesweepers advanced to clear the passage. Meanwhile the French squadron, which from its close range position had received several severe hits, was withdrawn, to be replaced by the reserve British squadron.

Of the main squadron, *Inflexible* had also receivd a hit which had wrecked her forebridge and started quite a serious fire – from that one shell she had been far more badly damaged than by anything fired from *Gneisenau*. She too was withdrawn for the time being.

Thus far the day had been entirely successful. At a total loss of perhaps forty men and some dented armour the forts had been silenced, and the clearance of the Narrows was underway.

The time was 1354 when the French pre-dreadnought *Bouvet* suddenly blew up.

Queen Elizabeth was still firing, but the noise was so enormous that it drew the men out of the turret for a moment, to watch the huge plume of smoke and the very rapidly disappearing hull of the French battleship.

'Christ, that must have struck her magazine,' Martin said.

Midshipman Barber gulped. 'Continue firing.'

Jack was back at the breach, while wondering how a shot from the all but dead batteries could have travelled so far with such accuracy.

Five minutes later, all replies from the shore again ceased, and the minesweepers advanced. Immediately the supposedly eliminated shore batteries opened up again, raising in Jack's mind serious doubts as to just how much damage the warships were actally doing. But now the relief squadron was closing in and shooting at short range. Again the forts were blasted, and the shore replies became desultory. Yet the fleet continued banging away to cover the minesweepers, who were finding their objectives, from the series of explosions which came from further into the strait.

By now it was 1600, and the bombardment had been going on for a very long time; Jack's mind was spinning with the noise. Round and round the ships went, heeling to the force of their broadsides, recovering as they lined up for the next salvo.

Ten minutes later, there was another of those dull, underwater explosions near at hand.

'Oh, hell,' Midshipman Barber commented.

Jack looked out of the turret, and his heart nearly stopped beating. *Inflexible* had taken on a distinct list.

114

'She must have struck a goddamned mine,' Martin commented.

'Maybe that's what did for *Bouvet*,' Jack said, gazing at where the picket boats and steam launches were still criss-crossing above the sunken battleship, looking for survivors.

'But where are the damned things?' Barber wailed. 'There aren't supposed be any south of the Narrows!'

He had barely spoken when there was an explosion from the British pre-dreadnought *Irresistible*, and she too took on a dramatic list, while unlike *Inflexible*, which was attempting to work her way back through the fleet and out of danger, she was absolutely immobile.

'Can they be mines?' Barber demanded at large. 'Do you think the Turks have some kind of deepwater torpedo?'

Jack reckoned it wasn't his business to debate with an officer on the imponderables, but the same thought seemed to strike the Admiral, together with the enormous hoohah which would result if he had to report that Britain's newest and most powerful battleship had been sunk, or even crippled, by a mine. A few minutes later the orders came to withdraw, and concentrate on picking up shipwrecked sailors.

'Hell,' Martin said. 'I thought we were just about through.'

But the tragedy of 18 March was not yet over. On instructions from the Admiral, the pre-dreadnought *Ocean* approached *Irresistible* to rescue survivors, and there was yet another of those terrible muffled explosions. Water shot hundreds of feet in the air, and *Ocean* began to settle.

Destroyers rushed in to pick up whom they could, and in an hour nearly all the crews of both ships were safe. But the two pre-dreadnoughts continued to drift, derelict, and slowly sinking.

'Christalmighty!' Martin said. 'What a bloody shambles.'

And still the day was not done. As *Queen Elizabeth* slowly, sadly steamed out of the Narrows, her crew watched *Wagram* moving into position where *Bouvet* had gone down an hour before, also searching for survivors.

'Oh, no,' Jack wanted to shout.

115

But he would not have been heard above the bang.

The appalled watchers on *Queen Elizabeth* saw water and steel and men hurtling into the air, and the ship immediately begin to heel.

Over she went, while men leapt into the sea. Jack knew the feeling so well, and his emotions were heightened not only by understanding that it could again happen to him for the third, and surely last, time, but also by the knowledge of what Pierre Tonnheur must be feeling as his first big command dissolved beneath his feet.

Wagram went down in seconds. Her captain was not amongst the survivors, although his body was later picked up.

PART TWO

Shot and Shell

CHAPTER 5

The Torpedo

'ADMIRALTY TO VICE-ADMIRAL DE ROBECK
'20 MARCH 1915
'WE REGRET THE LOSSES YOU HAVE SUFFERED
IN YOUR RESOLUTE ATTACK STOP CONVEY TO
ALL RANKS AND RATINGS THEIR LORDSHIPS'
APPROBATION OF THEIR CONDUCT IN ACTION
AND SEAMANLIKE SKILL AND PRUDENCE WITH
WHICH HIS MAJESTY'S SHIPS WERE HANDLED
STOP CONVEY TO THE FRENCH SQUADRON THE
ADMIRALTY'S APPRECIATION OF THEIR LOYAL
AND EFFECTIVE SUPPORT AND OUR SORROW FOR
THE LOSSES THEY HAVE SUSTAINED.

'*QUEEN* AND *IMPLACABLE* SHOULD JOIN YOU
VERY SOON AND *LONDON* AND *PRINCE OF WALES*
SAIL TONIGHT.

'PLEASE TELEGRAPH ANY INFORMATION AS
TO DAMAGE DONE TO FORTS AND ALSO FULL
CASUALTIES AND AMMUNITION EXPENDED.

'IT APPEARS IMPORTANT NOT TO LET THE
FORTS BE REPAIRED OR TO ENCOURAGE ENEMY
BY AN APPARENT SUSPENSION OF THE OPERA-
TIONS STOP AMPLE SUPPLIES OF FIFTEEN-INCH
AMMUNITION ARE AVAILABLE FOR INDIRECT
FIRE OF *QUEEN ELIZABETH* ACROSS THE
PENINSULAR.'

'Agreed?' the First Lord asked.

'Agreed,' the First Sea Lord replied. 'We must finish this
thing.'

The fleet was sullen and angry at the repulse. Most of the crews

119

were old hands, men who hated the concept of death being able to lurk beneath the waves. As they went about the business of retrieving the drowned, they growled their bitterness.

Jack volunteered for this task, and was on the scene when Pierre Tonnheur's body was recovered by one of the French boats.

'Will he be buried here?' he asked Martin.

Burial parties were already lining up on the decks of the ships.

'Fat chance. He's a Capitaine de Vaisseau. He'll be sent back to Paris for a big do.'

Helene, in widow's weeds, Jack thought. She'd enjoy that; she knew how well black suited her.

Admirals and captains, generals and aides-de-camp, converged on *Queen Elizabeth* for a conference.

'Now we're really going to let them have it,' Martin told his gun crew. 'Those Turks ain't seen nothing yet.'

Midshipman Barber had been doing some accounting, on orders from the bridge. He was really only concerned with A-turret, but he was an inquisitive youth with a mathematical turn of mind.

'Do you know,' he asked them, 'how many fifteen-inch shells this ship has fired during the past month? Three hundred and fifty-two.'

'Jesus Christ!' Martin commented. 'Begging your pardon, Mr Barber.'

'That is very nearly half our normal stock of shells,' Barber said triumphantly.

'Good thing these new barrels will take three hundred and fifty firings,' Jack commented.

Barber gave him a dirty look. He wasn't all that keen on able seamen who knew so much about the theory and practice of naval gunnery.

'What I want to know, Mr Barber, sir,' Martin said, 'is when the brass up there . . .' he jerked his finger at the bridge. 'Are going to let us start shooting again.'

'I don't like the sound of this telegram from De Robeck one little bit,' the First Lord said, looking at the members of the Admiralty War Group, hastily convened. 'Just to refresh your memories, I will read it to you:

'VICE-ADMIRAL DE ROBECK TO ADMIRALTY
'23 MARCH 1915 (RECEIVED 0630)

'AT MEETING TODAY WITH GENERALS HAMILTON AND BIRDWOOD THE FORMER TOLD ME ARMY WILL NOT BE IN A POSITION TO UNDERTAKE ANY MILITARY OPERATIONS BEFORE 14 APRIL STOP IN ORDER TO MAINTAIN OUR COMMUNICATIONS WHEN THE FLEET PENETRATES INTO THE SEA OF MARMARA IT IS NECESSARY TO DESTROY ALL GUNS OF POSITION GUARDING THE STRAITS STOP THESE ARE NUMEROUS AND ONLY SMALL PERCENTAGE CAN BE RENDERED USELESS BY GUNFIRE STOP THE LANDING OF DEMOLISHING PARTY ON 26 FEBRUARY EVIDENTLY SURPRISED ENEMY STOP FROM OUR EXPERIENCE ON 4 MARCH IT SEEMS IN FUTURE DESTRUCTION OF GUNS WILL HAVE TO BE CARRIED OUT IN FACE OF STRENUOUS AND WELL-EQUIPPED OPPOSITION STOP I DO NOT THINK IT A PRACTICABLE OPERATION TO LAND A FORCE ADEQUATE TO UNDERTAKE THIS SERVICE INSIDE DARDANELLES STOP GENERAL HAMILTON CONCURS IN THIS OPINION STOP IF THE GUNS ARE NOT DESTROYED ANY SUCCESS OF FLEET MAY BE NULLIFIED BY THE STRAITS CLOSING UP AFTER THE SHIPS HAVE PASSED THROUGH AND AS LOSS OF MATERIEL WILL POSSIBLY BE HEAVY SHIPS MAY NOT BE AVAILABLE TO KEEP DARDANELLES OPEN STOP THE MINE MENACE WILL CONTINUE UNTIL THE SEA OF MARMARA IS REACHED BEING MUCH GREATER THAN WAS ANTICIPATED STOP IT MUST BE CAREFULLY AND THOROUGHLY DEALT WITH BOTH AS REGARDS MINES AND FLOATING MINES

121

STOP THIS WILL TAKE TIME TO ACCOMPLISH BUT OUR ARRANGEMENTS WILL BE READY BY THE TIME ARMY CAN ACT STOP IT APPEARS BETTER TO PREPARE A DECISIVE EFFORT ABOUT THE MIDDLE OF APRIL RATHER THAN RISK A GREAT DEAL FOR WHAT MAY BE ONLY A PARTIAL SOLUTION.'

Churchill laid down the paper.

'I have to admit that I read that the first time with consternation. Is the whole operation now going to hang fire for nearly a month? I do not think we can permit that.'

'We always knew it was going to be a desperate business, First Lord,' Sir Arthur Wilson commented. 'And a costly one.'

'Costly,' Lord Fisher muttered. 'Costly!'

'We knew we might sustain casualties,' Churchill argued. 'Any attacking force sustains casualties. But so far it seems to me that we have got off very lightly. Hardly a hundred men killed and wounded. I am very sorry about *Bouvet* and *Wagram*, of course. I understand the loss of life there was quite severe. But the French are immediately replacing those losses.'

'It is the ships, not the men, that matter,' Fisher said.

'Oh, come now, First Sea Lord. *Ocean* and *Irresistible* were both due for scrapping. They were only kept in service because of the War. The same can be said about *Bouvet* and *Wagram*: both were pre-dreadnoughts. The only modern ship we have had damaged is *Inflexible*, and I am informed she will be back in service in six weeks at the outside. No, gentlemen, the only serious casualty we run the risk of incurring is time. De Robeck and Hamilton appear to imagine that they can call a halt to the entire proceedings, announce a moratorium, if you like, with the game to recommence on 14 April. What do you suppose the Turks will be doing between now and then? They know what we are about, now. They will certainly know we are putting an army ashore in Mudros. That army can only be

122

there to assault the Dardanelles. Do you not suppose they are working day and night to prepare for us? Our ships ran into an unexpected minefield on 18 March, one which clearly had been laid in the very short space of time that had elapsed since the area had last been swept. Do you not suppose the Turks will be laying more minefields, just as quickly as possible, for as long as they are given the time to do so? And what of submarines? We know the Turks have them. Given the time, they are going to start using them as well.'

The admirals looked sceptical. None of them had a very high opinion of the Turks.

Churchill cleared his throat.

'I have therefore drafted the following reply to De Robeck, which I would like to read to you before sending:

'YOUR 818. IN VIEW OF THE DANGERS OF DELAY THROUGH SUBMARINE ATTACK AND HEAVY COST OF ARMY OPERATION AND POSSIBILITY THAT IT WILL FAIL OR BE ONLY PARTLY EFFECTIVE IN OPENING THE STRAITS AND THAT THE DANGER OF MINES WILL NOT BE RELIEVED BY IT WE CONSIDER THAT YOU OUGHT TO PERSEVERE METHODICALLY BUT RESOLUTELY WITH THE PLAN CONTAINED IN YOUR INSTRUCTIONS AND IN ADMIRALITY TELEGRAM 109 AND THAT YOU SHOULD MAKE ALL PREPARATIONS TO RENEW THE ATTACK BEGUN ON 18 MARCH STOP AT THE FIRST FAVOURABLE OPPORTUNITY YOU SHOULD DOMINATE THE FORTS AT THE NARROWS AND SWEEP THE MINEFIELD AND THEN BATTER THE FORTS AT CLOSE RANGE TAKING YOUR TIME USING YOUR AEROPLANES AND ALL YOUR IMPROVED METHODS OF GUARDING AGAINST MINES STOP THE DESTRUCTION OF THE FORTS AT THE NARROWS MAY OPEN THE WAY FOR A FURTHER ADVANCE STOP THE ENTRY INTO MARMARA OF A FLEET STRONG ENOUGH TO BEAT THE TURKISH FLEET WOULD PRODUCE

123

DECISIVE RESULTS ON THE WHOLE SITUATION AND YOU NEED NOT BE ANXIOUS ABOUT YOUR SUBSEQUENT LINE OF COMMUNICATIONS STOP WE KNOW THE FORTS ARE SHORT OF AMMUNITION AND SUPPLY OF MINES IS LIMITED STOP WE DO NOT THINK THE TIME HAS YET COME TO GIVE UP THE PLAN OF FORCING DARDANELLES BY A PURELY NAVAL OPERATION.

'COMMODORE DE BARTOLOME WHO STARTS TODAY WILL GIVE YOU OUR VIEWS ON POINTS OF DETAIL MEANWHILE ALL YOUR PREPARATIONS FOR RENEWING ATTACK SHOULD GO FORWARD.'

When he was finished there was silence, while the admirals exchanged glances.

Then Sir Henry Jackson said, 'With respect, First Lord, but I do not think you can send that telegram.'

Churchill raised his eyebrows and looked at Fisher, who hitherto had been, as usual, somewhat slouched in his chair.

Now he sat up straight.

'Jackson is quite right, First Lord.'

Churchill had a surge of irritation.

'I'm afraid I do not quite understand,' he said. 'When I entered this room I was of the opinion that we had unanimously determined that the Dardanelles operation was to be carried through to a successful conclusion.'

'The success of any operation depends upon the opinion and resolve of the commander on the spot,' Fisher said. 'I went along with the idea because Carden said it could be done, and de Robeck appeared to agree with that opinion. De Robeck now says it cannot be done. You cannot override that opinion, and send a man into a battle he feels sure he is going to lose. If you disagree with him strongly enough, you can propose to this council that he be replaced.'

The two men glared at each other; it was the first real difference of opinion they had ever had.

All manner of thoughts flickered through Churchill's mind, from the memory that the British had once shot an admiral they regarded as not having tried hard enough to that of this very John Fisher declaring the battle must be won and sending two precious battlecruisers all the way to the Falklands to deal with Spee.

But he knew that to propose replacing De Robeck would not meet with the approval of the admirals; he could see it in their faces.

He also knew that if the assault on the Dardanelles was delayed for nearly a month, it would never succeed; unlike his admirals, he had a very high respect for the toughness and determination of the Turks – it was not so distant history when they had been the most feared soldiers in the world.

Was it then, a case of De Robeck or himself? He was very tempted to make it that issue. But resignation, unless over a point of honour, was a self-defeating sacrifice. It would damage the Government at a time when, with casualties mounting every day in Flanders, it needed all the support it could get. More important, it would not solve the situation at the Dardanelles, but rather make it worse; any new civil minister coming into the Admiralty would be completely dominated by these three very senior service chiefs.

'Is it therefore the majority decision of this Council,' he said, speaking slowly and deliberately, 'that Vice-Admiral De Robeck's proposal to delay any further operations in the Dardanelles for a period of at least three weeks be approved, and that I recall Commodore de Bartolome from his mission?'

'Oh, no, let de Bartolome continue,' Fisher said, suddenly jovial now he had won his argument. 'There is nothing like having a man on the spot to talk with De Robeck and report back on the true situation. But as for the delay, I do not think it is going to be as serious as you suppose. After all, Winston, it seems that the Army is ready to take over the show. Well, why not? It probably should have been their show in the beginning. And it'll tickle Kitchener.'

'The service will be held on Saturday morning,' explained Contre-Amiral Vaichy. 'A car will be sent for you, madame.'

He watched the widow as he spoke. She did not look the least overcome by her husband's death in action. But then, he had not really expected it. At least she was wearing a black dress.

'Thank you,' Helene said.

'The President of the Republic will attend.'

'That is very kind of him, monsieur l'amiral.'

Vaichy nodded. 'Have you heard from your brother, Madame Tonnheur?'

'Not as yet. His letters have to come through Switzerland.'

Vaichy gave a cold smile. 'I know that, madame. Well, I will see you on Saturday, at Notre Dame.'

'Yes,' Helene said, and watched the door close.

He loathed her. Hated her, perhaps. Well, she hated him.

Partly this was a defence mechanism. Since the beginning of the War and Pierre's departure from Paris, she had become very aware that when people had been nice to her before the War they had been being nice to Madame Tonnheur, wife of a French naval officer – not to Helene von Eltz, who just happened to be married to the Frenchman.

All of those gay parties, that gushing handkissing, the embraces she had received from her French guests and hostesses, had been utterly false.

And she had believed them.

In the seven months the War had been going on she had received hardly an invitation. She had been dropped as if she had been a hot potato.

And Pierre had refused to allow her to go home . . . but now Pierre was dead.

She felt no sense of loss, or grief. He had died for her when she had found out about his Monique. She had never forgiven him for that, and she never would. Nor for keeping her virtually a prisoner for seven months.

And now he was dead. She sat at her desk to write to Bruno; that funny little man Furrer would be coming along for a letter any day now.

Henri stood in the doorway.

126

'Will there be anything else, madame?'

There was a huge crowd milling about in the April sunshine outside the Cathedral of Notre Dame.

April in Paris, Helene thought; the best time of the year in the best city in the world – according to the French. But she would soon be rid of it.

Everyone stood in line to shake her hand and kiss her on both cheeks, even the President. Her veil went up and down as if spring-loaded, but only cheek high. No one could properly see her eyes, observe the anger and contempt she felt for all of these hypocrites. She did not care if she never saw any of them again.

Presumably the nice things they were saying about Pierre were genuine.

Contre-Amiral Vaichy escorted her to the waiting car after the service. 'I trust it was not too much for you, madame?'

Now Helene raised the veil on to the brim of her hat, so that he could see just how she felt.

'No, monsieur l'amiral. I have buried a loved one before. However . . . I would like a private word.'

'Of course, madame. Anything I can do to help.'

'Ride home with me.'

Vaichy hesitated, then inclined his head. 'It will be my pleasure, madame. Excuse me for one moment.'

He went off to mutter a few words at another admiral, then returned, and sat beside her in the back of the car as it rumbled slowly over the bridge from Isle de la Cité, giving way to the crowds of pedestrians who were also returning to their homes and jobs.

'It was an impressive ceremony,' Vaichy remarked. 'France can ill afford to lose such a distinguished sailor.'

'I would like to go home,' Helene said.

Vaichy glanced at her. 'We are on our way there now, madame.'

The fool was being deliberately obtuse. 'I meant, I would like to go home to Germany, monsieur.'

'Germany?'

127

'That is my home. I agree, Paris was my home as long as I was married to Pierre. I am no longer married to Pierre. I am an alien. I have no relatives here, nothing to do here.'

'And you would have something to do in Germany?'

'Indeed. I am sure I would be very busy running the estate at Schloss Elsjing in my brother's absence.' She thought dreamily of the river and the bridle paths, her horses and the dogs. And, from time to time at the least, Bruno.

'I am afraid it would be quite impossible for us to repatriate you to Germany, madame,' Vaichy said.

Helene's head turned, sharply.

'The negative propaganda value would be very great,' Vaichy explained. 'And besides, madame, Germany is not your home. You are a French citizen.'

'That is nonsense. I was a French citizen only when I was married to Capitaine de Vaisseau Tonnheur. I am no longer married to him.'

'Madame, French citizenship is not something you can put on or take off as you choose. You are a French citizen, and France is at war. It is your bounden duty to remain here and do everything you can to assist in our victory.'

The car was stopping outside the apartment building.

Vaichy opened the door for her 'I am sorry, madame, but . . .'

Helene did not even bother to reply. She went up the stairs, and the apartment door was opened for her by Henri. 'Monsieur Furrer is here, madame.'

'Ah, Furrer.'

Helene stalked into the drawing room and Furrer hastily got to his feet.

'Madame! I came to offer my condolences.'

For a moment Helene wasn't even sure what he was talking about, then she allowed him to kiss her hand. 'There is a war on, Furrer. And in wars people get killed.'

'Ah . . . yes, madame. I also wondered if you had anything for me to take . . . to Switzerland?'

'Yes. I have a letter. But I wish to write another. Wait for a few minutes. Henri!'

'Madame?' The butler had been hovering in the hallway.

'Give Monsieur Furrer a brandy,' Helene commanded, and went into the boudoir.

'Captain Harrison Krantz, junior, sir,' said Lieutenant Watson.

'Harry!' Geoffrey left his desk to advance to the door of the day cabin and shake Harry's hand. 'When did you blow in?'

'Four days ago.'

'And you're returning to the fleet? With promotion?'

'Promotion, certainly. But not to the fleet. This is a flying visit. I'm on my way to the Med, as you suggested. Where the action is.'

'There's not a hell of a lot of action down there either, at the moment,' Geoffrey said. 'The whole naval war seems to have come to a standstill.'

'Yeah.' Harry grinned. 'Maybe I'll be able to stir them up. Anyway, I couldn't go without dropping in to say hello. What's it feel like to be back at Scapa?'

Geoffrey walked with him to the port, to look out at the harbour, the rows of great ships, and the surrounding islands, bristling with gun emplacements and listening devices.

'Very good indeed. This place is as tight as a drum. I don't think a sardine could wriggle in here now. Where's Lizzie? At Silver Streams?'

'Not yet. Fact is, I ran out of furlough and had to come across on a destroyer. Lizzie comes on *Lusitania*, in a fortnight. Actually, the docs felt the delay would be good for both mother and baby, after everything. Boy, is it a relief that your government has lifted that ban on their big liners.'

'Well, as you said, Tirpitz must've had second thoughts about playing the pirate. And how's the boy? A month seemed very early.'

'Yeah. I was having kittens. But Geoff, Harrison Krantz the Third is just the greatest little guy in the world, even if he was premature. I know now how you feel about your Mark.'

'And Lizzie's all right?'

129

'Right as rain. So's the little fellow.'

'That's tremendous. Now, let's see about getting you a cabin.'

'Just for the one night. I must be off again in the morning. Say, Geoff, you okay?'

'Of course I'm okay,' Geoffrey said. 'Why do you ask?'

'You don't look so good to me. Maybe you're just tired.'

'I am perfectly all right,' Geoffrey said, somewhat irritably.

'Well, that's great. Say, any chance of your getting a furlough sometime soon?'

'I don't need a furlough, Harry. And I haven't the time. My name will come up, eventually. Why?'

'It's just that . . . Lizzie isn't travelling alone. Well, it didn't seem right after what she's been through. My folks and my sister Lorraine are coming over as well, to visit at Silver Streams. I sure would like you to meet them.'

'Well . . . how long are they coming over for?'

'They thought they might stay the summer.'

Geoffrey grinned. 'Aren't you still afraid the Germans are going to invade us?'

Harry flushed. 'I guess I got that one wrong. They were making such aggressive noises . . .'

Geoffrey clapped him on the shoulder. 'I'll try to get down there, to meet your people, Harry. Besides, I want to see Lizzie . . . and Krantz Number Three.'

'That,' said Harrison Krantz Senior, as he emerged from the theatre into the brilliant lights of Times Square, 'was one hell of a movie.'

They had been fortunate to get seats. The queues to see *The Birth of a Nation* stretched for blocks. But there were black market tickets available, and as they were off on the great adventure the very next day, Harrison had felt like splashing out.

He had never been to England, and to go for the first time while there was a war on seemed an enormous adventure. He even hoped to get across to France. Without the girls, of course. But Harry should be able to take enough time off to show him the ropes.

Now he grinned at them all. Margaret, like him, was in her fifties, and had put on weight. But the girl he had married could be seen again in Lorraine, tall and slim and dark – and a twenty-three-year-old spinster. Harrison Krantz couldn't understand that, but maybe it had something to do with the way Lorraine always looked as if she'd just fallen off a horse . . . all surprised and dishevelled.

Harrison remembered that young Harry had looked like that, before the Navy had got hold of him. Pity girls couldn't go into the Navy.

But he thought his daughter-in-law a treasure. Equally tall, but fair where Lorraine was dark, beautifully groomed and chic in her hobble-skirt, she was an eye-catcher, even if her Britishness was sometimes too good to believed. Perhaps her figure hadn't quite got back to normal yet; he didn't know about that, although he could see that her bust was presently outsize – but then, she was feeding.

Of her courage there could be no doubt. To undertake a sea voyage with a month-old premature baby . . . but she was determined to be near Harry. And she wanted to be with her family. Harrison could understand that. And she'd be in good hands on the voyage: Margaret and Lorraine would see to that.

But oh, she had courage, and determination.

Harry was a lucky guy. And she was the mother of Harrison Krantz the Third. She was perfect.

'So, what did you think?' he asked, as he walked them down the street towards their hotel; the May evening was warm and starlit.

'I think Lillian Gish is just the sweetest thing,' Margaret said.

'I wish that Stoneman character could've fallen into a vat of boiling oil,' Lorraine commented.

'I think it was all rather prejudiced,' Lizzie observed.

Harrison smiled at her; she was entitled to her opinion, and she didn't really understand about the Civil War, anyway.

131

'What's that boy shouting?' Margaret asked.

'Something about a ship . . .' Harrison stopped the newsboy and bought a paper. 'Hell! It says here one of our ships, SS *Gullflight*, has been torpedoed without warning by a German submarine. God damn.'

'Was anyone hurt?' Lizzie asked.

'Well, sure, honey, Some people were killed. How can the Germans do something like that?'

'Have you seen today's paper, Lizzie?' Margaret asked, when they had assembled for breakfast.

'No. Is there more about that *Gullflight* thing?'

'It's about the *Lusitania*.'

'Oh, no. Don't tell me they've cancelled her sailing!'

They were due to board that evening.

'No, it's this notice.'

She handed over the paper, and Lizzie read:

NOTICE!

Travellers intending to embark on the Atlantic voyage are reminded that a state of war exists between Germany and her allies and Great Britain and her allies; that the zone of war includes the waters adjacent to the British Isles; that, in accordance with formal notice given by the Imperial German Government, vessels flying the flag of Great Britain, or of any of her allies, are liable to destruction in those waters and that travellers sailing in the war zone on ships of Great Britain or her allies do so at their own risk.

IMPERIAL GERMAN EMBASSY
Washington, D.C.

'What do you reckon?' Harrison asked.

'I think it's a colossal piece of cheek,' Lizzie said.

'Yeah. But . . . you got any thoughts about cancelling?'

'Certainly not,' Lizzie said. 'I'm not scared of any German threats. Anyway, there's no submarine in the world could catch the *Lusitania*.'

'Attagirl!' Harrison said.

132

Oh, she had guts.

'Now that,' Harrison Krantz declared, 'is what I call a ship.'

Lizzie had to agree with him. Even if she had travelled on the *Lusitania* before, she was again astonished and impressed by the sea-going monster, rising as high as an apartment block alongside the Hoboken pier.

Some eight hundred feet long, displacing thirty-one thousand tons, with four great funnels towering above the boat deck – Lizzie knew only two of them were real – SS *Lusitania* looked exactly what she was, the queen of the North Atlantic. On her maiden voyage, eight years previously, she had broken the record time for the crossing from England to America, and since then only her sister ship, *Mauretania*, had challenged her.

She looked over her shoulder to see how Nurse Macguire was feeling. Nurse Macguire, a red-headed eighteen-year-old whose name was actually Molly, clutched Harrison Krantz the Third the closer to her ample bosom, and gaped.

'Time to board,' Harrison Krantz said.

'Oh, my,' Margaret said. 'I am so excited!'

And her excitement grew as she followed her husband up the covered gangway, and thence up the interior stairs to the first-class deck, and looked into the Louis Quinze lounge, at the huge, vaulted ceiling – a reproduction of one at Versailles – before emerging on to the promenade deck, the windows open now to allow the May sunshine and the gentle breeze and the cheers of the crowds on the waterfront to filter into the ship – although they would be firmly closed in the event of bad weather.

'I guess this is all old stuff to you,' she remarked to her daughter-in-law.

'I wouldn't say one Atlantic crossing makes one a veteran,' Lizzie said. 'I'm excited too, Margaret.'

Margaret had insisted they be on reciprocal first-name terms almost from the moment of their first meeting.

'I'll have to leave you to do the waving,' Lizzie added. 'It's time for Harry's feed.'

Molly was waiting in the stateroom with the baby. Lizzie had a stateroom all to herself, with a cot for Harry; Molly would be right across the hall, in one of the small cabins reserved on the first-class deck for valets and personal maids.

'Oh, Mrs Krantz,' she said. 'I ain't ever seen anything like this.'

'How did you get to America?' Lizzie asked, sitting in one of the easy chairs and unfastening her bodice. If she had been as frightened as anyone when, following that slight fall on the stairs of the Krantz house, the baby had started, she had to admit that it was a great relief to know it was over . . . and that Little Harry was perfectly healthy, even if he had weighed only five pounds at birth. Now it was her business to build him up . . . and she had the breasts for it.

And they were going home. Much as she had loved America, much as she had been welcomed into their home and their lives by the Krantzs, she still wanted to be back at Silver Streams with Little Harry . . . and hopefully Big Harry as well.

'Lordie, ma'am,' Molly was saying, 'I was born here. My folks, now, they came across steerage . . . on a Cunarder, too. But I guess the *Lusitania* hadn't been built then. Say, ma'am, do we put in at Ireland? I'd sure like to see the place.'

'I don't think we stop there,' Lizzie said. 'Not on the inward voyage. But it's our first landfall. You'll certainly see it.'

Lizzie actually finished feeding Harry in time to return on deck for the departure. She stood with Lorraine to listen to the sirens sounding and the band playing, watch the mooring lines being dropped and the streamers flying through the air, look up at the bridge where the Captain and the First Officer could occasionally be glimpsed as they emerged on to the wing to make sure the tugs were doing their job, and feel the immense throb as the huge vessel was slowly pulled away from the dockside.

Once Captain Smith looked down, and Lizzie waved, wondering if he remembered her from last year.

Whether he did or not, he waved back.

First night out, no one dressed for dinner; there was a sumptuous cold buffet laid out in the first-class dining room. On the second night, however, the Krantzs discovered that they had been placed at the Captain's table.

'Welcome aboard again, Mrs Krantz,' Captain Smith smiled at Lizzie; he had clearly done his homework with the passenger list. 'I understand there are two of you now?'

'There were two of us when last I sailed with you, Captain,' she replied. 'Only you didn't know it. Neither did I.'

The Krantzs were introduced to Mr Alfred Gwynne Vanderbilt, handsome, debonair and perfectly groomed.

He was the great-great-grandson of the famous commodore who had been one of the richest men in America, but was personally better known as a sportsman than a businessman: he had several brothers to attend to the family fortune.

He was also, it turned out, a bachelor, although, having spotted Lizzie's wedding ring, his manners were impeccable, if solicitous.

'Whatever takes a lovely young lady like you to England in time of war?' he asked.

'I happen to live there, Mr Vanderbilt.'

'But you're married to an American.'

'Who happens to be a naval attaché with the Royal Navy.'

'Ah! What a fortunate man.'

'I should be asking you the same question,' Lizzie said.

'I, unfortunately, am not an attaché. My visits to England combine pleasure with business. I'm actually going to make sure a stud I am interested in hasn't been requisitioned by the British Army. Can you imagine a thoroughbred worth perhaps a million dollars galloping across a Flanders mudfield filled with potholes?'

'No, I can't,' she smiled. 'Or what you would say if you saw it.'

'But seriously,' Vanderbilt went on, 'You're not at all upset by this advertisement the German Embassy has been running?'

135

'Propaganda,' Lorraine said, determined to muscle in on the conversation – after all, she was the unmarried member of their party. 'I'm not sure it isn't being paid for by the British, to make the Huns seem more Hunnish than ever. If you'll forgive me, Lizzie.'

Lizzie giggled. 'You could be right. But really, Mr Vanderbilt, even if I thought the Germans would consider for a moment sinking the *Lusitania*, I don't see how they can. They'd need half their High Seas Fleet just to catch her. Are you worried about it?'

Vanderbilt smiled in turn. 'No. But then, men are not supposed to be. There are some of the ladies who are a little nervous. You must let me introduce you to Mrs Frohmann. You can reassure her.'

By next morning an easterly breeze had sprung up, and *Lusitania* was plunging into a head sea. Plunging was the operative word. The huge bows would climb up the side of the swell, almost entirely exposed, and then fall down into the following trough, all sixty feet of topsides going into the green water, which bubbled up to the immense anchors and almost to where the name would have been – but the name had been painted out.

The motion was unsettling on the stomach, and separated the seagoers from the landlubbers. Lizzie had a cast iron digestion but the Krantzs, as well as Molly, all succumbed, which left her very little time to socialise as Little Harry needed a lot of looking after.

But she got to the saloon for meals, and was able to make the acquaintance of the other leading first-class passengers.

Charles Frohmann was a famous theatrical producer, full of interesting anecdotes about the players with whom he had been associated; his wife, if, as Vanderbilt had suggested, distinctly nervous when they first met, improved rapidly as Lizzie reassured her.

Elbert Hubbard was a writer and philosopher, who was also accompanied by his wife, and there were several other distinguished passengers, all of whom were delighted to pass the time with the pretty young mother.

Lizzie had had time since Little Harry's birth to replenish her wardrobe. She loved the latest American styles which were flattering, yet sophisticated – unlike so many of the leading European coutouriers. Her hair was no longer a wide Edwardian pompadour, but drawn back in soft waves over her ears to a neat chignon in the nape of her neck, leaving a small fringe curling over her forehead. She was pleased with the effect and couldn't wait for Harry's reaction.

When the skies cleared and the wind dropped the next day, the liner took on an almost festive appearance, as she raced through the calm water at a steady twenty-three knots. The ship was indeed surprisingly full, but as they were now within twenty-four hours of the Irish coast everyone was in a state of some excitement.

'Do you think we'll actually see a submarine?' asked Mrs Frohmann.

'Not if I can help it, ma'am,' said Captain Smith.

He was happy to explain to his favourite passengers that the Company, in conjunction with the Admiralty, had drawn up an impressive list of safety precautions to be carried out as soon as the ship entered home waters – the War Zone declared by Germany – the most important of which was to zigzag, that is, to follow one course for perhaps half an hour, and then alter to another compass setting for fifteen minutes, and then alter to another, some degrees different, and so on. This was to prevent any German submarine from being able accurately to aim a torpedo, which apparently took some time and required the intended victim to steer a steady course.

This was vastly reassuring, although the Captain then explained that zigzagging, even if the course alterations were slight and always in the general direction in which they were travelling, did not make navigation any easier.

'You mean we might miss England altogether, and wind up in Germany instead?' Alfred Vanderbilt asked next morning with his usual easy humour, as they lunched at the Captain's table.

'Not exactly, Mr Vanderbilt,' the Captain replied. 'We have our sextants and our chronometers to tell us pretty accurately where we are. But no skipper wants to be even a mile off course, especially when navigating the Irish Sea, and we'll be entering that tonight. I estimate that within another hour or so we'll sight the Old Head of Kinsale. That's a prominent headland on the south coast of Ireland, you know. That will give us an exact fix, and from then on we should be all right.'

'You mean we're about to sight land?' Mrs Frohmann cried. 'Oh, I shall be so glad to see it.'

'Then come up on the bridge when you've finished your meal,' Smith invited.

He left them right away, while they digested the fact that tomorrow was the last day of the voyage.

'I hardly feel I've been to sea,' Lorraine complained.

'We'll be sighting Ireland in a few minutes, Molly,' Lizzie said, hurrying down to the cabin. 'The Emerald Isle.'

'Oh, ma'am . . .' Molly's eyes were brimming with sentiment.

Lizzie put an arm round her shoulders. 'You go on out and have a look. Baby sleeping?'

'Snoring his head off, ma'am. Can I really go out?'

'Of course you can. I'm going too. We'll wake him up for his feed right after.'

She and Lorraine hurried up to the bridge, standing before the huge windows and watching the low green hills appearing in the distance.

Lizzie wondered if Molly was still tearful.

'How far off are we?' she asked.

'That we intend to discover exactly,' Captain Smith told her. 'Normally this is done by means of a running fix. That is, we take a bearing on a headland like that over there, and then, maintaining course and speed for an hour, take another bearing and lay it off on the chart. Where the two bearings cross is our position. However, as we know the exact height of the Old Head of Kinsale, all we have to do is line up on it, and as soon as we are close enough, take a sextant

138

reading. That relates the height of the headland to us, and tells us exactly the distance we are from it along the compass bearing we are steering.'

'Do you think Harry knows all of this?' Lorraine asked.

'Well, of course he does, Miss Krantz, it's basic navigation, and every officer knows that. But it's really very simple.'

'But . . .' Something was troubling Lizzie. 'You'll have to stop zigzagging while you do it.'

'Well, yes, of course, Mrs Krantz. But only for about ten minutes. That's why I'm using this method instead of the running fix. Not,' he added jovially, 'that there is the slightest chance of a submarine being in this exact neighbourhood at this exact moment. We'll be commencing now.'

Lizzie sensed that he needed to concentrate, and dragged Lorraine down to the promenade deck; by the time they reached the foot of the ladder *Lusitania* was steering on the headland, her wake as straight as a ruler.

'Now isn't that brilliant,' Margaret said, and walked with Lizzie to the rail to look down at the water, which was changing to green from deep blue as they approached the shore. 'Say, wasn't that a just perfect crossing?'

'Oh, yes,' Lizzie agreed. 'Just . . .'

She gazed at a peculiar line of white froth, under the green of the water, and racing straight at the ship. At the same time she heard shouts from the bridge, and the entire ship made an abrupt turn. So abrupt, she found herself lying on the deck.

'Mother!' Lorraine was shouting. 'Mother, you must get up.'

She and her mother had also been thrown to the deck by the force of the explosion, but she had regained her hands and knees.

It occurred to Lizzie that Lorraine must have been shouting for some time, because her face was quite red, but her own ears were ringing – her head had struck the deck when she fell and she must have been unconscious for a few seconds. She still felt too surprised, and too winded, to move, however she knew it was both ridiculous and unladylike to be stretched on the deck at two o'clock in the afternoon.

Then she saw Alfred Vanderbilt reaching down for her.

'Mrs Krantz?' he asked. 'Are you hurt?'

She stared at him in amazement because he was accompanied by his valet, who had never before appeared on the first-class promenade, and they were both wearing life-jackets.

Vanderbilt held her arm and assisted her up; the valet was doing the same for Margaret, and Lorraine was already on her feet.

'We must find you ladies a lifeboat,' Vanderbilt said. 'Have you no jackets?'

'Jackets?'

Lizzie was too confused to understand what was going on. It seemed as if the normally secure and ordered world of the great ship had gone mad, with sirens blowing and alarm bells jangling, people shouting and screaming all about her, and with the deck suddenly seeming to have developed a tilt, not sideways, as if the ship was rolling, but forward. As if she was . . . she turned round and looked at the bows; there was only a slight chop on the sea, and yet the bows were dipping under water . . . and not coming up again.

'Oh, my God!' she gasped.

'Yes,' Vanderbilt agreed. 'I think Smith should stop her. However . . . a lifeboat. But first, a jacket.' He took his off, draped it around Lizzie's shoulders, put her arms through the holes, tied the strap round her waist. 'George, Mrs Krantz senior.'

'Of course, Mr Vanderbilt.'

The valet did the same with his, for Margaret.

'But . . . we can't take your life-jackets,' Lizzie protested.

'You may need them, my dear girl. George will find us others, and one for you, Miss Krantz. But you had better get into a boat anyway. Come along now.'

His tone was quite brusque, because the slope of the deck was increasing. The boats were already being swung out, filled with women and the few children who were on board. Many of the women were crying, others were shouting out to their husbands, who were hanging back, but there was actually no panic.

Margaret and Lorraine were pulled on board a lifeboat, and Margaret suddenly shouted, 'Harrison! Where's Harrison?'

'I'm sure he'll be quite all right, Mrs Krantz,' Vanderbilt told her, and himself half carried the semi-conscious Lizzie to her place, in virtually the last seat, against the gunwale.

But Margaret's question had penetrated the fog of concussion which had hitherto been shrouding Lizzie's brain.

'Little Harry!' she screamed. 'Molly! Where are they?'

'I'll find them for you,' Vanderbilt promised. 'And get them into a boat.'

'I must come with you,' Lizzie gasped, trying to climb out, and being restrained by several pairs of hands. 'I must!' she shrieked.

'You really can't keep these good people waiting, Mrs Krantz,' Vanderbilt said. 'I will find your baby, I promise.' He gazed at her for a moment, and then, to her total consternation, leaned over the rail and kissed her on the forehead. 'God help you and keep you,' he said.

Lizzie's hand went up to brush moisture from her face – but it was blood, from the blow to her head. She fought for consciousness. 'Please . . .' she said feebly, but the lifeboat was already swinging away from the side of the ship, which was now listing as well as sinking by the bow. Some of the women, all first-class passengers, attempted to smile at her.

Margaret put her arm round her shoulders.

'Baby'll be all right,' she said. 'Molly was with him, wasn't she?'

Oh, God, Lizzie thought. Molly . . . and Harry!

'Harry!' she screamed, threw off their hands, and stood up, reaching for the rail. But the lifeboat was already being lowered. Lizzie fell across the intervening space, and as she caught hold of the ship's rail she felt her footing drop away beneath her, while someone, a sailor on the deck of the ship, started to prise her fingers loose.

'You don't understand!' she screamed. 'I must get up. My son is up there. My son!' she moaned, as the man freed one finger and then the next, and she felt herself starting to slip. The boat's descent had been checked, and hands were grasping at her legs and thighs. A moment later she had collapsed again into the bottom of the boat, and the deck was a good six feet above her head.

'My son!' she screamed, trying to get up again, and being restrained by Margaret and Lorraine. 'My son!'

'Jesus Christ!' muttered the sailor on the tiller. 'Why doesn't the old man reduce speed?'

Lizzie turned her head to look forward, and wanted to scream again, but now she couldn't utter a sound. For the ship was still plunging onwards, at a good twenty knots; her bows had completely disappeared, but were setting up a tremendous disturbance, racing away from the sides of the hull, a series of high and sharp waves into which the lifeboat was about to plunge.

'Jesus Christ,' the sailor commented again.

Lizzie felt herself flying through the air. Then she was in the water, going down, down, down, so deep into the green. At least the cold seemed to revive her. Desperately she tried to kick, and couldn't; the new style of hobble skirt designed to keep her ankles close together was like a straitjacket. Her lungs started to burst, and lights shot across her brain, then she suddenly broke the surface, gasped for air and swallowed water, vomited, and gasped again, kept afloat by the life-jacket which had already saved her life.

'Lizzie!' Lorraine was only six feet away.

The upturned lifeboat was only a few feet further; they struggled towards it and the women holding on to the safety lines – about half the women who had originally been in the boat . . . Margaret was not amongst them.

But the sailor was there too, and he caught Lizzie's arm to bring her to this temporary refuge, and then stared past her.

'Jesus Christ!' he repeated, as if those were the only words he knew.

Lizzie turned her head, and felt like echoing him as she looked at a sight she would surely never forget. The *Lusitania* was sticking out of the water at an angle of some sixty degrees, bows and foredeck and forward superstructure having disappeared beneath the waves, the stern high in the air and crowded with people, beneath whom the huge propellers were still turning.

The ship itself was absolutely motionless for the moment, and Lizzie understood why. As the Captain had told her, there were only three hundred feet of water here; thus the bows had hit the bottom, while the stern was still above the surface, because the ship was eight hundred feet long. Somehow that seemed the most incredible aspect of the entire incredible afternoon. It was simply not possible that a ship could be resting on the bottom, and still also be above the surface – and that her passengers and crew should be drowning. If only it could stay like that, an island, until rescue came.

But even as she watched, the stern began to sink, slowly at first, and then with increasing speed, while people threw themselves into the already crowded sea around the ship. Then the stern disappeared, and there was only bubbling water, surging about them, and the sailor began to weep.

The crowded sea . . . suddenly, mysteriously quiet after the recent tumult. But still crowded. People moaned, and sighed, and occasionally cried out, their voices immediately lost in the slurping of the waters, the wails of the sea birds.

Even Lorraine, clutching the length of rope which trailed from the upturned lifeboat beside Lizzie, and shouting over and over again, 'Motherrrrr! Motherrrrr!', seemed to be a long way away.

And enormous numbers of people made no sound at all, just drifted by, face down or face up, staring lifelessly at the heavens. It was not comprehensible to Lizzie to suppose that she was floating in the midst of so many people, in sight of land, and that so many were dead.

She was aware that she had unfinished business. That somewhere around here were Molly and Harry. But were they amongst the motionless ones?

Her brain was dull again. Added to the pain in her head was a seeping, growing despair. Her baby was gone! Then for a moment she thought she saw Harry walking towards her, smiling. He seemed to approve the new hairstyle. She waited for him to take her in his arms. But he didn't seem able to reach her.

One or two of the women were actually trying to sing; others preferred to shout at the few lifeboats which had reached the sea right side up; but they were all crowded and would not approach anyone in the water for fear of being swamped.

Suddenly the dream faded. 'Have you got my baby?' Lizzie shouted. 'Please tell me you have my baby!'

Apparently they didn't.

'Why didn't he reduce speed?' the sailor asked. 'Why didn't the old man reduce speed?'

'Perhaps he couldn't,' Lizzie said, fighting for sanity. 'The engine room telegraph must have jammed, or been destroyed.'

'Ah,' the sailor said. 'That must have been it.'

And as if he had just been waiting for an explanation, he released the rope and floated away into the afternoon.

Lizzie felt she should try to stop him, but if it was something he wanted to do . . . because she knew it was what she wanted to do too. Little Harry was dead. No doubt Alfred Vanderbilt was dead too. Everyone was dead. And she was so cold, and so tired, and so miserable . . . then the dream returned. Harry was just there. He would comfort her, if she could only reach him.

'Lizzie,' Lorraine said urgently. 'Don't go to sleep. Lizzie! Wake up. We'll be rescued any moment. Lizzie!!!'

Lizzie had released the rope, and was floating away behind the sailor.

It took just over an hour for the fishing boats from Queenstown to reach the scene of the catastrophe. High-bowed, they cautiously nosed thrugh the floating corpses and debris, seeking those who might still be alive.

They concentrated upon those who were in the water first, pulling them close with boathooks and hauling them on to the deck, only then worrying whether they were alive or dead.

At last they reached the upturned lifeboat, began dragging the women on board. Lorraine Krantz had no feeling as she was lifted from the water, no feeling even when her clothes were stripped off by two bearded young men, and she was wrapped in a blanket. Then she was given a cup of hot coffee to drink, laced with rum, and seated on the deck in the warm May sunshine, and slowly feeling began to return, in the form of agonising pins and needles.

'My mother,' she whispered.

'We'll find her, miss.'

'There's one!'

Lorraine watched the red-haired young woman being dragged on board; she wore a life-jacket and was clutching something in her arms. For a moment who she was didn't register.

Lorraine sat up. 'Molly! Is that you, Molly?'

The girl lay on the deck, panting, water running out of her clothes. The sailors knelt beside her and tried to take what she was holding before undressing her.

'No!' Molly screamed. 'Don't take the baby. Don't take the baby.'

The two young men looked at each other, and then at the girl again.

'But miss,' one of them said. 'Your baby's dead.'

CHAPTER 6

The Silent Service

'What kept you?' Lorraine Krantz asked.

Her voice was dull.

'Well . . . travelling about in wartime ain't the easiest thing in the world,' Harry explained. 'Believe me, I moved heaven and earth to get here. Why did you stay?'

'Because I knew you'd be coming. You want to go look at them?'

Harry nodded.

He held her hand as they walked down to the suddenly crowded cemetery. She looked as she had always done, untidy. But with reason, this time: she was still wearing borrowed clothes; presumably it simply had not occurred to her to buy new, or maybe there weren't any suitable shops in this little fishing village.

'There were all these reporters,' she said. 'With cameras. God, it was awful.'

Harry said nothing. He gazed at the mounds of earth.

'They say there are going to be headstones,' Lorraine explained. 'They also said we could take them back to the States, if we wanted to. Still can, I guess; it's just a matter of digging them up.'

'Who's down there?' Harry asked.

Lorraine sighed; tears were dribbling down her cheeks. 'Mom. And Little Harry.'

His head turned, sharply.

'That's it. We never even saw Dad after the torpedo struck. And Lizzie . . . she just drifted away. She'd been badly hit on the head. The nurse survived. She was a real heroine. She hung on to the baby until she was pulled out of the water. She didn't know the poor little mite

146

had been dead for an hour. I reckon you owe her one, Harry.'

'She'll get it.'

Harry turned away from the graves, and stared out to sea.

'Lizzie's somewhere out there,' Lorraine said. 'We saw these hills, from the water. I guess these hills saw us. You want to take them home, Harry?'

'No,' he said. 'I want them to stay here, so I can come back, every year, and remember.'

Harry reckoned Silver Streams would never change. He hoped it wouldn't.

He had been looking forward to coming here, every year for the rest of his life, with Lizzie, and Little Harry, and all the other kids they had been going to have.

Well, he supposed, he could still come here, whenever he felt like it. By himself. Every year, perhaps, after calling at Queenstown and gazing out at the sea from that Irish hillock.

Harriet no longer boomed. Well, how could she? He supposed that when one had six kids, one had to figure on losing one of them during one's own lifetime. But Harriet had now lost three, to all intents and purposes.

Mary was great. She embraced Lorraine, and she embraced him. She even embraced Molly Macguire. And then looked at her own children with a pensive expression. If there were three of her siblings down, there were still two to go, while the war went on.

Not to mention Geoffrey. She was a strange girl. When he first met her she had seemed so . . . straitlaced, boring, even sexless. Well, she wasn't exactly a Lillian Gish now. But she had developed a warmth, a zest for life which he'd not noticed before. Her conversation was lively and interesting. She seemed to be holding together the remains of her family. It was to Mary one turned now, at least in domestic matters.

One member of the family had been out of the firing line for four months.

147

Now Peter looked absolutely fit again, and he was wearing a thin gold band between his two thick ones.

'Well, congratulations,' Harry said.

'Came through only a couple of days ago. I've been passed fit for duty, so . . . I've been given a destroyer.'

'A destroyer? Hey! What's her name?'

'*Arrow*. Three-and-a-half thousand tons, six four-inch.' Peter grinned. 'That's out of the book; I haven't even seen her yet. But I go down to Portsmouth on Monday to take command.'

'And then?'

'We're assigned to the Grand Fleet, at Scapa.'

'Heck, you'll be near Geoffrey.'

'Yes. I might even manage to talk with him,' Peter said. Then his face became serious. 'Are your people going to do anything about *Lusitania*?'

Harry sighed. 'I wish to God I could say yes. There's just too many people over there don't want anything to do with Europe, any more.'

'But killing more than a hundred Americans . . .'

'One hundred and twenty-four,' Harry said. 'Yeah. They will have to be avenged, some day.' He gave a savage grin. 'You guys ever going to go out and take those bastards?'

'Yes,' Peter said. 'Oh, yes.'

'We had a letter from Geoffrey,' Mary said.

They sat together at the bottom of the garden. How many romances had blossomed in this very spot, Harry wondered.

'He sends you, well . . . "sympathy", "condolences",' all words sounded inadequate.

'Thank him for me. He's one hell of a guy.'

'Then there was the telegram. I mean, there were lots of telegrams. But this one was different.'

Harry frowned at her.

'It came from a place called Mudros. That's in the Aegean, isn't it?'

'Sure it is. It's the British base for this campaign they're running in the Dardanelles. Heck, I was there only ten days ago. Who's it from?'

'It wasn't signed. It just said: Most terribly sorry.'

They gazed at each other.

'You think it could be from Jack?'

'I'm sure of it.' The words were spoken almost under her breath.

'In Mudros. You mean he's a soldier?'

'I don't know.' She gave a deep sigh. 'If he was on a ship, he'd still have to use the shore office, wouldn't he?'

'Yeah,' Harry said. 'If he tried to have it sent from the ship to this address, questions might be asked. Son of a gun. And I was right there, ten days ago. What does the rest of the family think?'

'They don't,' Mary said. 'I never showed it to them.'

'What?'

'Well . . . I wanted to talk with you first, or Geoffrey. You happen to be here, first.'

Harry made no immediate reply.

'It's nice to know he still cares,' Mary said.

'Still cares? If he's in Mudros he's fighting on our side, Mary. I don't give a damn what he's supposed to have done, once upon a time. He's fighting for us. Look, when I get back out there – I'm assigned to *Queen Elizabeth* – I'm going to do a bit of detective work.'

'How? There are about sixty British warships in the Dardanelles.'

'You let me take that telegram with me, and see what I can find.'

Mary hugged herself. 'Do you really want to know?'

'Sure I do, and so do you, deep down inside.'

Mary was quiet for several minutes, then she asked, 'What did you feel, when you heard about *Lusitania*?'

Harry looked at her.

'I need to know,' Mary said. 'She was my sister. I felt as if I'd been stabbed to the heart. But . . . it's not the same as being married. And I . . .' she sighed.

149

'Yeah,' Harry said. 'You might get one of those telegrams about Geoffrey. I felt empty, Mary. I still do. I feel empty for them both. Heck, Mom and Dad . . . they'd been around a long time. Don't think I don't grieve them. But Lizzie . . . she had her whole life in front of her. And now I guess there won't be a Harrison Krantz III. Don't get me wrong. It isn't the name that's important. But I hardly even knew the little guy.' He gave a sad grin. 'We only met once or twice.'

'Of course there'll be another Harrison Krantz III,' Mary said. 'You mustn't think that way.'

'That's the way I want to think,' Harry said.

There were tears in his eyes.

The sun was slowly sinking into the shallow cloudbank sitting over the hills. Above the sky was clear, and it was still bright. It was an absolutely perfect May evening.

'Best time of the year, Pa always said,' Peter observed. 'I suppose I never really appreciated it till now.'

'Because you're leaving it tomorrow,' Mavis remarked.

They walked together over the downs behind Silver Streams. Walking had been one of the recommended recuperative processes for Peter, and they had walked together every afternoon for three months. When they had begun there had been snow on the ground. Now it was pleasantly warm.

'I'm not really leaving it,' Peter said. 'Certainly not tomorrow. But even when we do leave Portsmouth, we're only going up as far as Scapa.'

'Scottish springs aren't the same as English springs,' she pointed out.

He supposed she was right. She was right about most things, or at least she made her points with such devastating confidence that one felt she had to be right.

They had never even held hands on their hundred-odd walks together. How did one hold hands with a girl like Mavis? He thought he'd rather find himself and his destroyer beneath the guns of the entire German High Seas Fleet than have to face one of her devastating stares, and a remark like, 'Really, Peter!'

But he wanted to hold her hand. And more than that. If only he could be sure what the emotion really was. It could be just the shock of Lizzie's death, urging him to reach out to another human being. It could be just the concept of leaving Silver Streams again, of going back to sea and the possibility of battle, after four such splendid months.

Or it could be simply a desire to know the girl behind the impenetrable facade.

To know her, in a biblical sense? Oh, he wanted to do that, all right. He did not suppose Mavis would ever win a prize for beauty, but there was a lot of her, and everything seemed to be in the right place.

And she had such a delicious nose.

'I suppose not,' he conceded.

'Better be getting back,' she decided.

'Not yet.'

Mavis stopped walking to frown at him; it was the first time he had ever opposed her.

'I'd like to stay out a while longer,' he explained. 'And talk.'

'What about?'

'Well . . . us.'

'What about us?'

'Well . . . I'm a Lieutenant-Commander, now. Quite a senior position, you know. And captain of my own ship. That means, well, that I can arrange my life more to suit myself than . . . I'm not doing this awfully well, am I?'

'I have no idea what you are trying to do, or say,' Mavis pointed out.

'I'm asking you to marry me,' Peter said.

Her head jerked.

'Oh, really, Peter!'

Her stare wasn't half as devastating as he had expected.

'Well, will you?'

'Marry you? Marry?' She turned away, and he realised she was blushing.

He stood behind her, put his arms round her waist, and kissed her on the neck.

151

'Peter!'

She tried to free herself, and he held her tighter, then, determined not to stop after having started something he had wanted to do for weeks, he turned her to face him, holding her as tightly as he could.

'Peter!' she wailed.

'I love you,' he said into her ear. 'I love you, love you, love you.'

She tried to push him away, but couldn't.

She tried to take a step backwards, and he went with her.

'Peter!' she cried as she overbalanced on to the heather.

He fell with her.

They held hands as they walked home in the dusk.

'Periscope!'

The shout came from the fighting top, but immediately the alarm bells jangled and *Queen Elizabeth* jerked into life, men running to their battle stations, steam pinnaces being cast off, while the destroyers rushed to and fro.

This went on for half an hour, without anything being sighted. But there was no reprimand for the nervous lookout, and no one complained.

The entire fleet was nervous, because a German submarine had definitely been sighted off the Dardanelles the previous day.

'Had to happen,' Petty Officer Martin remarked.

On top of all this, a Turkish torpedo boat had sunk the pre-dreadnought *Goliath*, the day before that.

Everyone was like a cat on hot bricks.

If *Queen Elizabeth* was to stop one . . .

As if it mattered, Jack thought, as he gazed into the green waters, translucent beneath the fierce May sun which dominated the Dardanelles.

The news of the sinking of the *Lusitania* had arrived ten days ago. That had been the biggest shock of the War so far, but it had then been an impersonal shock. The emotions had been anger, of course, determination to avenge such a wanton act, of course . . . but equally a kind of detachment:

152

the sort of people who travelled on ships like *Lusitania* were no longer in his social ken.

Until the arrival, two days ago, of papers from England, with complete passenger lists, and complete lists of those passengers known dead and those 'missing, believed drowned'.

Jack hadn't even intended to look at them, but Midshipman Barber had, and had given a low whistle.

'Alfred Gwynne Vanderbilt,' he said. 'Mr and Mrs Charles Frohmann . . . reads like a page of *Who's Who*. Holy Smoke! Elizabeth Krantz. Wife of Captain Harrison Krantz Junior . . . do you know, I've met that fellow? He was naval attache with the Grand Fleet up at Scapa last year, when I was with *Bellerophon* before joining *Queen Elizabeth*. He'd just got married to one of the Dawson girls. Remember the Dawson scandal, oh, ten years ago? I met the youngest brother, you know. Giles. He's the one earned all that credit back in February. He's a DSC now.'

Lizzie! Jack had read about the marriage in a paper. And now . . .

'May I look, sir?' he asked.

Barber gave him the paper.

There was no doubt: Mrs Elizabeth Krantz, wife of Captain Harrison Krantz Junior, USN. And then, Mr Harrison Krantz, of New Haven, Connecticut. Harry's father? And then, Mrs Margaret Krantz, of New Haven, Connecticut Harry's mother? And then, Master Harrison Krantz III (one month). Harry's child?

And Lizzie's? But Lizzie, gone? Lizzie, who had never harmed a soul, or even had a cross word for a soul, in her entire life, floating around the sea, a waterlogged corpse?

He had been unable to read any more, unable to understand why he, who had nothing to offer anyone any more, should twice have found himself in the ocean and twice survived, and Lizzie should have drowned.

He had gone ashore and sent a telegram of condolence, without counting the possible repercussions. So now he just wanted to see a German submarine, and blast it out of the water.

Instead, that evening orders arrived for *Queen Elizabeth* to return to England.

'They think we're too valuable,' Martin growled.

'Well . . . we've done all we can, Petty Officer,' Barber argued. 'It's up to the Army now.'

The sailors did not agree. It had seemed a good idea, in the beginning, to have the Army take over the Turkish forts as the Navy softened them up, and thus advance, hand in hand, to Constantinople. But things were not working for the Army either. The initial landings had been made on 25 April, three weeks before. The soldiers had swarmed ashore in several places with tremendous elan, and run straight into the most determined resistance. The Turks had indeed used their five-week respite well, and where there had been isolated forts there were now complete zones fortified with trenches and barbed wire, and defended by the bravest of men.

The Army had got nowhere, and they were still there, slogging it out within sight of the beaches.

And of the Navy.

No one was apparently despondent. They were told that a vast reinforcement was on its way from England and Australia, and that these new troops would sweep the Turks aside. That might be so, but the Navy was left with a painful sense of unfinished business.

And now to be commanded to steam away and leave their comrades to the battle . . . no one could be happy about that.

It was on the voyage home that the crew of *Queen Elizabeth* received a series of supreme shocks – as did all members of the fighting forces anywhere.

They had not yet got to Gibraltar when the captain announced to the crew that Lord Fisher had resigned and been replaced by Sir Henry Jackson.

Why had Fisher resigned? Because of the losses at the Dardanelles?

'Has to be,' Martin said.

154

The real bombshell arrived as they reached the Channel approaches. The Government had fallen, and Churchill was no longer First Lord of the Admiralty. In the new coalition Government which had been formed, and which retained Mr Asquith as the Prime Minister, it was a former Prime Minister, Arthur Balfour, who took over at the Admiralty.

Gina once threw a brick at him, Jack thought. But he had been in office when *Dreadnought* had been authorised, so his heart had to be in the right place.

Jackie Fisher had also been in office then.

Jack received a bombshell himself just after they docked in Devonport for their refit: he was summoned to the Captain's day cabin.

'Able Seaman Smith,' Captain Crawford said, studying the sheet of paper in front of him. 'You have had a most unusual War, Smith. I would say, unique.'

'Yes, sir.'

'However, it also appears to have been a very gallant one, and I have had the highest reports of your seamanship and general ability from your immediate superiors.' He leaned back in his chair to look at Jack for the first time. 'I intend to recommend you for promotion to Petty Officer.'

'Sir?'

Crawford's somewhat stern face relaxed. 'Don't sound so surprised. It's the logical next step up the ladder. How old are you, Smith?'

'Ah . . . forty, sir.'

He knew he looked at least that, and the figure had to correspond with the age he had given when he had joined up.

'Well, I would say you'll make CPO at any rate, before this War is finished. Now, first thing, you are to attend an investiture at Portsmouth to receive your DCM. Congratulations. Then you will require some training on shore before being reassigned, and I doubt very much that you will be re-assigned to *Queen Elizabeth*. So, good luck!' He stood up and held out his hand.

Jack shook it, then stepped back and saluted before being marched out of the cabin.

'Congratulations.' Martin slapped him on the back. 'Maybe we'll serve together again sometime.'

'I'd like that,' Jack responded.

But his mind was elsewhere, and far less on his promotion than on London. Because he also had a week's leave after reporting to Portsmouth, and before being re-assigned.

The investiture took place on the parade ground of the Gunnery School. It was crowded with wives, parents and sweethearts, all beaming with pride as their loved ones each received his medal. There were cheers and clapping.

Awaiting his turn, Jack swallowed hard, trying to smile, trying to mask the misery that threatened to swamp him. He didn't bother to look at the rows of smiling faces, because Pa and Ma would not be there, or his brothers and sisters. He could not even expect that Denise would have known about it and travelled down . . .

Then a familiar face caught his eye; Peter was standing in the front row of officers. He had clearly recovered from his wounds, and had also been promoted. He wouldn't know he was watching his brother receiving the DCM, but at least he was there. And Peter had never believed him guilty.

Jack's face spread into a genuine smile and he allowed himself to beam out over the happy faces . . . and then he saw Denise waving frantically at him. Bless her heart! She *had* taken time off work to get down here. He allowed himself to drop an eyelid in her direction, before straightening his face and standing rigidly to attention as the Admiral read his citation.

The Prince of Wales, a small and limp young man, had virtually to stand on tiptoe to pin the multicoloured ribbon on Jack's breast.

But it looked, and felt, awfully good.

He hurried to find Denise as soon as the investiture was over, resisting the temptation to rush across and shake Peter's hand. Oh, how he would have loved to have done that, but

Peter was already surrounded by fellow officers, two of whom were showing him their new decorations. Anyway, he couldn't inflict the secret on his brother; it would put Peter in an impossible position.

'Hello!' A feminine voice reached him from behind.

'Denise?' He swung round, and there she was, elbowing her way through the throng.

Fortunately Peter was too preoccupied to notice her, and Jack held her arm and hurried her away.

'Jack! Congratulations.' She was in his arms. 'What are your plans now?'

'I intended heading for London. And you. We could try the same hotel.'

'Let's try my place instead.'

'To your flat? You sure?'

'Yes, I'm sure.'

They were fortunate to have a train compartment to themselves.

'Oh, Jack!' She kissed his mouth, his nose, his eyes, his cheeks . . . he had dreamed of a woman loving him this much, but had never expected to have it happen. He returned the kisses as passionately.

At last she sat back and straightened her hat. 'About Lizzie . . . oh, Jack. I'm so sorry. And the baby, too, poor little mite. Her husband must be devastated.'

'Yes,' he nodded sadly. 'Poor Harry.'

They took a cab from Waterloo to her flat. It was a tiny apartment, with a single bedroom and what could hardly be called a kitchenette. It was dark when they arrived, and drizzling.

'This war . . .' she sighed. 'And the weather . . . It makes you feel so beastly. Even when you don't want to.'

'Yes,' he agreed again. 'Isn't your landlady going to cause a rumpus when she finds out you're entertaining a man up here at night?'

'She can do what she likes. Jack . . . I'm pregnant.'

He looked down at her always petite figure. Her dress fitted snugly round the waist, but there was no visible bulge.

157

'It's only four months. I'm not showing yet. But it's there. He's there. Our baby, Jack.'

He thought about Master Harrison Krantz III (one month). But his baby was going to live. 'Will you marry me?'

'When?'

'I only have a week. We'll get a special licence. "Won't you need a birth certificate?" He shook his head. 'When I joined up I told them I was born overseas. They didn't argue. They won't know. I'm a hero. What about your folks?'

'Yes. Well . . . I don't suppose you could tell them the truth?'

'I can't, Denise. I'd be sent back to prison.'

She smiled. 'Then I'm to be Mrs Jack Smith, wife of Able Seaman Jack Smith. They'll have to put up with it.'

'Actually, you're going to be the wife of Petty Officer Jack Smith.'

'Promotion already? Oh, wonderful. But . . . I still think you had better let me handle Mummy and Daddy.'

'Aren't you afraid they'll cut you off without a shilling?'

'I suspect that's just what they'll do, when they learn I'm in the family way out of wedlock. Will that bother you?'

He kissed her. 'I think we can manage on a PO's salary.'

Again he had to wonder why he could be so happy, when all around him was gloom.

But happiness was Denise. Everything about her.

'Can we?' he asked, when they went to bed.

'Why not?'

'Well, what about the baby?'

'He'll love it. And you'd better make the most of it. Next time you get leave it might be more difficult.' She giggled. 'I don't think we should waste any time.' She unbuttoned the neck of her dress.

They honeymooned for three days.

'Do you want to talk, about afterwards?' he asked.

'Do you?'

'I don't want you to be a PO's wife for the rest of your life.'

'I want to be your wife for the rest of my life, Jack. Let's get things in their proper order. I want you to survive this crazy business, and come back to me, safe and sound. Then we'll talk about what comes next.'

'Can we really justify such a thing as torpedoing a ship like *Lusitania*?' Bruno von Eltz asked.

'There is no doubt that she was armed. Or that she was carrying munitions, unlisted in her manifest,' Hipper said. 'Our Washington Embassy has confirmed this.'

'The British deny it.'

'Well, they would, wouldn't they?'

'But even if she was carrying munitions, to murder fifteen hundred civilians in cold blood . . .'

'It was not meant to happen like that,' Hipper argued. 'Something went wrong. The ship actually seemed to steam beneath the waves. It is assumed that the explosion beneath the bridge in some way damaged the telegraph system. Where she was, within a dozen miles of Ireland and in a calm sea, she should have been able to put down all of her boats and take off all of her people before she sank. There should have been very little loss of life.'

'Very little loss of life,' Bruno muttered. Lizzie Krantz . . . Lizzie Dawson. He was not even sure he remembered her. Had she been at Silver Streams during his visit? He simply could not remember.

But she was a Dawson. What an unhappy family they had become, to be sure. And he had started that ball rolling.

'There would have been some loss of life, no matter how slowly she sank,' he said.

'We are fighting a war, Bruno. There is always going to be loss of life.'

'It should be confined to soldiers and sailors,' Bruno grumbled.

'You are speaking of an ideal world. However, I have some good news for you. You have been promoted. Well, not in the

159

sense that you have advanced a rank, but you have advanced a ship. You are being transferred to *Brunswick*.'

Bruno raised his head, frowning.

'As her captain, of course. You should be pleased. She is every inch a dreadnought battleship.'

'You mean I am regarded as a failure as a battlecruiser captain?'

'Why do you always think in terms like failure, or success? Well, if you will have it so, you have not been an entirely successful battlecruiser captain. I am not criticising your professional skill; that is of the highest. It is your attitude. We are being forced to fight this war in a way none of us likes, but you like it least of all, to an extent which is felt, in some quarters, to put your efficiency at risk. Well, now you are wanted for a battleship, and you can be sure that you will never again have to bombard a seaside resort or run away from the enemy; when you put to sea in *Brunswick* it will be to engage the British Grand Fleet.' He peered at his erstwhile protege. 'For God's sake, cheer up. It is a step up for you, and I have no doubt at all that you will continue to be stepping up. I shall be sorry to lose you, but Ingenohl is very pleased to have you. Good luck, Bruno.'

Bruno shook hands, and left the cabin.

He wondered why he was not pleased. He had never enjoyed the hit-and-run role ordained for the battlecruisers and this was, as Hipper had said, another step up the ladder. From captain of a super-dreadnought the only next step was Konteradmiral. It was a dream he had long held. But it did mean he was being pushed up and away from the more active role of the battlecruisers. Not that even Hipper had been allowed to go to sea since their defeat off the Dogger Bank in January.

He was overwhelmed with this constant feeling of malaise. He returned to *Roon*.

'Well, Carl,' he said. 'We are leaving.'

'Leaving the Navy, Herr Baron?' Carl asked eagerly. He suffered from seasickness.

'No, no, Carl. We are being transferred. To a battleship. You will like that much better; it is bigger, and will not roll so much. Now tell me, has Herr Furrer telephoned?'

'Not yet, Herr Baron.'

Bruno frowned. Furrer was four days overdue with Helene's latest letter.

He went ashore and telephoned Reuger.

'Anton! Tell me, when last did you see Furrer?'

'I have not seen him for some time, Herr Baron.'

'Does he not visit you regularly?'

'Well, he does, Herr Baron. But it so happens he has not been here for a fortnight.'

'I would like you to get hold of him, Anton, and ask him to get in touch with me immediately. Will you do that, please?'

'Of course, Herr Baron. I will get on to it right away.'

Bruno returned to *Roon*, frowning. Whatever was that nasty little man up to now?

'Welcome aboard, sir.' Lieutenant Ganning shook hands with his new commanding officer, Lieutenant-Commander Giles Dawson. 'How's the arm?'

'The arm is fine,' Giles told him. 'How's the ship?'

'All repairs completed, sir. She's ready for sea.'

Giles slid down the ladder into those so familiar surroundings. In Mudros Harbour, with the summer sun glaring down from a cloudless sky, everything was hot – the interior of the submarine, despite the fans, was like an oven. But it was so good to be back.

Giles had not been the least upset at not being sent home while recovering from his wound; he had had no desire to leave the Dardanelles theatre. He had in fact been relieved that *C17* had been laid up as long as himself, having the damage to her conning tower repaired; that meant she had not been sailed by anyone else in his absence.

Now she was his. Somewhat earlier than he had expected. And of course it was very sad that Manly had died. But Manly had received a posthumous VC for sinking that Turkish battleship. Now it would be his turn. He had been given

161

the DSC for bringing the ship home. He could hardly wait to get back at the enemy again; he had been as upset as anyone by the news of Lizzie's death. Now he wanted to give them something of what they had given *Lusitania*.

But things had changed, as he was warned when briefed by the Flotilla Captain.

'The army aren't making any headway at all,' Gillespie told him. 'There are constant rumours of new reinforcements and new attacks, but right now things are stagnant. The Turks are dug in depths, and they seem prepared to fight to the last man. The fleet is simply stymied, and there are so many German U-boats and Turkish torpedo boats about that none of our surface craft dare venture into the straits. So, offensive action is all up to you chaps. Just remember that this time they're waiting for you.'

C17 slipped away from her mooring at dusk, to make the journey to the strait on the surface. In June the nights were short, even in the Mediterranean, and it was ten o'clock when they left Mudros; in hardly more than six hours it would be light again.

It was uncanny to be motoring on the surface, on a clear night and in a calm sea, with the sounds of battle only a few miles away, clearly audible, and visible from time to time. They could hear rifle shots as they approached the headland, and every so often a star shell would arc into the sky, turning its immediate vicinity as bright as day, before disappearing to increase the darkness.

'Poor blighters,' Ganning commented. 'I'm glad I'm a sailor.'

At four AM they dived, the strait now open ahead of them, and proceeded dead slow into the narrows. There were a great many more minefields, now, than when Giles had first ventured here, but British submarines had been regularly slipping in and out and they were well marked. More disturbing was the constant surface activity, the patrol boats rushing to and fro, causing Giles to drop below periscope depths every so often. But Marmara was reached without too much difficulty, in the middle of the afternoon.

During the journey up the strait Giles had used the periscope when he could, to examine the Turkish defences, which had indeed quadrupled in quantity, and, he suspected, quality, since he had last seen them.

Marmara was open, however, although here also there was a great deal of activity. But *C17* was able to surface at dusk, after a very long eighteen hours, and almost the entire crew came on deck to take great gulps of fresh air, while Giles and Ganning inspected the horizon with their glasses.

'Nothing worthwhile,' Ganning grunted.

'We'll make for Istanbul,' Giles decided, and *C17* glided through the night.

At dawn they submerged, the minarets of the city well within sight, and a considerable amount of shipping both outside the harbour and using the Bosporus, the northern strait which connected Marmara with the Black Sea.

'Again, no big stuff,' Giles said. 'It must all be north of the city. Have any of our chaps ever penetrated the Bosporus, Harry?'

Ganning gazed at him in consternation.

'We have a chart of it,' Giles reminded him. 'And as far as I know, it's not mined.'

'That'd be some show,' Ganning said. 'There's nothing in orders about it.'

'There's nothing in orders against it, either,' Giles pointed out.

Relying on the element of surprise, Giles determined to enter the Bosporus on the surface; that way he could travel faster, and see more of what he was about. As soon as it was dark, *C17* came up for air, and then slipped forward. The growl of her diesel seemed very loud on the conning tower, but he doubted anything was being heard in Constantinople itself; there was no suggestion that Turkey was at war in the bright lights and occasional bursts of loud music emanating from the city.

163

But then, Giles reflected, Constantinople was not subject to raids, either by zeppelins or surface craft.

Soon after midnight he sighted several ships coming down the channel, again fully lighted. He stopped engines and let *C17* drift until they were past, then resumed his passage. The Bosporus was less than half the distance of the Dardanelles, and the submarine emerged into the Black Sea well before dawn. Their way of course took them past the Golden Horn, and Giles had a good look at the land-locked harbour through his glasses. But to enter there would be virtual suicide, and he could see nothing large enough to justify hazarding his ship.

North of the strait, however, there were several ships lying at anchor, no doubt feeling entirely safe from Allied attack. In the darkness. Giles could identify none of them, and so elected to wait for daylight, which meant spending the day in these unfamiliar waters.

C17 put out to sea, and when well away from land, was able to surface and lie wallowing in the gentle swell. Giles maintained six lookouts to keep an eye in every direction, but although they saw smoke more than once, and prepared to dive, no ship approached them.

That afternoon, the submarine dived again, and returned to within sight of Constantinople submerged to periscope depths.

'*Goeben*!' Giles said.

'Are you sure, sir?' Ganning asked.

'Take a look for yourself,' Giles invited, and relinquished the eye-piece.

'There's a prize,' Ganning muttered. 'She's well-protected.'

'As one would expect. We'll attack at dusk.'

He returned to the periscope himself, studying the enemy, while *C17* cruised very slowly up and down. The battlecruiser was indeed well protected; there were several large vessels moored around her, and an outer ring of torpedo-boat-destroyers and patrol boats. On the other hand, these were nearly all moored as well; the Turks had no concept that an enemy submarine could possibly have passed the Bosporus. It was simply a matter of lining up the largest opening leading to the big one; what happened afterwards would have to be played by ear.

The sun drooped ever further into the western sky, and Giles found himself looking directly into the rays. Equally, however, *Goeben* was becoming silhouetted against the bright evening glow. And he had found his gap; it was temporarily closed by a patrol boat, but the steam pinnace was moving . . .

'Stand by,' he said. 'Stand by. Fire bow tubes.'

'Number One gone, sir,' said Sub-Lieutenant Gibbons. And a second later, 'Number Two gone, sir.'

'Take her down, Number One,' Giles snapped, closing the periscope and withdrawing it. 'One hundred feet, steer oh five oh.'

Directly away from the Turkish ships.

C17 dropped into the depths even as she turned. She was already on her new course when they heard a water-muffled explosion, and then another.

'Do you think we got him?' Ganning asked.

'We got something,' Giles replied. But he would have expected a battlecruiser to make more of a bang.

'Propellers,' said Petty Office Langham.

'Stop engines,' Giles said. 'Take her down, Number One.'

The engines stopped, and *C17* again sank into the depths, while above their heads patrol boats rushed to and fro. Giles knew that the Admiralty were developing a new method of attacking submarines: underwater explosives called depth charges. But he doubted the Turkish Navy possessed anything as sophisticated; they would have to rely upon first of all determining where the enemy craft was, and then on keeping it submerged until it was forced to surface for air. At night, that was a forlorn hope.

C17 sank silently into the depths until, at a hundred and seventy-five feet, she found the bottom. This was close to her hull's pressure capabilities, and there were one or two minor leaks, but nothing the engineers could not cope with. Giles remained there for an hour, then restarted his engines, rose off the bottom, and slipped slowly away, again to the north-east.

The Turks had correctly estimated the most likely direction a maurauding submarine might take, but the hour's total disappearance had caused them to disperse their forces. When next Giles, having risen to a hundred feet, stopped engines, there was not a sound to be heard. He then rose to periscope depths, and found nothing near at hand, although there were a great number of flashing lights in the distance.

A few minutes later *C17* was on the surface, flooding itself with life-giving air, while the diesel was re-charging the batteries.

Giles and Ganning levelled their glasses at the distant lights of Constantinople. There was no evidence of anything on fire, but if they had struck anything, their target would have long since sunk.

'We'll just have to wait and see,' Giles said. 'When we get home.'

He knew this was going to be a long and difficult business. *C17* remained on the surface for the rest of the night, submerged at dawn, and cautiously moved to a position a few miles north of the entrance to the Bosporus. Here, through the periscope, Giles could monitor the shipping movements in and out of the strait, and could watch too the considerable patrol boat activity, both there, and around the vessels anchored north of the strait. To his chagrin, he could make out the tripod masts of the *Goeben*, thus proving that he had not not hit his target – but he reflected that he must have sunk something, going by the explosions, and to attempt to make another attack, with the Turks alerted, would be suicide. His business was to get his ship and his men back to safety, and he was relieved to observe, during the afternoon, that the patrol activity in the mouth of the strait had diminished. No doubt the Turks were assuming that the attacking submarine had already made its escape.

'We'll have to do this submerged,' he told Ganning. 'They won't have relaxed to that extent.'

Ganning nodded, his face grim.

But Giles was as confident as ever. He had made a careful note of all the courses steered on the way up, and the length

166

of time on each leg; now it was simply a matter of steering, and measuring, reciprocals.

They entered the strait at dusk, and made their way steadily south, helped by the current which flowed constantly from the Black Sea into Marmara, and thence through the Dardanelles into the ever-evaporating Mediterranean. Through the periscope Giles saw the lights of the various villages drifting by, and saw too the various patrol boats which were still active, but these were easily avoided by dropping below periscope depths for a few minutes.

An hour passed, and he could see the lights of Constantinople; just beyond that was Marmara, where he intended to spend the next day before tackling the Dardanelles. And what a tale he would have to tell – the first British submarine to enter the Black Sea. He felt a rising excitement, and then a sudden coldness on his shoulders and the back of the neck as there was a scraping sound along the hull, and *C17* came to a halt.

All eyes turned on the captain. Giles moved the periscope round a full three hundred and sixty degrees, and saw nothing, save the lights on the shore. The submarine was almost exactly opposite the Golden Horn, and there was a great deal of activity there, judging by the moving lights – but that was over half a mile away.

Then he saw, closer at hand, a line of markers on the surface, bobbing and bubbling under the weight of the submarine.

'We've fouled a net,' he said. 'Hard astern, Number One.'

The propellers went into reverse, and after several agonising seconds the submarine came free. But they were still on the wrong side of the net.

'The bastards,' Ganning commented. 'Do you reckon it's right across?'

'No. The passage is too wide. We'll have to find a way round.' Giles inspected the situation through the periscope, while feeling an increasing sense of anxiety; he had underestimated the vigour, both mental and physical, with which the Turks would respond to his attack.

The decision facing him was starkly simple. He could go to the right, which would take him into the glare of the lights from Constantinople and Galata, the suburb on the northern side of the Golden Horn, or he could go to the left, to the Asiatic shore – but his chart told him that it was shallow over there.

He gazed at the Golden Horn. There was a lot of activity outside of the harbour, and it seemed to be spreading in their direction; obviously the Turks had had a boat waiting at the end of the net, and it had felt the vibrations set up when the submarine had become snagged. They knew he was there, somewhere, and were waiting for him to show himself.

He looked at the Asiatic shore. That was in darkness. Therefore the Turks clearly felt it was too shallow for the submarine to make a passage. But it was his best bet.

'We'll go for the eastern end,' he told his men. 'Slow ahead.'

The submarine inched its way to the east, having to steer north-east to avoid being swept back into the net by the current. Giles watched both the line of marker buoys and the approaching shore, as it crept closer. He anticipated the coming grating sound a second before it happened.

They were still perhaps a cable's length, two hundred yards, from the land, and he could see the end of the line of markers, perhaps fifty feet away.

'All right, Number One,' he said. 'Take her up.'

Air hissed into the buoyancy tanks as the water was forced out, and *C17* came up. Giles emerged into the conning tower, and looked down at the net markers, then up at the cliffs above him; they looked frighteningly close, but *C17* was floating.

'Now,' he said. 'Slow ahead, Number One, and we'll see if we can creep round this net.'

'Aye-aye,' Ganning said enthusiastically.

C17 came round in a tight circle, the end of the net now well to starboard, but the cliffs very close; Giles knew

168

there could not be more than a few feet under the hull, but then, he was only a few feet from deep water on the far side of the net, and safety: Marmara was less than a mile away.

Then a great white light shone into his eyes, and all hell broke loose.

CHAPTER 7

The Fleet

'How's your mother taking it?' Harry asked. He had nearly completed his furlough, and tomorrow would be on his way north to Scapa Flow to rejoin the Grand Fleet. He was glad to have been here when this fresh catastrophe had struck the family, even if he could not help but wonder how many more tragedies lay in wait for these so attractive people.

Harriet had read the telegram without a change of expression, but after handing it to Mary she had retired to her bedroom and not been seen for the rest of the day.

'I think she's more upset by the idea that Giles is a prisoner-of-war than if he had been killed,' Mary said. 'A prisoner, of the Turks. Imagination conjures up such terrible pictures . . .' She gave a little shiver.

'This is the twentieth century,' Harry said reassuringly. 'They'll obey the Geneva Convention.'

'I'm not even sure they signed it. What was he doing in the Black Sea, anyway?'

'It was quite a feat. I'd say the Admiralty must be proud of Lieutenant-Commander Giles Dawson.'

'Even if he lost his ship?'

'By all accounts he took one of theirs with him. And he's alive, Mary. That's what counts. He's alive.'

'I wonder what it's like?' she said. 'Death.'

This was a subject she kept returning to with alarming regularity, almost as if she expected Geoffrey to be the next victim. What's it like? Harry thought. But he had spent some months in the Dardanelles, and had gone ashore several times. So what is it like to lie in a stinking slit trench with your bowels ripped out by an enemy bayonet and flies settling all over you?

170

But then, what of feeling the rush of cold water through your nostrils as you drown? Like Lizzie.

He always came back to that.

'It's pretty grim,' he said solemnly, and then forced a grin. 'Not that I've ever experienced it, you understand.'

They were alone at the table; Lorraine had taken Joan out to play, and nurse had Mark upstairs.

Mary rested her hand on Harry's arm.

'It's been very good having you here. One gets so . . . well, introspective just reading the newspapers. Experiencing the War at second-hand, as it were.'

'That's all I've been doing.'

'But actually seeing. Harry . . . I'm so sorry you didn't turn up anything on Jack. Right this minute . . .'

'Even he would have been welcomed home. Sure. You know something? I have a notion he could've been on *Queen Elizabeth*.'

'Why?'

'Because it was such a near miss. I apply to be sent to the Dardanelles. I'm told I'll be berthed on board the *Queen*. I get as far as Mudros, and am recalled to Ireland because of Lizzie's death.' After four months he could just say it without wincing. 'So I come back, and then return to the Dardanelles. And in my absence *Queen Elizabeth* has been returned to England for refitting. I hunted through most of the other ships, casual visits, talking to the men, asking about their experiences, just what an attaché is supposed to do. I covered them all pretty thoroughly. If Jack had been on one of them I'd have recognised him.'

'The police said he'd grown a beard when he absconded.'

'I'd still know him.'

'Well,' she said. 'Now you're going to Scapa. *Queen Elizabeth* will return there, after her refit.'

'Yeah.' He glanced at her. 'And you'd like me to find him?'

'Oh, God, I wish I knew what to say. Finding him can only cause trouble, but . . .' She got up, walked to the window, looked out at the garden. 'Will you be seeing Geoffrey?'

'I'm being berthed on *Anson*.'

171

'Will you give him my love?'

'Sure.'

He also got up, stood behind her at the window.

'And tell him . . . it'd be awfully nice to have him down here for a visit.'

'When last was he here? He was going to come down in May.'

'Well, he never did. I haven't seen him for a year.'

'Heck. That is a long time. I guess, as ship's captain, he feels he has to give himself less leave than any member of his crew.'

'I suppose,' she agreed. 'But you'd think *Anson* would be due for a refit herself around now.' She turned, so suddenly that she found herself in his arms.

For what seemed the longest second of her life, Mary stood there, gazing at him. Because she wanted him to kiss her. Maybe she wanted Geoffrey to kiss her, and as Geoffrey wasn't here . . . she could tell by the look in his eyes that he wanted to kiss her too.

But she wasn't Gina. She had never had a promiscuous thought in her life. Until now. Because after he had kissed her, she wanted him to . . .

'Oh, heck,' Harry said. 'I think the sooner I'm on that train north the better, for both of us.' He released her. 'I'll give Geoffrey your love, Mary. And tell him he'd better sure as hell give himself some leave.'

'Carl, this bottle is empty,' Bruno said.

'Yes, Herr Baron.'

'Well, fetch me another.'

'Do you not think it would be best for you to lie down, Herr Baron?'

'Fetch me another bottle, you rascal, or I will have you thrown off this ship.'

'Yes, Herr Baron.'

Carl dutifully placed a new bottle of brandy on the table, gazing at his master as he did so. Bruno's collar was awry and so was his tie; his normally immaculate hair was rumpled.

Carl poured, and Bruno drank. He had been drinking now for more than two hours, but Carl was sure his master was not drunk.

'What is that noise?' Bruno asked.

'It is a whistle, Herr Baron. The boatswain's whistle.'

'Well, tell him to stop it,' Bruno snapped.

'Yes, Herr Baron.'

Carl turned towards the cabin door, checked as it opened after the most perfunctory of knocks.

'Herr Kapitan! Herr Kapitan!' It was Oberleutnant-sur-Zee Richter, in a state of some alarm.

'What is it, Richter?'

'Vizeadmiral Scheer is on board, Herr Kapitan.'

'What is he doing on my ship, unannounced?'

'Well, Herr Kapitan . . .' Richter, a fresh-faced young man with yellow hair, licked his lips. 'I think he is coming to see you.'

'Then show him in.'

'Yes, Herr Kapitan.'

Richter looked at Carl, and Carl looked at Richter. They were both aware that their captain was in no proper state to receive an admiral, either in his dress or his attitude.

Then Carl shrugged.

Richter left the cabin.

'May I assist you, Herr Baron?' Carl stood by the chair.

'Assist me to do what?'

'Well, Herr Baron, your tie . . .'

Carl attempted to straighten it and received a cuff which sent him reeling across the cabin. Before he could make another attempt to help his master, Scheer was in the doorway, Richter hovering at his elbow.

The Vice-Admiral took in the situation at a glance.

'Thank you, Oberleutnant,' he said. 'You may go.'

Richter hesitated, then saluted and retreated.

'What is your name?' Scheer asked.

'Carl Mayen, Herr Vizeadmiral.'

'Yes. Well, leave us.'

Carl also hesitated, then backed through the doorway.

'And close it,' Scheer commanded.

Carl closed the door.

Bruno was endeavouring to stand, and had stumbled against the table; the full bottle of brandy fell over, and Scheer picked it up; amber liquid rolled across the table to soak the newspaper before dripping on to the carpet.

'Why do you not sit down, Bruno?' Scheer recommended, 'Before you fall down.'

He took off his cocked hat, laid it on a chair, and sat down himself.

'I would like to apologise, Herr Vizeadmiral,' Bruno said. 'I do not feel very well.'

'Would you like leave, Bruno?'

'Leave, Herr Vizeadmiral?'

'Do you not wish to go home to Schloss Elsjing for a few days? I am sure there are things which require your attention.'

'I have no wish to return to Schloss Elsjing, Herr Vizeadmiral.'

'Well then, Berlin? See a few shows, eat at some good restaurants?'

'Herr Vizeadmiral, I wish to go to sea and fight the English. That is why we are here, is it not?' He waved his arm. 'There are sixteen dreadnought battleships in this harbour, Herr Vizeadmiral. And not one of them has ever fired a shot in anger, although the War has now been going on for more than a year. Are we to spend the entire War sitting in port?'

Scheer sighed. 'I am not any more happy with the situation than you are, Bruno. The trouble is, the British have twenty-eight dreadnoughts. Twenty-nine when *Queen Elizabeth* has completed her refit. That is very nearly two to one, and they also have twice our number of battlecruisers.'

'We were to whittle that strength down,' Bruno said.

'And we have not succeeded in doing so. Nor were we very successful in January at destroying Beatty's squadron. The High Command feels it is too risky to attempt that again, just for the sake of the British battlecruisers.'

'So we sit in port.'

'The day will come,' Scheer mused.

174

Bruno studied him. He could tell that the Vice-Admiral was as fed up as anyone. Only Ingenohl did not seem to feel the prevailing frustration. The Commander-in-Chief was perfectly happy with the situation. He had the second greatest fleet in the world to look at, and the future to think about. He also had a superficially sound strategic argument, that the mere presence of the High Seas Fleet, poised for action, kept the Grand Fleet in Scapa Flow.

The point was, the Grand Fleet in Scapa Flow was where it wanted to be, conducting a most efficient long distance blockade of Germany which was already beginning to bite. The task of the High Seas Fleet had surely to be to move the Grand Fleet from Scapa, if possibly, decisively.

And Scheer knew that as well as anyone.

The Vice-Admiral stood up.

'I will take my leave now, Bruno. Permit me to offer you some advice. Medical advice, perhaps.'

'Yes, Herr Vizeadmiral.' Once again Bruno struggled to his feet.

'Send your man ashore, and tell him to come back with a woman.'

'Here, Herr Vizeadmiral? That would be highly irregular.'

'It is permitted to be irregular once in a while. You are being highly irregular at this moment. I should not like any of your crew to see you in this state, so you will remain here until you have sobered up. But have a woman. It is what you need more than anything. Good night to you, Bruno.'

The Vice-Admiral closed the cabin door behind him. Carl waited in the companionway.

'I have something for you to do, Mayen,' Scheer said.

As a petty officer Jack found his duties pleasantly changed; he gave orders now as well as receiving them, had charge of one of the seamen's messes, and also one of the six-inch secondary batteries on board *Queen Mary*.

She was a splendid ship. But then, all six ships of the Battlecruiser Squadron – *Lion*, *Tiger*, *Princess Royal*, *New Zealand* and *Indefatigable* were the others – were fine ships, manned by the most confident of men. They remembered Dogger, and they remembered the Falklands. They had tasted blood, and they were eager for more.

Fortunately, from Jack's point of view, *Invincible*, *Inflexible* and *Indomitable* had been detached from Beatty's command and formed into a separate squadron, under Rear-Admiral Horace Hood, to scout for the Grand Fleet. Jack had to presume that Peter was back on duty again by now, and it really would be chancing his arm for them both to be stationed in Rosyth.

All any man in the squadron now wanted was for the Germans to come out again.

But for some, concentration upon that aim was more difficult than for others. Jack's thoughts kept drifting down to London, and Denise's tiny flat. She was due any day now. At least here in Rosyth he could telephone her regularly. She always sounded perfectly cheerful and happy, although he knew that as she had both given up her job and again quarrelled with her parents – over her marriage so far beneath her – she must be unutterably lonely. As the wife of Petty Officer Jack Smith she couldn't even turn to her old school friends like Mary.

But then, according to her, she and Mary had drifted apart anyway.

But oh, how he wanted the German Navy to come out and fight.

Denise telephoned in the middle of October to say that she had given birth, two weeks prematurely, to a little boy, who she was going to name Jack, if that was all right with him.

For a moment he was speechless with excitement.

'Jack? Jack, are you there?' she called over the telephone.

'Yes. Oh, my darling, yes. That sounds splendid. Are you sure you're all right?'

'Right as rain. I only wish you were here.' Her voice mirrored his happiness.

'I'm on my way,' he promised her. 'Just as soon as I can get away. And I'll celebrate with the lads tonight.'

In the circumstances, a week's furlough was easy to come by. The three of them spent the seven days inside the flat, only going out to shop. For the rest, their life centred around Baby Jack, a lusty and hungry, if terribly little, fellow.

'He'll grow,' Denise promised. 'He'll be as big as his father.'

But she didn't have enough milk, and the midwife was already advocating a switch to bottles.

'And guess what,' she said. 'I had a phone call from Mummy. She's coming down, as soon as you go back.'

'Well that's wonderful. When do I stop being persona non grata?'

'Give it time, lover. Give it time.'

'Now for the bad news. Coming down here now, I won't be one of the lucky ones at Christmas.'

'When, do you reckon?'

'Well . . . not before April.'

Denise smiled. 'I'll have Mummy licked into shape by then. And Daddy too.'

Jack had just regained the squadron when the news came through about Nurse Edith Cavell, shot by the Germans for assisting British and French prisoners to escape into Holland.

The world was shocked, and a feeling of cold anger ran through the fleet.

In November, Denise wrote to say that she had found a new job – as a bus conductress. Apparently the Government had decided to allow women to take on various types of employment hitherto reserved for men. She had found a woman to babysit Little Jack, who was now entirely bottle fed and beginning to put on weight. She was as pleased as punch.

Jack reckoned she was having a more active time than he was. The battlecruisers put to sea occasionally, and swept up and down the North Sea, and there were rumours that the Grand Fleet was also out, but of the Germans there was no sign, while the battles in France got bloodier and bloodier.

They did also in the Dardanelles, with even less Allied success, and in December the project was abandoned, having cost over two hundred thousand casualties, of which at least twenty-five thousand were known dead.

And quite a few were prisoners. Including Giles. But Jack had a notion Giles was capable of surviving even a Turkish prison camp, despite the gruesome stories that went the round of the messes about forcible circumcision. Anyway, there was talk that he was going to receive a VC, for being the first submarine captain to penetrate the Bosporus. That would be worth a bit of hardship, if it were true.

The fleet was left to brood on might-have-beens: if Fisher had not got cold feet and resigned; if Churchill had not been sacked; if Carden had not been taken ill . . . and most of all, if Robeck had done a Farragut, shouted 'damn the torpedoes', and battered his way into Constantinople, even if it had meant the loss of half his ships.

It seemed the quality of British leadership was not what it had been. And the man who everyone knew had the Nelsonian touch could do nothing about it. Sir David Beatty took his ships out and brought them back, inspected them and their crews, stopped to stare at the big, bearded petty officer – they had met many years before – and brooded on what the Germans were doing.

At least his potential was recognised at Whitehall. Early in the new year, four huge ships steamed into the Firth of Forth to join the Battlecruiser Squadron. Known as the Fast Battleship Squadron, and commanded by Rear-Admiral Hugh Evan-Thomas, it consisted of *Queen Elizabeth*'s four sisters, *Barham*, *Malaya*, *Valiant* and *Warspite*. *Queen Elizabeth* herself was still refitting after the enormous amount of firing she had done at the Dardanelles, but the arrival of the new ships meant that Beatty had been given command of the most powerful ten-ship fleet the world had ever seen.

By a happy chance, Peter obtained a Christmas furlough as well as Geoffrey; for a week, despite the family tragedies of

178

the past few years, Silver Streams was almost as boisterously happy as it had been in the old days.

They even had Mavis indulging in some horseplay, but all she wanted was to be alone with Peter. She had continued to live with her parents after the wedding, and Peter spent most of his time at the vicarage.

'Presumably another grandchild will soon be on the way,' Harriet predicted hopefully. She had temporarily regained her spirits, but her voice no longer boomed as it used to, and her large frame seemed to have shrunk; the crumpled skin of her face was like a well-worn shoe. Repeated wounds of bereavement had left her permanently scarred.

Peter was on top of the world, delighted with his destroyer and, like everyone else, praying for action. His stationing at Scapa meant that he had been able to see Geoffrey regularly; the Captain made a point of entertaining the Lieutenant-Commander to dinner once a week.

Lorraine was apparently remaining in England until the War was over, or at least until Harry could personally escort her home. Harriet did not object to having the American girl as a permanent house guest, and Mary was delighted. Lorraine was her own age, a good companion who fitted easily into their routine, and there were too many empty places at table crying out to be filled.

Besides, her presence meant that Harry would be coming back, some time.

That was a terrible thought to have, but Mary was slowly coming to realise that her marriage to Geoffrey had not fulfilled her early hopes. But then, did any marriage? Were not most marriages, from the woman's point of view, based on girlhood fantasies – the 'happy-ever-after' dreams of childish fairy stories?

She had criticised Georgina so much for her passionate exuberance and for lacking serious attention to her father's authority and to household domestication. Her clothes had been too brightly coloured, her hair dressed too fussily, and her manner with strangers far too open – particularly with men. But ever since Gina's death, and since determining to be a far

179

more suitable wife for Geoffrey than ever her sister might have been, Mary believed she had become, quite unwittingly, more and more like Gina.

She looked down at the frilled lace blouse she was wearing, the wine velvet skirt and matching jacket with its nipped-in waist; the dress rings she had added to her wedding and engagement bands – and the collection of fine silver bangles on her arms.

Oh, yes. And not only her looks had changed . . . so too had her feelings. Not that she didn't love Geoffrey any more: she admired him and looked up to him as she always had. But nowadays, just occasionally, she wondered about their kind of loving. Was it her imagination, or did it truly lack the fire she sometimes detected amongst other young couples – and envied. Why had Geoffrey never aroused in her that delicious sensation that welled low in her stomach and spread down her thighs whenever Harry walked into the room?

But Geoffrey would be shocked even to think she might ever feel that way.

Of course maybe the war could be blamed, their long separation which left them looking at each other like strangers . . . but she was starting to wonder if this marriage would ever achieve a fairy tale quality.

She had wanted virtually nothing when she had got married, save to be Geoffrey's wife. And he had apparently wanted nothing, save to be married and a father. Neither of them had felt more deeply about each other than that, and she at least had been too innocent to want more.

Now, despite his evident pride in his two children, there was a remoteness in his eyes which utterly excluded her from any mental intimacy.

As for the other, when she lay beside him in bed after the most perfunctory intercourse, she could not stop herself thinking back to Lizzie and Harry, so obviously, magnificently, erotically happy during that so tragically brief honeymoon, Lizzie's laughing confession that they never wore clothes in bed . . . but what a thought to be having when lying next to one's husband.

180

Geoffrey always wore pyjamas.

Early in the new year, Admiral von Ingenohl was retired. In fact, he was sacked. Even the Kaiser was becoming fed-up with his dilatoriness, his reluctance ever to risk his precious ships at sea.

People were asking what the High Seas Fleet was for, where was the spirit of Spee. And the blockade was growing slowly tighter; in February there were food riots in Berlin.

Ingenohl's successor was, predictably, Reinhard Scheer. and the new Commander-in-Chief had not been in office longer than a fortnight before he called a captain's conference, which included Vice-Admiral Hipper and the battle-cruiser skippers as well, in the wardroom of his flagship, *Kaiser Friedrich der Grosse*.

He wasted no time in greetings; he knew them all too well.

'What I have to say to you is absolutely confidential,' he said. 'But we have it in our power to win a great victory, and perhaps turn the entire tide of the War.'

He paused to let that sink in before continuing.

'The strategic plan has always been, as you are aware, on the one hand to whittle down the Royal Navy's lead in capital ships, and secondly, to bring to battle, where possible, an enemy squadron and by opposing it with overwhelming force, destroy it or badly damage it. As the Grand Fleet always puts to sea with its full complement of dreadnoughts, which far outnumber ours, the force on which our efforts necessarily have had to be based was the Battlecruiser Squadron of Sir David Beatty.

'Now, as we all know, neither of our plans has so far been successful. Only one dreadnought has been sunk, and that was a long time ago. And our attempt, a year ago, to bring Beatty to battle ended in disaster. There were several factors involved in this. One was the composition of our Battlecruiser Squadron, which should never have included *Bluecher*. A second was the slowness with which the High Seas Fleet left harbour. Hopefully, in view of the amount of time we have spent on improving procedure, this will not again occur. But perhaps the most important factor telling against us was pure luck: that Beatty and his ships happened to be at sea on the very day we chose for our action, so that Vizeadmiral Hipper's squadron encountered them several hours earlier than had been projected, and therefore before the High Seas Fleet could get to sea.'

He smiled.

'We may also claim to have had bad luck in that *Lion* was crippled. Had she not been, Beatty might well have continued the chase right into our arms.

'Be that as it may, it was subsequently felt by Admiral von Ingenohl that the risk was too great, in sending our entire strength to sea to lure five ships to destruction. I did not entirely agree with him, but my decision to resume that earlier strategy is based upon an additional factor which has just come to my notice. Gentlemen, Beatty has been reinforced, by the four new fast battleships of the *Queen Elizabeth* class. Now, I need hardly tell you that for us to sink or cripple those ten ships would be a victory which would reverberate around the world.'

He held up his hand as there was a rustle of movement and whispered comment.

'Now, make no mistake about it; these ships are very fast, and they are armed with fifteen-inch guns. That makes them, individually, more than a match for anything we possess. It is absolutely essential, therefore, that each of those ships is brought to battle by two of ours. Now, the plan will be as before, with certain vital changes. Vizeadmiral Hipper will make a sweep towards the British coast, and draw Beatty out. He will then run for home, with the British in pursuit. The changes will be that the sweep will take place at night, when there is more chance of good visibility, and that the High Seas Fleet will already be at sea, and this time, waiting, just far enough away to draw Beatty into a trap he cannot avoid. Because this time we are going to succeed, gentlemen. Gentlemen, I have chosen a date: 24 April. I will wish you good fortune. Thank you.'

At last, Bruno thought. We are going back into action.

But Scheer's plan did not meet with general approval. Tirpitz was against it, and Scheer had to argue it to the very top, with the result that it was sanctioned by the Kaiser, and Tirpitz resigned. He was succeeded as Navy Minister by Admiral Eduard von Capelle.

There was actually more to Tirpitz's a resignation than Scheer's determination to take the High Seas Fleet into battle. The real point at issue was the future of submarine warfare.

The furore caused by the sinking of the *Lusitania* had been such, especially in America, that the Kaiser had announced that no more merchantmen would be attacked without warning. This had mollified world opinion to a certain extent, and the German Government had then also accepted full responsibility for the tragedy and agreed to pay the United States an indemnity.

Other vessels had been attacked and sunk since, but each time it was blamed upon some misinterpretation of orders.

That the U-boat could however be a very potent weapon of destruction had been made clear to everyone, and now, as 1916 dawned, there were these crippling food shortages; in March, rationing had to be introduced.

It had therefore become a very obvious fact to the Kaiser and his advisers that hard as the German army was fighting, Germany was on its way to losing the War simply through starvation. Something had to be done, and on a drastic scale.

The first and best option would be to win the War in the field. With this in mind a massive offensive was launched in February against the key French fortress of Verdun. It was not supposed that so strong a position could be taken; the concept of the new Chief of the Imperial General Staff, Falkenhayn, was that the French would be 'bled white' attempting to defend their famous citadel.

In fact, the French fought with a tenacity that had surprised even Falkenhayn, with the result that the casualties were as severe on the German side, and what had begun as a strategic sideshow had developed into the major battle of the War.

Thoughts had then turned to Britain. If France was proving such a tough nut to crack, might not the British, reeling from the Dardanelles disaster, prove less resilient if real pressure was put upon their home front? This could only be done by means of the submarine.

Capelle was a profound advocate of the use of submarine warfare, indiscriminately, to inflict upon Britain some of the hardships the blockade was causing Germany.

Tirpitz opposed this view, less on moral grounds – not only was this clearly going to be a fight to the finish which would involve the utter destruction of either Germany or Britain, and in such circumstances moral considerations had no part, but he had been an original advocate of the unrestricted use of U-boats which had culminated in the sinking of the *Lusitania* – than because he had been deeply disturbed by the amount of indignation that tragedy had caused, and he was certain a resumption would inflame neutral, and especially American, opinion to breaking point.

Capelle conceded this, but in turn could point out that the United States was in an election year, and that both the Republican and the Democratic parties had repeatedly reiterated that under no circumstances would they allow their country to be dragged into the European conflict; it seemed certain that this stance would dominate the election – all commentators were agreed that it would be political suicide for any candidate, such as ex-President Theodore Roosevelt was doing, to advocate immediate entry into the War on the Allied side – and this peace pledge would surely tie the hands of any president for at least a year following the election.

By mid-1917, perhaps sooner, Capelle was sure unrestricted submarine warfare would have forced Great Britain out of the War, and left France helpless and also alone save for the uncertain assistance of Italy and the crumbling Russian effort.

It was left to the Kaiser to decide between the two points of view, and he opted for Capelle.

So Tirpitz went. The whole episode was viewed with some concern by the Navy. Few sailors, except those who actually volunteered for the submarine service, cared for the concept of unseen death striking from beneath the surface without warning, and all were well aware that if the new policy did not succeed in forcing Britain to her knees they might well one day have to contend with the American Navy as well, and by the spring of 1916 the US Fleet included ten dreadnoughts, with two more already launched.

Equally, there was not a man in the fleet who had known any other Navy Minister than Tirpitz; the role had been specifically created for him eighteen years before.

On the other hand, Capelle was prepared to give Scheer a free hand in the North Sea. The plan went ahead.

On the morning of Sunday 23 April, the alarm bells jangled throughout the Royal Navy; the Germans were coming out.

Room Forty had informed Jellicoe that there would be a battlecruiser raid on the East Coast during the following afternoon, and that supporting the cruisers would be several units of the High Seas Fleet.

The following morning Geoffrey and Harry stood on the bridge of *Anson* and grinned at each other as line after line of battleships steamed out of Scapa. The destroyer flotillas, Peter's *Arrow* amongst them, were already lost in the mist.

In Rosyth there was no less activity as the Battlecruiser Squadron put to sea, followed by the big battleships. Anticipation hummed through *Queen Mary*, although for Jack it was a bitter blow; he had been down for a furlough, leaving that very afternoon for the south. Now all shore leave was cancelled.

On the other hand, it sounded like the battle everyone had waited for so long was about to be fought. No man of the lower deck of course had any concept that the German naval code had been broken; they just assumed their admirals were acting on information received, perhaps from some scouting submarine or destroyer.

They steamed south-east, to intercept the German battle-cruisers as they returned from their mission. During the night news came in that Lowestoft and Great Yarmouth had both been bombarded. Every man was on deck looking for a first sight of the enemy. But nothing was seen, and as the darkness began to fade so came up the mist again, limiting visibility to less than a mile.

Beatty stayed at sea until two in the afternoon, and then called it off.

The battleships turned wearily round and made back for Scapa, as did the battlecruisers for Rosyth.

'The point is,' Geoffrey said. 'Was the High Seas Fleet there at all, or did Room Forty get it wrong?'

This consideration pervaded the entire senior structure of the Navy.

Jack got ashore on the Thursday morning to telephone.

'Oh, my darling,' Denise said. 'I thought you were hurt, or something. I've been chewing my nails.'

'I'm as right as rain. Pretty fed up, though. Everyone is. We really thought this was going to be the big one. Trouble is, now the Germans are again showing some activity, there will be no leave at all for the next couple of months. So . . . I'll see you in the summer, maybe.'

'That'll be nearly a year,' she said sadly.

'A near miss,' Scheer told his officers.

He had his private reservations about what had happened. An unfortunate illness had kept Hipper from command of the Battlecruiser Squadron – the Germans called it the Scouting Force – on the appointed day, and although Rear-Admiral von Boedicher, assuming command, had carried out his bombardment faultlessly, he had taken too cautious a route home afterwards, and that, combined with the dawn mist coming up sooner than had been anticipated, meant that he had never sighted any British ships – no one knew if Beatty had even put to sea.

But Scheer kept that opinion to himself.

'We will have to try again,' he said. 'Raiding the British coast simply does not seem to work. So we will change our strategy. It is known that the British are conducting a considerable trade with Norway, and thus obtaining Swedish

186

iron as well as timber and other essentials. Our next purpose will therefore be to send the Scouting Group against this trade on the Norwegian coast. Its presence will immediately be reported by British agents, who we know are stationed on both the Danish and Norwegian coasts and equipped with wireless sets. That should bring Beatty to sea, with his ten ships. But this time, we are going to use all our resources, and really force him to battle. Firstly, Vizeadmiral Hipper will, after showing himself on the Danish/Norwegian Coast, then turn towards England as if intending to continue his operation with the usual bombardment of East Coast ports – one or other of these manoeuvres has simply got to draw Beatty; secondly, we are going to use our zeppelins to track Beatty's movements, and make sure he has no support from the Grand Fleet; thirdly, Admiral von Capelle has agreed that for this operation our submarines will be withdrawn from their commerce-destruction duties and concentrated in an area between the Scottish coast and the Norwegian coast. With fortune, Beatty will this time steam into a real trap; and fourthly, the High Seas Fleet will already be at sea, and waiting. When the British have been attacked by our U-boats, then will be the time for us to fall upon them. It could be the decisive battle of the war. The operation will commence on 15 May.'

'What do you make of this report from Room Forty, Sir John?' asked Vice-Admiral Sir Doveton Sturdee, as the admirals in command of the various squadrons of the Grand Fleet assembled in the wardroom of *Iron Duke* for their weekly conference. 'They report an exceptional number of submarines putting to sea, but no orders as to hunting areas. This is against the normal pattern.'

'They could be going to operate as a pack,' suggested Vice-Admiral Sir Thomas Jerram.

'That could pose a problem,' Vice-Admiral Sir Cecil Burney remarked.

'Or it could be connected with some proposed move against our coasts,' Admiral Sir John Jellicoe said.

His admirals exchanged quick glances. They had all lear-ned from experience that their commander was a man more concerned with grand stategy than the mere business of leading a fleet, hopefully into battle.

Just as he had steadfastly refused to allow his ships to return to Scapa Flow until it had been fortified, so he held the opinion that the two prime duties of the fleet, as it had been in Nelson's day, were firstly to blockade the enemy and secondly to prevent the invasion of the British Isles. Should the High Seas Fleet attempt to break the blockade by force, or should it put to sea as a cover for a German invading army, then he would be happy to take them on. Until they did either of those things, he was equally happy that they should remain in Wilhelmshaven.

That, with the German army being bled white before Verdun, engaged against Russia, and also in conquering Rumania, an attempt at invasion was so unlikely in the spring of 1916 as to be considered impossible, and that from the beginning of the war the High Seas Fleet had shown not the slightest intention of attempting to smash the blockade, had apparently made no difference to these twin resolves.

For the squadron commanders, it was galling. The Grand Fleet disposed of thirty-three super-dreadnought battleships. Five of these were normally being refitted, but that still left twenty-eight – against a known German maximum of sixteen. It would be a fight with such favourable odds it could not possibly be lost.

But would it ever be fought?

'We will await some more information before taking any action on this submarine force,' the Commander-in-Chief decided.

Two days later, Room Forty reported that the High Seas Fleet was showing an unusual amount of activity, and that the battleships were concentrating on Wilhelmshaven. Taken in conjunction with the equally unusual submarine activity, Room Forty suggested that some major move in the North Sea was imminent.

'If they're right,' Jellicoe commented. 'Ask for confirmation,' he told his flag-lieutenant. 'It's only three weeks since they sent us to sea on a wild goose chase.'

'Well,' Sturdee commented, looking out of the port at the grey skies and the trees bending before the wind. 'It's no weather for an invasion, at any rate.'

The weather broke on 15 May, and for the next fortnight it blew a gale, with sweeping rainsqualls and heavy low cloud. The great ships rasped on their anchor chains as they rose and fell; bedding could not be aired; food and drink was spilled, and life became generally uncomfortable.

Thoughts of battles occurred to no one.

Scheer called his admirals together on the morning of 30 May, with the wind still howling and the rain sheeting down.

'It cannot be said that the elements are fighting for us, gentlemen,' he told them. 'This weather has been quite abominable. As a result of it, not a single zeppelin has been able to take the air, and now I am informed that our submarines, which have been out in the North Sea waiting for us for the last fortnight, have reached the end of their endurance, and must return to port within the next three days to replenish their supplies.'

He paused to look from face to face.

'In these circumstances, I am forced to make the decision of either calling the operation off for at least another month, or commencing it immediately. I have determined to commence immediately.' He smiled. 'The weather men tell me this wind is going to drop, at last, tonight. They cannot promise much else, at the moment, but the entire weather trend seems to be improving, and I am reluctant to postpone our venture. Once those submarines come home, it is likely we shall not get them again: the Admiralty is anxious to start its unrestricted campaign against British shipping.

'In these conditions, there seems little chance of the zeppelins being of any use at all, now; I am told that the cloud cover will remain too low for the next twenty-four hours at least. However, the odds on the Grand Fleet being at sea in this weather are remote. We are still going to take out Beatty, if we can. The Scouting Group will sail at 0100 tomorrow morning, and the High Seas Fleet ninety minutes later. Gentlemen, I will wish you good hunting.'

'Signal from Admiralty,' said Flag-Captain Chatfield. 'To Grand Fleet but repeated to Battlecruiser Squadron.'

'Read it,' Beatty suggested.

'CERTAIN INFORMATION RECEIVED THAT GERMAN BATTLECRUISER SQUADRON WILL LEAVE JADE ESTUARY TOMORROW MORNING AND HEAD NORTH ALONG DANISH COAST FOR NORWEGIAN SHIPPING LANES STOP POSSIBLE ELEMENTS OF HIGH SEAS FLEET WILL SUPPORT STOP DISPOSITIONS WILL BE MADE AS FOLLOWS STOP GRAND FLEET TO TAKE UP POSITION ONE HUNDRED MILES EAST ABERDEEN STOP BATTLECRUISER SQUADRON WILL SWEEP TO WITHIN NINETY MILES OF SKAGERRAK AND THEN TO THE NORTH TO RENDEZVOUS WITH GRAND FLEET STOP SHIPS TO BE AT SEA BY DAWN.'

'Message timed 1740,' Chatfield said.

Beatty looked out of the nearest port at the grey skies; although it was not yet six o'clock in the afternoon, and Midsummer's Day was only three weeks off, yet the lowering clouds made it almost dark.

'I wonder if they've got it right this time,' he said.

At midnight the British ships started moving out of Rosyth. The destroyers went first, followed by the light cruisers. Then the battlecruisers, forming up in line ahead as they reached the sea: *Lion*, flying the Vice-Admiral's pennant; *Tiger* flying that of the commander, under Beatty, of the First Battlecruiser Squadron, Rear-Admiral Osmond de Beauvoir Brock, and followed by by *Princess Royal*, and *Queen Mary*; after these came *New Zealand*, flying the pennant of the commander of the Second Battlecruiser Squadron, Rear-Admiral W.C.

190

Pakenham, with the other ship of this squadron, *Indefatigable*, bringing up the rear.

Rear-Admiral Evan-Thomas's squadron took its place to the left of the battlecruisers: *Barham*, *Warspite*, *Valiant* and *Malaya*.

The two lines were about five miles apart.

All hands had been piped to duty, and Jack had his six-inch gun crew alerted and ready. Obviously they would play a minor role in any big-ship long-distance gun duel; it was their business to take care of any destroyers or submarines which might manage to sneak through their own destroyer screen.

The men were, unfortunately just a little bit blasé about this hurried putting to sea. They had done so too many times already, only to return to port with nothing to show for it but the business of coaling.

Jack's thoughts kept straying to Denise and Little Jack as *Queen Mary* surged into the darkness, exactly in the wake of *Princess Royal*.

When a misty dawn broke at 0245 the two squadrons were steaming east-by-north across a slate-grey sea; the wind had dropped but the waves remained big enough to cause a shuddering jar every few minutes.

Accurate shooting in these conditions could present a problem. Jack's forehead was pinched into a frown.

Getting out of Scapa Flow took considerably longer, both because the entrance was not as straightforward as the Firth of Forth and because there were so many more ships.

The destroyers went first, feeling their way past the buoys which had been hastily put down to guide them through the tortuous channels, and which would be taken up again the moment the fleet was at sea.

'What do you reckon, Brooks?' Lieutenant-Commander Peter Dawson asked his Executive Officer. 'Will this be what we've been waiting for?'

'We have to be lucky one day,' replied the lieutenant. 'Maybe this is going to be it.'

191

Behind the destroyers came the light cruisers and then the armoured cruisers.

There were two armoured cruiser squadrons. The first consisted of four ships, including *Defence*, and was commanded by Rear-Admiral Arbuthnot; the second also comprised four ships. All of these vessels were armed with nine-point-two-inch guns as their main strike weapons, the more modern with six, the older with four.

After the armoured cruisers there emerged the Third Battlecruiser Squadron of Rear-Admiral Sir Horace Hood: *Invincible*, *Indomitable* and *Inflexible*.

Then the battleships themselves began to emerge.

Iron Duke flew the pennant of the Commander-in-Chief. With her, comprising the First Battle Squadron, were *Marlborough*, flying the flag of Vice-Admiral Sir Cecil Burney, *Revenge*, *Hercules*, *Agincourt* – the name which had been intended for the sixth Queen Elizabeth had instead been given to one of the Turkish battleships taken over at the start of the War – *Colossus*, *Collingwood*, *Neptune*, *St Vincent*, and *Anson*.

All of these were armed with twelve-inch guns, save for *Iron Duke*, which had thirteen-point-fives, and *Revenge*, which had eight fifteen-inch.

Vice-Admiral Sir Thomas Jerram commanded the Second Battle Squadron and flew his flag in *King George V*; he was followed by *Ajax*, *Centurion*, *Orion*, *Monarch*, *Conqueror* and *Thunderer*. Every ship of this squadron was armed with thirteen-point-five inch guns.

Vice-Admiral Sir Doveton Sturdee commanded the Third Battle Squadron, and flew his pennant in *Royal Oak*. She was followed by *Superb*, *Canada*, *Erin* – the other renamed Turkish battleship – *Benbow*, *Bellerophon*, *Temeraire* and *Vanguard*. This squadron was also armed with thirteen-point-fives.

'Some sight,' Harry commented, as he gazed through the darkness at the myriad bow waves, the flashing signal lamps, listened to the immense hum of the turbine engines. 'Any idea how many ships this little armada comes to, Geoff?'

'Why, yes,' Geoffrey said, relaxing somewhat now that *Anson* was clear of the narrows and out into the North Sea. 'Not including the fleet from Rosyth, but taking in all our destroyers, we have ninety-nine ships at sea, with a total of two hundred and seventy-two heavy guns. If we include Beatty's fifty-six, we have a total of a hundred and fifty-five ships, with three hundred and forty-four heavy guns.'

'Heck! Can the Germans match that?'

Geoffrey grinned.

'By just over half, maybe.'

At 0100 SMS *Lutzow*, flying the flag of Vizeadmiral Hipper, led the First Scouting Group out of the Jade; behind her were *Derfflinger*, *Seydlitz*, *Moltke* and *von der Tann*. *Lutzow* and *Derfflinger* were armed with twelve-inch main batteries, the remainder with eleven-inch.

At 0220 the High Seas Fleet put out. Admiral Scheer flew his flag in *Kaiser Friedrich der Grosse*, followed by the First Battle Squadron: Vizeadmiral E. Schmidt's flag flew from *Ostfriesland*, and then came *Thuringen*, *Helgoland*, *Oldenburg* – these four, like the fleet flagship, armed with twelve-inch guns – *Posen*, *Rheinland*, *Nassau* and *Westfalen*, the last four carrying eleven-inch.

The Third Battle Squadron followed: Konteradmiral P. Behncke in *Koenig*, then *Grosser Kurfurst*, *Markgraf*, *Kronprinz*, *Kaiser*, *Prinzeregent Luitpold*, *Kaiserin* and *Brunswick*. These all carried a main armament of ten twelve-inch.

Lastly came the Second Battle Squadron: Konteradmiral F. Mauve led in *Deutschland*, followed by *Pommern*, *Schlesien*, *Schleswig-Holstein*, *Hannover* and *Hessen*. These were all pre-dreadnoughts, armed only with four eleven-inch main guns. Poorly armoured and with a maximum speed of under twenty knots, they had never been envisaged as part of a dreadnought trial of strength – in fact they were known in the German Navy as 'five-minute-ships', five minutes being their estimated time of survival if they were ever engaged by a British battleship. But their captains had all pleaded to be taken along, and Scheer had rather weakly, in Bruno's opinion, agreed.

They added a spurious suggestion of strength, he supposed, looking astern from the bridge wing of *Brunswick* at the altogether smaller old battleships, ploughing into the seas, which grew bigger as they left port . . . if they did manage to catch up with Beatty's squadron, they would have odds of three to one.

He felt good. He had not heard from Helene in a month, and Scheer's personal advice had certainly proved effective. He should have taken it long ago instead of spending his time brooding on that so illicit love.

Or on that earlier tragedy. If he was doomed never to have a worthwhile relationship with any decent woman, then he must be content with whores for the rest of his life.

At least you could not hurt a whore . . . or be hurt by her.

But how he hoped and prayed that today, at last, they would have action.

CHAPTER 8

The Battle

By late morning the Grand Fleet was steaming through choppy but decreasing seas, approaching its rendezvous. It was hazy, but visibility was improving, and there were even occasional suggestions that the sun might come out.

The fleet made a dazzling sight, the six lines of dreadnoughts, maintaining perfect stations, the battlecruiser squadron out in front, the light and armoured cruisers just visible beyond them.

Further on yet, the destroyers were out of sight, performing their task of not only looking for enemy surface craft, but also searching for submarines. Although the sea was going down all the time, there were still sufficient holes to make even the battleships shudder every few minutes; Geoffrey imagined Peter must be having a bumpy ride.

But being Peter, he would be enjoying every minute of it.

The boy had recovered very well, Geoffrey thought, from all the traumas his family had been forced to undergo, as well as from his wounds. He had a splendid career ahead of him, and he had accumulated a fine, no-nonsense type of wife, who would make the ideal partner for a future admiral.

The same might have been said of Giles, had he not had the misfortune to be captured by the Turks. Of course he was a hero, recommended for the VC, and it must have been a tremendous feat of navigation and courage to have taken his submarine right through the Bosporus as well as the Dardanelles – not that Geoffrey was prepared to admit there was anything good about submarines.

But now . . . even if the boy survived his captivity, would he ever be the same, if all one read about the Turks was true?

But the Dawson family as a whole had recovered from the

disaster to Giles as they had ridden all the successive body-blows fate had inflicted on them. Except, perhaps, Mary. This was at once a disappointment and a surprise. He had always put his wife down as the most level-headed and competent member of the Dawson tribe. And it was only on this last furlough that he had found her the least different to that estimate.

No doubt it was the war.

And perhaps him as well, he supposed. On that furlough he had had more chest pains than usual. He had almost told her about them, and then decided against it. Once she knew, Mary would insist on his seeing a doctor, and once that happened, he might be placed on the inactive list. He couldn't risk that until after the war. And as if to prove that he was doing the right thing, he had never felt better than he did today. Because this was what he had been waiting for, for very nearly two years. A chance to fight the enemy.

But he wished he could discuss Mary with someone, was tempted to raise the subject with Harry, who had seen much more of her over the past eighteen months than himself.

But one simply didn't discuss one's wife with a fellow officer.

He glanced at Harry, and Harry glanced back, and grinned.

'Some show. Say, I wonder what Jellicoe feels like, as he stands up there on the bridge of *Iron Duke* and looks around him. There is no admiral in history has ever commanded such an armada, in terms of power. Boy, I wish I could see him now.'

The time was 1235, 31 May 1916.

Admiral Jellicoe was at that moment digesting a message from the Admiralty which had just been decoded, informing him that according to Directional Wireless signals, the German High Seas Fleet had not yet moved from the Jade estuary.

Direction finding by radio is a relatively simple matter, with the proper equipment. As radio beams travel in straight lines, and can be isolated, a ship wishing to ascertain its position can, if it is possible to pick up signals from two known shore stations, reasonably presume it is situated where the beams cross, or close by, allowing for various forms of deviation. A third station providing a third line establishes position beyond doubt; the three lines very seldom cross exactly, but the triangle enclosed by them, known as a cocked hat, is where the ship is, and the smaller the cocked hat, the more accurate is the position. Similarly it is possible for two shore stations to ascertain the whereabouts of a ship, or ships, if they both pick up signals from that vessel.

Room Forty had presumably picked up signals from some of the High Seas Fleet, emanating from inside Heligoland.

They had been correct often enough in the past to give the Commander-in-Chief some confidence in them.

'Another wild goose chase,' he commented. 'However, we'll complete our exercise, wait for Vice-Admiral Beatty to join us at the rendezvous, and we'll all go home. What a life.'

Beatty was no more happy about the Admiralty signal, but he was also determined to complete his task; the squadron stopped more than once to check out trawlers and identify neutral steamers, but by 1410 it had reached the outer limit of its designated sweep, ninety miles west of the entrance to the Skagerrak, the broad inlet which separates the northern tip of Denmark's Jutland Peninsular from the southern tip of Norway, and gives access to the Baltic Sea.

Beatty now gave the order to turn, and steam north-west to make the rendezvous with the Grand Fleet.

As the two battle squadrons were in the process of completing their swing round, however, one of the flanking light cruisers, *Galatea*, having seen smoke to the south-east and gone to investigate – it was a Danish steamer, the *Fiord* – reported that she could see more smoke, further to the south-east yet.

A few minutes later gunfire rumbled across the morning.

'There are some of them out,' Beatty snapped. 'Someone's shooting at *Galatea*.'

'Those weren't heavy guns,' Chatfield pointed out. 'Six-inches at best. A light cruiser squadron, perhaps.'

197

'Well, we'll have something out of it,' Beatty determined. 'Alter course to close *Galatea*, and make to all ships to follow. Use flags, not wireless; we don't want Jerry to discover we're here.'

Instantly *Lion* altered course, and the other five battle-cruisers, in line behind her, followed without hesitation, despite the fact that the abrupt turn and the smoke clouding from *Lion*'s funnels as she increased speed, tended to obscure the signal just hoisted. Admiral Evan-Thomas's Fifth Battle Squadron thus did not see the command and continued to steam north-west; the two squadrons were streaking away from each other at a combined speed in excess of forty knots.

'You'd think he'd understand what we're doing,' Chatfield said. 'Shall I use wireless?'

'No,' Beatty said. 'Flash him with a searchlight.'

This was done, and at last the Fifth Battle Squadron turned and began to chase the battlecruisers, but at a distance of ten miles.

The time was 1440.

The course was south-east, and the six great ships went leaping forward, watching the smoke and listening to the exploding guns.

'Poor bloody cruisers,' commented Able Seaman Partridge, Jack's chief loader. 'We'll never get a look-in.'

Jack saw a seaplane soaring into the sky above them, for one of Beatty's squadron was the seaplane carrier *Engardine*. Lacking the speed of the battlecruisers she had dropped behind, but had obviously been signalled to find out exactly what enemy strength lay ahead.

And twenty minutes later course was altered to starboard, south-south-east, as a note of exultant urgency ran through the squadron.

'Enemy battlecruisers in sight on port bow.'

Jack could envisage the situation, and the reason for the alteration of course. Given its position when the British squadron had first steered south, Hipper's squadron, to port, had to be closer to the Jutland peninsular than themselves; therefore the Horn Reef, which protruded from the base of the peninsular, was between Hipper and home; if Beatty could take his faster ships to a position adjacent to the Horn, there would be no chance of Hipper escaping without having to fight his way through the British battlecruisers.

He cast a quick glance aft. The four battleships were still several miles away. But did that matter? Another glance forward showed the Germans, five ships in line ahead, and now turning, as anticipated, to withdraw. But even without the Queen Elizabeths, Beatty had six.

'Range, eighteen thousand yards.'

Too far, as yet, But it was closing.

'Give me the position of our High Seas Fleet,' Franz von Hipper snapped, staring through binoculars at the British battlecruisers. He could not yet see the Queen Elizabeths behind them.

'Fifty miles south, Herr Vizeradmiral. But where are the other British ships?'

Hipper grinned, and pointed at the distant columns of smoke. 'They have made a mess of things and have lost touch. But they will follow their admiral.' He smashed his right fist into his left hand. 'Then we have them. After eighteen months, gentlemen, Beatty is in our grasp.'

'Range, seventeen thousand yards.'

'When, do you think?' asked Chatfield.

'When we're sure to hit.' Beatty grinned at him. 'We have superior speed and power. And Evan-Thomas is closing. This time, Chatfield, that bugger Hipper is not going to get away.'

It was the Germans who fired first, *Lutzow* delivering the first broadside at fifteen thousand yards.

The time was 1548.

'Christalmighty!' Partridge exclaimed, as huge plumes of water rose to either side of *Queen Mary*. 'That's bloody good shooting.'

Jack had to agree. The Germans seemed to have found the range immediately, while the British shells were pitching over and beyond the enemy squadron.

But the faulty range-finding was quickly adjusted, and hits began to be scored; from time to time the distant shapes became sparked with red. The two lines, both steaming south-south-east, naturally fell into a ship-to-ship duel, but thanks to the British superiority in numbers, both *Lion* and *Princess Royal* were able to engage *Lutzow*, while *Queen Mary* fired on *Derfflinger*, *Tiger* on *Seydlitz*, *New Zealand* on *Moltke*, and *Indefatigable* on *von der Tann*. Obviously when the four Queen Elizabeths caught up the Germans would be totally overwhelmed, but as yet the battleships were out of range.

And the Germans were still firing the more accurately. The watchers from *Queen Mary* saw both *Lion* and *Princess Royal* struck, and a huge gush of flame from *Lion* amidships.

'Heck,' Partridge growled. 'Not Dogger again,' remembering how the action had been broken off when a British victory had been in sight because of damage to the flagship.

None of them knew how close *Lion* had come to being lost altogether.

An armour-piercing shell had struck directly on the midship Q turret, killing every member of the gun-crew save for the commander, Major Hervey of the Royal Marine Artillery, and his sergeant, and Major Hervey had both legs blown off.

Hervey lay amidst the wreckage, surrounded by flames and dead men and blood, much of it his own, only semi-conscious, and aware that he was about to die himself. Then he observed a horrifying sequence of events. The force of the explosion had knocked the two thirteen-point-five inch guns out of position, and one of them had been left pointing crazily at the sky. Now, as the major watched, the breach opened, and the loaded cartridge slowly slipped back out.

Why it had not gone up in the earlier explosion was a mystery, but now it was immediately ignited by the flames, and in turn ignited the rest of the waiting charges. The flash flame whisked at the ammunition trunk connecting the turret with the magazine fifty feet below in the bowels of the ship. Hervey knew what was about to happen, and seized the voice tube to shout, 'Close magazine doors and flood magazines.'

His order was obeyed immediately, split seconds before the searing heat shot down the shaft, killing every man in the lower crew, and causing the huge gush of flame which had been seen from the other ships. Hervey died in that instant. But instead of flying to the sky as her magazine exploded, *Lion* continued to send shots screaming at the enemy, thanks to the major's determined act of self-sacrifice.

Five minutes later, at 1605, *Indefatigable* did explode.

Possibly the same thing had happened there, with no one to give the vital order. The watchers from the other ships had no idea what had caused the catastrophe. One minute *Indefatigable* was exchanging shots with *von der Tann*, and had even appeared to score a hit on her opponent, and the next she was a huge pillar of smoke rising to the sky, her bows pointing in the same direction before disappearing beneath the waves.

Two destroyers turned back to pick up any survivors, while Jack and Partridge looked at each other, and then at the younger members of the guncrew.

'Bloody hell!' one of these remarked. His bell-bottomed trousers were wet.

'Here come the big boys,' Jack said to encourage them.

For the Queen Elizabeths were now within range, and opening fire with their enormous fifteen-inch guns. The German squadron was continually straddled by the pluming white water, and although they continued to return fire, and accurately, too, there seemed little doubt that in a few more minutes they would be destroyed.

Jack was considering ruefully that he had now been in three naval battles and had not yet personally fired a gun – he could hardly count the bombardment of the Dardanelles as a battle – when he lost consciousness.

The time was 1625.

The lieutenant gulped.

'*Queen Mary* has blown up, sir,' he said.

Beatty stepped on to the bridge wing to look back at the great pall of smoke, then without a word stepped inside again. As he did so there was a huge whoosh and a salvo smashed into the sea immediately astern of *Lion*.

Or had it been into the sea? The noise was tremendous, and all the watchers could see was another huge cloud of smoke and water.

The lieutenant licked his lips as he stepped inside.

'*Princess Royal* has blown up, sir.'

Beatty glanced at him, then at the Flag-Captain.

'Something seems to be the matter with our bloody ships today, Chatfield,' he remarked. 'Alter course two points to port.'

Bringing his ships nearer to the enemy.

And a few moments later *Princess Royal* emerged from the waterspout which had enveloped her, relatively undamaged.

Hipper knew he had been lucky, up to now. He had never dreamed of being able to sink two British dreadnoughts in half-an-hour. But the coming few minutes were going to be critical. The British shooting was slowly improving in accuracy, even if their shells, when they did strike home, were doing far less damage than had been anticipated, and the delivery from the Queen Elizabeths was terrifying, even when the shells struck only water, while their superior speed meant they were closing the range every minute. He therefore sent in his destroyers to slow up the British advance and disrupt their shooting.

It was a suicide attack, but it worked to a certain extent. The British destroyer screen advanced to meet the enemy, and for some minutes there was a wild melee of the small ships between the opposing battle lines, from which the Germans retired with heavy losses, having never got within torpedo range. The British ships then followed up with an attack of their own, and actually made a hit on *Seydlitz*, although she remained afloat and even kept her place in the German line.

But yet the destruction of Hipper's squadron appeared certain to the British observers, a result which would have more than made up for the losses they had suffered. Only eight minutes after the sinking of *Queen Mary*, however, *Lion* received a wireless signal from Commodore Goodenough, in charge of the light cruiser squadron which was further to the south than the battlecruiser engagement.

'Battleships in sight!'

Beatty and Chatfield looked at each other in consternation.

'The High Seas Fleet? It's in the Jade,' Chatfield said.

'Like hell it is. Those bloody boffins have got it wrong as usual.'

Beatty's brain was racing. He had been led into a trap, and with eight ships was about to be confronted by sixteen dreadnoughts, not to mention the still firing battlecruisers. But behind him was Jellicoe and the Grand Fleet.

'Ships will come about and steer north,' he said. 'At full speed.'

Jack realised he had been swimming, instinctively while only half conscious, for several minutes. The water was cold, and this helped to dull the pain, because there was a great deal of pain. From where he had no idea. It seemed to shroud his entire body.

And his mind. He could remember nothing of the explosion. Obviously the magazine had gone up.

And he had escaped destruction.

Third time lucky. Or was it?

He listened to a gasping, choking sound, discovered Partridge, beside him in the water. Partridge must have saved his life, kept him moving. But now the seaman was barely able to sustain himself.

'Thank God you're awake, mate,' he panted.

'My watch,' Jack told him, and took hold of Partridge's armpits to keep him up in turn.

Desperately he looked around him, but they were utterly alone. The air was still filled with the sound of gunfire, but the ships, although just visible, were several miles south of him.

All of the ships. He did not suppose they would be coming back on this occasion . . . at least in time to save him.

Or Partridge. The seaman's head was sagging, and Jack had to jerk him to keep his nose from dipping into the water.

'Hey, Jim,' Jack gasped. 'Wake up.'

There was no response. Jack's arms were like lead, and he knew it would only be a few minutes until he could no longer keep even himself afloat. The temptation to release Partridge was enormous. The man was unconscious. He would drown without feeling a thing – and he was going to drown anyway. Releasing him would buy another precious few minutes of life for himself . . . but he couldn't possibly just let his messmate drown. He gritted his teeth and kept his feet moving.

It was some minutes later that he saw a wooden lifefloat, which must also have been blown from the deck of either *Indefatigable* or *Queen Mary*, or dropped by a destroyer. He kicked his way towards it.

'Just a few seconds more, Jim my lad,' he panted.

He reached the float, threw his arm over it. He tried several times to get Partridge up, but lacked the strength, and if he released the unconscious man to get up himself, he would never get him back, he knew. But at least he had something to hold on to. Something to support Partridge.

'Enemy in sight, Herr Kapitan,' said Oberleutnant-zur-See Richter.

Every pair of binoculars on the bridge of *Brunswick* was immediately levelled to the north.

They had seen the smoke and heard the rumble of the firing for some time. Now Hipper's beleaguered battlecruisers could be seen, several of them in flames, and astern of them, the four remaining ships of Beatty's squadron. Behind them again, just emerging over the horizon, were the four Queen Elizabeths.

'They have fallen into the trap,' Korvettenkapitan Muller said exultantly.

'And they know it,' Bruno commented, as Beatty's ships turned sharply about, steaming close past *Barham*, Evan-Thomas's flagship, signals streaming from *Lion*'s masthead.

But once again the Queen Elizabeths were slow to react, and kept on heading south for some minutes more, blazing away at the German battlecruisers.

'Range fourteen thousand yards.'

'Message from flagship, Herr Kapitan. Fleet will open fire on near ships.'

At last, Bruno thought. At last. The moment he, and every other German officer, had been waiting for since the beginning of the war. Revenge, at last. Because after everything that had happened, only a German victory could bring peace of mind.

The Queen Elizabeths were smothered in smoke and flame and flying water, and at last they turned to follow Beatty north. They had suffered extensive damage, *Warspite* in particular, but they were so heavily armed and armoured that not one of them had even lost speed, much less ceased firing; indeed, *Grosser Kurfurst* and *Markgraf*, the two leading German battleships, had both taken hits.

At 1730 the British were out of range. But Scheer still ordered a chase. The British ships might be faster, but now it was his turn to think in terms of cutting the enemy off from his base. For some reason Beatty was steering almost due north; Scheer steered west of north to position himself between the British and Rosyth.

It was time to take stock.

'Make to Vizeradmiral Hipper and inquire the condition of his squadron,' Scheer commanded.

The message came back a few minutes later: all fires under control; *von der Tann*, no guns able to fire; *Lutzow* and *Seydlitz* badly damaged but operational; *Derfflinger* damaged; *Moltke* minor damage.

Scheer ordered *von der Tann* out of the battle, but commanded the remaining four battlecruisers to continue to steam flat out. As he did so, grey fingers of mist started to drift across the horizon.

Jack came to with a start. Had he been asleep . . . or unconscious? His fingers remained hooked into the wooden slats of the float, and were so cramped he was not sure he could free them even if he wanted to. His entire body was freezing, but the cold helped to combat the pain. Or maybe the pain was just easing.

Partridge was still there, pinned against the float by Jack's body. But still unconscious.

'If you'd wake up, old son, you'd be company,' Jack muttered.

He grinned. He had survived a third disaster. And he would survive, no matter how long he had to wait for rescue. Denise and Baby Jack were waiting for him.

It had been noise which had roused him. The noise of great engines, of exploding guns, and screaming shells.

He supposed he must be dreaming. It was so close . . . but the battle had gone away from him over an hour ago.

He raised his head, blinked his eyes. A mist had come down, and he could not see very far. But then he made out a line of ships racing through the murk, perhaps three miles away. They were shrouded in smoke and flying spray and he could not identify them, but he knew they were battlecruisers.

Steaming north!

Five minutes later their wakes reached him, and he was left gasping and bobbing on the rippling water.

'Oh, hell! Mist,' Geoffrey groaned, staring through the bridgescreens at the wispy grey which was threatening to ruin the afternoon.

'That would be a real shame,' Harry agreed.

The battleships had a pretty good idea of what was happening to the south of them. Even if Beatty had been maintaining radio silence, they had picked up the various reports from the light cruisers. They knew there had been an engagement, they knew the British had lost two ships, and they knew that Beatty had turned away and was running up to them, hopefully leading the High Seas Fleet to destruction.

What they did not know was exactly where all this was happening, and until they did . . .

'Your boss will have to deploy before he can fight,' Harry remarked.

206

'Yes,' Geoffrey agreed, and stepped out on the bridge wing to look at the ships around him. Twenty-four dreadnoughts in six columns of four, the whole of which would have to be brought into line. That was going to take time. But Jellicoe couldn't make a decision as to which wing to deploy until he had precise information as to the whereabouts and course of the German fleet.

'Who'd be an admiral?' Harry commented, fully understanding the problem.

The time was 1740.

'Far enough,' Beatty said. 'Hipper mustn't spot Jellicoe until he's right up to him. Make to all ships; turn back and engage enemy.'

The crews were happy to do so. Hipper's squadron had already started to draw ahead of the High Seas Fleet, and the mist now obscured the battleships although no one doubted they were still there. For a few minutes it was again a contest between the two battlecruiser squadrons. And this time the British had the range and the power while the Germans were surprised by the unexpected manoeuvre. *Seydlitz* was hit several times more, and fresh fires broke out. *Derfflinger* began to take water, but she kept in the fight, as Hipper once again ordered a withdrawal.

'That should do it,' Beatty said with some satisfaction. 'Fleet will resume course.'

'Gunfire,' Chief-of-Staff Schultz said. 'Hipper has caught Beatty.'

Scheer frowned; he knew that was impossible. But he could not see through the mist – he had to conjecture.

'Beatty has turned back,' he decided. 'He is trying to break through in order to make a run for home. Make to all ships; course will be altered north by east, towards the sound of the guns.'

'Listen,' Peter Dawson said, as they heard the distant gunfire.

'Big stuff,' Lieutenant Brooks remarked.

'There, sir,' said Sub-Lieutenant Richardson.

All the officers, as well as the crew of the destroyer, were in a state of high excitement. But that surely went for the whole flotilla, hurtling through the water at more than thirty knots in their search for the enemy.

Peter levelled his binoculars at the ships emerging from the mist.

'*Lion*', he said. 'Beatty. I wonder where the Germans are.'

'They can't be far,' Brooks said. 'Shall we signal?'

'Radio silence,' Peter reminded him. 'Jellicoe will see them soon enough.'

And meanwhile, he and his fellows were charging straight at the High Seas Fleet.

'You know what,' Brooks remarked. 'I think vis is improving.'

The time was 1800.

'Message from Admiralty, sir,' said the Flag-Lieutenant.

Jellicoe took the piece of paper.

'CAN NOW CONFIRM HIGH SEAS FLEET HAS LEFT THE JADE MAKE NECESSARY DISPOSITIONS.'

The admiral handed the message back.

'There are times,' he remarked, 'when one either has to laugh . . . or cry.'

'What the hell is that?' cried Harry Krantz as the battlecruiser came into view.

'That is HMS *Lion*,' announced Commander Rutledge.

'And there are *Tiger* and *Princess Royal*, and *New Zealand*,' Geoffrey agreed. 'But . . . they're not supposed to be here.'

From what calculations they had been able to make, the Grand Fleet had estimated Beatty to be several miles further east, and had in fact been steering to put themselves on the flank, and hopefully behind, the High Seas Fleet. But here were the battlecruisers directly in front of them.

Lamps started winking from *Iron Duke*:

WHERE IS THE ENEMY?

Lion replied:

208

ENEMY SITUATED TO THE SOUTH-EAST.

It was an unsatisfactorily imprecise reply, and Geoffrey could only imagine what Jellicoe was thinking, and probably saying.

But a few minutes later the orders came:

FLEET WILL DEPLOY ON THE PORT WING.

'He's made his decision, blind,' Harry commented.

If it was the wrong one, they might never see the Germans at all.

But visibility was steadily improving – although clearly it was going to be a misty night. And as the British battleships took up their stations, making as they did so a huge gentle arc, several miles long, with Beatty's squadron at the south western end and Horace Hood's three battlecruisers at the eastern, over the horizon steamed the German battlecruisers, followed by the High Seas Fleet.

The British stared in disbelief, because, having made a decision, blind as Harry had remarked, Jellicoe had miraculously crossed the enemy T: the Germans had been south rather than south-east of the Grand Fleet, and were steaming straight into the centre of the arc.

FLEET WILL COMMENCE FIRING.

'Holy Hallelujah,' Harry commented.

The time was 1810.

The next two hours were not to be forgotten by any man who was there, and even by those who read of it.

Bruno gazed at the immense array of battle power in front of him, and swallowed. He had sought revenge . . . and found destruction.

Even as the realisation entered his mind, plumes of water rose around *Brunswick*, and a moment later there was a shattering crash from aft.

'Keep firing,' he commanded. 'Damage control, Herr Korvettenkapitan.'

But did it matter? The entire north-eastern horizon was a sheet of flame.

Caught in the middle between the two battle fleets were several light and armoured cruisers, as well as the destroyers. Almost immediately the big shells started falling amongst these, and the destruction was horrifying. *Defence* exploded; *Warrior* was turned into a floating wreck, while a few minutes later the super-dreadnought *Warspite*, already having suffered considerable damage, fell out of the line, her rudder jammed so that she performed endless circles.

On the German side, the cruiser *Wiesbaden* was a burning hulk, and almost all the battleships received hits within the first few minutes of the action, while the battlecruiser squadron was being cut to ribbons.

'Message from flagship,' panted Leutnant Richter. 'Fleet will make a one-hundred-and-eighty degree turn to starboard and steam south-west.'

He stared at his captain in consternation. Could it be done?

Togo had done it at Tsushima, and Scheer had had his fleet practice such a manoeuvre in the Baltic.

'Course is two two five,' Bruno snapped at the coxswain.

The wheel spun, and the battleship rolled as she came round almost in her own length. Every other ship was doing the same. Bruno stepped on to the wing to make sure no other ship was coming too close, glanced aft at the fire which was now under control . . . and found himself lying on the deck.

For several seconds he had no idea where he was. His ears were singing and he smelt burning, and a distant pain which was slowly coming closer.

He gazed up at the bridge. But there was no bridge. A shell had struck the starboard side and demolished it. He had just happened to be standing on the port wing, and thus had been blown . . . on to the foredeck of his ship. Above him were the barrels of his forward twelve-inch guns, silent now as *Brunswick* had turned away.

But she was turning again. With no one on the helm, indeed, with no helm, she too was making circles; the other battleships were leaving her behind as they surged into the evening.

Desperately Bruno attempted to push himself up, and found that he could not. And now the pain was very close.

Men were bending over him.

'Korvettenkapitan Muller,' he gasped.

'He is dead, Herr Kapitan. And you are wounded . . .'

'Help me up, God damn you.'

The men exchanged glances, and then obeyed.

Bruno screamed in agony, and looked down at himself.

From the waist down his uniform was a mass of blood.

'Here!' A stretcher party arrived, and the captain was laid on the canvas.

'My ship!' he shouted. 'Get my ship under control. Fetch an officer.'

'I am here, Herr Kapitan.'

Bruno blinked at the young lieutenant.

'Dorf,' he said. 'You are in command.'

The boy gulped. 'Yes, Herr Kapitan.'

'Get to the aft steering position and resume course.'

'Yes, Herr Kapitan.'

'Have that fire doused.'

'Yes, Herr Kapitan.'

'And keep firing your stern guns.'

'Yes, Herr Kapitan.'

Bruno fainted.

The time was 1831.

'Got one of them,' Geoffrey shouted with excitement, watching the red-tinged smoke billowing skywards from the German battleship. It was impossible to identify the ship hit, just as it was impossible to say if *Anson* had fired the shot which had caused so much damage, but it was worth believing.

He had never felt so elated, so exhilarated, in his life. This was what he had been born to do, take part in the greatest naval conflict in history.

'More than that,' Harry said. 'Look . . .'

He never finished the sentence. The horizon to their left suddenly filled with smoke, and the reverberations of the explosion came slicing through the evening.

Invincible had blown up, carrying with her Admiral Hood.

211

'Great Scot!' Geoffrey cried.

'Seems to me these battlecruisers don't have what it takes for a major engagement,' Harry said.

Because although none of the German battlecruisers had actually sunk, they had all been badly mauled.

But the remainder of the High Seas Fleet was fleeing west just as fast as it could, and disappearing into the mist.

Geoffrey and Harry looked at each other, expectantly. The Germans were still only a few miles away, even if they were invisible. Now surely was the time for GENERAL CHASE.

Instead, to their consternation, came the command: FLEET WILL RESUME CRUISING FORMATION AND STEER ONE EIGHT ZERO.

'Due south?' Harry asked incredulously.

Once again they looked at each other. Neither would say it, but they shared the same thought: Togo would have ignored the danger of torpedoes and closed the enemy.

Reinhardt von Scheer peered into the mist. The firing had stopped, and the enemy were invisible. There could no longer be any thought of trapping Beatty; he had been trapped himself. The British were to the east of him, and between him and the Skagerrak, which seemed his best hope of escaping. And they would almost certainly still be deployed in line.

His nerve had failed him half an hour ago. Now he must smash through that line and escape, or he would be left outnumbered and outgunned when the mist lifted.

'Make to all ships,' he told his Flag-Lieutenant. 'The fleet will come about and steer due east.'

'Must do as the man says,' Harry remarked, watching the expression on Geoffrey's face.

The orders were given, and the Grand Fleet began forming once again, this time into four columns of six. While this was going on there was considerable bunching as some ships reduced speed to fall into their allotted place and others increased speed for the same purpose.

'Goddamn,' Harry remarked. 'As I have probably said

212

before, the way you guys toss thirty thousand tons of metal about . . . holy shitting cows!'

Geoffrey turned his head at his friend's ejaculation, and saw what he meant. Emerging from the mist, and virtually at point blank range – certainly not more than five miles away – were the German battle squadrons, coming straight at them.

Geoffrey didn't wait for orders from the flagship. He grabbed the telephone.

'Open fire!' he shouted. 'Open fire!'

Apparently every other captain had reacted similarly: the entire Grand Fleet became a blaze of light as every gun which could be brought to bear blasted at the Germans.

Every head on the bridge of *Friedrich der Grosse* turned towards the Admiral.

Scheer gulped as he realised that for the second time in an hour he had led his fleet into disaster. Instead of a long line of British battleships taken by surprise, there was the whole Grand Fleet, bunched together and firing together too. Even as he gazed at the wall of red in front of him, the flagship trembled as a shell struck home. The ships to either side were also being blasted.

'Make to all ships,' he snapped. 'Reverse course. Reverse course!' Then he went into the wireless room himself, seized the microphone. 'Hipper!' he shouted. 'Vizeadmiral Hipper! This is the Fleet Commander. Charge the British. Use your battlecruisers. Use everything you have, but charge them!'

Without hesitation, Hipper gallantly obeyed, and led his already battered battlecruisers against the full might of the Royal Navy.

The Germans ships were smothered in flying spray and flaming red. *Lutzow* fell out of the line, a blazing wreck; *Seydlitz* caught fire once more, as did *Derfflinger*; only *Moltke* yet again miraculously escaped serious damage, and Hipper immediately summoned a destroyer to transfer his flag. It was actually going to be another hour before he managed to get on board *Moltke*, for at that moment, the mist curtain having once

213

again closed down over the High Seas Fleet, Scheer recalled the battlecruisers. In their place, he sent in his destroyers in the hopes of slowing up any pursuit with a torpedo attack.

The miracle was that none of the battlecruisers was sunk in the brief action – although *Lutzow* did finally founder before she could get home.

'Destroyers!' came the message from the masthead.

Binoculars came up, and the little German boats could be seen darting forward in an attempt to divert the British.

Successfully.

FLEET WILL ALTER COURSE TO PORT.

The command had to be obeyed, even if it was again galling.

'Oh, hell,' Harry shouted. 'That's actually turning away from the enemy. Why don't we just blast through the bastards?'

Geoffrey felt the same, but he gave the order in obedience to the command. Then he went on to the bridge wing to watch the British destroyers racing towards the enemy.

'You'll catch them up again,' Harry said reassuringly, regaining his optimism. 'After your destroyers have dealt with those chaps.' He grinned. 'It's Peter's turn.'

The time was 1915.

FLOTILLA WILL ENGAGE.

Hurrah!' shouted Lieutenant Brooks. 'Hurrah!'

Peter peered through the bridgescreen . . . there was no sheltering roof on a destroyer's bridge, and the wind was whistling around his ears as the little ship leapt forward at more than thirty knots.

Her sisters raced beside her, their washes causing each other to roll and plunge.

'Range eight thousand yards.'

But closing at a mile a minute.

'Stand by,' Peter said into his telephone.

'Range six thousand yards.'

FLOTILLA WILL FIRE AS SOON AS POSSIBLE.

The Germans were now clearly visible. They were slewing

off to the east in an attempt to attack the battleships, but they were never going to get within torpedo range.

'Range five thousand yards.'

'Fire.'

The four-point-one-inch on the foredeck barked. It was impossible to say where the shell had gone; the entire sea in front of them was a mass of plumes of white water.

And now the Germans were replying; red flashes rippled through the evening, and plumes began exploding amongst the British ships.

'Evasive action.'

The helm was twisted to and fro and the destroyer responded; she had no armour and a direct hit from even a four-inch shell could send her to the bottom. But the constant weaving also made accurate shooting all but impossible. Still, the quick-firing was kept up, and now the Germans were turning away; several of them were on fire.

'Hurrah!' Brooks shouted. 'Hurrah!'

FLOTILLA WILL RESUME STATION.

The time was 1930.

'Where is *Brunswick*?' asked Admiral Scheer.

Konteradmiral Schultz peered into the gloom. The mist had closed around the German fleet.

'She has left the line, Herr Admiral.'

'Her bridge was demolished, Herr Admiral,' said the signal lieutenant.

'Damn,' Scheer said. Poor Bruno, he thought.

But he had more important things on his mind. The High Seas Fleet, accompanied by those of the battlecruisers still able to maintain any speed, was steaming south-west. Jellicoe had disappeared behind the mist curtain, but Scheer knew he was to the east, just as he knew that the British ships were faster than his own.

He also knew he could not continue steaming south-west, or he would run aground on the English coast. Somehow he had to work out a way of getting his ships home.

The first step was obvious.

215

'Make to all ships, course is one eight zero.'

Schultz raised his eyebrows. 'Due south, Herr Admiral?'

That would take them straight down the North Sea towards the Straits of Dover.

'For the time being, yes,' Scheer said wearily.

He went into the chartroom, began to make some calculations. There were three swept channels through the minefields which surrounded Heligoland Bight since the action there in the early days of the war, any one of which would take him and his beleaguered ships to the safety of the Jade estuary – obviously another attempt to make the Skagerrack was out of the question: Jellicoe would surely have ships over there now, sewing mines, and probably supported by destroyers and submarines to block the entrance. The westernmost passage, to the mouth of the Ems, was also out of the question: although he was actually steering for it now, it was by far the farthest and would require him keeping the sea until the next evening. That left the Heligoland passage itself . . . or the passage inside the Horn Reef. But a simple calculation of speed and tide told him that he could reach neither until just about daybreak the next morning . . . and the British would be there before him.

But would they cover both passages? Could they, in sufficient force? At present, they did not need to. They were to his east: it was up to him to make the next move.

He could be under no illusions as to what would happen should he arrive at either passage in daylight and good visibility, and discover Jellicoe waiting for him. His fleet had done marvellously well; three British capital ships had gone down, and no German as yet – although obviously one or two of the battlecruisers were in a sinking condition, and he did not know about *Brunswick*. But he had only been saved from annihilation by his own prompt action in turning away, and now by the mist. If he encountered the Grand Fleet at the beginning of an entire day, it would be catastrophe.

He sank into a chair, staring at the map.

Waves of pain seeped up to envelop Bruno's sagging mind. Followed by waves of lucid thought.

216

'What is that firing?'

'We do not know, Herr Kapitan. We can see nothing; the mist is very thick.'

That they were big guns was very obvious.

'What is our course?' he demanded.

'Two two five, Herr Kapitan.'

Bruno tried to think. Big guns meant the fleets were again engaging. Thus Scheer had turned, probably to the south; no longer having a wireless, the message would not have reached *Brunswick*.

'What is our speed?'

'Eighteen knots, Herr Kapitan.'

'That is not fast enough.'

'It is all she will make, Herr Kapitan. We are taking in water.'

'Are the pumps going?'

'Yes, Herr Kapitan.'

'Where is the Fleet?'

'I do not know, Herr Kapitan. We have lost contact with them and we have lost our wireless aerials.'

'Then where is the enemy?'

'I do not know, Herr Kapitan. There is thick mist.'

Isolated in the middle of the sea, and the middle of a battle, Bruno thought. But he was going to take his ship home. He was determined on that.

'Alter course one eight zero.'

'Yes, Herr Kapitan.'

'What time is it?'

'Twenty past eight, Herr Kapitan.'

'Where is my valet, Carl Mayen?'

'Mayen was in your cabin when the bridge was struck, Herr Kapitan. He has not been seen since.'

Poor Carl, Bruno thought. He had always hated the sea.

'You must make sure the men are fed.'

'Yes, Herr Kapitan.'

Twenty past eight, Bruno thought. It was still daylight. And he really had no idea where he was. The mist might lift at any moment, and discover him next to the Grand Fleet.

The Surgeon-Commander was at his bunkside, holding a glass and some pills.

'What are those?' Bruno demanded.

'They are morphine, Herr Kapitan.'

'Morphine? How can I take morphine, Liebermann? I have a ship to command.'

'Herr Kapitan, you are very seriously wounded. Without the morphine your pain would be unbearable.'

'You mean you have given it to me already?' Bruno tried to sit up, and sank back as a tremendous shock of pain struck upwards from his shattered legs. 'Will you have to amputate?'

'I am hoping not, Herr Kapitan. But . . .'

Leutnant Dorf stood beside him.

'Yes, Dorf, what is it?'

'There is no sound of firing, Herr Kapitan.'

'And the weather?'

'The mist is very thick, Herr Kapitan. In addition, it will soon be dark.'

'Yes. That is good. You must show no lights, Dorf.'

'Yes, Herr Kapitan.'

'But maintain your course.'

The destroyer flotilla had been commanded to probe forward into the mist and see if it could discover the whereabouts of the Germans. The excitement of the brief battle with their opposite numbers had faded, and Peter had ordered hot soup for all hands, to be served at their posts, as there could be no standing down for dinner. At least he still possessed an undamaged ship and had not yet suffered a casualty, but then, he was sure the battle had not yet actually commenced.

'God to be able to see,' Brooks grumbled. 'What happens if we run smack into the High Seas Fleet?'

'We signal in clear,' Peter told him.

'And then get blown out of the water,' Richardson grinned.

'Object on starboard bow,' remarked the petty officer signalman.

Peter felt a tightening of his stomach muscles as he brought up his glasses. It was dark, and very low . . . a submarine? He knew this was the Commander-in-Chief's greatest fear, that he would be led into a submarine trap.

'Use your lamp, Petty Officer,' he said. 'Signal leader and ask for permission to investigate suspicious object.'

Permission was granted immediately, and *Arrow* pulled out of the line to close the object.

'It's a liferaft, sir,' the Petty Officer said.

'With two men clinging to it,' Brooks added.

'Do we pick them up, sir?' Richardson asked eagerly.

'Yes,' Peter said. 'They may have information. Stop engines, lower cutter.'

Arrow came to a halt, rolling in the swell, while the cutter was put down.

'Make haste, Mr Richardson,' Peter called from the bridge wing. 'Or we shall lose the flotilla.'

Which was already almost hull down in the mist.

The cutter nosed up to the raft, and he watched the two men being dragged on board. But he was more interested in the flotilla, kept his glasses trained on them, and the cutter had barely been hoisted clear of the water when he ordered full speed ahead to catch up.

'Well, Mr Richardson?' he asked as the sub-lieutenant regained the bridge.

'A seaman and a petty officer, off *Queen Mary*, sir. The seaman is dead.'

'And the petty officer?'

'He's unconscious, but the surgeon says he may pull through. He's a big, strong fellow. In fact, sir, I have the strangest notion that he could be that man Smith.'

'What man Smith?'

'You remember Smith, sir? The fellow who was with *Good Hope* when she was blown up, and rescued by the Germans. Then went down with *Scharnhorst* and was rescued by *Invincible*. Why, you were with *Invincible* then, sir.'

'Yes,' Peter said, peering forward to pick out the Aldis lamp signals being shown from the stern of the flotilla leader. 'Then he went to *Queen Mary*, eh?'

219

'And got blown up again,' Brooks remarked. 'It seems to me that any ship on which this fellow Smith finds himself is on a hiding to nothing.'

Admiral Jellicoe looked through the bridgescreens at the gathering gloom; the mist was so thick he could hardly see any of his other ships.

'No word from the destroyers?' he asked his flag-lieutenant.

'They have found nothing, so far, save for a couple of half dead seamen. British seamen. Off one of the sunken battlecruisers.'

'Can you make contact with Vice-Admiral Beatty?' the Admiral was not terribly interested in stray survivors at that moment.

'I'm afraid not, sir. His aerials must have been shot away.'

'Well, call a destroyer alongside. I must have communications. The fleet will continue on its present course in cruising formation.' He glanced at the young officer's expression. 'I have no intention of blundering after the Germans in the dark and getting hit by another torpedo attack. What time do you calculate we will sight Heligoland, Charles?'

Rear-Admiral Sir Charles Madden, the Chief of Staff, had been busy making his calculations. 'Just on dawn, sir. Two forty-five.'

'That will be satisfactory. Scheer cannot get there before then. We must prepare for action at that time. Meanwhile, we must consider the likelihood that he will launch another destroyer attack, and we know he is behind us. I wish the destroyer flotillas to take up station five miles astern of the Fleet, and maintain the same speed as ourselves; that way they will not only protect our rear, but we are left free to blast any destroyer sighted in front of us without waiting to identify it. I wish this order implemented immediately. It goes without saying that no lights must be shown, and that as we approach German waters, every possible lookout must be kept for mines and submarines.'

Madden nodded in acknowledgement.

220

'Bloody Blind Man's Bluff,' Geoffrey growled, staring at the darkness.

His earlier exhilaration had dissipated itself in furious frustration, and regret that he had that bowl of soup and slice of bread forced on him by his orderly . . . he was suffering from acute indigestion.

'The boss seems to think we're going to find them,' Harry commented. 'But not until tomorrow morning. Why don't you take a nap, Geoff? You look done in.'

'My business is to be here,' Geoffrey reminded him, and took another turn up and down the bridge.

The time was 2105.

'Coffee, Herr Admiral?'

Chief-of-Staff Schultz stood beside the chart table, at which Scheer was still sitting.

'Thank you, Herr Konteradmiral.' The Admiral took the cup, sipped. 'Where do you suppose Jellicoe is, Schultz?'

'Well, Herr Admiral . . . he has either abandoned the fight and turned back for Scotland, in which case he is . . . about here . . .' he placed his finger on the chart, roughly abeam the Skagerrack. 'Or he is holding on in the hopes of finding us again when visibility improves. In which case he would be about here.' Again he stabbed the chart with his finger, indicating a position to the south-east and inside the marked German position.

'You think he will continue steering for Heligoland?'

'It is logical, Herr Admiral. If he moves east to cover the Horn, he will be exposing the Heligoland Passage. And he knows we are west of him. We cannot reach the Horn Passage without an encounter.'

'So that if we maintain this course, he will most certainly find us again, come morning.'

'If he has held on, Herr Admiral. But Jellicoe must know that every moment takes him closer to our minefields, and as far as he knows, our submarines as well.'

The battle had so far been fought at such a speed and over such great distances that the German U-boat screen had been useless; not a single submarine had even been sighted, by either fleet.

'But he is Jellicoe,' Scheer pointed out. 'He is a British Admiral. He is the heir to a tradition that stretches back beyond Nelson. He will not give up, for the sake of a few mines and torpedoes. We must outthink him, Schultz.'

'Yes, Herr Admiral,' Schultz said doubtfully.

'So, let us create a scenario, eh? It is four o'clock tomorrow morning, it is broad daylight, and this mist has cleared . . . and Jellicoe is in position north of Heligoland, expecting us to appear over the north-western horizon at any moment. Agreed?'

'Yes, Herr Admiral.'

'If we appear, there will be a real battle instead of a mere exchange of shots. And in that case I very much fear we will get the worst of it. In fact, we will be annihilated. So . . . it is our business to get between him and Jutland, some time tonight, no matter what the risk involved. If we can do that, and he is covering Heligoland, the Horn Passage will be open. So . . . using the lowest possible power, you will make the following signal to all ships: Our main body is to proceed in. Course will be south-south-east-a-quarter-east, speed sixteen knots.'

Schultz gulped.

'South-south east, Herr Admiral? But . . .'

'Jellicoe is south-east of us? If our calculations are correct, Herr Kapitan, the Grand Fleet is already a good distance ahead of us. The course I have laid should take us across its stern. If our calculations are not correct and we run into the entire British fleet again, well . . . at night and in poor visibility is our best chance of surviving a battle. But I think I am correct. We will cross the British stern and get inside them and Jutland. Then, when Jellicoe turns back to look for us, we will be closer to the Horn than he. It is our best hope of saving the fleet, Herr Konteradmiral. Give the order.'

The time was 2114.

Blearily Jack opened his eyes, gazed at the sickbay orderly. Who grinned encouragingly. 'You took a ducking.'

222

Memory flooded back. Three times lucky! That surely had to be his lot. But Partridge . . .

'Partridge!' he gasped. 'The man who was with me.'

'Sorry, Petty Officer. He didn't make it. Here, have a drink.'

A tumbler of rum was held to Jack's lips, and he took a long gulp. He was beneath a layer of blankets, and the sickbay was warm, but he still trembled with cold.

'What time is it?'

'Half past nine.'

And *Queen Mary* had gone up at about half past four; he had been in the water for getting on for five hours. And now . . . he could tell he was on board a destroyer, from the movement and the slaps of the waves on the thin steel hull only inches from his hed. A destroyer steaming quite fast, but not flat out.

'What happened to the battle?'

The orderly grinned again. 'Hasn't been one yet. We're still looking for Jerry. We reckon to find him at first light.'

'I must report to your captain.' Jack tried to sit up.

'You just take it easy, Petty Officer. You need rest, and warmth. The old man knows where you are. He'll be down for a chat when he has the time.'

'God, for some visibility,' Peter groaned, slapping his gloved hands together; it had become quite chilly. 'How the devil can we keep a lookout for enemy subs when we can hardly see each other?'

'Well, maybe the subs won't be able to see us, either,' Brooks suggested.

The flotilla droned into the night and the mist. The hum of their engines filled the air, obscured even the hiss of the waves past the hull. Every man knew there were destroyers to either side of him, in front of him, and behind him, just as he knew that the Grand Fleet was some five miles in front of him – but no one had any idea where the Germans were, save that they were somewhere to the west, no doubt also hurrying south as fast as they could.

'Coffee, sir,' said Able Seaman Whittaker.

Peter took the cup in both hands, sipped the boiling liquid.

He had now been on this bridge for some twenty hours, save only for natural calls. He was exhausted. So were all of his men. And there was the prospect of another battle at dawn.

But no one wanted to go to bed.

Wearily he made another sweep of the limited horizon with his glasses . . . and gasped in horror.

'What in the name of God is that?'

Brooks was also staring into the western night, and gaping at the monstrous shape which was materialising out of the gloom.

Behind it was another.

'They must be ours. They must . . .'

Brooks never finished his sentence, as the battleship saw the destroyers and opened fire with her six-inch secondary battery. The sea became peppered with waterspouts, and the coxswain put the helm hard over without any orders from Peter.

'Make to flotilla leader,' Peter shouted. 'Enemy battleships to starboard. Open fire all guns. Prepare torpedo tubes.'

Their abrupt turn combined with the poor visibility had confounded the German shooting for the moment, and now the entire flotilla had turned into action, popping away with their four-inches, which naturally had not the slightest effect on the battleship's armoured sides. But there could be no doubt that the destroyers were being charged by the entire High Seas Fleet as dreadnought after dreadnought came into sight, identified almost entirely by their guns, as they showed no lights.

'Message from Flotilla Leader, sir: LAUNCH TORPEDO ATTACK NOW.'

'Helm to starboard,' Peter said. 'Well, chaps, here we go.'

For their torpedoes to be effective, they had to be within four thousand yards' range. It was a matter of racing straight at those guns, letting off the great steel fish, and hoping to be able to turn and escape before being blown out of the water.

'Full speed!'

Arrow hurtled forward almost as if she had indeed been fired from a bow. And now the entire night exploded. Hitherto the Germans had been seeking only to scatter the mosquito fleet upon which they had come so unexpectedly.

Now, as they realised their danger, they opened up with everything they had, even their twelve-inch whenever they could be sufficiently depressed. The evening became a kaleidoscope of flashes, weirdly reflecting from the mist.

Peter was aware of the noise and the explosions, but remained staring at the nameless warship he had selected as his target.

'Range five thousand,'

'Prepare to fire.'

'Range four thousand five hundred.'

'Stand by.'

'Range four thousand.'

Brooks looked at Peter, but the order was not given.

Flying spray was now cascading over the open bridge, and soaking their greatcoats. Ahead of them the German battleship loomed like a mountain, her sides a sheet of flame as her six-inches barked again and again.

'Three thousand five hundred.'

'Fire all tubes.'

There was a hiss which made the ship shudder, and the torpedoes splashed into the waves.

'Hard to port.'

The destroyer heeled almost to her scuppers as she came round, still miraculously undamaged. Peter and Brooks watched the streaks as far as they could.

'The bugger's turning,' Brooks shouted. 'He's seen them.'

'Damnation,' Peter snapped.

The German had taken evasive action in time and the torpedoes had missed.

'We have to stop them,' Peter growled. 'Reload tubes.'

He looked to left and right, gulped as he saw the shattered shell of what had once been a destroyer slipping beneath the waves, her flaming decks giving off huge hisses as they reached the water. There was no time to think of survivors at the moment; the poor devils would have to wait until this unbelievable fracas was over.

'Tubes ready, sir.'

'Helm to port.'

Arrow came round again, this time lining up on another ship. Still blazing away, the Germans were nearly through the thin British rearguard.

'Steady, full speed ahead!'

This time, surely, Peter thought, staring ahead. Then the ship shuddered, and there was an explosion from aft.

'We're hit!' Brooks said, looking down on the afterdeck.

'Damage?'

It had not been a very large explosion.

'Doesn't look too bad. Something . . .'

'Sub-Lieutenant Richardson here, sir,' said the voice tube. 'We have taken a six-inch shell which luckily failed to explode. But the tube firing mechanism is dead.'

'Oh, shit on it!' Peter snapped.

They were now well within range, racing at the battleship, with only the useless four-inch guns.

'I'm going to stop the bastard,' he said. 'No matter what. Call the forward gun crew aft.'

Brooks stared at him for a moment, then gulped, and gave the orders. The man abandoned their gun and fled behind the bridge, not too unwillingly, as the four-inches had no turrets, and they had been standing there behind a small, thin, metal shield, virtually exposed to the flying shot all around them.

The battleship was so close now that even her six-inches could not be sufficiently depressed to hit the tiny destroyer. Peter could see men lining her rail, actually firing at him with sidearms and rifles.

'Got you, you bastard,' he muttered, seconds before the impact.

'Listen!' Harry Krantz said.

Hitherto the night had been quiet, save for the hum of the engines, as the Grand Fleet had continued on its way. Now the darkness was punctuated by a series of explosions, coming from astern.

Both Harry and Geoffrey went on to the bridge wing to look aft, but they could see nothing save for the shape of the battleship behind *Anson*.

Geoffrey returned inside. 'Make to flagship, FIRING ASTERN,' he told Lieutenant Wilkinson.

'Don't you reckon Jellicoe has heard it?' Harry asked.

'If he has, why aren't we doing something about it?'

'Reply, sir: MESSAGE RECEIVED AND UNDERSTOOD STOP NOISE INDICATES LIGHT GUNS STOP SUSPECT FLOTILLAS ARE DEALING WITH GERMAN DESTROYERS STOP THAT IS WHAT THEY ARE THERE FOR STOP MAINTAIN COURSE AND SPEED.'

'Sounds a bit testy,' Harry commented. 'I'm not surprised.'

'Something should go back,' Geoffrey growled, and went on to the wing again. Harry watched him standing there, listening, using his binoculars in a vain effort to see something . . . then suddenly he collapsed, his knees giving way so that his body crashed straight down.

'What is that noise?' Bruno asked, struggling up to his elbow.

'Firing, Herr Kapitan.'

'Where?'

'To the south-east of us, Herr Kapitan.'

'Tell Leutnant Dorf to alter course towards it.'

The orderly hesitated a moment, then snapped to attention.

'Yes, Herr Kapitan.'

Jack listened to the shouting of orders above his head, the sudden increase of speed, was thrown from left to right as the destroyer made several rapid alterations of course. While above the engines there now came the roar of the guns.

He sat up, and fell out of the bunk. On his hands and knees he faced the orderly, who had been outside.

'Now look here, mate,' the orderly protested.

'You can't keep me down here in the middle of a battle,' Jack begged. 'Where are my clothes?'

'Well . . .' the orderly pointed. 'But they're not dry yet. You're going to catch your death.'

'One way or another,' Jack grinned, dragging on his pants and buttoning his tunic; his cap seemed to have disappeared.

He ran into the corridor, and up the nearest ladder, while *Arrow* trembled to the discharge of her torpedoes. He emerged into the waist, and a sight he had never expected ever to see. *Arrow* was in the centre of a storm of shot and blazing lights and huge dark shapes; the water was a maelstrom of surging white foam. Aft there was a small fire, but it seemed to be under control; forward the four-point-seven-inch was blazing away, but as he watched, the gunners abandoned their position and ran back to the shelter of the superstructure amidships.

Several of them crouched close to Jack. 'He's going to do it,' one of them panted.

Jack looked past them. *Arrow* had stopped twisting and turning, and was now maintaining a steady course, while beneath him the engines screamed as they reached their maximum speed of some thirty-four knots.

In front of them loomed the immense dark bulk of a battleship, the sides of which were lined with red explosions, some large enough to be six-inch guns, but others small enough to be rifles. To either side of the destroyer the sea leapt and bubbled as the shot slashed into it, and from time to time the destroyer shook as she was struck. But she was racing at her huge adversary, and now she was too close to be hit.

'Hold on!' shouted one of the men nearby.

Jack threw both arms round a stanchion, and a moment later there was a terrifying impact, which almost tore his arms loose, accompanied by a screech of tortured metal and the sound of an explosion closer at hand. He gazed up at the immense bulk of the battleship looming above his head, could even make out the heads of the German sailors looking down at him, while they continued to fire into the impudent destroyer, then, again accompanied by that mind-paralysing screech of tortured metal, the German vessel drew away into the darkness.

The destroyer sagged in the water, her bows crushed. Releasing the stanchion, Jack waited for orders and alarms, but there were none. He scrambled his way forward, pushing men left and right, and gasped. Not only was the bow crushed, but the bridge had also collapsed, whether under the weight of the impact or by a direct hit from a six-inch shell he couldn't be sure.

He scrambled up a ladder and reached the remnants of the controls. Several bodies lay huddled beneath the wreckage; none of them was moving.

'My God!'

Jack raised his head and looked at a very young officer, wearing the single wavy stripe of a sub-lieutenant in the Royal Naval reserve, who had apparently come from aft.

'They're all dead,' Richardson gasped. 'They're all dead!' he shouted. 'We're sinking. We must abandon ship.' He looked left and right. 'How do I tell them to abandon ship?'

'You don't, sir,' Jack snapped. 'She won't sink. Close the forward bulkhead doors and she'll float for hours.'

Richardson gazed at him in consternation.

The controls were still available. Jack closed the watertight doors himself.

'There are men down there!' Richardson protested.

'It's half a dozen men, sir, supposing they're still alive, or the whole ship's company,' Jack told him. 'There's the aft steering position, sir. You get back there and take command.'

Richardson hesitated. 'You come with me, Petty Officer,' he said, as he left the shattered bridge.

The Signal-Lieutenant stood to attention beside the Admiral.

'We have decoded the Admiralty message received at 2241, sir.' The young man was clearly very excited.

Jellicoe took the piece of paper:

'GERMAN FLEET ORDERED HOME AT 2114 BATTLECRUISERS IN REAR COURSE SOUTH-SOUTH-EAST-THREE-QUARTER EAST SPEED SIXTEEN KNOTS.'

He handed it to Madden.

Who gulped.

'That means they're not making for either Heligoland or the Ems. They're trying to get to the Horn. That firing we heard must have been them breaking through our destroyers.'

229

'Supposing this message is correct,' Jellicoe said. 'We have received such a mishmash of mistakes from the Admiralty these past twenty-four hours . . . if that was the High Seas Fleet, how come not a single report has been made that the destroyers were engaging battleships?'

Madden had no answer to that.

Jellicoe brooded for a few moments, then he made his decision.

'The Fleet will maintain course and speed, for Heligoland.'

The time was 2330.

Dawn came quickly, just after half past two. It was still misty, but far less thick than the previous night.

The light revealed the twenty-seven dreadnoughts of the Grand Fleet still steaming majestically south, accompanied by the battered battlecruisers – few of the battleships had taken any damage, save for the Queen Elizabeths, and they had stood up to it marvellously well. Only the mishap to *Warspite*'s steering had caused her to leave the fleet – and she was safely on her way home.

Now every eye was turned to the north and west. But there was nothing to be seen.

'Position,' Jellicoe said.

'We are forty miles north of Heligoland, sir,' replied Madden.

'Make to all ships to reduce speed, and then the fleet will come about. We've obviously outstripped them. And find out from *Anson* the state of Captain Young's health.'

Geoffrey's collapse had been reported the previous evening.

The messages went out, and the battleships began to slow, and then each column began to turn.

The signal lieutenant stood beside the Admiral.

'*Anson* regrets to report that Captain Young died an hour ago, sir. Commander Rutledge has taken command.'

'Damn. There's a fine career gone down the drain. Why the devil didn't he report sick?' Jellicoe stared at the morning. 'Where the hell is Scheer?'

'Message from Commodore Tyrwhitt, sir.'

'Yes?'

'HAVE NOW ASCERTAINED HIGH SEAS FLEET FOUGHT ACTION WITH DESTROYERS BETWEEN 2130 AND MIDNIGHT WHILE STEAMING SOUTH-EAST.'

Jellicoe looked at Madden, who looked back.

'Calculate their position,' Jellicoe said quietly.

They did not need to.

'Message from HMS *Albion*, sir. HAVE SIGHTED GER-MAN HIGH SEAS FLEET ENTERING SWEPT CHAN-NEL INSIDE HORN REEF.

'Damn,' Jellicoe said. 'Damn, damn, damn.'

'Shall we go over there, sir?'

'Fifty-plus miles? They've made it, Charles.' The Admiral stared at the morning for a moment, then squared his shoulders. 'Make to all ships. Squadrons will return to base. A careful watch will be kept for submarines.'

'And survivors, sir,' Madden suggested.

'Oh, indeed. And survivors.'

The day got steadily brighter. The Glorious First of June, the British called it, Bruno remembered, in celebration of a victory gained over the French off Ushant in 1794.

They had come so close to having another one.

'Position?' he asked, when Dorf came down to see him.

'We are fifty miles from the Ems Estuary, Herr Kapitan.'

'The Ems?'

Dorf swallowed.

'I made the decision, Herr Kapitan. *Brunswick* is very badly damaged. She could not take part in any fleet action.'

'You disobeyed my order.'

Dorf stood to attention.

'Yes, Herr Kapitan.'

'And you have brought her all the way down here. No enemy in sight?'

'No, Herr Kapitan. We will be in this afternoon.'

Bruno sighed, and sank back. He was so very tired, although

obviously the morphine had a lot to do with that. He had taken as little as possible, in an attempt to keep his brain working, and at times, as Liebermann had warned, the pain had been quite unbearable. Now his ship was all but safe. Now he could just relax and go to sleep; Dorf would take her in.

Having disobeyed his captain's command in order to save his ship. There was something Nelsonian about that.

He must recommend Dorf for promotion.

'Report,' Scheer said.

Chief-of-Staff Schultz got out his list. 'Sunk: Battlecruiser *Lutzow*; pre-dreadnought battleship *Pommern* – as you know, she was torpedoed by a British destroyer just before we reached the Horn; cruiser *Wiesbaden*; light cruiser *Frauenlob* – during our breakthrough; light cruiser *Elbing* – rammed by one of our own destroyers; light cruiser *Rostock*, torpedoed at dawn, probably by a British submarine. Also five destroyers. It is a total of sixty-one thousand tons by my reckoning, Herr Admiral. And there are two thousand five hundred known dead.

'The damage report is more extensive. *Seydlitz*, *Derfflinger* and *von der Tann* will be out of action for months. Not one of them has a main battery capable of firing. It is indeed a miracle that *Seydlitz* was kept afloat. I have been aboard her, and she is an absolute shambles. In addition, every one of our battleships has been hit at least once and requires repair; two of them were rammed by British destroyers – they threw themselves at our ships without the slightest hesitation.'

'What of *Brunswick*?'

'I can report that *Brunswick* is in the Ems Estuary. She is the worst damaged of all, but she is afloat, although I understand her pumps have to be kept going.'

'But Bruno von Eltz brought her home. I am pleased about that. Still . . . the British suffered too, eh, Schultz?'

'Oh, indeed, Herr Admiral. Oh, indeed.'

'Report,' said Admiral Jellicoe.

Sir Charles's Madden's face was grim.

232

'Battlecruisers *Indefatigable*, *Queen Mary* and *Invincible*; there were only half a dozen survivors from all three.

'As you will know, sir, Rear-Admiral Hood went down with *Invincible*.

'Also sunk are the armoured cruisers *Defence* and *Warrior*. *Defence* was lost during the initial exchange; *Warrior* was badly damaged in that exchange and I am afraid she has now sunk. *Black Prince* was sunk during the German breakthrough. Rear-Admiral Arbuthnot was lost with her. In addition we have lost eight destroyers. The total is one hundred and fifty-five thousand tons.'

'Casualties?'

'I'm afraid those are rather heavy, sir. We have at least six thousand known dead. Of course, three-quarters of those went down with the three battlecruisers.

'However, when we come down to the damage report, things are much brighter. All the surviving battlecruisers took a hammering, of course, and so did the Queen Elizabeths. But they are all fully repairable, and the work will be put in hand at once. There is also a considerable damage list for the light cruisers and destroyers, but I have to say that they behaved magnificently. Two of them even rammed German battleships when their torpedo attacks failed. *Arrow* regained port with her bows crushed and her decks awash, but they kept her afloat. Unfortunately her captain was killed. Peter Dawson.'

'Dawson! My God, what an unfortunate family that is! Who brought her in?'

'Her junior officer, Sub-Lieutenant Richardson. Lieutenant Brooks, her executive officer, was also killed. But, you won't believe this, according to Richardson's report, she was actually brought in by Petty Officer Jack Smith. Richardson admits he rather lost control for a while, and it was Smith took over.'

'Well done, Smith. He must be given a leg up. What's his record?'

'Sir John, this is *the* Jack Smith.'

Jellicoe frowned at him. 'I'm not with you.'

'This is the man who went up with *Good Hope*, and then with *Scharnhorst*, and then, believe it or not, with *Queen Mary* during the battle itself. He was picked up by *Arrow*.'

'And brought her in,' Jellicoe mused. 'He must be quite a fellow. I'd like to meet him, Charles. And you say he's a Petty Officer? What kind of age?'

'Oh, middle, late thirties, I believe.'

'We must get him a stripe. Yes, I'd like to see him, Charles. Now tell me about the Grand Fleet.'

'Ah. Now there the news is very good. Apart from the fact that *Marlborough* was struck by a torpedo but sustained very little damage, all our battleships are virtually untouched. We could put to sea again tomorrow and fight the battle over again, sir.'

Jellicoe sighed. 'Scheer will still claim a victory.'

'In terms of materiel and casualties, I suppose he can.' Madden smiled. 'But I think you could say we held the field, sir.'

'You are to be congratulated, Herr Admiral,' said Admiral von Capelle. 'It is a great victory. The Kaiser is very pleased. Do you realise this is the first time the Royal Navy has been defeated in something like two hundred years?'

'Have you seen the figures, Herr Admiral?' Scheer asked.

'Indeed I have. The British losses are more than double our own.'

'In ships sunk and men killed, but half their casualties can be attributed to the blowing up of their three battlecruisers – a design fault they will presumably now rectify. Herr Admiral, I have hardly a ship in my command in a fit state to put to sea. And we were lucky. Desperately lucky. In so many ways. We were lucky with the weather. We were lucky that the British were commanded by Jellicoe. He was so terribly cautious. Far more cautious than we had any right to expect. I suspect that had Beatty been in command we might not have got off so lightly. But above all, Herr Admiral, we were lucky in the inferior quality of the armour of the British battlecruisers, and even more, the inferior quality of their shells. They kept breaking up on impact instead of penetrating our armour and then exploding. Otherwise I would have lost half the fleet. And even our armour-piercing shells, which did so much damage to the battlecruisers, did almost none to their battleships. The fact of the matter is, Herr Admiral, that if the point of bringing the Grand Fleet to battle was to lift the blockade . . . then I have been defeated. The North Sea is still a British province.'

Capelle regarded him for several seconds, then remarked, 'You are a very tired man, Herr Admiral. It was a tactical victory, and we shall claim it. Oh, yes, we shall claim it as loudly as we can.'

Harriet sat with the telegrams on her lap. Mary was one side of her, Mavis the other.

They had not spoken for some time.

Mavis got up. Her face was composed; she was a very composed young woman.

'I'll come in again this evening,' she said. 'Mrs Dawson . . . I am so terribly sorry.'

Harriet watched the door close. Had she ever loved? she wondered.

Mary also stood up. 'Peter died in action,' she said in a low voice. 'Pa would have been pleased about that.'

'Geoffrey died in action,' Harriet pointed out.

'But not of action. There was no need for him to be *there*! Oh, if only he'd told me . . .' she was bitter.

Harriet held out her arms. 'Mary . . . you're the only one left.'

Mary went to her.

'I'd like your thoughts, Captain Krantz.' Admiral William Sims, US Navy, was on a fact-finding tour of England. 'Just who did win the battle?'

'Great Britain, sir.'

'Despite losses three times that of the enemy?'

'Granted, sir. And Scheer and Hipper both carried out a series of brilliant tactical manoeuvres, far superior to anything

235

the Royal Navy tried. But . . . the battle was fought for control of the North Sea, sir. The Royal Navy controls the North Sea.'

Sims stroked his very brief goatee.

'What was wrong with those battlecruisers?'

'Insufficient armour on the gun turrets, sir. There could have been a fourth. *Lion* was only saved by the gallantry of Major Hervey.'

'Seems there was a lot of gallantry about,' Sims remarked. 'I've been reading about this boy named Cornwall. Just a kid.'

'Yes, sir. Boy Cornwall stayed at his gun although everyone else in the turret was killed, and he himself was mortally wounded. He's to get the Victoria Cross, posthumously. Then there was this fellow Smith, who brought a crippled destroyer in; he's to get the VC as well – his commanding officer gets one posthumously for having rammed a German battleship. But there was, as you say, a lot of gallantry about, most of it unrecorded.'

'Save for the Commander-in-Chief, eh?'

'Sir?'

'Well, shucks, Krantz, from what I've read, Jellicoe had more than one chance to get right in amongst those German battleships, at odds of two to one, and he didn't take any of them. That's no way to fight a war.'

'Do you know, sir,' Harry said. 'I thought so at the time, as well. And there's no doubt he was overly worried about losing ships to torpedoes. Actually, torpedoes seem to have been discounted as a battle weapon. The German battlecruiser *Seydlitz* was torpedoed, as well as being very heavily damaged by gunfire, but she's alongside in Wilhelmshaven right this minute. The British dreadnought *Malrborough* was torpedoed, and it didn't even reduce her speed. The only ship of any size which actually sank from being torpedoed was the pre-dreadnought *Pommern*, and no one is ever going to put a pre-dreadnought into a battle line again. They were useless, and they slowed Scheer up.'

'Then you agree with me?'

'I thought at the time that Jellicoe could have smashed the High Seas Fleet to bits by following them west at half past six, with another couple of hours daylight left, yes, sir. Maybe I still wish he'd done it. Then I started to think, what would I have done if I'd been Jellicoe? Sure it would have been great stuff for him to steam into the midst of the Germans, like Nelson, blazing away. Difference is, sir, that Nelson never fought any battle in fog, and he never had to worry about any enemy weapon he couldn't see. Suppose Jellicoe had gone in, and maybe sunk half a dozen German ships, but lost twice that number of his own to mines and torpedoes; he didn't know then that the torpedoes weren't going to be all that effective. That would have upset the whole balance of naval power. His business was to maintain the blockade, and make sure that the German High Seas Fleet never could become . . . a high seas fleet. And that's what he accomplished, in my book.'

'Hm. That's an interesting concept, Captain. I'll want it all in writing.'

'Yes, sir.'

'And then I want you back home. You've been hanging about over here long enough. Three years, isn't it?'

'Yes, sir.'

'Well, I've a command for you.'

'Yes, sir!'

But Harry was not entirely enthusiastic, as Sims could see.

'You'd rather be here, I guess, where the action is. Well, I'll tell you something, Krantz. I know what all the politicians are saying back home. They don't have any choice, it's an election year. But between you, me, and that door, all of us are pretty damned fed-up with this U-boat business. I can't tell you if we'll ever go to war about it, officially. But I can tell you that if it doesn't stop pdq we are going to take action to protect our shipping and our nationals. And that means the Navy.'

'Yes, sir!'

'So when can you leave?'

'Ah . . . is it possible to have a week's furlough first, sir? There's something I have to do.'

237

Harry sat beside Mary on the bench at the foot of the garden, beside the rustling stream.

'Were you with Geoffrey when he died?' Mary asked.

'Yeah.'

'How did it happen?'

'He just collapsed. The Surgeon-Commander said it must've been his heart. Did you know about that?'

'He never mentioned a word. I feel so sorry . . . I mean, that's a silly thing to say, but he'd waited all his life to take a ship into action, and then . . .'

'You mean he'd have been happier if he'd stopped one. Yeah. I agree with you.'

They gazed at each other.

'I know words don't mean much, at a time like this,' Harry said at last. 'But it's not all black. I mean, you have two brothers, and they're both getting the VC. There can't be too many families in that position.'

'I *had* two brothers, Harry.'

You had three, he thought sadly. 'Giles is still alive.'

'Is he?'

'What I'm trying to say is, you have one hell of a lot to be proud of, Mary. Geoffrey too. He died captaining his ship in battle. No man could ask for any better fate than that.'

Mary sighed.

'Well,' Harry said. 'That's about it, for me. I'm been ordered back to the States.' He grinned. 'I'm getting a command, at last.'

'Oh, Harry!' She held his hands. 'I'm so glad. And you deserve it. You must have seen more action than anyone else in the United States Navy.'

'Could be. And I wish I was staying to see some more. Supposing the High Seas Fleet ever comes out again.'

'Will they?'

'That I doubt. I guess Lorraine has told you that she's staying on.'

'Well, of course. She's part of the family now. So are you, Harry.'

238

'I know. I'm really happy about that.' He leaned forward and kissed her on the cheek, then stood up. 'So long.'

She watched him walk up the path towards the house, and called out. 'Harry, will you be coming back?'

'Oh, sure. If you want me to.'

'Yes,' she said. 'I want you to.'

He stopped, and turned to look at her.

'In that case,' he said. 'I'm going to be back just as soon as I can.'

'Oh, Jack!' Denise clung to him. 'I am so very proud of you.'

'For doing what comes naturally?'

'I'm proud of all of you. I wish there was some way we could let your mother know . . .'

'So do I.'

'You don't suppose . . . well, now you're to be both a VC and an officer, we could tell the truth?'

'No. At the very least there would have to be an inquiry, and I'd be out of the war.'

'I'd like that,' Denise said. And sighed again. 'But you wouldn't.'

He held her close. The Germans aren't beat yet, not by a hell of a long shot.

PART THREE

Success and Sadness

CHAPTER 9

The Widow

The band played and the flags flew above Buckingham Palace. The crowd was immense, pressing forward to gain a glimpse of their majesties. But for the moment, the principals were indoors.

The recipients waited, in an antechamber, to be called. They were a mixed group, mostly officers, from all three of the services, several wounded. Then there were mothers or fathers of the men for whom the awards were posthumous. There were only four non-commissioned officers and half a dozen private soldiers. Jack was the only Petty Officer, and indeed the only non-commissioned seaman present.

Save that he was about to be commissioned.

Denise, resplendent in a new frock, clung to his arm. She had never been so happy. Quite apart from the medal, she had had him all to herself for the past two months. He might have risen from his sickbed to bring *Arrow* home, but the prolonged immersion and the shock of what had happened had bitten more deeply into that giant frame than even he had understood, and the result had been an attack of pneumonia which had lingered longer than expected, and had been followed by a month's recuperation leave.

Now he appeared as strong as ever. Even Denise could only guess at the inroads made into his personality by the knowledge that the ship he had brought home had belonged to his brother, whose twisted body lay amidst the wreckage of the destroyer's bridge.

But she was so proud of him.

And anxious for him. People were still arriving, and to her consternation she saw, coming through the doorway on the far side of the room, Mary Young. Mary wore black, for both husband and brother, and a black veil . . . yet the yellow hair and the build were unmistakable to an old school friend. With her was another woman, also in black and wearing a veil, but there was nothing familiar about her.

'She'll recognise me,' she whispered. 'I must go, Jack.'

'Damnation,' he muttered. But he knew she was right.

Denise squeezed his arm and hurried from the room.

Mary and her companion looked around the assembled company, and then were engaged in conversation by one of the senior naval officers present, and Jack could allow himself a long breath of relief. Yet when he went forward to receive his Victoria Cross he was very aware of his exposure. He marched as smartly as he knew how, coming to attention in true lower deck fashion.

Facing him were both the King and the Prince of Wales.

'Smith,' remarked the Prince. 'I gave you a medal at the beginning of the year.'

'Yes, sir!'

'You're making a habit of it, eh?'

'Very gallant deed,' mumbled his father. 'Very gallant deed.'

'Thank you, sir!'

Clutching his priceless little box, Jack marched back to the waiting ranks, aware that Mary was gazing at him. Well, she would be anyway. It was an ordeal that had to be endured. The moment the ceremony was over, the two women were escorted towards him by the Rear Admiral with whom she had been standing.

'Petty Officer Smith!'

'Sir!' Jack stood to attention.

'This lady is the wife of Commander Dawson, and this is his sister.'

'Ma'am!' Jack stood to attention.

'At ease,' the Admiral told him.

Mary gazed into his eyes, and he knew she had recognised him. He could only wait.

'I wished to thank you, Mr Smith, for bringing my brother's ship home.'

244

'Thank you, Ma'am. He was a fine officer.'

'Did you ever serve with him?' Mavis Dawson asked.

'Ah . . . not exactly, Ma'am. But we were on *Invincible* together for the voyage home from the Falklands.'

'Of course,' Mary said. 'Have you no relatives to share this occasion with you?'

Jack hesitated for a fraction of a second. But he had been seen to arrive with Denise, by the Rear Admiral. 'My wife is here, Ma'am. But she was taken poorly just before the ceremony began. Nerves, I expect, Ma'am.'

'Your wife,' Mary said thoughtfully.

'Yes, Ma'am.'

Once again the long look into his eyes. 'You must give her my regards,' Mary said. 'It has been a great pleasure meeting you, Mr Smith.'

'Will she spill the beans?' Denise asked, when they left the Palace.

'I don't think so,' Jack said. 'There's only her and me left, now.'

'What about the other one? Peter's widow?'

'I don't think she had any idea who I was. So, unless Mary tells *her* . . .'

'Oh, Jack . . .' she clung to his arm. 'To be able to go back to Silver Streams . . .'

'I want that more than anything.' He looked down at her. 'Well, almost more than anything. It'll happen, Denise. One day. That's a promise.'

'I simply have to tell someone,' Mary wrote. 'And there is no one else I can possibly confide in. In fact, even were Geoffrey and Peter still alive, I would still be unable to confide in them, for fear of the consequences. And while I would dearly love to be able tell Mother, I think that too is impossible right this minute. Mavis is of course quite out of the question; in any event, it's no business of hers.

'Harry, you were right all along. Jack is alive, and well, and serving in the Navy, and he has just received the Victoria

245

Cross. He is none other than the famous Jack Smith, the seaman who survived two blowings up before Jutland and another there, and then brought Peter's ship home. I don't know if he knew it was Peter's ship at the time or not. Anyway, he is again a hero.

'I almost fainted when I was introduced to him. I knew who it was immediately, of course, although he has put on weight and wears a W.G. Grace type beard and there is a lot of grey in his hair. And I think he knew I recognised him, although he gave no sign of it.

'He is apparently married, although I did not meet his wife. As he has been serving on the lower deck I imagine she cannot be anyone from a good family. But now he is to become sub-lieutenant. It is an amazing world.

'This letter is of course in the strictest confidence, but I did want you to know and I should love to hear your opinion . . .'

'Bruno!' Reinhard Scheer bent over the hospital bed to shake hands. 'You're looking well.'

This was a lie, as Bruno well knew. 'I am fit for nothing, Herr Admiral.'

'That is nonsense. You are a hero. You know that you are to receive the Pour le Merite?'

Bruno nodded. 'What of Dorf? It was he actually brought *Brunswick* home.'

'Dorf also. That is unique, you know, two officers from the same ship receiving our country's highest award. The Kaiser is very proud of you both. And we want you back on the bridge of a battleship, Bruno. The High Seas Fleet cannot afford to lose one of its finest commanding officers. There is even talk of promotion. I think that would be most appropriate.'

'A one-legged Konteradmiral,' Bruno said bitterly.

'There have been very many famous seamen with only one leg, Bruno,' Scheer said severely. 'Now, you must shake off this depression and get well. We have demonstrated that we can take on the British ship for ship and get the better of it. Now that official approval has gone ahead for the commencement

246

of an unrestricted submarine campaign . . .'

'Unrestricted, Herr Admiral?'

'I know. I do not like it. But we must face facts. The British blockade is having an increasingly severe effect. Our people are starving, our war effort is being gravely hampered. We have no option but to strike back with whatever weapons we possess, and the submarine is the most potent. It is calculated that six months of unrestricted submarine warfare will bring Britain to her knees, where she will have to make peace, or starve, and should Britain pull out, then the French will also do so. As for the Russians, they are on the verge of collapse anyway.

'But do not suppose the British will surrender without a fight. When the going really gets hard, they will send every ship they possess to sea to combat the U-boat menace. That will be our chance. And when the chance comes, Bruno, I want you with the fleet. Remember this. Now get well.'

The Admiral saluted, and left the room. Bruno stared at the closed door. How could one not be depressed, he wondered, in a world going criminally mad?

Meanwhile, he had to inform Helene that he was alive and even going to recover, even if he would be a cripple for the rest of his life; she would be going mad with worry.

He picked up the telephone which had been placed next to his bed, and called Reuger, the Managing Editor of the Eltz Newspaper Group. 'I wish to see Furrer,' he said. 'Just as quickly as possible.'

'Admiral Vaichy,' Helene said, as reasonably as she could. 'My brother has been most dangerously wounded. Surely, on sheer humanitarian grounds, I should be allowed to return to Germany. I am his only living relative.'

'I am sorry, madame, but it is not possible.' Vaichy sounded tired.

'You are treating me as a prisoner of war!' Helene stormed.

'I am very sorry about your brother, madame. But he was injured fighting against France. There are thousands of men being killed and injured every day. I believe your brother is

247

one of the lucky ones, in that he has survived. Now I must ask you to leave. I am a very busy man.'

Helene stalked past Henri as she entered her flat. She had never been so angry, and so frustrated, in her life. When Pierre had been killed, over a year ago, now, and she had been refused permission to return home, she had been angry, but had forced herself to be patient. The war would be over in another year, everyone said. Over a year ago!

Now Bruno lay wounded, terribly wounded . . . his letter had been so brave. But then, he was a brave man. And her brother. And the only man she had ever loved. And these pompous French idiots would not let her go home.

'Has Monsier Furrer called?' she asked.

'No, madame.'

'Oh . . . fetch me a brandy.'

Helene sat down and stared at the wall. It was now five weeks since Furrer had last called, bringing her news that Bruno had lost his leg. Up to then he had been coming every fortnight. What on earth had happened to him? She had two letters ready for Bruno, and she desperately wanted to receive another from him, reassuring her that he was going to be all right.

Henri brought her the drink, and she sipped, and then sat up straight. Suppose Furrer had not come simply because there was nothing to bring? Because Bruno had died!

But in that case, Furrer would surely have come immediately to tell her?

She finished her brandy, went to the window, and looked down on the street, watched the peoeple bustling about. They always bustled. She was going mad, caught in this alien lunatic asylum simply because she had been so stupid as to marry Pierre Tonnheur.

She went into her bedroom, sat on the bed.

Gabrielle immediately appeared.

'Can I fetch you something, madame?'

'No, no, leave me alone.'

'Of course, madame.'

248

Gabrielle closed the door behind her.

Silly girl, Helene thought. She was as irritating as any of them. Oh, for poor Lisa. But Pierre had insisted that Lisa be left behind in Germany.

Everything she valued was in Germany, Bruno most of all. And it did not look as if this war was ever going to end. Therefore . . . She realised that every muscle in her body was tensed, while her brain seemed to be flying on wings, way above the ordinary concept of things.

Why had she not thought of it before? Because she had become used to being Pierre's wife? Being ordered about, as Vaichy had ordered her about after the funeral, or again today?

She was Madame Tonnheur, widow of a dead hero. That was in France. Once out of France, she was Fraulein Helene von Eltz, sister of the Baron von Eltz. Who could possibly stop her going where she pleased?

Why should not Madame Tonnheur go shopping in Geneva, if she chose? No border guard was going to prevent her. All she had to do was go.

Secretly, of course, or they might try to stop her here in Paris. But she would be in Switzerland before anyone even knew she had left.

Helene was amazed at the simplicity of it all. But then, secrecy, stealth, playing her own part to the exclusion of all else, was the dominant aspect of her personality. She recognised this, and relished it.

She spent a very quiet day at home, made herself even if obviously pleased to see the servants. And she thought about every possible eventuality. She slept soundly, and was up early. She breakfasted, dressed herself in a carefully nondescript brown tunic dress and a velvet hat, said goodbye to Henri and Gabrielle, and went for a walk.

She went out most days, for a walk in the wood.

'I think I shall lunch out today, Henri,' she said casually, as he opened the front door for her.

Henri bowed.

She carried nothing with her, save for an umbrella and a light coat. 'In case of rain,' she told Gabrielle.

And of course, her handbag, in which there were several hundred francs. She would have liked more, but that would have meant going to the bank, and to withdraw a larger sum of money than usual might be to arouse suspicion. Once she was in Geneva she would telegraph Reuger and obtain all the money she needed.

She walked well away from the apartment building, and then summoned a fiacre and rode to the Gare du Lyons. There was no difficulty in getting a train from there to Lyons – she was travelling away from the war zone.

She sat in a corner of her compartment and watched other travellers come and go. Surprisingly few were soldiers, and if the men cast interested glances in her direction it was obviously because of her looks.

She boarded the train at ten o'clock, lunched in the dining car, and arrived at Lyons at four in the afternoon.

There she bought a ticket for Geneva, and disappeared into the tunnels by the Barrage de Genissiat. At seven o'clock she was at the border, and the douanes were wandering through the carriages.

'Passports! Passports!'

Helene had hers ready.

'Madame Tonnheur?' The man frowned at her.

'I am going to Geneva for a few days,' she explained.

'Ah!' He looked at the passport again, then handed it back to her. 'Bon voyage, madame.'

He continued on his way, and she waited for the train to recommence its journey. It was still light, and she could clearly see Geneva in the near distance, with the waters of the lake shimmering beyond it.

Then another officer presented himself in front of her. This man's uniform was decorated with gold braid.

'Madame Tonnheur?' He looked vaguely embarrassed. 'Will you come with me, please?'

Helene raised her eyebrows. 'With you?'

'It is a formality, madame. It will not take a moment.'

Helene hesitated, glanced at the other passengers, who were staring at her, then shrugged and rose.

'What sort of formality?' she asked, as the officer escorted her down from the train and on to the platform.

'A formality,' he repeated, now speaking somewhat brusquely, and showed her through the gates into the station courtyard, where she discovered that, in addition to a gawking crowd, there were several policemen. 'Will you get into the car, please, madame?'

He indicated the Renault at the foot of the steps.

'The car? I am going to Geneva, by train.'

'Possibly later, madame. Now, please, you are coming with me. I would request you not to make me use force.'

Helene goggled at him. She simply could not believe her ears.

'Ha!' she commented. 'I suppose Admiral Vaichy has sent you.'

Obviously that swine Henri must have become suspicious when she had told him she was lunching out . . . but to have gone straight to the admiral – she had not expected anything so prompt as that. And anyway, how had he known where she was going? They could hardly have sent out an alert to every railway station in France.

'The car, madame,' the officer said.

Helene got in, and he sat beside her. There was another gendarme in the front seat, beside the driver, who was also in uniform.

'Are you taking me back to Paris?' Helene asked, as they drove off. Just like a truant schoolgirl, she thought.

'If necessary, madame.'

They were actually driving back to Lyons. It was dark when they got there, and she was taken straight to the Central Police Station.

There an inspector was waiting for her. 'Madame Tonnheur,' he said without preamble. 'You are under arrest.'

Once again Helene's breath was taken away. 'Under arrest? What am I supposed to have done?'

'The charge is one of spying, for Germany.'

Helene stared at him, then burst out laughing. 'Of all the absurdities.'

'Let us hope so, madame. Now, I wish you to be searched. I have arranged for Sister Wenceslaus to take care of it.'

Helene turned, gazed at the three nuns.

'If you will come with me, please, madame,' invited the eldest, who was apparently the Sister Wenceslaus.

'Where?' Helene demanded.

'Somewhere private, madame.'

Helene glared at her, and then at the inspector.

'It would be best for you to co-operate with us, madame,' he recommended.

Helene stamped into the recesses of the station, and found herself in a small, windowless room, lit by a single electric bulb, and furnished with a bench and table.

The nuns came in behind her and carefully closed and locked the door.

'Will you please undress, madame,' Sister Wenceslaus requested.

Helene gave her another glare. 'That is absolutely unnecessary. I have nothing on me of the least value to anyone. Here, you may search my handbag.'

She placed it on the table, and at a nod from Sister Wenceslaus one of the younger nuns emptied its contents and began going through them.

'Now will you please undress, madame.'

'I have said I will not.'

'If you will not, madame, I will have to call in some of the gendarmes to assist me. Do you wish that?'

This must be some kind of a nightmare, Helene thought. But the woman obviously meant what she said; the turtle-like face indicated her determination.

Helene undressed, laid her gown and petticoats on the bench, then stood straight, breathing deeply.

'Everything, madame,' Sister Wenceslaus insisted.

Helene gritted her teeth before she was really rude to the woman, removed her shift and corset, rolled down her garters and stockings, unlaced her boots and took them off. 'Are you satisfied?'

'And the drawers, madame.'

I shall strangle her with my bare hands, Helene thought. Even if they guillotine me for it.

Then she found herself wondering if they guillotined spies. She was so agitated she slipped down the drawers without further protest. The other young nuns gathered the clothes up and began testing the seams and prodding the boots.

'You have obviously done this before,' Helene commented.

'Of course, madame.'

'Well, would you please hurry up? I am cold.'

'We are being as quick as we can, madame. Now, would you please bend over the table, with your legs apart.'

'Do *what*?'

'It is necessary for me to search you as well, madame.'

'I have never heard of such a thing. Do you realise who I am?'

'You are the widow Tonnheur.'

'I am the sister of the Baron von Eltz!' Helene shouted.

'That is nothing to be proud of at this moment, madame. You are admitting to being a Boche.' Suddenly Sister Wenceslaus' voice was harsh. 'Kindly bend over.'

'I absolutely refuse to do such a thing.'

'Very well, madame. Sister Veronique, would you kindly ask the inspector to step in here, with . . .' she sized up Helene, 'four of his people.'

'You would not *dare*!' Helene shouted.

Veronique went to the door.

'My God!' Helene gasped. 'Stop.'

Veronique waited.

Helene bent over the table.

'Madame Tonnheur. Please be seated.'

There was a single straight chair before the desk, and Helene sat on it. She was still experiencing feelings she had never known before. Her very clothes felt alien to her.

She was also exhausted. She had left home early that morning, and now it was nearly midnight; when the nuns

253

had finished with her she had been left sitting in that damnable room for four hours. No one had paid the least attention to her protests – and all she had had for supper was a bowl of soup and some bread. Not that she had felt like anything more; she had even refused the glass of wine.

But perhaps the end was in sight. The man behind the desk, wearing civilian clothes, middle-aged and paunchy, did not look as antagonistic as the policemen and the nuns.

'My name is Malraut,' he said. 'I am an examining magistrate. Do you understand this?'

'Yes. I wish to make the strongest possible complaint about my treatment by your police.'

'Indeed, madame? Are you hurt in any way?'

'Hurt? Well, nothing that will show. But I have been abused by three nuns, acting under the orders of your police inspector.'

'You mean you were searched. It is an unpleasant business. But then, so is spying.'

'Spying?' Helene demanded. 'For God's sake, how can I be spying? What have I got to spy about?'

'That is what I am hoping you will tell me, madame.' Malraut untied the piece of blue ribbon confining the folder on his desk. 'The reason there has been some delay in bringing you before me is that I have had to study your file. You have been corresponding with your brother, who is an officer in the German Navy, ever since the start of the war. Did it never occur to you that this was a criminal act?'

'I have corresponded with my brother ever since I married the late Captain Tonnheur. That was before this war was ever thought of. Is that a crime?'

'It was certainly unwise, especially after war was declared. However, we have evidence that you were a German spy even before the outbreak of war. Indeed, that you only married Capitaine de Vaisseau Tonnheur in order to pursue your objective. I have here copies of several of these letters, including the very first one you wrote after arriving in Paris. You keep referring to a "secret",

254

and to your "plans". Will you tell me what you mean by these references?'

Helene stared at him. Tell this man of her relationship with Bruno? 'I will not. It is none of your business.'

Malraut did not seem disturbed. He turned over one or two more letters.

'And just how did you get those letters, anyway?' she demanded.

'Some are copies. Others are originals, which were confiscated after the outbreak of war. We needed these to make sure that the copies were genuine.'

'Who did all of this?'

'Your butler, Henri Couronne. He has been an agent for the Deuxieme Bureau for some time. As soon as you arrived in Paris they placed him in your apartment to keep you under surveillance.' Malraut shrugged. 'It was very simple for him, as you always gave him your letters to post. At least, up to September 1914.'

'You mean he stole my letters to Bruno? I always knew he was a swine.'

'Some people would prefer to call him a patriot, madame, who is to be congratulated on bringing a known spy to justice.'

'I am not a spy,' Helene interrupted. 'I keep telling you that.'

'How do you explain the affair of Lieutenant Dawson, of the Royal Navy?'

'That was a joke. Everyone knows it was a joke. I signed an affidavit that I obtained nothing from Lieutenant Dawson.'

'Ah, but did you try, madame?'

Helene realised that her mouth was open, and hastily closed it again.'

'I must tell you, madame,' Malraut went on, 'that it is the opinion of the Deuxieme Bureau that your letters to your brother, and his to you, contain a code. It will go much better for you were you to confess to me now what that code was, and what information you were giving to your brother.'

'Oh, for God's sake, I have never heard anything more absurd. Look, monsieur, I have never written anything in code

255

in my life; I wouldn't know how to start. I have never conveyed any information to my brother in my life. I exchanged letters with my brother because he is the only living relative I possess. There was no other reason. Monsieur, I am very tired. I wish to go to bed. Let me go to bed, and I will talk to you again tomorrow.'

'You will go to bed, madame, when you have finished talking to me now. Tell me, when you discovered that your letters were not getting through to Germany, following the declaration of war, you employed a go-between to carry your messages to your brother and from him to you. Is that correct?'

Helene hesitated. But if Henri had really been spying for the Secret Service they would know about Furrer already.

'Yes. It was the only way we could be sure our letters would get through.'

'This man's name was Furrer, was it not?'

'Yes. His name was Furrer. He is a Swiss journalist.'

'On the contrary, madame. He may carry a Swiss passport, to enable him to travel freely in and out of this country, but his real occupation was spying . . . for Germany.'

Once again Helene's jaw sagged. 'That wretched little man? A spy for the Fatherland? That is not possible.'

'It is very possible, madame, and very true. Herr Furrer was arrested a fortnight ago, and has confessed. I may say that he is also sure that you and your brother corresponded in code. He took the liberty of opening some of your letters, and later pretended that this had been done by the French authorities.'

'He has admitted this?'

'Yes, madame.'

She'd always distrusted that little rat.

'So, will you not now confess?'

'I have nothing to confess to,' Helene insisted, spreading her palms across his desk in exasperation.

'Then tell me this: why were you attempting to flee France?'

'I wished to go shopping in Geneva.'

'Madame, please do not suppose I am a fool. You wished to go shopping in Geneva, from where you could not possibly

256

have regained Paris before tomorrow evening, and yet you carried no change of clothing, no nightdress, not even a toothbrush? Were you not desperately trying to get out of France because you knew that Furrer had been arrested, and that therefore your own arrest must soon follow?'

'That is absurd. If you wish the absolute truth, I was leaving France because I wished to go home.'

'To Germany. I think that almost amounts to a confession.'

'It is a confession of nothing!' Helene shouted. 'I have nothing to confess about. I wished to go home because my brother is very badly wounded and needs me.' She paused, panting, and as Malraut continued to regard her, perhaps even a little sympathetically, continued in a lower tone. 'What will happen to Furrer?'

'Well . . . he is a Swiss national. I should imagine he will be sent to prison for a very long time.'

'He should be guillotined.'

'I agree with you, madame. But the law must be observed. However, I consider that there is sufficient evidence against you to send you for trial. And madame, I should warn you, that as you are a French citizen, if *you* are found guilty . . . you will be shot.'

'Anton! Anton!' Bruno shouted into the telephone. 'Is this report true?'

'That they have charged Frau Tonnheur with spying? Yes, Herr Baron, I am afraid it is true.'

'My God! Of all the absurdities. It must be stopped, Anton.'

'Ah . . . yes, Herr Baron,' Reuger said, uncertainly.

'I wish you to print a lead article condemning the French Government for their high-handed and immoral act in arresting an innocent woman.'

'Yes, Herr Baron,' Reuger said, more doubtfully yet. 'You do not think that may inflame French opinion?'

'I do not care what it does. I wish my sister out of there. The thought of her in a French prison . . . my God!'

'Yes, Herr Baron,' Reuger said, a third time.

257

Bruno went to see Capelle, limping on his crutches – he had not yet got the hang of using only one.

'I have spoken with Admiral Scheer and Viceadmiral Hipper, and they seem to think that nothing can be done.'

'They are right, Herr Baron,' said the Grand Admiral.

'The correspondence between Helene and myself was perfectly innocent, Herr Grosseadmiral.'

'Perhaps it was, but it was still very foolish of you to conduct a correspondence with a national of a country with whom we happen to be at war. Why, do you not realise that we could arrest *you* for spying for France?' He smiled at Bruno's expression. 'Only a joke, Herr Baron.'

Bruno was not amused. 'And my sister, Herr Grosse-admiral?'

'I'm afraid we must hope for the best, Herr Baron, and put our faith in the well-known gallantry of the French. That is all we can do.'

Bruno returned to the convalescent hospital, and wrote letters. He wrote to the Pope and the President of France; to Mr Lloyd George and to Mr Wilson. He swore on his honour as a German naval officer that Helene was innocent.

He never got any replies.

'I hope they guillotine her,' Harriet said.

'I think she should be boiled in oil, along with her brother,' Mary suggested. Somehow the thought that, because of his liaison with Helene, Jack had been forced to serve as an ordinary seaman, even if he had won fame and promotion, made her even more angry than the thought that he had been sent to prison.

Lorraine looked from one to the other; she had never heard her in-laws sound quite so vicious.

'Here's a letter from Harry,' she said. 'He's been given a cruiser.'

'Why, that's splendid,' Harriet said. 'Now, if your people

258

were to start putting their ships to proper use . . .'

'Is there any possibility of him getting over here again?' Mary asked, her voice quiet.

Lorraine shook her head. 'Not a chance, the way things are right this minute.'

'Oh, that looks tremendous.'

Denise stood back to admire the thin stripe she had just finished sewing on Jack's sleeve.

'It's been missing a long time,' Jack agreed.

Denise glanced at the letter lying on the table. 'Have you any idea what they want?'

'To offer me employment, presumably.'

Denise scratched her nose. She had been close to the Navy long enough to know that senior officers did not usually wish to meet sub-lieutenants – especially sub-lieutenants promoted from the lower deck – merely to inform them that they had been appointed to such-and-such a ship. But no doubt all would be revealed in due course; she counted every day that he had been left in their London flat a blessing.

Besides, there was great deal else on her mind. 'Jack . . . have you seen the news from Paris?'

'Yes.'

'I hope they hang her.'

'Even if she's innocent?'

'She can't be innocent. Can she?'

'Mm . . . I don't know,' Jack said, slowly. 'Look, my love, I have to go; I'm due at the Admiralty in an hour.'

Even if she's innocent? he wondered, as he went down the stairs.

He had an uneasy feeling that Helene was actually on trial for their abortive affair, ten years ago.

It had been the longest, most miserable summer of Bruno von Eltz's life. Quite apart from the horrific mess that had been made of his body, the days of physical pain and the weeks of mental anguish as he had groped towards an acceptance of the fact that he had lost a leg, the slow crawl back to health . . .

259

there had been the unacceptable realisation that the battle for which he, and so many others, had waited all of their lives, had fizzled out in a panic-stricken attempt to escape the guns of the Royal Navy.

That the attempt had been successful, indeed, triumphantly so, could not disguise the fact, known to every German sailor, that the High Seas Fleet had run away.

While all summer Helene had been fighting for her life, and he had been quite unable to help her. He could only sit and wait, and read the reports of the trial as they filtered through to Germany.

And pray.

'Madame Tonnheur, if you cannot tell the Court the truth about the "secret" you refer to in your letters to your brother, I regret there is little I can do to help you.' Advocate Francois Maurier removed his spectacles, produced a large white handkerchief from his pocket, and proceeded to clean them, repeatedly holding them up to the light to check his progress. He was a huge man, grossly overweight, but with a pleasant, if purple, face, full of humour, topped by a thatch of thick, straight grey hair, badly cut and sticking out from his head like a hedgehog.

Considering he was a Frenchman he had been very kind, always giving Helene the impression that he genuinely wanted to help. And now he was giving her the opportunity, yet again, to save herself. Helene's elbows were on the prison table between them, and now her head drooped, to be supported by her hands. For the millionth time she was tempted to save herself and admit everything. Avoid the fusillade of bullets which would mutilate the body in which she had always taken such pride . . . which Bruno had once loved . . . just once.

Oh God! Little had she realised that the penalty for that glorious hour of defiance of all convention and morality would be death. Or . . .? What was the alternative? To ruin Bruno, the one person in the world she truly loved? He would not only be cashiered and drummed out of society, but probably imprisoned, for wasn't incest a criminal offence?

260

Bruno! The innocent. Oh, yes, he had been innocent of any crime. She had been the instigator, the temptress, when he was too drunk and miserable to resist. Bruno, the decent, the brave, the Baron von Eltz, attempting to uphold the honour and tradition of their dear, dead father. Bruno, who had died inside when Georgina Dawson had killed herself because of him, who had cringed with shame and horror at the memory of what had happened between them . . . even to the extent of himself attempting suicide.

And now she had this last chance to decide between dying – or the destruction of the brother she adored.

Well, there was no choice: what life could there be for her if she took the latter course . . . and revealed all to an euphoric press?

Helene sighed as she sat back, spine rigid, chin high. 'I thank you for your kindness and patience, Monsieur, but I will not break a pledge of secrecy.'

'Madame, not even to save your life?' Maurier asked gently.

'Monsieur, what is life without honour?'

A telegram arrived at Schloss Elsjing from Reuger, on 2 September:

'MOST DREADFULLY SORRY TO INFORM YOU MADAME TONNHEUR TODAY FOUND GUILTY AND CONDEMNED TO DEATH BY FIRING SQUAD. SENTENCE TO BE CARRIED OUT IMMEDIATELY.'

Bruno stared at the words for several seconds, then he discovered that tears were dribbling down his cheeks.

'Well?' inquired Captain Lesseur.

The warder shook his head. 'She is not yet awake.'

'They don't usually sleep at all.'

'Not when they are guilty.'

'You think this is the sleep of the innocent?' the Captain asked. Lesseur had no sympathy for spies, even if they were reputedly as beautiful as this woman; he had only seen a rather poor photograph in a newspaper.

The warder shrugged.

The Captain looked at his watch; it was five o'clock, and dawn was only a few minutes away. 'Well, you must wake her. She must be prepared. I will give you fifteen minutes.'

The warder nodded, and went off to give his instructions to the nuns who tended the female prisoners. Lesseur stamped up and down; it was chill September morning, and his hands were cold.

The warder returned. 'She is awake.'

'Who else is here?' the Captain inquired.

'Mother Stanislaus and Father Maurice are waiting.' The warder led the way into the prison. All the other inmates were awake, and they shouted abuse at the soldier as he marched towards the condemned cell. The priest and the nun stood outside it.

'Open the door,' Lesseur commanded.

Mother Stanislaus crossed herself, and then opened the door; the Captain gazed at Helene Tonnheur.

Helene was dressed and sitting on the edge of her bed sipping a cup of coffee. Although the tunic dress she had worn on the day of the trial was now looking a little tired, and her hair was no longer chicly coiffed but pulled straight back from her face and tied with a piece of cloth at the nape of her neck, she looked every inch a calm aristocrat.

Unable, despite the efforts of Sister Stanislaus, to persuade her to confession, Father Maurice could not grant her Absolution, but he was moved by her obviously sincere penitence as he laid his hand on her head and called for God's blessing and mercy on her soul.

Declining the proffered brandy, Helene walked in front of the Captain, past the cells full of screaming, shouting inmates, looking to neither left nor right. She blinked as she stepped into the pale daylight of the courtyard, but continued without hesitation to the stake. The twelve men of the firing squad were standing in a group, smoking cigarettes, muttering. They had of course been chosen by lot, but none of them liked their assignment, the more so as their victim was to be a beautiful woman. They would be no good for days after this, Lesseur thought.

The Captain stood in front of Helene, holding a length of black material. 'I will tie this over your eyes, madame,' he explained.

'That won't be necessary, Captain.'

Lesseur hesitated, then turned and signalled to the waiting sergeant, who came forward with the length of cord.

'Is this absolutely necessary?' Helene asked.

'It is necessary, madame.'

She gave a slight shrug, and stood with her back to the stake. The sergeant pulled her arms behind her, and behind the stake as well, and secured her wrists together. Helene breathed deeply.

'If you please, Father,' Lesseur muttered. He was becoming as affected as his men.

Accompanied by Sister Stanislaus, Father Maurice went to stand beside Helene, while Lesseur retreated against the wall and drew his sword. Presumably the priest and the nun were praying, although he could not hear them; the noise from inside the prison was enormous.

The soldiers were being lined up by the sergeant. Lesseur took another step back, and checked as his legs touched the lip of the waiting wooden coffin.

Father Maurice and Sister Stanislaus stepped away from Helene, and returned to the prison doorway.

'Present!'

Lesseur could see the muzzles of the rifles moving as the men trembled.

He raised his sword, and looked at Helene as he did so. She seemed to stiffen, and then forced her mouth into a smile, staring straight ahead of herself at the black muzzles.

Lesseur's arm dropped.

The volley was very ragged, and Lesseur watched the splinters of stone flying from the wall behind the woman. But there was blood scattered across the bodice of her gown, and her body was sagging, kept from collapsing altogether by the bound wrists to the wood of the stake.

Lesseur hurried forward, and stood beside her. More blood was welling through the lace and satin with every breath, and

263

she was still breathing quite strongly; he didn't think she'd been hit by more than three bullets.

Her eyes were open. 'I am innocent,' she whispered. 'Of spying against France. I swear this.'

Lesseur drew his revolver and pressed the muzzle against the back of Helene's neck, pointing slightly upwards. He wanted not a vestige of that face to remain, to haunt him forever.

CHAPTER 10

The Killers

'Sub-Lieutenant Smith, sir,' said the secretary, opening the door to allow Jack to enter the office.

Commodore Keyes looked up from his desk. He exuded energy, and determination, and pugnacity. 'Well, Smith.' He stood up, and Jack saluted. Keyes then held out his hand, and Jack clasped the fingers before again coming to attention.

If he was both curious and exhilarated at his summons to the Admiralty, he was also feeling a sense of detachment; he had picked up a paper on his way here from the Underground Station, and read of Helene's execution.

What a chapter in his life that had been!

'Sit down,' Keyes invited.

Jack did so, and heard the door close behind him. He was alone with the Commodore.

'I assume you are fully recovered from your illness?' Keyes inquired.

'Fully, sir.'

'Good. I'm afraid times are going to get harder before they begin to improve, Smith. I am not speaking of the situation in France, although God knows it is severe enough, and it is difficult to see the end of it. But as long as we can maintain our armies in the field, and the Navy can maintain its blockade of German ports, ultimate victory is certain. It is the problem of maintaining that blockade that concerns us. The U-boat, Smith. The U-boat. It is the most vicious, and properly used, the most effective, weapon ever devised for sea warfare. Unseen, unheard, until it delivers its frightful blow . . . our losses these past couple of months have been enormous, and they look like growing more enormous still. I am not going to give you any figures; they are absolutely confidential. But

I can tell you that they are so severe there is every probability of the Government introducing food rationing for the civilian population this winter. I'm sure you'll agree that is a pretty horrendous thought, eh?'

'Yes, sir,' Jack said, thinking of Denise and the baby.

'So, what's to be done about it, eh?'

He clearly was not expecting a reply, so Jack did not offer an opinion.

'I can tell you,' Keyes went on, 'that there are several schemes being mooted. I'm not going to go into the question of convoys. Convoys worked very well against Napoleon, but that was a hundred years ago. The enemy could be seen coming. There is considerable doubt as to whether in modern conditions we would not be throwing ships away by accumulating them in a group, thus presenting more of a target to the U-boats. No, to my mind, there is only one way to deal with this menace: destroy the enemy. Now, there are two ways of doing that.

'One is to prevent the U-boats from putting to sea at all. That means either capturing their more important bases or blocking them up. I can tell you that plans are going ahead with both of those objectives in mind; I am speaking, of course, of Ostend and Zeebrugge, the Belgian ports which, being on the North Sea Coast, give the Germans such an extended range, but which are really within the scope of a determined offensive on the part of our armies.

'However, we must also attempt to deal with them at sea, and the problem is, how to get them to show themselves, except when actually attacking. The answer is, there is no way of accomplishing this. Now, as I am sure you know, Lieutenant, we have taken steps to arm as many of our merchantmen as possible. The difficulty is that when attacking any ship of any size, the submarine stays beneath the surface and uses its torpedoes. It is only when faced with a ship not worth the expenditure of a torpedo that the U-boat surfaces, and sinks its victim by gunfire.

'This raises some interesting points. Some of our smaller ships have given quite good accounts of themselves, and one or two have even driven the U-boat away. Bully for them. But this is not what we want. We want to sink the bastards. Now of course it is a bit much to ask merchant seamen, who wish only to proceed about their lawful business in peace, to do anything more than defend themselves when attacked. But suppose there was a ship at sea, or several, hopefully, which looked like a small coaster or trawler, an obviously easy mark for a U-boat's gun, but which, in fact, was manned entirely by naval seamen, and was armed with a powerful, totally concealed weapon? And whose sole purpose was to wait to be attacked. What about that, eh?'

'It sounds a brilliant idea, sir,' Jack ventured.

'It's not as simple as it sounds, Smith. As I have said, our aim is to sink the bastards, not frighten them away. In other words, this disguised warship cannot, must not, open fire the moment the U-boat is sighted, or the enemy will merely submerge and slip away. It must accept fire, and whatever damage may be thereby incurred, until the U-boat is close enough for its destruction to be certain. That is going to require a high quality of fortitude and discipline upon the part of the captain and crew of the decoy. If they make a mistake, their lives will be in danger. You understand this?'

'Yes, sir.'

'Very good. Well, then, we would like you to take command of one of these decoys. Q-ships, we are going to call them.'

'Yes, sir.'

'Your command is being fitted out in Glasgow. Her design is top secret, of course, and so is everything I have told you here today. Not a word of it is to go beyond these walls. Your crew will be all volunteers who know only that they are to undertake a highly dangerous mission. You will sail under sealed orders, and no member of your crew is to know what you are about until you are at sea. Understood?'

'Yes, sir.'

Keyes allowed a brief smile to flit across his face. 'I did not ask you if *you* volunteered, Smith.'

'No, sir.'

'But you do?'

'Yes, sir.'

Keyes stood up and held out his hand. 'Then, good hunting, Lieutenant.'

'An independent command?' Denise was delighted. But she knew too much about the Navy not to be amazed also. 'A sub-lieutenant?'

'It's a very small kind of patrol boat,' Jack explained. He hated lying to Denise – the only person in the entire world he had never lied to before – but he had no choice.

'When can I see her?'

'Well . . . I'm afraid you can't. She's a very new, top secret type of vessel.'

'You mean we're back to a *Dreadnought* situation.' But instantly she was contrite and squeezed his hands. 'I'm sorry. I didn't mean that. I understand. But . . . if she's a very small ship, you won't be going very far afield.'

'Probably not.'

'Well, there's a relief. I think you've been sunk quite often enough for one war.'

'Well, Bruno.' Reinhard Scheer stood up to shake hands; Bruno could now walk with a single crutch. 'It is good to see you looking so well.'

Scheer had indeed been somewhat afraid of what he would see, in all the circumstances. But Bruno looked remarkably fit, even if his face had changed, become tighter.

'Thank you, Herr Admiral.'

'When will you be ready to return to sea?'

'I am ready to return to sea now, Herr Admiral.'

Scheer frowned. 'The medical report indicates that you require a further period of convalescence. Three months is suggested.'

'I am ready now, Herr Admiral. I wish to fight the British.'

'The British? Or the French?'

Bruno's mouth twisted. 'They are both our enemies, Herr Admiral. But there are no French warships in the North Sea.'

'Bruno . . . you understand that there is no room for personal vendettas in wartime. When next you go to sea, it will be in command of a battleship, indeed, when you are promoted, which will happen as soon as you are entirely fit for duty, you will command a squadron. That means you will be responsible for the lives of several thousand men.'

'I understand that, Herr Admiral. I have no personal vendettas with any officer in the Royal Navy.' Again his lips twisted. 'I do not even know any of them, now.'

Which was true enough. Jack Dawson was long disappeared, Peter Dawson and Geoffrey Young were both dead, and Giles Dawson was in a Turkish prison camp.

'But you still wish to be avenged for the death of your sister.'

'I wish to fight the enemies of the Fatherland, Herr Admiral. It is what I understood we were going to do. And now that Jellicoe has been replaced by Beatty as commander of the Grand Fleet . . .'

'You suppose the British will be more eager to fight. You may be right. However, the situation is changing dramatically. Do you know the total of British shipping we have sunk this year? Over two million tons. That is far more than they have been able to build in that period. Our U-boats are winning the war, out there in the Atlantic, Bruno. Now we shall have to see what the British intend to do about it.'

'You are hoping they will use units of the Grand Fleet to go after the submarines?'

'We shall have to wait and see.'

'May I ask what is the American attitude to this, Herr Admiral? Now that Wilson has been re-elected?'

'They issue protests whenever one of their ships happens to be attacked,' Scheer conceded. 'But Wilson was re-elected on a platform of keeping America out of the war. He must honour that pledge. In any event, if America becomes too bellicose, we have plans in that direction also. When you consider that Russia is in a shambles, that there is disaffection in the French Army . . .'

'They repulsed us at Verdun,' Bruno pointed out.

'This is true. But at what cost? We also anticipated that they would fight for Verdun with everything they possessed. Our object was to kill as many Frenchmen as we could, and this we have done. No, no, Bruno, 1917 is going to be a very good year for us. But for the time being, we in the High Seas Fleet must be patient, and save ourselves for the climactic battle, when Britain is so close to starvation that she must risk all. And achieving that must be left to the U-boats.

'But we must be prepared. And so I wish you to take up your new command just as soon as you are able. It will be the super-dreadnought *Kaiser Wilhelm I*. She is just completing in Hamburg; she was launched eight months ago. It is estimated that she will be ready for sea trials in the Baltic in another three months. I would very much like to think you will be on her bridge when she sails.'

'I shall be there, Herr Admiral.'

'Good. When your promotion is confirmed, *Kaiser Wilhelm I* will become the flagship of your squadron.'

'Thank you, Herr Admiral.'

'Now, I wish you to draw up a list of officers you would like to have serving under you. Most of your old crew have been re-assigned, of course, but I will see which of them can be reassembled.'

'Thank you, Herr Admiral. I shall do this immediately.'

To go back to sea, he thought. As commander of a squadron of super-dreadnoughts! And avenge Helene.

He would need the very best.

'Herr Kapitanleutnant Dorf, Herr Baron,' announced Adolf the butler.

Bruno stood up; movement was becoming increasingly easy as he got used to his crutch and his new sense of balance, even if he was aware that conditions at sea would be vastly different to those obtaining in the peace and stability of Schloss Elsjing. 'Dorf! How good to see you. I must congratulate you on your promotion.'

'Thank you, Herr Kapitan.' Dorf saluted, and then shook hands. 'It was good of you to invite me. May I . . .' he hesitated, 'offer my condolences?'

'Thank you. My sister was innocent, you know.'

'Indeed, Herr Kapitan. I understand this.'

'Now all we can do is avenge her. I am to command *Kaiser Wilhelm I*.'

'My congratulations, Herr Kapitan.'

'Naturally I wish as many of my old people with me as I can. You will be gunnery officer.'

'Ah . . . regretfully, Herr Kapitan, I must decline.'

'Decline?' Bruno could not believe his ears.

'I should be able to think of no one I would rather serve with, Herr Kapitan. But I have been given a command of my own.'

'Some destroyer?'

'An *Unterseeboot*, Herr Kapitan.'

'A U-boat?' Bruno was scandalised.

'After the battle, Herr Kapitan, when I was given a short spell of leave, I visited some of these craft in Wilhelmshaven. It was at a time when the Navy was appealing for volunteers to take the fight to the enemy. Herr Kapitan, I knew at once this was the way to do that. Think of it, sir. We have been at war now for two and a half years, and the High Seas Fleet has been in action only once. As a U-boat commander I will be in action every day I am at sea. And I shall be winning the war for Germany.'

Bruno gazed at his face, so handsome, so dedicated. This boy could be the son I never had, he thought.

'You are not concerned that you will be engaged in a kind of latter-day piracy?'

'I will engage in anything, Herr Kapitan, in order to win this war for Germany.'

Bruno nodded. 'Let us hope that is still possible, Dorf. I will wish you success in your command.'

'What are these?' Harriet boomed, gazing at the neat pile of booklets.

'Our ration books,' Mary explained. 'They tell you how much meat, and eggs, and butter, you may buy each week. There's one for each of us, and for each of the staff as well.'

'Rations? I have never heard of anything so ridiculous in my life,' Harriet declared.

Mary sighed. 'You are going to have to get used to them, Ma. I'm sorry, but there it is. Now, you must remember to take your books with you whenever you go shopping. They cover clothes as well. Here is the list of all rationed items. You won't be able to buy anything on that list without producing the requisite coupon, and allowing the retailer to tear off the slip.'

'Absolutely absurd,' Harriet insisted.

Mary went to the window to look down at the garden where the children were playing with their Aunt Lorraine. There was no way Lorraine could go home now, even if she wanted to, with the submarines sinking several hundred thousand tons of Allied, mainly British, shipping every month. But the American girl seemed determined to stay to the end, regardless of the discomfort.

Or the possibility of a British defeat?

She felt so alone. More so, indeed, than ever before. Because of seeing Jack, of knowing he was alive and well, and fighting the war in his own way. How she wanted him to be able to come home, even if she did not know the answer to what had happened between him and Helene von Eltz back in 1906. The fact that Helene had been shot as a spy seemed to confirm Jack's guilt . . . and yet, at the investiture he had looked so noble, so formidable, indeed – and so strong. How she wanted to be able to lean on strength, somewhere.

Harry Krantz? She knew now that he was a man she could love. Far more than Geoffrey had ever been. Geoffrey had been a girlhood dream who had developed into a real-life situation. They had shared no true intimacy because Geoffrey did not believe in that sort of thing. She had shared more with Harry, in their few brief wartime meetings, than ever with Geoffrey.

But Harry too was gone. And to know that Jack was there, perhaps available at the end of a telephone, was the most tantalising situation she had ever known. Because it was also mutually self-destructive.

If only Giles would come home. But she did not even know if Giles was alive.

'What do you reckon?' Ganning asked.

He knelt beside Sub-Lieutenant Gibbons, wiped sweat and flies from the boy's forehead.

'He's very ill,' Giles Dawson said. 'Christ, who wouldn't be, in this climate?'

The prison camp appeared to be situated in the middle of a desert. Actually, it was only separated from an oasis by a low hill. Over there was a village, sweet water, people and animals. On this side of the hill there was nothing, save rock and sand, and a cluster of buildings. The prisoners' food and water was brought across from the village once a day.

It was a good situation in which to lose weight, Giles supposed.

He personally had weight to spare. Few others did. When they had first been taken prisoner they had had more immediate matters on their minds, such as tales of forcible circumcision or worse. Actually, they had not been ill-treated, save for a few buffets and bruises, nor humiliated save for being paraded through the streets of Constantinople before a jeering crowd, and having their photographs taken by a Turkish newspaper correspondent. Giles had even been relieved to discover that he and his officers were to be left in the company of their men, while his interrogation by a Turkish naval commander had informed him that although he had missed the *Goeben* and sunk only a supply ship, his very appearance in the Black Sea had caused the most utter consternation.

He had also been relieved when the Turkish officer had told him that a complete list of the survivors – and there had been no casualties – would be forwarded to London so that next of kin could be informed. It had all seemed very civilised.

273

Then had come a train journey, which had more and more left civilisation behind, and then a march on foot over very rough ground and beneath a pitiless sun, to reach this camp.

The crew of *C17* had been the first inhabitants of the camp, and had remained so for several months. That had been a relatively good time. Although the food had been strange to them, and never quite enough, there had been space and, in any event, they all knew each other very well. Boredom had been their principal enemy, for the guards had been good-natured, if lazy. Giles had therefore organised them as he had organised them on board ship, with regular hours set aside for exercise, for games, and for discussions.

In the beginning these discussions had centred mainly on the possibility of escape, which had slowly developed into an understanding of the *im*possibility of escape. Even supposing it might have been practical to overpower their guards – who outnumbered them in any event and were well armed – there was a squadron of cavalry in the village, and even if they might suppose it were possible to cross the hills and valleys and open country with which they were surrounded faster than the horsemen, without food or water, they did not actually know where to make for, because they did not know where they were.

Certainly they had travelled east and then south-east for several days before arriving here. The topography of the country indicated that they were in northern Mesopotamia, and the high mountains in the near distance suggested they were close to the borders of Armenia, which meant that the Caucasus and Russia might not be all that far away, but it would still be an incredibly difficult journey. Any other direction just took them towards more and more Turks. But there was also a Turkish Army in the Caucasus, fighting the Russians.

In any event, by the time they had reasoned all of that out, it was winter, and they had been able to do nothing more than huddle in their huts for warmth . . . and they were no longer together.

It had been during the early autumn that they had first been joined by other prisoners, from the Army, taken on the Gallipoli Peninsular. British, Australians and New Zealanders, these men were confused and bitter, having been led to believe that the Turks would offer them virtually no resistance as they marched on Constantinople. There were numerous incidents and fights, and as the numbers had grown, the Turks had decided to separate officers from men. Giles and Ganning and Gibbons had stood to attention to watch the seamen from *C17* march out, under the command of Petty Officer Langham. Giles had felt unashamedly like crying. They had been through so much together. Now he had no idea where his people were being sent, whether he would ever see them again.

In their place had arrived a batch of officers who regarded the Navy trio virtually as aliens.

Actually, with the camp, ontaining only comissioned prisoners, conditions had to a certain extent improved. The Turks regarded all British officers as gentlemen, and allowed them the privilege, from time to time, and under guard, to go into the village. But these expeditions only convinced them that the possibility of escape had retreated further into the distance. The village was growing as a military establishment. A hospital had been set up, and to it came Turkish wounded, mainly from the south. It bustled with people and officialdom, and the squadron of cavalry remained as a garrison, while all around was the pitiless desert.

Additionally, as time had drifted by, their already short rations had been shortened further. Dysentery had soon made its appearance and a general weakness had set in.

It was hard to believe that they had now been in this camp for well over a year, their uniforms in rags. Most depressing of all was the complete absence of any news from outside. Down to the end of 1915, the arrival of other prisoners had at least meant information as to what was happening, and the guard commander had himself announced to the inmates with much pleasure, at the end of the year, that the Allies had accepted defeat, evacuated the peninsular and abandoned their campaign.

That had been a stunning blow, as only by a general Turkish surrender could they envisage any hope of release.

Then for an entire year they had been virtually cut off, their only certainty that the war continued. Their Turkish captors had not even bothered to feed them propaganda victories. They had certainly claimed to have defeated an Anglo-British Army at Kut-el-Amara on the Tigris, and taken a large number of prisoners, and had been able to prove it – several English officers from that force had come into the camp. The news they had brought had been all bad, of massive French and British casualties on the Western Front, of ever-growing German power, and, worst of all for British seamen, the story of how the British Grand Fleet had been defeated by the Germans in the North Sea.

This was quite unbelievable, yet the Turks swore it was true.

The news of Jutland had renewed talk of escape, but now it had to be very discreet talk. There were too many loudmouths around. It had, in fact, come down to Giles himself, Ganning, and Gibbons. They had naturally stuck close together over the months of their incarceration, and now, with things obviously in a desperate state, it was the three of them who had realised that it was up to them.

The decision was not lightly taken. The dangers had, if anything, increased. But England clearly needed every man who could command a ship. Thus they had determined, no matter what the risk, to chance the desert and mountains and try to make for the Russian lines, just the moment the snows melted.

There was no snow to be seen now, in the spring of 1917. And now Gibbons was down with a raging fever, with which was developing a rash.

Giles went to see the Camp Commandant. As a Lieutenant-Commander he was no longer the Senior British Officer, for one of the Kut prisoners was a half colonel, but he was certainly the senior officer in terms of residence in the camp, and he and Colonel Rafsi were old acquaintances, if not exactly friends.

'Lieutenant Gibbons needs a doctor, urgently,' Giles told him. 'I think he should be in hospital.'

Rafsi himself came to look at Gibbons. 'It is typhus,' he announced.

'Typhus?' Both Ganning and Giles spoke together. The camp had been free of the dread disease so far.

'Hush,' Rafsi said. 'No one must know of this. Yes, he will be removed to isolation.'

'We would like to go with him,' Giles said. 'To make sure he is properly treated.'

Rafsi wagged his finger at them. 'You are trying to play a game with me, Commander Dawson.'

'Look, my officer is genuinely and most seriously ill,' Giles pointed out. 'You cannot deny that.'

Colonel Rafsi couldn't. Gibbons was taken from the camp in a truck and driven round the hill to the village, where he was placed in an isolation ward. Giles and Ganning went with him, under heavy guard, and saw him as comfortable as possible.

'Is he going to be all right?' they asked the Turkish surgeon.

'Who can say.'

The sergeant of the guard jerked his head, and they realised they were required to return to the camp. They followed him outside.

'I think he will die,' the Sister said.

Giles' head jerked in surprise. The Sister was Turkish, not very old – certainly not much over thirty – with a strong rather than pretty face; the rest of her was completely obscured beneath her flowing robes. They had seen her often enough during visits to the village over the preceding six months, when she had first arrived, but up to now she had been rather a remote figure.

Now she wrinkled her nose, most attractively, at their surprise. 'I studied in England, before the war.'

'Ah! And you say he will die?'

'If it is typhus, you will probably all die. It is very contagious, and very deadly. You need to bathe, very much, and with disinfected water.'

'Chance would be a fine thing. In our camp?'

'I will see what can be done,' she promised.

'What do you reckon?' Ganning asked. 'An English-speaking nurse? Who has actually lived in England?'

'Something to think about,' Giles agreed.

But for the moment it was more important to think about the typhus. By the next day there were four more cases, and Colonel Rafsi was becoming agitated, even if he appeared more worried about himself and his guards than his prisoners. Giles had by now told him what the nurse had suggested, but he was sceptical.

'Sister Bakr is full of new-fangled ideas,' he grumbled.

'Don't you think it's worth a try?' Giles asked. 'Or you could wind up with a camp-full of corpses.'

'Do you not realise, Commander, that there is a water problem, here?' the Colonel demanded.

Giles went off to speak with Lieutenant-Colonel Adams, who had had previous experience of typhus and was feeling very gloomy. 'We're all goners, old boy,' he said. 'When typhus takes hold . . . it's worse than the Black Death.'

'Which is all the more reason for trying everything we, or anyone else, can think of,' Giles argued.

They had hoped to be allowed to visit Gibbons again, but instead he was brought back to the camp, which was placed in quarantine. But a doctor and some nurses came in to see what could be done, and amongst them Giles saw the English-speaking Nurse Bakr.

She gave him no great welcome apart from a nod of greeting, but over the next couple of days he observed both that she seemed unhappy with much of her work – which was reasonable as she now was as likely as anyone to catch the disease – and that whenever he was in her company and looked at her he found her looking at him.

On the third day it was his turn for an inspection; by then a good third of the camp was down with fever.

'Do you still think we are going to die?' he asked, as she opened his shirt and peered at his chest.

'Very probably.' This time she did not look at him.

'Yourself included?'

'Very probably.'

'But I haven't got it yet?'

'There is no rash, and you have no fever. How are your bowels?'

'As good as can be expected. How about Lieutenant Ganning?'

'He also seems to be surviving, so far.'

'I told the Commandant what you suggested,' he muttered. 'But he seemed to think it would be a waste of water.'

She nodded. 'These people have no knowledge of medicine.'

'These people? Aren't you one of them?'

She looked up. 'Yes. I am one of them, Commander. That is why I am here. That does not mean I have to approve of everything they do. Or do not do.'

They gazed at each other, and an idea began to take shape in Giles' mind.

'I would like to speak with you, in private,' he said.

'Why should I wish this?'

'Because I think we may have something in common.' He grinned. 'Apart from typhus. At least we speak the same language.'

She hesitated, and then shrugged. 'Now that we are here, some of us are remaining on duty all night. I have volunteered for the first week. But we nurses are sharing a room, in the guard building.'

'Can you not leave it?'

'I can leave it. Can you leave your barracks?'

'Yes. Your guards do not take their duties too seriously, unless someone tries to get through the wire. Tonight then. At eleven o'clock, when the camp is quiet. I will meet you by the latrines.'

Her nose wrinkled in that so attractive fashion of hers. 'You wish to have sex with me?'

Again she surprised him. 'Would you allow that?'

'No,' she said. 'If that is what you wish, I will not come.'

'I wish to speak with you,' he told her. 'I will not touch you. I give you my word.'

'As an officer and a gentleman,' she remarked, and began another examination.

Giles did not even tell Ganning what he was planning; time enough for that, later, if there was any prospect of his plan working out. He had to confide his intention of leaving the officers' quarters that night, so that they could cover for him just in case there was a surprise visit from the guards, but left Ganning to assume he was attempting a liaison with Sister Bakr.

And just what was he attempting? To suborn a woman from her duty and her loyalty simply because she might be of use to him, and because he felt, purely by instinct, that she was vulnerable? He would be asking her to risk her life. Yet he could not stop now. Seeing her, in private, had suddenly become important, for all his promise.

There was a single searchlight emplaced on the camp's one watchtower, and this slowly swept its way round the the compound, but its movement was so measured that avoiding its beam was a simple matter. And Sister Bakr was already waiting for him when he reached the area behind the latrines, which, if smelly, was concealed from the light.

She wore a blue cloak over the white uniform, for the nights were chill.

'You wish to escape,' she said.

She was a continuous surprise.

'How did you work that out?'

'There must be some reason for wanting to meet with me.'

'Well, I can think of several . . .' he held up his hand. 'Don't worry, I promised. Yes. As you said, if we stay here we are going to die.'

'You think the whole camp will be able to escape?'

'Unfortunately, I do not think that will be possible. Believe me, I do not like leaving them. But I believe that Lieutenant Ganning and I have the strength, and the will, to escape . . . providing we can obtain a little help.'

'From me?'

'Yes.'

'Why?'

'Well . . . we haven't come across anyone else we could turn to.'

'I meant, why do you think I should help you? I would be betraying my country.'

'I have a feeling that you do not altogether go along with what your country is doing.'

He could not see her eyes properly in the darkness, but again his instincts told him to press forward.

'Tell me what is wrong,' he invited.

She gave a little sigh. 'You are asking me to betray my country,' she said again.

'I would hope we might be able to help each other,' he said. 'Tell me what is troubling you. Or let me guess.' Again he was following his instincts, and his knowledge of recent Turkish history. 'Some of your family was involved in the revolutionary movement, before the war.'

She gave a little shiver. 'My father was shot for conspiring against the Sultan.'

'I'm sorry. Then you have every reason to hate the Government.'

'The Government of the Sultan, yes,' she said fiercely. 'Most Turks hate that disgusting old man. And his henchmen.'

'But they fight for him.'

'They are fighting for Turkey. There are many Turks who look forward to the overthrow of the Sultan. To a Turkey free of Ottoman rule.'

'Yet you are also fighting for Turkey. But you would rather not. Have you family?'

'No,' she said. 'They shot my mother too.'

'Good God!'

281

'I had a brother, but they sent him into the Army. He was killed in the Dardenelles, two years ago. By the British.'

'I am sorry about that, too. But don't you see, the sooner this war is ended, the sooner will your Sultan fall from power.'

'If I could believe that.'

'It will happen, Sister Bakr. By the way, what is your first name?'

'Anja.'

'I like that. Anja.'

'And you think that helping you to escape will bring the end of the war closer? What will you do when you escape? Go back to killing Turks. The Turks are my people. It is only the Government which is vile.'

'*I* will not be killing Turks. If I escape I will go back to the Navy, to fight the Germans. It is the defeat of Germany that matters. Once that is done, Turkey will have to make peace, and your people will be able to get rid of the Sultan.'

'What makes you think the Germans are going to lose? We are told they are winning everywhere.'

'That is propaganda,' Giles assured her.

She stared into the darkness. And he had been away from the barracks too long.

'I must go back,' he said. 'Will you not at least think about what I have said?'

'If I were to do my duty, I should report what you have said to the Commandant.'

'But I do not think you wish to do that.'

She turned her gaze on him. 'No,' she said. 'I do not wish to do that.'

'Will you think about what I have said, and meet me here again tomorrow night?'

She looked at him for several seconds longer, then walked into the darkness.

Giles could have no doubt as to the risk he was taking. Anja Bakr had made no promises, even of not handing him over to the guards. She was clearly a deeply upset young woman;

into which direction her uncertainty might lead her he had no idea.

It was a matter of waiting, not helped by Ganning being unable to resist asking, 'Well, how was she?'

'I'll let you know,' Giles replied.

But there were knowing winks and nods all round when that night he went out again.

Once again, Anja was there before him. 'What your propose is madness,' she told him. 'Suppose you managed to get out of the compound. Where would you go?'

'I am hoping you will tell me.'

'To the south is a Turkish Army. To the north is Anatolia, the Turkish heartland. To the west is a Turkish Army.'

'And to the east? The north east?'

'There is a Turkish Army there too.'

'Fighting the Russians.'

'There has been a revolution in Russia,' she said.

'A revolution?'

'The Tsar has abdicated. Russia is finished.'

'Good Lord!' That was quite the worst news he had ever heard.

'But the east is still our best hope,' Anja said. 'In the mountains of Armenia there are people who have suffered, and are suffering, much at the hands of the Turks. They will help us.'

'Us?'

'If I help you to escape, you must take me with you.'

'I should like nothing better. But . . . are you sure of what you do?'

'As you say, I do not wish to fight for these people any longer.' Her teeth showed as she smiled. 'Besides, I will be escaping the typhus, will I not?'

Anja reckoned it would take several days to organise the escape; her spell of duty inside the camp ended the next day, but she would be returning at the end of three days, and hopefully would by then have made all the necessary arrangements. In that time, another dozen men died. Giles could only pray that neither he nor Ganning came down with the disease or, even more important, Anja herself.

Or that Ganning, when the plan had been confided to him, did not break it to any of the other officers. But the young lieutenant, although obviously far too happy and confident for an inmate of a camp suffering from typhus, managed to keep the secret until, on the third night, they both stole out to the meeting behind the latrines.

They had seen Anja during the day, but she had given them only the most perfunctory greeting, which had made them distinctly apprehensive that she might hve changed her mind. But to their enormous relief she was waiting for them, and had brought them Bedouin haiks and burnous to wear, and also a revolver and ammunition apiece. 'I had hoped to disguise you as women,' she said. 'But you are too big, Commander. Now listen. Outside of the camp there are horses, and food for three days. I have also some water. We must get to those and make our escape. To do this we must get past the gate. To do *this* it will be necessary to kill the guards.'

'Kill them?' Ganning was alarmed. As a naval officer he had never had anything to do with hand-to-hand fighting.

'You must understand that if we fail to do this, you will be severely punished, and I will be executed.'

Ganning gulped. Giles felt like gulping himself.

'We will not fail,' Giles promised her. 'How many men?'

'Four men. I will distract them, but they must all be killed.' Now she handed them each a long-bladed knife. 'You must not use your firearms.'

Giles glanced at Ganning, who swallowed; neither of them had any training in personal combat. Neither really knew if he was capable of knifing a man to death, much less four.

'Can you do this?' Anja asked.

'Yes,' Giles said.

'Then let us make haste. Keep out of sight until I call you.'

Without another word she walked towards the gate. Giles and Ganning followed her at a distance, staying in the

284

darkest shadows, and throwing themselves to the ground as the searchlight passed by them.

Anja was apparently well known to the men on the gate, for they welcomed her with some warmth, and a moment later she was in their midst. Giles and Ganning crept closer yet, unnoticed by the men who were apparently fondling the nurse and oblivious to everything else. They had the sense to step away from her when next the light passed over them, then clustered close again, and at the same time Anja said, in English, 'Now!'

Giles and Ganning were on their feet in an instant, and against the first two of the guards a moment later, throwing their arms round the men's necks while they drove their knives into their bodies. Giles felt a roll of revulsion in his stomach as he felt the hot sticky liquid spurting over his hand and arm, then he let the man fall to the ground to get at the others. Of these one was already dead, knifed by Anja herself. The fourth did not have the time to understand what was going on, before Giles reached him.

'God!' Ganning was kneeling and vomiting.

'Hurry!' Anja was already pushing on the bars to the gate. She was not even panting. Giles joined her, and forced it open. The searchlight was again creeping round.

'Will they not see the dead men?'

'They will look for nothing if the gate is closed.'

They pushed it open just far enough for them to get through, pulled Ganning behind them, and lay on the ground as the light came back. This was the longest moment of Giles' life, but the light did not pause for more than a few seconds on the gate, which had been pushed shut. At a distance the watchers on the tower would not be able to tell that the bars were not in place. Nor did they apparently find anything amiss that none of the guards could be seen. The beam continued on its way.

'Quickly,' Anja whispered, and they stole away into the darkness.

'How much time do we have?' Giles asked.

'Very little. Sooner or later the men on the tower will wonder where the guards have gone. In any event, they are due to be relieved at four o'clock.' Which was three hours off. 'That is our maximum time.'

There were four horses tethered in a valley just outside the village, being held by a young man.

'This is Semih. He will help us,' Anja said.

Again there was no time for asking questions, although a great number were by now roaming through Giles' mind. They mounted, Anja riding astride with the skirt of her haik pulled up to her thighs, and walked their horses into the darkness. Behind them the glow of the searchlight lit up the sky, but they had not been away from the camp for more than half an hour when distantly they heard the blaring of a bugle.

'They have found the dead men,' Anja said. 'Ride, as fast as you can!'

They weren't even being granted the three hours of grace.

They kicked their horses, the two naval officers hanging on as best they could. Giles had at least been brought up with horses at Silver Streams, and had ridden all of his young life, although he had not done so for some years now; Ganning had apparently only ever ridden hacks on rare occasions. Both were weak after the bad food they had endured for so long. But they stuck to it with determination, and after about ten minutes Anja waved them to a walk as the horses were becoming blown.

They could hear nothing behind them now.

'It will take a little while for them to work out what has happened,' Anja said. 'But they will soon pick up the trail. We must try to lose them.'

She clearly knew the country very well, and directed them to the north-east. They walked their horses through the darkness, each entirely bound up in his or her own thoughts, and just as it was getting light found themselves on the banks of an extensive lake.

'Well, glory be,' Giles remarked. 'I had no idea there was this much water close to us.'

286

'It is salt,' Anja told him. 'But it is not deep. We must cross it.'

Ganning did another of his gulps, but there was nothing for it. Anja dismounted and tucked the skirt of her haik into the waist band of her ankle-length pantaloons, then held her horse's bridle and walked into the water. The three men followed her. They soon sank to their waists and occasionally were just about swimming, mainly because in places the bottom was liquid mud, but their progress was steady, if slow, and smelly.

Giles looked over his shoulder after half an hour, and was surprised at how far away the shore was . . . but they would still be very conspicuous to any pursuers who might arrive. Yet no one was in sight, for the moment at any rate.

'How much longer?' Ganning asked. 'I'm exhausted. And thirsty.'

'We cannot stop now,' Anja told him. 'It will be another hour, at least.'

'An hour. God!'

He was nearly at the end of his endurance. Giles, with his much greater size and strength, was also feeling pretty exhausted, but he stayed near Ganning's shoulder just in case, and sure enough, a few minutes later, the lieutenant stumbled and disappeared beneath the water.

Giles dragged him up and set him on his feet, while Anja looked over her shoulder, somewhat impatiently.

'He can go no further,' Giles told her. 'He will have to ride.'

'That will make him conspicuous,' she complained. 'And tire the horse.'

'It's his life we're talking about,' Giles insisted.

He helped Ganning into the saddle, and they resumed their journey; he didn't in any event see what Anja was worried about, as the bank behind them was lost in the heat haze as the sun rose higher, and those to either side were also invisible – presumably she was steering by the sun.

The wade became nightmarish as minute after minute passed, and sweat poured out of his hair to soak the

287

burnous and run down his shoulders to meet the water of the swamp. But Anja never hesitated or slackened her steady movement through the water for a moment, and Semih followed obediently at her shoulder. While Ganning slouched in the saddle.

There were several small wooded islands in the swamp, and, as they approached the eastern bank, a good deal of reed growth. Soon they were completely obscured from any watchers.

'It will not be long now,' Anja said.

At last the water began to shallow, and at about ten o'clock – Giles' watch had been taken when he had been captured, so he had to work on sun height – they were only ankle deep. A few minutes later they staggered on to dry ground, baked into hard flakes by the sun.

'We will rest over there,' Anja said, and pointed to a clump of trees.

Gratefully Giles dragged Ganning from the saddle and held one of the water bottles to his lips. Anja and Semih prepared food, but when it was offered to Ganning the lieutenant shook his head. 'Couldn't eat a damn thing,' he muttered, attempting a grin.

A moment later he vomited.

'Oh, Christ!' Giles said.

Anja knelt beside them.

'It must be the heat,' Giles said.

'Can you lift him up?'

'Yes.' Giles lifted Ganning's inert body, while Semih came to help.

Anja pushed the haik up to Ganning's shoulders, opened the torn shirt beneath, looked at the rash. 'He has typhus.'

'Damn, damn, damn.' He gazed at Anja, who was gazing at him.

'He is going to die,' Anja said.

'No, he isn't. If we can get him to these friends of yours . . .'

'They are not friends of mine,' Anja said. 'They hate all Turks. I am hoping they will be friends of yours. But it will be some days before we reach them. We cannot carry your friend.'

'You mean we leave him here? To die of hunger and thirst?'

'That would be cruel,' Anja said. 'It would be the more cruel, because the soldiers at the village will employ Bedouin Arabs to track us. They will already have done so. They will have told the Arabs that they do not wish us alive. Therefore the Arabs will feel free to do as they wish with any of us they may catch. They may even have women with them.'

Giles licked his lips.

'The decision must be yours,' Anja said. 'But it must be made, now.'

She got up and walked away. Semih went with her.

Giles chewed his lip as he looked at the unconscious Ganning. It was not a situation he had ever imagined he would have to face. He and Ganning had served together now for three years, and the two years in the prison camp had made them as close as brothers.

He shook Ganning's shoulder. 'Bill,' he said. 'Bill.'

Ganning opened his eyes.

'Look, Bill . . . do you know who I am?'

'Yes,' Ganning whispered.

'Listen . . . you have typhus.'

Ganning's nostrils dilated.

Giles licked his lips. 'Bill, we can't take you with us. Do you understand this?'

Ganning's lip twitched. 'Of course you can't. I'll just wait here for the jolly old Turks, eh?'

'Yes, but . . . Nurse Bakr thinks that it won't be the Turks. That they will be employing Bedouins to find us . . . maybe with orders not to bring us back.'

Ganning's eyes had closed, and Giles shook him awake again.

'Listen to me. She thinks they will torture any of us they catch.'

289

'So I'm for the high jump,' Ganning said.

'Listen. You have your revolver. If the men who come towards you are Turks, you can surrender. If they are Arabs . . .'

'They tickle my testicles,' Ganning giggled.

'Bill . . .'

'I know. I'll blow my brains out. Okay. I understand.'

Giles looked at his friend. 'Do you know how sorry I am?'

'I think I do. Giles . . . let the old man know what happened, will you?'

'I'll do that. If I make it.' Giles stood up, and saluted.

'And when you get back, sink some of those bastards, eh?'

'I'll do that, too.'

Giles walked to where Anja and Semih were waiting with the horses.

'You did not shoot him,' Anja said.

'He'll do that himself.'

'Do you think he will be capable? You are a fool, Commander. And you are wasting a revolver.'

'He'll do it himself,' Giles repeated. 'Now let's get the hell out of here.'

They mounted, and rode out. They had ridden for about five minutes when they heard the sound of a shot.

'That will tell everyone within half a mile where we are,' Anja grumbled.

'Wouldn't they have heard if I'd shot him?' Giles asked.

'We would have had the extra gun,' she pointed out.

They rode into the afternoon heat. Giles had never felt so absolutely miserable in his life. Not even when Jack had been sent to prison. Jack had always been a somewhat remote figure, the eldest brother, the head of the family, an athlete and a sailor whose experience none of the others could ever hope to match.

Bill Ganning had been a very close friend.

290

Perhaps even Anja, who had revealed an aspect of womanhood Giles had not suspected to exist, understood the depths of his emotion. When, after alternately riding and walking their horses throughout the afternoon, seeing no one as they traversed the bleak landscape, she finally called a halt for the night, and he collapsed in exhaustion, she came to sit beside him.

'He was a brave man,' she said. 'It was not his fault that he became ill.'

'If I become ill, will you shoot me?' Giles asked.

'It would be necessary,' she said seriously. 'But I do not wish you to become ill.'

'Because I'm your passport to safety, through the Armenians,' he remarked.

'That is true. But also because I like you.'

He looked into her eyes, and she smiled.

'I am too forward. But this is a primeval situation.'

She went away, and with Semih prepared food. This she brought back to him, and offered him a drink.

It wasn't water. Cautiously he sniffed it.

'It is raki,' she said. 'Turkish alcohol. Very strong.'

'I thought Muslims didn't drink?'

'We do not drink wine. We drink raki.'

He sipped it. It was indeed strong.

'Are we safe now?'

'No. But we are safer than we were. We have travelled a long way. Would you like to have sex with me?'

Once again he looked at her. 'No.'

She raised her eyebrows. 'You do not like me? I thought, at the prison camp, that you liked me.'

'I do like you.' He could not explain that it would be like mating with a black widow spider. 'It's just that I am too exhausted to have sex with anyone.'

She smiled. 'You are young, and strong. You will feel like it when you hold me in your arms.'

'I thought all Turkish women were virgins when they married?'

'I will never marry.'

'Why not?'

She shrugged. 'I was raped, when I was a girl.'

'When your father was arrested?'

'Yes.'

'Yet you stayed in Turkey.'

'Where else should I go? Yes, my brother and I stayed, to work for the revolution. Even after I got a scholarship to go to London to study nursing, I came back, to help the revolution. But the war . . . my brother was conscripted . . .'

'And killed.'

'Yes. So, I did what I had been trained to do, and forgot about the revolution. Until you. Now . . . I would like to have sex with you.'

'What about Semih?'

'Semih will keep watch.'

'I meant, what is your relationship?'

'Semih loves me.'

'And he is just going to sit there and listen to us?'

'Yes. I have told him to do this.'

Giles looked to where the young man sat, with hunched shoulders, looking back at the way they had come. Then he looked at Anja as she lay down beside him, pulled her haik about her waist and slipped her pantaloons over her thighs. With the pantaloons went the knife with which she had stabbed one of the guards.

Giles had had very little to do with women outside of the obligatory visit to a brothel which was considered part of becoming a man. The traumas which had afflicted his family just as he had been leaving school for Dartmouth had limited his friendships within his own sex, and quite precluded the slightest temptation to get too close to any of his classmates' sisters, while the other possible source of female companionship, his own sisters' friends, had also dried up at the same time and for the same reason.

Thus he really had no idea how to cope with a woman as forceful and demanding as Anja, even had he been truly sure he wanted to. But as she had prophesied, she was not to be resisted once he was in her arms, and could feel her naked groin against his. They surged tumultuously for several seconds, while the wildest of thoughts went through his brain . . . of turning up at Silver Streams with Anja in tow. Whatever would Ma say?

But suddenly it was something he wanted to do.

They continued their journey all the next day, once again under a pitiless sun, but without seeing or hearing any signs of pursuit. In mid-morning they came to a village, which Giles would have avoided but, as they were low on food, Anja elected to go into it. They were perfectly safe, as there were neither telephones nor radios out here in the desert, and the stop was well worthwhile, because there were horses available, and Anja sold their worn-out mounts and purchased three fresh ones. She seemed to have quite a large store of money, and Giles found himself wondering for how long she had been considering just such a move as this, while patiently waiting for the Christian prisoner who would see her to safety with the Armenians.

Two days later they came to the foothills of the mountains, and the following morning were halted by a rifle shot which kicked up dust and earth a few feet in front of them.

The horses whinnied and reared, but were soon under control, while Semih and Giles looked to Anja for instruction; no one doubted that she was their commander, while, as she had come to Giles on each night since their escape, he understood that he was completely under her spell.

'Raise your hands,' Anja said, setting an example. 'And you, Giles, come forward.'

Giles obeyed, guiding his horse with his knees.

'Tell them who you are,' Anja said.

'Will they understand me?'

'They will understand Turkish.'

Giles had picked up sufficient of the language in the camp. He took a deep breath, and shouted. 'I am an English officer, escaped from a Turkish prison.'

His voice echoed to and fro between the hills, but for several

293

minutes there was no reply. Then, from surprisingly close at hand, a voice commanded, 'Throw down your weapons, and dismount.'

Giles glanced at Anja, who nodded. He threw his revolver and knife to the ground in front of his horse. Anja did likewise, and Semih dropped his rifle. Then they dismounted.

'Walk away from the weapons and the horses,' the voice commanded.

They obeyed, for perhaps fifty feet.

'Stop,' the voice said.

They waited, and men appeared amidst the rocks. They wore a variety of clothes, and carried a variety of weapons, from very old muskets to modern rifles and revolvers. They came up to the three fugitives and peered at them.

'These are Turks,' someone said.

'I am English,' Giles repeated. 'These people helped me to escape.'

His captors peered more closely at him. 'Speak English,' one commanded, in English.

'My name is Lieutenant-Commander Giles Dawson, and I was the captain of His Majesty's Submarine *C17* which was captured in the Bosporus in July 1915,' Giles said, as distinctly as he could. And to help matters, he raised his burnous, to reveal the remnants of his naval uniform.

'But these are Turks,' repeated his English-speaking interrogator.

'Yes. But they are against the Government of the Sultan. They helped me escape.'

'And where you wish to go now?'

'Russia.'

'In Russia, there is revolution. In Russia, you will be shot.'

'Well . . .' Giles' knowledge of Middle Eastern geography was sketchy, once one left the sea. 'India? I wish to get back to England, to fight against the Germans. And the Turks,' he added.

'You think England will win the war?'

'Of course. England does not lose wars.'

The Armenians muttered amongst themselves.

'Are they going to help us?' Anja asked.

'I think so. But we must be patient.'

'When the war is over,' the English-speaking Armenian said, 'and Turkey is defeated, will the English allow us our own state?'

'I am sure of it,' Giles said.

'Then we will help you.'

'I can promise you the gratitude of my Government.'

'But not them. They are Turks.'

'Now, listen,' Giles said. 'They helped me to escape.'

'Because they hoped to escape also.'

'That doesn't matter. They are my responsibility.'

'You have no more responsibilities, Englishman. Save to kill Germans. And Turks.' The man made a gesture with his hand.

Giles spun round to look at Anja and Semih as there was a flurry of rifle fire.

CHAPTER 11

Q

'Ma!' Mary said, standing in the bedroom doorway, the telegram clutched in her hand. 'Ma!'

Harriet raised her head. She looked tired. But she always looked tired, nowadays. The war had simply been going on too long, claimed too many lives. Too many lives in her own family.

'Ma,' Mary said. 'Giles is coming home.'

'Giles?'

'He escaped from his Turkish prison camp, Ma. He's in Persia, with the British there. He's coming home! Oh, Ma!' She ran forward to kneel beside her mother's chair and hug her.

'I'm so happy for you,' Lorraine said. 'Oh, so happy.'

Mary kissed her. The two were almost like sisters now. And now they shared an even closer bond. Since the American declaration of war on Germany, Harry was out there fighting as hard as any of the Dawson boys had ever done . . . and taking the same risks, as well.

Would he ever find himself in England? He had to, Mary knew. And then surely he would call.

But Giles, coming home, after two years! That was too good to be true.

'Jack! Wake up.'

Normally Denise would never have awakened him; she knew how exhausted he was whenever he managed to get home for a few days' leave in between voyages in his so mysterious patrol boat. But this was something special.

Jack opened his eyes.

'It's in the paper.' Denise brandished *The Times*. 'It says, "With the British forces in Persia, Lieutenant-Commander Giles Dawson, RN, VC, DSC. Lieutenant-Commander Dawson, captain of the first British submarine to penetrate the Black Sea, was taken prisoner by the Turks but now, after nearly two years, has made a hazardous escape through the mountains of Armenia."'

Jack was sitting up. 'Let's see.'

He frowned at the paper. 'Well, glory be. Baby brother.'

'When last did you see him?'

'Giles? God, eleven years ago. I wonder what he looks like.'

'But he's safe, Jack. Oh, your mother and sister must be so happy about that.'

'Yes,' Jack said. 'Yes.'

'And one day they'll know they have two sons. They will know that, won't they, Jack?'

'One day,' Jack promised her.

There was the usual crowd of wives and sweethearts and wellwishers to cheer *U76* as she slipped from her mooring in Wilhelmshaven and made for the Jade Estuary and then the open sea. The crowds were always enthusiastic, but this time there was a touch of sadness, amongst the women at least: when she had completed her voyage *U76* would be returning to Zeebrugge, where she was normally stationed – for the last month she had been in Wilhelmshaven to be overhauled.

There was also a good deal of pride, pride in which the crew could share. Because no one could argue that it was the sailors of the submarine service who were doing most to win the war for the Central Powers. Allied shipping losses were simply staggering, and even the belated introduction of a convoy system was not making any immediate impact. Everyone knew it was a race against time. Despite their successes in the East, against a collapsing Russia, Germany, and more especially Austria-Hungary, were coming close to starvation, not only of food, but of the sinews of war. No doubt Britain and France were equally suffering. It was matter of whether the U-boats could bring Britain to her knees before the Americans could enter the war in any strength, to complete the destruction of the Kaiser's war machine.

Korvettenkapitan Dorf did not doubt that they could. He already claimed seven victims, was fast being hailed as one of the great U-boat commanders. On this voyage he intended to claim several more, especially as the approach of summer meant calm seas, and even more important, short nights.

Certainly the shallow waters of the Jade were calm enough, today. But Dorf was in a hurry to gain the depths of the North Sea.

Mary Elizabeth slipped her mooring just before dawn, and moved down the Firth of Forth for the Minches. No one saw her go, and the growl of her diesel engine was lost in the growls of the several other engines as the fishing fleet put out.

Mary Elizabeth was not part of that fleet, nor did she moor with them. She put to sea with them, however, in the darkness, and then peeled away from them as soon as they reached the open sea. She was a ship of mystery as far as the seafaring folk of Glasgow were concerned. No doubt a great deal of gossip went on about her, and her various sisters, in the pubs, and no doubt some of the guesses were on target, but it was difficult to suppose any of the gossip reached Germany, or would have mattered if it did; at sea, one trawler looked very much like another.

Jack had named his command himself; there had been no ceremony, and if he had chosen to commemorate his two sisters that was his business. In every way, externally, *Mary Elizabeth* looked totally conventional of her class, just over sixty feet long, with her bridge deck and accomodation well forward, and her after section open deck, in the centre of which was the hold for the catch. Knowledgeable onlookers might realise that she was made of steel instead of wood, and was powered by a diesel instead of steam, and might argue about the obviously new-fangled ideas of her owner; a diesel at least had the advantage of requiring a smaller crew; that it also provided a quicker turn to full speed would have seemed irrelevant, in

298

a trawler. Only the crew knew that there was no hold, that in the bowels of their ship there was a gun platform on which was mounted a four-point-seven inch. The trawler's topsides were designed to fall away to expose the gun, only some three feet above the waterline, at the appropriate moment.

So far, however, to the disgust of Jack and his crew, there had not been an appropriate moment.

The crew of *Mary Elizabeth* numbered only seven, including her captain. All volunteers, and sworn to secrecy, the others consisted of Petty Officer Mann and five ratings. They had been picked because they had all been real trawlermen, at one stage or another of their lives, and therefore could appear to be hauling their nets in a convincing fashion, just as they had discarded their uniforms and wore seaboots and heavy turtle-necked sweaters, with woollen hats.

It was, in many ways, a holiday job. They put to sea, became separated from the rest of the fleet, and 'inadvertently' found themselves farther offshore than was usual. Then they drifted about, apparently fishing, but whatever catch was brought on board was always released into the sea again at nightfall . . . save what might be required for supper.

Their business was waiting.

But they understood the dangers, too. Not only that a submarine might decide after all to waste a torpedo on them – and a single hit from a torpedo would blow *Mary Elizabeth* to pieces – but that when their intended victim did appear, and do all the right things such as surfacing, they would yet be on a hiding to nothing, until the enemy was so close they could not miss.

Yet there was not a man of the crew who was not impatient for the sight of an enemy, whatever the risks that might follow. And so far, they had seen nothing.

There was always the next voyage.

'Ship on starboard bow,' said Oberleutnant Albrichtson.

Dorf leaned his elbows on the conning tower rail to steady his binoculars. *U76* was on the surface, rolling slowly in the long Atlantic swell. It was nine thirty in the evening, and Dorf had surfaced early, because there had been nothing in sight until this lone vessel, a very long way away; it was just a blob against the sunset.

'Steer to close,' Dorf said.

'Do you wish to submerge, Herr Kapitan?'

'He cannot see us, and it will be dark in half an hour. We will close him on the surface.'

The orders were given, the diesel's growl became louder, and the U-boat slipped rapidly through the low swell.

'Range estimated fifteen miles, Herr Kapitan,' Albrichtson observed.

'He is a fishing vessel,' Dorf said.

'Will you attack?'

Dorf considered.

'It is strange, to find a trawler alone,' Albrichtson said. 'Do you suppose he can be one of these disguised warships that we have been warned about?'

'We shall have to see,' Dorf decided. 'Reduce speed. We will maintain our station until dawn.'

'There,' said Petty Officer Mann.

Jack levelled his binoculars. The sun was all but gone now, but it was going to be a bright night, and although the darkness to the east was more intense than anywhere else, after a few seconds he picked up what Mann had spotted, an ever-recurring splash of phosphorescence gleaming through the gloom.

The sea was too calm for the glows to be be wave crests.

'She's very low in the water, sir,' Mann said, trying to keep the excitement from his voice.

'Oh, she's a sub,' Jack agreed. 'Question is, is she one of ours or one of theirs?'

'One of ours would hardly be stalking us,' Mann argued.

'Could be. She can't identify us either, you know.'

'Shall I alter course to close her?'

'No. She mustn't know we've seen her. We'll just maintain course and speed, and wait for her to make the first move. Stand the watch below down. It's going to be a long night.'

300

Dorf slept for a few hours, and was awakened by his orderly at two thirty.

'Darkness is fading, Herr Kapitan.'

Dorf nodded, pulled on his seaboots, went up on to the conning tower where Albrichtson was slapping his gloved hands together; even in June, it was chill on deck at dawn.

'He is still there, Herr Kapitan. I do not think he has seen us.'

'We will submerge,' Dorf said. 'And take a closer look at this fellow.'

'Periscope astern,' Mann reported.

Jack had a look. 'Right. Start hauling our nets.'

The crew fell to, even if they could not help glancing astern every few minutes. Jack remained on the bridge, watching the telltale wisp of white wake trailing away from the periscope. It made him think of a shark, circling its victim, keeping its distance until it was certain . . .

'I do not think she is a Q,' Dorf said. 'She is fishing normally.'

'Has she seen us, Herr Kapitan?'

'It would not appear so.'

'Shall we surface, and send her down?'

Dorf continued to survey the trawler for a some minutes longer. 'No,' he said at last. 'She has a wireless aerial. She would get off a message before we could hope to sink her, and there may be Royal Navy units in the vicinity.' He stepped back and brought the periscope down. 'Time enough for that sort of thing when we are on our way home, Albrichtson. Not on the way out.'

'Damn,' Jack said.

Mann came up to the bridge. 'Where is he?'

'Disappeared.'

'Preparing an attack, you mean, sir?'

'I don't think so. But tell the men to stand by.'

Half an hour passed, and there was no sign of the submarine.

'Damn,' Jack said again.

'It's hard to believe it's worth it, sir,' Jack told Commodore
Keyes. 'We've been out on five patrols, seen one U-boat, and
he didn't attack.'

'Patience is the name of the game, Lieutenant. We have
had a couple of successes. And quite a few near misses. We'll
get the bastards yet.'

Jack thought the odds were very long and he, and his men,
were becoming bored. But at least he was in no danger. And
Giles was coming home.

'Good heavens, sir.' The butler stared at the tall young man in
naval uniform standing at the front door of Silver Streams.
'You'll be Mr Giles.'

'And you are Rawlston?'

'That's right, sir.'

Giles held out his hand. 'Pleased to meet you again,
Rawlston.'

'It is a great pleasure, sir. Let me take that bag. The ladies
are in the garden, sir.'

But Mary had come into the house at the sound of the bell.
She was standing at the inner end of the corridor.

'Giles,' she said. 'Oh, Giles!'

They moved forward together, and were in each other's
arms.

'You've lost weight,' she murmured.

'I've put weight on, recently.'

She held him at arms' length, the better to look at him. He
was smiling, but there was so much sadness lurking behind his
eyes.

'Ma,' she said, and held his hand to lead him into the garden.

'This is your Uncle Giles,' Mary explained. 'You don't
remember him, do you?'

The children stared at the big man, sitting beside his mother
on the garden bench. They couldn't remember Grandma ever
looking so happy, either.

'And this is Lorraine,' Mary said.

'Gee,' Lorraine said. 'I've heard so much about you.'

'Do you want to talk?' Mary asked.

It was after dinner, but in June was still light, and the pair of them were alone in the garden, Lorraine having tactfully elected to read the children a bedtime story.

'I think I probably do,' Giles said. 'But . . .' His mouth twisted. 'You tell me, first.'

'Tell you what?'

'About Peter, and Geoffrey.'

'Jutland.' She told him how they had died.

'I wish I'd been there.'

'I'm glad you weren't. But Giles . . . can you keep a secret? The most deadly secret in the world?'

'If it's your secret.'

'It's mine, and Harry Krantz's.'

'He was the American attache who was married to Lizzie?'

'He's also Lorraine's brother, remember.'

Giles nodded, slowly. 'And you and he have a secret?'

'Yes.' Mary told him about Jack.

He listened in silence, then commented, 'Son of a gun.'

'You understand that we can't tell anyone. Not even Ma, much as I'd adore to be able to do it. We must wait for Jack to feel he can reappear.'

'Of course. But you say he's married?'

'That's what he said.'

'Do you think his wife knows who he really is?'

'I doubt it. He'd be taking too much of a risk.'

'What a show. I wonder if I'll ever run into him.'

'It's a big navy.'

'Um. Oh, sis, if you knew how much that has cheered me up.'

'Life was pretty grim in that camp, eh?'

He hesitated. 'As a matter of fact, relatively speaking, life in the camp was pretty good. It was after I left the camp, that . . . well, let's say I came into contact with feelings and emotions I'd never known before.'

'Tell me.'

'Do you really want to know?'

'What are sisters for?'

It was her turn to listen.

'Were you in love with her?' she asked, when he had finished.

'I have no idea. I made love with her.'

Mary said nothing; this was a subject about which she still felt uncertain.

'The point is, she regarded me as her safeguard. She only helped us on that condition. And I did nothing, while she was shot to death.'

'From what you have said, you did not have the time to do anything.'

'That does not alter the fact that I watched her die. Just as I rode away from Bill Ganning, knowing that he must die.'

Mary sighed. 'Perhaps it is a privilege, to watch people who mean a lot to you, whom you love, die. I have never seen anyone die, save for Pa, and that was peaceful.'

He knew she was thinking of Geoffrey. And probably Peter and Lizzie as well.

And Gina?

But he understood what she was feeling. She was surrounded by death, nowadays on a scale the whole world had never supposed possible, but she knew of it only at second hand.

He squeezed her hand, and she looked up with a quick, tearful smile. 'Anyway, you're home for . . . how long?'

'I don't know. Their lordships just told me to go home and recuperate.'

'We'll see that you do that,' Mary promised.

'I will be going back, you know.'

'I know.'

'I owe it, to Anja, and Semih . . . and Bill Ganning.'

'And to Jack,' she reminded him.

'Oh, indeed. I wish I knew what he was doing now.'

'Astern of us,' Petty Officer Mann said.

Jack levelled his glasses. *Mary Elizabeth* was forging slowly ahead, making only two knots, as her crew handed their nets. And once again there was that telltale wake, dogging them.

It was the third time they had been inspected by a periscope this summer, without anything coming of it. Yet he had to follow the drill.

'Tell the lads,' he said, and Mann slid down the ladder, while Jack stood by the helmsman, Bob Meeker, the youngest member of the crew.

'What do you reckon, sir?' Meeker asked.

'We'll just have to wait and see. We'll just have . . . by God, he's coming up.'

The grey-painted conning tower was breaking the surface. The submarine was half a mile away, but Jack could make out the heads appearing in the tower, and the men clambering down the ladders on to the still awash foredeck to uncover their gun.

He stepped on to the little bridge wing. 'Let the net go,' he said quietly. 'And stare at her. That's what you would do.'

The crew slipped the net, while peering at the now fully exposed submarine. In the same instant there was a flash, and a moment later a plume of water rose about fifty yards to their right.

'Good shooting,' Mann muttered, as he joined Jack on the bridge. 'Do you reckon that was a summons to surrender, sir?'

'We'll take it as such, Petty Officer. Strike the flag.'

Mann himself went aft, over the exposed after deck, to haul down the Red Ensign. Meanwhile the submarine came closer, and Jack could make out the officers on the tower inspecting him through their binoculars. His crew were gathered in a group just aft of the superstructure, as they might have been expected to do, as that was the only possible shelter if the U-boat decided to keep on firing.

They were also only a few feet from the hold.

A light winked from the conning tower. Jack seized a pad of paper and wrote down the Morse code message, which was in English.

'Stop your engine.'

Jack put the gear lever into neutral, and *Mary Elizabeth* rolled slowly in the long swell; with a diesel – its exhaust close to the waterline – the German would not be able to tell that he had not actually lost power, as no telltale smoke would escape from *Mary Elizabeth*'s false funnel.

'Abandon ship,' was the second message.

Mann was at the foot of the ladder. 'He's well within range, sir.'

'We want him where we can't miss. Break out the boat,' Jack told him. 'But slowly. Have trouble with it.'

Mann nodded, and waved his arm to summon three of the crew forward to where the dinghy was stowed.

'You go down,' Jack told Meeker.

'Aye-aye.' The boy slid down the ladder to join the one man remaining by the hold; that was John Chidgey, the gunlayer.

The light was blinking again. 'You have five minutes,' Jack wrote down on his pad.

He glanced forward. Mann and his men were slowly taking the tarpaulin from off the dinghy. *Mary Elizabeth*, no longer making way, had turned broadside on to the submarine, so the Germans could obviously see they were preparing to abandon ship.

And the U-boat was now only just over a quarter of a mile away. Jack reckoned four hundred yards could be considered point blank range.

'Stand by,' he said to Chidgey.

'Aye-aye, Captain.'

There was a second flash of light, and a second shot plunged into the sea, this time much closer.

'In one minute I will sink you,' the light flashed.

Jack could now read the number on the conning tower: *U47*. That surely approximated the whites of their eyes.

'All hands,' he shouted, and stepped outside, himself to hoist the second ensign, the White Ensign, on the halliard immediately behind the bridge.

Mann and his men abandoned the dinghy, which had just been lifted up on its falls, and ran aft. Chidgey was already diving into the hold, followed by Meeker, and as they did so, Jack pressed the lever which caused the topsides to drop away and uncover the gun. He felt a tremendous surge of excitement, but even as the four-point-seven swung to find the range he was picked up by a massive force and hurled aft.

For several seconds he was unconscious, then he realised that Mann was shaking his shoulder.

'Mr Smith, sir. Mr Smith!'

Jack's ears were ringing and there was blood on his hands, but he did not think he was badly hurt. He rose to his knees as the entire ship heaved to the explosion of the four-point-seven.

'The bastard!' Chidgey shouted.

Jack reached his feet, and saw the submarine already half-submerged.

'Stay and fight!' Meeker yelled, waving his fist.

Jack looked left and right. The shell had landed on the foredeck, and blown the dinghy overboard, as well as carving a great hole in the high bows; the blast had blown him off the bridge wing on to the afterdeck, but the bridge itself seemed intact – and the flag still flew. Had the trawler been made of wood, as was usual, she would be sinking now. On the other hand, there were flames forward.

And the submarine was now gone, save for a froth of white water.

'Oh, the cowards,' Mann growled.

'Fire drill!' Jack snapped, and ran for the bridge ladder. Once submerged, and a reasonable distance off, and knowing now that she was engaged with a warship, the U-boat might well decide to settle it with a torpedo.

He reached the wheel, treading on the shattered glass of the windshield, which had also been blown in by the blast, thrust the throttle ahead to gain way, and watched Mann and his men playing their hose on the burning woodwork beneath him.

He spun the wheel, and brought *Mary Elizabeth* round in a tight circle, seeking some sign of where the submarine might be. But now even the confused water was settling; the enemy had sunk out of sight.

Mann arrived, panting. 'Fire under control, sir.' He surveyed the sea. 'Swine,' he said. 'What do we do now, sir?'

'Put back to port.'

'You mean we've lost him?'

'I'm afraid we have, Petty Officer. Him. There'll be others. But we are going to have to improve our technique.'

'Jack,' Denise said. 'Oh, Jack.' She touched his face; the various cuts and bruises were just beginning to heal.

'Even U-boats sometimes come close inshore,' he said.

'I thought you were taking a break from being blown up.'

'This fellow Dorf is doing very well,' Scheer commented. 'He has now sunk fifteen ships. You must be very proud of him, Baron. Proud to have trained him.'

'Yes, Herr Admiral,' Bruno agreed. 'But I am also ashamed that the submarine service is the only part of the Imperial Navy that is making any attempt to confront the enemy.'

He could hardly describe what Dorf was engaged in doing as fighting.

'I know, it is a frustrating time. The fact is, Bruno, you know, and I know, and every officer in the Navy knows, that we were very lucky the last time. Do you remember that the Royal Navy once fought a battle called, simply, The Glorious First of June?'

'Against the French, in 1794, four hundred miles west of Ushant.'

'That is correct. Tell me of the battle.'

'The French fleet was escorting a food convoy from America to Brest, and the British fleet was searching for them. The two fleets came into contact during the last week of May, but were prevented from fighting because of low cloud and bad visibility. In the fog, the convoy escaped.'

'But on 1 June the mist lifted,' Scheer said, 'And there were the British, and there were the French, in perfect visibility and good weather. The French fleet was all but annihilated. Suppose that had happened last year, as it could so easily have done?'

'With deepest respect, Herr Admiral, where our ships could see, they proved they could shoot just as straight as the Royal Navy. And more successfully.'

Scheer shook his head. 'They were successful against the British battlecruisers. We were quite unable to do any serious damage to the battle*ships*. And they outnumbered us two to one. No, no, it would have been a catastrophe.'

Bruno could not believe his ears. 'Do you mean we will never attempt to engage the enemy again?'

Scheer sighed. 'The Kaiser is also a student of history, Bruno.'

'He has forbidden the High Seas Fleet to put to sea?'

'The rules are the same as before. We engage when we have some prospects of victory. When we can catch the enemy napping. But we will engage, Bruno. We will engage. Meanwhile, let us drink a toast to the Dorfs of this world. They could yet still win us this war.'

Curly brown hair floating in the breeze, Lorraine Krantz cantered across the green fields below Silver Streams. She had done this often enough since taking up residence with the Dawsons, usually in the company of Mary. But over the past few weeks Mary had stayed at home, and allowed Lorraine to enjoy Giles.

Mary, being Mary, had been prepared to admit she had a reason. 'You will do him good,' she said. 'He has had a difficult time.'

As Giles had not confided his prison camp experience to anyone save his sister, Lorraine had no idea what she truly meant, and her imagination, having been stoked by what she had read of the Turks, or Muslims in general, had indulged in the most dire possibilities. Giles seemed fit enough, certainly after he had spent a week or so eating good food and enjoying the fresh air and relaxed atmosphere of the Dorset countryside, but there was certainly a remoteness in his eyes, and disconcerting breaks in his conversation, when he would stare at her in a very off-putting fashion.

Perhaps he was not seeing her at all, but was remembering. Equally perhaps, though, he might be seeing her very well, and wondering if he would ever be able to do with her any of the things a man might wish to do with a woman – another aspect of life she had only read of in novels.

But she liked him enormously, as she liked everything about this so traditional, and yet so tragic family, torn apart by the dreadful reality of war.

Giles drew rein as they came in sight of the house. 'I feel so guilty,' he remarked. 'All the time.'

'Has it not simply been a matter of survival of the fittest?' she asked, and bit her lip. Perhaps she should not have said that. But it was the only point of view that had enabled her personally to survive.

He glanced at her, then led the way down the slope towards the paddock. 'Do you believe that?'

'I have to believe it, Giles. Or I would have committed suicide, long ago.'

Old Dalton, very old now, was waiting to take their bridles as they slipped from the saddle. And once again Lorraine wondered if she'd made a mistake, as Giles made no further comment, but stepped aside to wait for her to go towards the house.

Mary stood in the doorway. 'There's a letter.' Her voice was dull.

Giles stepped past her, picked up the OHMS envelope, slit it with his thumb, took out the single sheet of paper and scanned it, a smile slowly spreading across his face. 'I've got a K,' he said, wonderingly.

'A knighthood?' Mary shrieked. 'Oh, Giles, I thought it was a new posting.'

'It is a new posting, not a knighthood.' He hugged her as he saw her expression change. 'But to one of the very new, big, K-Class subs. As captain, with promotion to Commander. Oh, Sis, this is really something.' He smiled past her at Lorraine. 'Really something.'

Now it was Lorraine who sat with him in the garden after dinner.

'When must you leave?' she asked.

'Sunday afternoon. I am to report for duty at Portsmouth first thing Monday morning.'

'And are these new ships really so magnificent?'

'They are absolutely the last thing in subs.'

'Can you tell me about them? Or are they terribly secret?'

'Well . . . they are, I suppose. But I can tell you that they are simply the biggest submarines ever built, that they make over twenty knots on the surface, and that they carry three guns.'

'That sounds enormous, for a submarine.'

'Well, it is. Of course, they're not intended for ordinary submarine work, sneaking up on an enemy or that sort of thing. They're designed to be scouts for the fleet, able to cruise to within sight of the enemy, send off his position, and then submerge and safely regain station.'

'Sounds tremendous. I wish I could be coming with you.' She gulped, and flushed, and bit her lip, all at the same time. 'I mean, I so envy you men, like Harry and yourself, able to rush off and fight your wars, while we have to sit at home and twiddle our thumbs.'

He nodded. 'I wouldn't like to be a woman. But then . . . we couldn't risk having women out there, being killed.'

'What's so different about a woman being killed?' she demanded. 'We're flesh and blood.'

He stared at her, and she knew she had opened Pandora's Box.

'There is a lot of difference, Lorraine,' he said, quietly. 'Did you see Lizzie die?'

'No,' she muttered. 'I didn't *see* anyone die. I mean, people were dying all around, but I guess I was just too busy thinking about myself.' She hesitated, then, as he didn't speak, felt compelled to go on. 'But you have. Seen a woman die.'

'Yes,' he said, quietly.

'Someone you were . . . fond of?'

311

'She had been my mistress, yes.'

'Oh.' Lorraine couldn't think of a response to that, made to rise, as she couldn't think of any way they could possibly continue the conversation, either, and then sat down again as he continued speaking as if she hadn't moved.

'She helped me escape, you see. She was a strange woman. A nurse.' He glanced at her. 'A Turkish nurse.'

'That must have been . . . different.'

His smile was sad. 'It was. Unexpected, I suppose. I couldn't imagine what Ma and Mary would have said had I managed to get her back here.'

'I'm sure they would have liked her very much.' Now she did stand up.

'Perhaps.' He stood up as well. 'It is very good of you, to allow me to bore you with my memories.'

'I don't find them boring at all. I . . .' she flushed. She had spoken so quickly. 'It's very good of your mother and sister to put up with me, all the time and for so long.'

'I think they'd be very upset, should you leave,' he pointed out. 'You're part of the family, now.'

'I guess I am,' she said sadly, and they walked back towards the house together. 'Are you looking forward to getting back to sea?'

'Oh, indeed. Especially as a scout for the Grand Fleet. I only hope that the Germans come out, for one last time.'

Capital units of the High Seas Fleet did put to sea, in mid-November, but this was purely to cover mine-laying activities north-west of Heligoland Bight. Thanks to Room 40, however, the Royal Navy knew they were coming, and attempted to force an engagement. Shots were exchanged and some minor damage done on each side, but the visibility was poor and the Germans regained port without loss.

Kaiser Wilhelm I, flying the flag of Konteradmiral Baron Bruno von Eltz, was not one of the German ships engaged.

Dorf went to visit his old commanding officer at Christmas. This was partly because he worried about the old boy, who seemed to get gloomier and gloomier every time he saw him, and partly to show off his Iron Cross First Class with Oak Leaves: he now sported two of Germany's highest military awards.

'How many is it?' Bruno asked.

'Nineteen, Herr Konteradmiral. It could have been more, of course. One sees so many possible targets, but one does not always have sufficient torpedoes.'

'Oh, quite,' Bruno said drily. 'But one can always surface and use your gun.'

To him that was what naval warfare was all about.

'Indeed, Herr Konteradmiral. But surfacing to attack requires careful reconnoitering, to make sure that one is not entering a trap.'

'Such as being caught by one of these Q-ships we are reading about,' Bruno suggested, somewhat contemptuously.

'Exactly.'

'Have you ever seen one?'

'It is difficult to say. There was an occasion last spring when I came across a trawler behaving suspiciously, you know, entirely on her own, and further away from land than is usual.'

'But you did not investigate.'

'Oh, I kept her under surveillance for several hours. But then I decided she was not worth the risk.'

'It is better to find an unarmed merchantman,' Bruno commented, more contemptuously yet.

Dorf was apparently impervious to sarcasm. 'Absolutely. We are in this business to win the war, not engage in heroics.'

'Can we win this war, Dorf?'

'Why, Herr Konteradmiral, we *are* winning it. Now that Russia has sunk into a state of total revolution, there are only the British and the French left.'

'And the Americans.'

'Oh, they are nothing. Anyway, we shall have defeated the British and French long before any American presence can make itself felt.'

'I hope you are right, Dorf. I hope you are right,' Bruno said.

313

Dorf stood up, and saluted. 'I must take my leave, Herr Konteradmiral. May I wish the High Seas Fleet good hunting when next it engages the Royal Navy?'

Bruno wondered if he was as insensitive to sarcasm as he had appeared. 'I am sure we will do very well, Herr Korvettenkapitan,' he said. 'And may I suggest that the next time you encounter what may be a Q-ship, you send it to the bottom?'

'What do you think of her?' asked the Flotilla Captain.

Giles' eyes gleamed. 'I have never seen anything quite so magnificent, sir.'

'Yes, they are splendid looking ships, aren't they?' The Captain pulled his nose. 'I must warn you that there have been one or two teething troubles on trials. We've had to modify the bows, make them higher and more robust, and you'll see we've had to do away with the forward three-pounder gun; it simply wasn't workable. But you have the two four-inches aft of the tower. You're still far more heavily armed than any German.'

'Oh, quite, sir.'

'Well . . . good luck and good hunting. Here are your orders. It's only a trial cruise, of course, and as you see you'll be in the company of two others. Portman is flotilla leader for the exercise. You'll join the fleet under my command when it's complete.'

Giles saluted, and boarded the pinnace which was waiting to take him out to the huge submarine. His heart was pounding. He had always believed that submarines were the future of sea warfare, and equally, that they would grow bigger with each design. Here he had the biggest submarine in the world, under his command. That *K4* had several sisters only made him the more proud. She, and they, measured three hundred and thirty-seven feet overall, with a beam of twenty-six and a half feet and a draught of sixteen. They displaced eighteen hundred tons on the surface and two thousand six hundred submerged. And they could make twenty-three and a half knots on the surface.

314

Which, even with two guns instead of three, made them quite the equivalent of any destroyer, when their ability to submerge and their ten torpedo tubes were taken into account.

The entire crew of fifty-two was on the afterdeck to greet their new commanding officer.

'Lieutenant Briggs, sir.'

Giles shook hands.

'Sub-Lieutenant Carter, sir.'

'Sub-Lieutenant Marsham.' The engineer officer.

'Chief Petty Officer Mallinson, sir.'

More handshakes, and then an inspection of the crew. Many of them surreptitiously looked at the crimson ribbon on his breast. He wondered just what they were thinking: exhilaration at serving under a VC, or apprehension at the thought that this man had already lost one ship?

'Carry on, Number One,' he said, and went below to inspect the interior, which was even more staggering that the exterior; for the first time in a submarine he felt he had room to breathe. Two of the ten torpedo tubes were even mounted in the funnel superstructure, for on the surface *K4* was powered by two oil-fired steam turbines, with an eight hundred horsepower diesel engine in reserve; submerged she was conventional, with four battery driven electric motors.

'Some ship, don't you think?' Briggs asked, following him into the office which opened off the amazingly spacious captain's cabin. Briggs was a short, somewhat plump young man with a red face and curly hair.

'Some ship,' Giles agreed. 'Prepare for sea, Number One. For our trials we are to operate as a flotilla under the command of *K1*.'

'Aye-aye, sir.'

Briggs hurried away, and Giles could allow himself to lean back and smile. He felt he was enjoying a glimpse of the future. And it was his future, as well.

With his officers he was in the conning tower when the signal to drop moorings was given. Thin wisps of steam issued from the funnel – utterly incongruous in a submarine – as the ship moved

315

away from her buoys and out of Portsmouth Harbour.

'Squadron will proceed at half speed in line ahead, to a position two miles from the Nab Tower,' came the command from *K1*; on the surface of course they could communicate by radio.

Giles gave the order, and the submarine increased speed to pass between the Spit forts guarding the eastern end of the Solent. *K4* was in the centre, with *K1* ahead and *K3* astern. The sea was calm in these sheltered waters, and the submarines rode through them effortlessly. People gathered on the now distant shore to watch and wave.

'How is it, cox?' Giles asked down the tube.

'Bit heavy on the steering, sir.'

'She'll improve with speed, I should imagine.'

There was certainly an immense feel of power beneath his feet. He grinned at Briggs, and Briggs grinned back.

Half an hour later they were off the Nab. 'Squadron will move into line abreast, two cables' length apart.'

K1 reduced speed to allow her sisters to catch up with her.

'Course is two six oh, speed sixteen knots.'

The submarines began to make their way down Channel, past the southern cliffs of the Isle of Wight . . . and into quite a choppy sea. Immediately *K4* began to move to left and right of her course, slewing back and forth. Giles went down the ladder to the control room, saw the coxswain red in the face as he wrestled with the helm.

'Can't hold her, sir,' the seaman gasped. 'She's yawing about all over the show.'

'My bet it's that bow,' Briggs commented, having also come down.

'Double up on the helm,' Giles ordered. 'She'll improve at full speed,' he added. She has to, he thought.

He considered reporting the problem to *K1*, but had not yet made up his mind when the order came to dive. 'Squadron will maintain course; speed eight knots, for one hour, then surface.'

Giles gave the order, himself went up to make sure all the various watertight vents were properly closed. With a steam

316

engine, diving could not be the instantaneous business it had been on a conventional submarine, and required a full fifteen minutes; at that, *K4* appeared to be ready before either of the others.

He went to the control position. 'No yawing about now, cox,' he warned.

'Oh, she's easier to hold, sir, at this speed.'

And under water, Giles thought. That didn't sound too good for her allotted task.

He was even less happy as he accompanied Briggs through the ship. Several of the vents were not working very well, and water was getting in everywhere.

'Shall we surface and report, sir?' the Lieutenant asked.

'No,' Giles decided. 'Keep your pumps going; it's only an hour. We'll prepare a list of all our faults together.'

And it's likely to be a long one, he thought grimly.

The hour dragged by, and every man on board *K4* was relieved when the command came to surface again; despite the pumps, in some places men were standing ankle deep in water.

'Pump her dry, Number One,' Giles said, as he climbed into the conning tower.

He wondered how the other two had got on; it could not only be his command which leaked like a sieve.

'Squadron will increase to full speed; course two seven oh.'

They were virtually in mid-Channel, and could steer due West. But full speed . . .

'Double up on the helm again,' Giles ordered down the tube.

Steam issued from the funnel, and *K6* began to move through the water at an ever-increasing speed, matched by her sisters.

Briggs appeared on the bridge. 'It's all hell down there, sir,' he said. 'I have three men on the helm, and she's still slewing about.'

'I can see that,' Giles said, gazing at the wake. He could also feel the unhappy motion.

'I think this is dangerous,' Briggs commented. 'Look, those others aren't doing any better.'

317

All of the wakes were a pattern of different white streaks across the water, almost as if they were zigzagging on purpose. Thus Commander Portman had to be aware of the problems.

'We must presume he knows what he's about,' Giles said.

'Signal from flagship, sir.'

Giles glanced at the note. 'Squadron will make one hundred and eighty degree turn to starboard, maintaining speed, and steer oh nine oh.'

'For God's sake,' Briggs muttered.

'He's putting us through our paces,' Giles reminded him. 'Hard a starboard, cox,' he said into the tube. 'Course oh nine oh.'

Due East, or back the way they had come. Still yawing her way through the waves at twenty-three knots, *K4* came round. Her sisters were doing the same, but the turning circles were far larger than Giles has expected, and the big submarine was still yawing to and fro in a most alarming fashion as she encountered her own wake. There were two cables' lengths – four hundred yards – between each of the ships, but where *K1* had managed to come round fairly tightly, *K4* was finding it difficult to come off of due north, and the gap was narrowing rapidly.

Officers on the conning tower of the flagship were waving and pointing, and Giles could hear the wireless crackling below him, but he had no time for messages now. He grabbed the tube. 'Reduce speed,' he bellowed. 'Keep that helm hard over. Keep . . .'

Even as he gave the orders he knew he was too late to be of any use. *K1* was directly in front of him, and although *K4* was slowly turning, she wasn't going to make it in time. A moment later there was a screech of tortured steel as the two hulls met.

'There will have to be a court martial, of course,' Commodore Keyes said. 'And until it takes place, you are relieved of duty, Commander Dawson.'

'Yes, sir,' Giles said. He had never felt so shattered in his life. He had seemed to have everything going for him, and now . . . the last of the Dawsons. And the true disgrace. Jack was a hero, whatever disguise he was forced to lurk beneath. Peter had been a hero, even if he was dead. And Giles was a hero, who had destroyed two ships and had the death of ten men on his conscience, those who hadn't been able to get out of the interior of *K1* before she had plunged to the bottom of the English Channel.

Keyes studied his expression. 'Don't take it too much to heart, Dawson,' he said. 'Every commanding officer of one of the K-Class has reported the handling difficulties, and we have a letter from Commander Portman exonerating you of all blame. We shall of course have to go on using them, as they are being built, but they do appear likely to be the biggest white elephants in naval history, barring perhaps that round battleship the Russians once attempted to build. The point is, I suspect the court martial is going to be a formality. So you go on home, and relax, and stop worrying about it.'

That winter the tide in the Atlantic began to turn. Not only was the convoy system beginning to work, but more and more American warships were now at sea, sharing the burden of tackling the U-boats. Shipping losses began to decline, while U-boat losses increased. This was very important in view of the huge numbers of American troops which were now being shipped across the Atlantic.

No one supposed the end of the war was in sight. In March 1918 the new Communist masters of Russia signed a separate peace with Germany, and the Kaiser's generals were able to transfer masses of troops to the Western Front in an attempt to knock Britain and France out of the struggle before American aid became effective. In this spring the two sides were locked in a titanic battle in north-western France, with the Allies only just holding on.

'Backs to the wall,' Harriet said sombrely.

'Oh, really, Ma, the newspapers are always saying things like that,' Mary pointed out.

'This isn't the newspaper.'

319

Mary gave her mother an old-fashioned look, as Harriet was undoubtedly holding *The Times* in front of her eyes.

'I mean, the newspaper is quoting what Sir Douglas Haig has said,' Harriet added. 'You have to admit that the situation is serious.'

'A gambler's throw,' Mary asserted. 'Look, there's the postman.'

She always kept an eye on the front drive during the morning, at least until the post had been. Now she ran into the corridor, to encounter Rawlston on his way to her, with the mail.

Mary sorted them as she returned to the parlour. 'Bill, bill, bill, invitation . . . letter.' Addressed to her, she saw with quiet satisfaction, and bearing a United States stamp.

Lorraine arrived from the garden, as breathless and untidy as ever, followed, more slowly, by Giles. Of course it was splendid having Giles home again so soon. But naturally he was both miserable and tense, waiting for his summons to the court martial.

He spent a lot of his time with Lorraine. In his frame of mind, Mary did not see anything very positive developing there, and she wasn't sure she wanted it to – Lorraine was two years older than her baby brother. On the other hand . . .

'Was that the postman?' he asked.

'It was.'

'Is there anything . . .' Lorraine bit her lip.

'Nothing very exciting. Save one from the States.'

'From Harry!' Lorraine squealed.

'I would say so.' Mary smiled at her. 'It's for me. But I'll tell you what he says.'

Up to a point, she thought, she she retired to her bedroom and slit the envelope. But she was back a moment later, waving the single sheet of paper. 'He's been assigned to the European Theatre,' she shouted. 'He's coming to England.'

Lorraine had never seen her sister-in-law so excited.

'Ship, two points on the starboard bow,' reported the look out.

320

'Make to flotilla leader,' the Captain said. 'Ask if we should investigate.'

'Message from *Brigham Young*, sir,' said the Petty Officer on the bridge of the light cruiser USS *Joseph Smith*. 'He wishes to know if he should investigate.'

Captain Harry Krantz, commanding the destroyer flotilla, turned his binoculars in the indicated direction, as did his staff.

'A ship, but no smoke,' Lieutenant Bridges remarked.

'Diesel engine,' Harry grunted.

'Unusual, sir. She looks like a trawler.'

'Yeah. Make to *Brigham Young*. Affirmative, and report.'

The message was winked across the turbulent spring seas, and they watched the destroyer leave its position and make its way towards the small vessel which could now be seen with the naked eye.

'It *is* a trawler,' Bridges commented.

'Yeah,' Harry agreed. He was finding it difficult to keep his thoughts on the job. The flotilla was bound for Scapa Flow, and on arrival there would be shore leave. Scapa was at the opposite end of England from King's Martin, but he certainly intended to get down there. After all, he had not seen his sister in more than a year.

And Mary would be there as well.

'A trawler, with a diesel?' Bridges commented again.

'It's the latest thing,' Harry commented.

He wished he could come to a decision about Mary. He had never questioned their mutual attraction, since that never to be forgotten day they had found themselves in each other's arms. But there had been an ocean of emotion and sentiment between them: his friendship for Geoffrey, and his previous marriage to Lizzie. He hadn't been sure that Mary could ever replace her sister, not only in his heart, but in the more intimate aspects of a relationship. Lizzie had bubbled with erotic excitement. Mary had suggested no such enthusiasm. Yet the excitement, and the eroticism, were there, he knew. Just waiting to be aroused.

Something Geoffrey had never done, apparently. She was a woman who needed to be aroused.

But then the ready-made family had been an offput.

And there was the fact that they shared an immense secret. Could a husband and wife risk that?

'Message from *Brigham Young*, sir,' said the Petty Officer.

'Yes?'

'Ship reported as trawler *Mary Elizabeth*, out of Glasgow, Master Jack Smith.'

'Understood,' Bridges said. 'Maybe someone should tell that guy that he's just begging for trouble, this far offshore.'

'*Mary Elizabeth*,' Harry muttered. 'Jack Smith. Son of a gun.'

'Sir?'

'That guy knows what he's doing,' Harry said. 'He's a Q-ship.'

'Sir?'

'He's a decoy, waiting to be attacked by a German submarine.'

Bridges tilted his cap over his eyes. 'You ain't even seen him close to, Captain. How can you know that?'

'Wanna put money on it?' Harry went on to the bridge wing to watch the trawler dropping out of sight. Good old Jack. Doing as dangerous a job as anyone's in the whole Navy.

But somehow, that had just made up his mind.

'Are you sure it was Jack?' Mary asked, as they sat on the stone seat at the foot of the garden. 'There must be hundreds of men in the Royal Navy named Jack Smith, for one reasion or another.'

'Who also name their ships *Mary Elizabeth*?'

'I never thought of that. Oh, that's tremendous, Harry.'

'Yeah. Kind of makes everything worth while.'

'Everything.' She shuddered. 'It just seems to get worse and worse.'

'Don't you believe it. This German push is being held, and it's the very last throw of the dice, as far as Jerry is concerned. Our guys are pouring into France like water from a bust pipe, and Kaiser Bill knows it. Come next year, we'll be ready to roll him up all the way to Berlin.'

'Next year,' she said. 'Another whole year. God, I can hardly remember 1914.'

He grinned. 'I sure can. I can remember coming here, with Lizzie . . . she'd been out collecting flowers, and she wasn't too pleased to see me. But your Ma invited me to stay for lunch. Say, that was the day we heard Jack had absconded from his parole. What were you doing?'

'Being Geoffrey's wife, in London.'

'Yeah.' He was suddenly serious. 'It does seem a long time ago, at that.'

'And now, you say, another year . . . it'll seem like forever.'

'Not if you have something worth waiting for. You have, Mary. The two kids . . . heck, they're gonna inherit this world we're so busy putting to rights.'

Mary's smile was wan. 'Are we putting it to rights, Harry?'

'Well, that's what it's all about, isn't it? We have to believe that, Mary. Think of the end of it. Think of Jack coming home, and Giles . . . say, what's the news about him, anyway?'

'He's in Portsmouth. The summons came last week. The court martial is about to start.'

'Don't brood on that too much. The word is that he'll be honourably acquitted. Those K-Class boats, God, they've turned out to be a disaster. They tried to use some of them in a fleet exercise a couple of weeks ago, and it was a total shambles. Mary . . .' he held her hands. 'Some day, some day soon, this is all going to be over, and then we're going to have to start picking up our lives again. Being normal, if you like.'

'Do you think of that a lot?'

'I have to.'

'What will you do?'

'I'm a professional naval officer, Mary.'

'I know. I meant, with Lorraine, your family home . . .'

'I'll think of something. You ever been to the States?'

She shook her head.

'Well, you know, you folks have put up with Lorraine for just on three years now. I reckon you owe us a return visit. With the kids, of course.'

'I don't think I could leave Ma.'

'We're looking ahead. But . . . maybe Ma could come too.'

'That would be quite an adventure.'

Harry picked up her hand. 'When I asked Lizzie, it just kind of came out. I guess it was because the war had just started, and everyone was excited . . . I sure was.'

'Are you asking me something?' Mary asked.

'I guess so.'

Her gaze was very solemn.

'You want to, don't you?' Harry asked, anxiously. 'I had an idea you might be keen on the idea.'

'I couldn't possibly leave Ma.'

'You know that's exactly what Lizzie said when I asked her? But like I said, when it comes time to return to the States, your Ma will come too.'

'If she'd ever leave this place. Oh, Harry . . .'

'I love you, Mary. I know maybe you think that's a bit much, after having loved Lizzie . . .'

'I don't think that at all. I'm very flattered.'

'And?'

'Well, of course I love you too, Harry . . .'

He took her in his arms. For how long had he wanted to kiss this woman?

When she got her breath back, and it took some time because she had never been kissed like that before, she asked, 'When did you have in mind?'

'I have the licence in my pocket,' he told her.

'Well, what do you know?' Denise asked, sitting up in bed to read the newspaper. 'It says here that last Sunday Captain Harrison Krantz the Second of the United States Navy was married to Mrs Geoffrey Young, widow of the late Captain Geoffrey Young, RN, at the parish church of King's Martin.'

'Let me see that!' Jack had been lying on his back with two-and-a-half-year-old Jack on his chest. Denise obligingly held the paper above them both.

'I think it's tremendous,' she said.

'I couldn't agree with you more. What's that?'

324

He was looking at the headlines.

'Oh, something about Commodore Keyes led a raid on Zeebrugge and Ostend to sink blockships and seal the harbour.'

'Take Jackie.' Jack sat up to appropriate the paper.

'It seems to have been successful,' Denise said. 'According to the paper.'

'Damn,' Jack said. 'Damn, damn, damn.'

'What's the matter, lover? Isn't it good news if two of the principal U-boat bases have been put out of action?'

'I have spent the last eighteen months floating about the Atlantic Ocean in a crummy disguised trawler waiting to get the drop on a U-boat, and now there aren't going to be any more.'

Denise frowned at him. 'Is that what you've been doing?'

Jack glanced at her, and bit his lip. 'Sorry. It slipped out.'

'You've been skippering a Q-ship, all this time?'

'Well . . . yes. It's very secret.'

'I can imagine. Oh, Jack! Why?'

'Because their Lords of the Admiralty told me to do it.'

'Their Lords of the Admiralty,' she said contemptuously. 'The men who thought you were a spy.'

'Well, they had their reasons.'

'Then that time you were wounded, you'd been fighting a U-boat.'

'Not very successfully. The blighter got away. And now, according to the newspaper, there won't be any more.'

'Oh, Jack,' she said, and hugged him, to a squeal from Baby Jack. 'I'm so glad about that.'

In August, Scheer was replaced by Hipper as Commander-in-Chief of the High Seas Fleet. This was part of a general reshuffle. Capelle went from the Ministry of Marine, and Scheer was kicked upstairs. The Navy as a whole greeted the change with some scepticism. No one could argue that Hipper had proved himself the most talented commander of the war, perhaps, indeed, on both sides. But after so long sitting in port there were not many who actually wished to be sent to sea, even under such a leader, to engage a Royal Navy which was now stronger than ever – and reinforced by several capital units of the US Navy.

Even the most warlike amongst the officers doubted whether the new appointment had come in time.

Only Bruno von Eltz greeted the news with undisguised pleasure. 'Now, surely you will take us to sea to fight,' he said, when he got the new Admiral alone.

'It would be a suicide mission,' Hipper said gloomily.

'Better that than sitting here.'

'We shall have to see,' Hipper said. 'There are still the submarines.'

For Keyes' raid, brilliant though it was, had not entirely closed the Belgian ports. Passages were found round the sunken ships, and the ships themselves were demolished by high explosives. When *U76* put to sea at the end of August, *Indomitable* was nothing more than a rusting hulk in the centre of the estuary.

Yet Dorf, and his men, were sufficiently sombre. The Battle of Amiens had been fought, and lost. The first day of that battle, when the British tanks, for the time used in squadrons instead of piecemeal, had swarmed irresistibly across the German trenches, had been described by Field-Marshal von Ludendorf himself as 'the black day of the German Army'. The war was lost, and all that could be retrieved was honour.

And revenge.

But Dorf knew even that was going to be difficult. The convoy system was now so well-developed, and each convoy so heavily protected, there were no easy pickings to be had. And Dorf, for all his undoubted courage, was not a man to indulge in suicide attacks. Thus this foray was a failure from the first. He and his men sighted sufficient targets, but could not get close enough for a kill. They fired their torpedoes from long range, and then desperately sought the safety of the depths, while enemy depth charges boomed around them, and the engineers tightened rivets and patched leaks. But when they finally turned for home, for the first time they had to accept the fact that they had scored no kills.

Until, in mid-September, as they made their way towards the north of Scotland, homeward bound after a fruitless voyage, they sighted a lone trawler, apparently drifting as her crew hauled their nets.

CHAPTER 12

Scapa

'Periscope astern,' Mann said.

Jack levelled his glasses. How many times had he done this, seeking a repeat of that one engagement, which he had definitely lost? Since then, he and his men had rehearsed their drill time and again, without having the opportunity to put his ideas into practice.

But there was always a first time.

'All right, Meeker,' he said. 'Time to change.'

'Aye-aye,' Meeker acknowledged, and went below. Mann took the helm, while the crew, alerted by Meeker, continued to haul their net, slowly and carefully, chatting amongst themselves.

The sky was heavily overcast, promising bad weather in the near future, but for the moment the sea was like glass, the Atlantic swell undulating slowly up and down; the sliver of white foam cut by the U-boat's periscope was easy to pick up.

Jack watched it veer away to starboard, and muttered a curse. But it did not disappear, instead slowly moved forward until it was abeam of the trawler, at a distance of just over half a mile. Once again Jack thought of a shark, circling its victim, deciding whether to attack . . .

Perhaps it could be encouraged. He stepped on to the bridge wing, away from the submarine. 'Chidgey,' he said. 'Spot the periscope and have hysterics. Bishop, when he does, run aft and lower the ensign. Williams, you try to stop him. Start now.'

'We have seen this trawler before,' Dorf remarked. 'I recognise the name, *Mary Elizabeth*. Always by herself. There is something strange about her.'

328

'Shall we leave her?' Albrichtson asked.

'Perhaps . . . they have seen us. My God, they are panicking. One of them is pointing and jumping up and down. Another is running aft to strike the colours. One of the others is trying to stop him. And their skipper is on the bridge wing, shouting and waving his arms. They are terrified.'

'Do you not suppose it could be a trap, Herr Kapitan?'

'I do not care if it is. We will have this bastard, Albrichtson, so we will take at least one success back to Germany with us. Surface, and tell the gun crew to put a shot across her bows.'

'Well done, lads,' Jack said. 'He's coming up.'

The sailors gathered in a knot amidships, as usual. Williams had so far succeeded in 'preventing' Bishop from striking the flag so that it still flew. Now they watched the grey conning tower breaking the surface, the officers immediately appearing on the bridge, the gunners gathering on the foredeck as it too emerged out of the sea, water cascading down its sides.

Meeker reappeared on the bridge, having changed his clothes. Although he still wore canvas trousers and a heavy sweater, these were of excellent quality, and a sub-lieutenant's epaulettes had been sewn on to the shoulders of his sweater, while he wore an officer's cap. There was of course no way any genuine Q-ship captain would be seen in such revealing gear, but the Germans would not know that.

'Good lad,' Jack said. 'Stand by.'

The gun on the submarine's foredeck flashed, and a moment later the shell splashed into the sea, some hundred yards away. The trawler trembled, and spray scattered across the bridge shield.

By now the lamp on the conning tower was winking.

'All right, Bishop, strike the flag,' Jack said, at the same time putting the engine into neutral.

Bishop hurried aft, and the Red Ensign fluttered down. Bishop folded it up and tucked it under his arm.

The lamp winked again.

'Break out the dinghy,' Jack said.

Mann and three of the crew hurried forward. Chidgey was keeping out of sight. The cover was taken off the boat, the falls attached, and it was winched up the mast and swung over the side.

The lamp winked.

'You have three minutes,' Jack called down, by now keeping out of sight himself on the port wing.

The boat splashed into the water, on the side of the ship overseen by the U-boat.

'All right, Meeker, do your stuff,' Jack muttered.

Meeker slid down the ladder and hurried forward, carrying the satchel which would undoubtedly contain the ship's papers. He climbed down the ladder into the waiting boat, which the crew then pushed off, and began to row away from the trawler, and out of the line of fire.

'Stand by,' Jack called down to Chidgey, who was already in the hold, and would be loading the gun.

'Shall I call the Englanders over for interrogation, Herr Kapitan?' Albrichtson asked.

'They cannot get very far. We will sink the trawler first,' Dorf decided, still inspecting *Mary Elizabeth* through his glasses. The ship looked utterly deserted, yet he had an instinctive gut feeling that all was not as it should be: the abandonment had been too quick, too subservient – but he intended to sink it, anyway. 'Range?' he inquired.

'Six hundred yards, Herr Kapitan.'

'Close. We wish to send her down as rapidly as possible.'

U76's diesels growled and she turned towards the trawler.

'Damn,' Jack muttered, crouching in the lee of the bridge. Head-on the submarine presented less of a target. But he was still determined to get her.

He could only imagine Chidgey's feelings; the gunlayer would have no idea of what was going on.

'Five hundred yards, Herr Kapitan,' Albrichtson said.

'Very good. Put a shot on to her waterline, amidships.'

Through his binoculars, Jack watched the gun being depressed, and knew he could not afford to wait any longer. He ran into the wheelhouse and put the throttles ahead, spinning the helm to starboard as he did so. Then he ran out on to the after platform and set the White Ensign, at the same time pressing the button which caused the topsides to drop away and expose the gun.

'Fire as you bear,' Dorf said, and then stared in consternation as the trawler suddenly surged forward, at the same time turning towards him.

Almost in the same moment there was a flutter of white from the halliard above her bridge, and he found himself looking at a four-point-seven-inch gun.

His own gun exploded, but because of the sudden burst of speed the shot plunged into the sea astern of its target, and now the trawler, having turned a complete circle to bring herself within four hundred yards of him, was losing way as her engine was again thrust into neutral, and he watched a big man sliding down the ladder to the deck, and then the hold where the gun was.

Dorf grabbed the speaking tube. 'Dive, dive, dive,' he shouted. 'Gun crew below.'

But it was too late. At such a range even a near miss was most effective. The trawler's gun exploded and in the same instant a tremendous fountain of water arose from the stern of the U-boat.

'Herr Kapitan!' The voice came up from below. 'We are hit! We are taking water!'

The deck was already awash, and the gun crew were swarming up the ladder.

'Reverse order,' Dorf snapped into the tube. 'Surface and bring me an accurate damage report. Get down and resume firing,' he told the Petty Officer in charge of the gun. 'Sink that ship.'

'Hurrah!' Chidgey shouted, throwing his cap in the air.

331

'We need another,' Jack told him, forcing a fresh round into the breech. 'Traverse left and raise.'

The gun barrel swung and came up, while Jack watched the submarine cease submerging; her guncrew were back on deck, splashing through ankle deep water.

'Fire!'

Chidgey jerked the lanyard, and the trawler rolled to the recoil. And more than that, as there came an explosion from forward; the Germans had fired at almost the same time at themselves, and with more accuracy, for Chidgey's second shot had raised only a waterspout.

Stopped, of course, the trawler was an easier target than the U-boat, which was still moving, but the range was only two hundred yards. In terms of cannon they were eyeball to eyeball.

'Traverse right,' Jack yelled. 'Depress . . .'

Not for the first time in his life, everything went black. He found himself lying on his back, staring at the sky, while a tremendous noise rang in his ears. He forced himself to sit up, gazed at Chidgey, or what was left of him. The German shell had landed just astern of the gun, and a piece of metal flying from the afterdeck had taken Chidgey's head off as cleanly as any headsman could have done; there was blood everywhere. The blast had also dismounted the gun, which lay with its barrel pointing at the sky.

That water was seeping over the floor of the hold hardly seemed relevant.

'Got the bastard,' Dorf said, with some satisfaction, as he watched the pillar of smoke rising from the trawler's gun emplacement.

'Shall we put another shell into him?'

'He is sinking,' Dorf said. 'Where is that damage report?'

'Here, Herr Kapitan,' said the engineer, at the head of the ladder. 'The British shell landed in the sea close by our stern, and forced several rivets. We took in some considerable amount of water. But the damage is being repaired, and the water is being pumped out now.'

'Can we submerge?'

'Within ten minutes, Herr Kapitan.'

'Ten minutes, Dortmann. Albrichtson, signal that Englander boat to come alongside. As the crew of a Q-ship, they are prisoners of war.'

'Yes, Herr Kapitan.' Albrichtson turned to the signalling lamp, and looked past it at the trawler. 'Herr Kapitan!' he shouted. 'Herr Kapitan!'

Jack knew that his ship was taking water; it concerned him far more that she was now disarmed and helpless. Or was she? Two hundred yards . . . he leapt to his feet and scrambled up the ladder, reached the bridge, and again thrust the throttle forward, seizing the helm to steer.

Dorf gazed at the hundred tons or so of metal charging him. 'Fire!' he shouted at the guncrew. 'Dive, dive, dive.' He virtually pushed Albrichtson down the ladder.

The gun exploded, but at the rapidly closing range the shell passed over the top of the trawler to explode in the sea astern.

'Hurry,' Dorf shouted at the gun crew, as they scrambled up the ladder, only just ahead of the water, which was already swirling over the deck. Dorf saw them down, stepped into the hatchway himself, and looked up at the bows of the trawler, only feet away.

Jack was holding on to the wheel with all his strength, steering straight for the conning tower. He knew he was badly wounded, could feel waves of pain seeping up his body, understood that he might only have a few minutes of consciousness left . . . but he intended to have this U-boat. Now he looked down, on the rapidly sinking conning tower, the officer who was standing in the hatch staring up at him, and a moment later there was a shattering crunch which threw him away from the wheel and half across the bridge.

He turned on his knees, held on to the broken windshield, ignoring the glass which cut into his fingers, and pulled himself to his feet. *Mary Elizabeth* had ridden over the submarine's deck, and he looked down at the grey hull, rolled half on its side by the impact. For the moment it was beneath him, and he could see the officer on the conning tower, blood streaming from a head wound; he had been thrown against the bulkhead, as *Mary Elizabeth* had struck just aft of the tower.

But now, engine screaming its protest, she was trying to get right across the after deck, and instead slipping sideways, tortured metal screeching against tortured metal, until she slid off the stern.

Jack reached for the wheel again to bring her round. The U-boat was wallowing, low in the water, certainly, and unable to dive because of the great gash at the foot of the conning tower, but still very much afloat. As he watched, men came out of the conning tower again, and some of them were attempting to regain the deck, thigh deep in water, and use the gun.

Round came *Mary Elizabeth*. Jack could hear gurgling noises from beneath him, and he was losing speed; she must be holed beneath the waterline. But her diesel engine would operate just as long as it was receiving air from the intake; he had a few minutes yet.

The German seamen saw him coming back and yelled their fear. The gun crew abandoned their attempts to fire again and leapt into the sea. The wounded officer on the tower waved his arms; he had been joined by another man who was staring at the trawler as if hypnotised.

But there was nothing any of them could do. For a second time, *Mary Elizabeth* slammed into the U-boat's hull.

This time the jar was even greater, as *Mary Elizabeth* was now lower in the water, and therefore could not ride up over the submarine's hull. Once again Jack was sent staggering across the bridge to come to rest against the after bulkhead.

From the series of crunching thuds which kept coming from forward he knew that the trawler was trying to forge ahead, her shattered bow now firmly locked to the huge gash she had opened in her adversary. When he pushed himself back to the helm, he listened to a crack which resounded even above the

334

shouts and the throb of the engines and the seethe of the water, and realised that one of the officers on the conning tower had fired a revolver at him.

He grinned. That wasn't going to make any difference now, and the officer was not going to have the chance to fire again, as men crowded up the ladder from below, where hundreds of gallons of water were pouring into the hull, to jostle him aside.

Jack put the throttle astern, and there was an even louder scream of tortured metal. For a few moments nothing happened, then *Mary Elizabeth* pulled back, taking with her a sizeable chunk of U-boat. Even as Jack watched, water gurgled into this, and the submarine sank like a stone, her crew desperately throwing themselves away from her.

But *Mary Elizabeth* herself clearly only had a few minutes to live. Her shattered bows were very low in the sea, and water was flowing across her foredeck, while now the diesel finally died. Jack dragged himself on to the bridge wing, aware that there was suddenly a great silence, save for the shouts of the men in the water, but that his own ears were still singing.

He looked across the sea and spotted the lifeboat, about a quarter of a mile away, but pulling back towards him. It was time to go.

He slid down the ladder to the main deck, landed up to his ankles in water. Only seconds now. He pulled off his sea boots, wondering at the amount of blood which was running down his legs, as he felt no pain at all, and stepped off the deck into the water, which was considerably colder than he had expected. His head went under, then he was on the surface again, and swimming as vigorously as he could.

Deja vu. Visions of *Good Hope*, and *Scharnhorst*, and then *Queen Mary*, surged across his mind. He supposed he had never had it so good, since *Scharnhorst*. Here again was a bright day, even if it was autumn instead of summer, and a calm sea . . . but he was so cold. Colder than he remembered even in the North Sea in May. And no matter how hard he was swimming, he didn't seem to be making a great deal of progress.

A wave rolled over him, and he was sucked down by a tug on his legs. *Mary Elizabeth* had gone. Desperately he fought his way back up, gulped at the fresh air, and turned on his back to float.

He listened to shouts. The Germans, presumably.

But at least one of the shouts was in English. 'Hold on, Mr Smith. Hold on.'

That was Petty Officer Mann. A good man, Petty Officer Mann. Jack smiled at his own joke. He was still smiling when the dinghy reached him.

Bruno von Eltz sat in his day cabin on board *Kaiser Wilhelm I* and drank coffee while he studied his newspaper. Poor Dorf. No one knew what had happened, as the British had made no claims. But the fact was that *U76* had not returned from its last patrol. It was now a month overdue, and it had to be accepted that it was lost.

Still, Dorf had had a good innings, earned himself several additional medals to wear beneath his Pour Le Merite, and a good deal of publicity. And he undoubtedly had died fighting the enemy, or the sea; both were worthwhile opponents.

While we rot in port, he thought bitterly.

But the following day he was summoned to a senior officers' meeting on board *Friedrich Wilhelm der Grosse*.

'Gentlemen,' Hipper said. 'There can be no doubt that the war is lost. Our armies are holding on by the skin of their teeth, and more and more Americans are landing in France every day. But more important is the situation on the home front. Our people are starving, and as a result they have lost their will to continue this struggle. Total collapse can only be a matter of time.'

He paused to let that sink in before continuing.

'The question remains, therefore, as to what we are going to do with the fleet. We have here one of the mightiest fighting forces the world has ever known; it is the second most powerful fleet in the world. Are we going to sit here and wait for the allied soldiers to appear on the dock and demand our surrender? Or are we going to put to sea and at least inflict as severe losses on the enemy as is possible?'

'We must put to sea,' Bruno declared.

'My own feelings entirely. May I take it we are unanimous about this?'

He looked from face to face. Not all the other admirals looked quite as enthusiastic as Bruno, but there were no dissents.

'Very good, gentlemen. It seems to me that we can hardly improve on our previous dispositions. I know it is late in the year, but the weather will be the same for the British. My orders are therefore as follows: The First Scouting Group will put to sea on the morning of 15 October, and make for the English coast. They will carry out bombardments of coastal towns, as in the old days. The High Seas Fleet will follow them, and take up a position between Rosyth and Aberdeen, one hundred miles off the coast. From there we will cover both the British Battlecruiser Squadron in Rosyth, and the Grand Fleet in Scapa Flow. When they come out, as assuredly they will, we will offer battle. And this time, gentlemen, there will be no hurrying back to port because we are outnumbered. We will fight it out to the end. Is this understood.'

'Understood, Herr Admiral,' Bruno said.

He returned to *Kaiser Wilhelm I* and summoned Flag-Captain Becker, who had last served with him, as a lieutenant, on *Roon*.

'Good news, Becker,' he said. 'The best news. We are going after the British.'

'Herr Konteradmiral?'

'Admiral Hipper is taking us to sea, to seek and destroy the British. Is that not splendid news?'

Becker scratched his ear.

'I wish you to issue my instructions to all members of the crews of the squadron. Next Thursday, October 15, this squadron will put to sea as part of the High Seas Fleet on a mission to engage the Grand Fleet.'

'With respect, Herr Konteradmiral, if that order is issued now, there will be time for it to be leaked, and perhaps picked up by a British agent.'

'That does not matter,' Bruno said ebulliently. 'We are going to fight, this time. We do not care if the British are waiting for us off Heligoland. In fact, that would suit us better.'

'Yes, Herr Konteradmiral.' Becker continued to be doubtful.

'Draft that order, and have it circulated, Becker. Tell the men this is the moment for which we have been waiting for more than four years. Tell them that this time we are going to conquer or we are going to die, for the Fatherland. Understood?'

Becker saluted, and withdrew.

Bruno dined, had a couple of glasses of champagne, and went to bed in a happier frame of mind that he had done for four years. In his imagination he saw a battle such as had been fought of old, with the great ships engaging at almost point blank range, blowing each other out of the water. Of course he was going to die. But that was what he most fervently wanted to happen, if it could be done fighting the British, taking as many of them as possible down with him.

He slept soundly, was awakened by his new valet, Heinrich, soon after dawn.

'Kapitan Becker is here to see you, Herr Konteradmiral.'

'Ah!' Bruno got up, put on the dressing gown Heinrich was holding for him, inserted his crutch into his armpit, and went into his day cabin. 'Has the message been circulated, Becker?' Then he frowned. Becker looked as if he had seen a ghost. 'What is the matter, man?'

'Herr Konteradmiral . . . the men are refusing to put to sea.'

Bruno's frown deepened. 'What are you saying?'

'I have received a deputation from the crew, Herr Konteradmiral. It is headed by the Petty Officers. They are saying that the men refuse to sail to fight against the British.'

'Why not?'

338

'Because, they say, they, we, the German Navy, will be destroyed.'

'Are they not aware that they are committing mutiny?'

'They are aware of that, Herr Konteradmiral.'

'Well, they must suffer for it. Have a wireless message sent to the other ships in the squadron, commanding them to train their guns upon the flagship.'

'Herr Konteradmiral . . . all the other ships are also refusing to go to sea.'

Bruno stared at him, then limped on to the gallery, to look across the harbour at his squadron. On each ship, the entire company was assembled on deck, standing to attention as if about to undergo an inspection. The officers stood on the various bridges.

He looked down at his own ship; there too the men stood to attention, while immediately beneath him his own officers were also gathered, muttering uncertainly to each other.

Bruno went to the wireless room, where the operators waited. 'Get me Admiral Hipper,' he snapped.

One of the telegraphers immediately sat down and made the call.

'I wish to speak with the Admiral personally,' Bruno said.

'I am here, Herr Konteradmiral,' Hipper said a few moments later. His voice sounded more tired that Bruno had ever known.

'Herr Admiral, I have to report a catastrophe,' Bruno said.

'Your men have mutinied,' Hipper said.

'But . . .'

'So have mine, Bruno. There is no ship in this entire fleet willing to put to sea.'

'But . . . Herr Admiral. What are we to do?'

'Accept that everything we have ever stood for, ever fought for, ever believed in, has come to an end, Bruno. I will wish you good fortune.'

The radio went dead.

339

Bruno looked from face to face. His officers looked bewildered, uncertain, even afraid. None of them had ever envisaged anything like this happening, in their wildest nightmares. But then, neither had he.

He managed a smile. 'Well, gentlemen,' he said. 'It seems that we are to have a holiday.'

When next the High Seas Fleet put to sea, it was following the German surrender of 11 November, and under the terms of the Armistice, eleven battleships, five battlecruisers, eight light cruisers, fifty destroyers, and every remaining U-boat, steamed into Scapa Flow past the guns of the Allied Fleet, to surrender.

Konteradmiral Bruno von Eltz was second-in-command of the surrendering fleet.

The hired trap drew up at the gate of Silver Streams, and Mary frowned at the somewhat small woman in black getting down, and then helping the child to the ground before paying the driver.

The child was a boy, about three years old, holding his mother's hand but walking sturdily beside her as the pair of them came down the drive; the woman carried a valise in her other hand.

And Mary suddenly recognised her, even if they hadn't seen each other for more than ten years.

'Dalton!' she shouted. 'Out front.'

She dashed outside herself.

'Denise!' she cried.

'Mary!'

Dalton arrived to relieve Denise of the suitcase, while Mary peered at the little boy.

'My son,' Denise said. 'Jack.'

Mary gave her a suspicious glance. 'I had no idea you were married.'

'I got married nearly four years ago.'

'Oh!' Mary's glance was even more suspicious as she looked at the boy again.

340

'Yes. I'm afraid Jack is nearly three and a half.'

Mary gulped. 'You'd better come along inside. Ma,' she called. 'You remember Denise Robertson? Or . . . what is your name, now?'

'Dawson,' Denise said.

Harriet had just come in from the kitchen, and Lorraine in from the back yard, where she had been playing with Joan and Mark.

All three of the women stared at Denise.

'I haven't come to make a nuisance of myself,' Denise told them. 'I came because I thought you might like to see your grandson, Mrs Dawson. And because I thought you should know about Jack, now.'

'Jack?' Harriet whispered. 'You married Jack?'

'Yes,' Denise said.

'But . . .' Mary looked at the black dress. 'Oh, my God!' Now that the war was over, she had dreamed of Jack coming home, with his wife, of course.

'Jack rejoined the Navy as an Ordinary Seaman,' Denise explained. 'And rose to be a Sub-Lieutenant. He got the VC. Then he was given command of a Q-ship, to fight the submarines. He was killed in an action with a submarine last October. I . . . I didn't know what had happened. He simply didn't come home on leave as he usually did. I only learned the truth yesterday. The Admiralty wouldn't allow details to be released until yesterday, because of the secrecy surrounding those ships.'

'Jack?' Harriet sat down.

'That's why I felt I could tell you, now. I promised never to do so while he was alive. To the Navy, he died as Sub-Lieutenant Jack Smith. But I told them who he really was.'

'What did they say?' Mary asked.

'Well, they have to check into it. But I think we may be able to clear his name.' She sat beside her mother-in-law. 'He was a hero, Mrs Dawson. I think he probably saw more action than anyone else in the Navy. Shall I tell you about it?'

Harriet stared at her, and then looked at Little Jack, was was standing shyly in the doorway. 'Please,' she said. 'I would

341

like that.' She held out her arms. 'Won't you come and give your grandma a hug, Jack?'

'Is everything prepared?' asked Konteradmiral Reuter.

The various officers standing around the cabin of *Friedrich Wilhelm der Grosse* nodded, as the Admiral looked from face to face.

'Very good then,' Reuter said. 'I do not know what the British reaction will be, but at least I am sure that they will not shoot us. The world would not stand for that. And I want you all clearly to understand that this is no wanton act of destruction that we are going to commit. The Allies have seen fit to impose the most stringent terms upon our country, and our so-called Government has accepted them. We are therefore forced to make the decision between handing over our ships to our enemies, or acting in accordance with our honour as German officers. What we are to do will resound through the pages of history, and with fortune, will inspire those who come behind us and who will once again raise the flag of the Imperial German Navy.'

He shook hands with each man in turn. 'I thank you all,' he said, and saluted.

Bruno's steam launch was waiting to take him back to *Kaiser Wilhelm I*, and Becker was waiting for him on the bridge.

'It is to be tonight,' Bruno told him, and went into his day cabin.

Becker followed. He worried about his superior. Of course every officer in the Navy had undergone a traumatic nine months, beginning with the mutiny of last October, then the surrender of Germany and the Fleet, and now this long six months' wait here in the remotest part of the British Isles. But during this period all of the dead wood had been removed, leaving only skeleton crews, men who were absolutely reliable and trustworthy, and who almost from the day of their surrender had had no doubt what they needed to do. And would do.

Men who therefore had been enabled to recover from the mood of deep depression that had swept the fleet, who felt they still had something to contribute to the history of Germany, however negatively.

Becker had never doubted that his commanding officer fully shared all of those sentiments. But Bruno had hardly ever smiled since that October day. Of course, he had not smiled all that often before it. His had been a life of almost unrelieved tragedy.

But over the past week he had seemed even more depressed than before. Becker had no doubt of Bruno's courage or determination; it had been proved time and again. But still. . .

'Will you give the order, Herr Konteradmiral?' he asked.

Bruno nodded. 'When it is time. I will inspect the charges, first.'

'Yes, Herr Konteradmiral. Herr Konteradmiral . . . the officers and I would be honoured if you would dine with us in the Wardroom, on this special occasion.'

Bruno looked up, obviously surprised. Although he was sure of his officers' respect, he had never endeavoured to make friends of them.

'We would also be pleased, Herr Konteradmiral.'

'That is very good of you, Becker. But I think I would prefer to dine alone, on this special occasion. We will inspect the charges at eleven o'clock.'

Becker hesitated, then saluted, and left the cabin.

Bruno opened the English newspaper which lay on his desk. It still felt strange, to be reading a paper other than one of his own. But that was behind him now. Reuger had his instructions; the von Eltz Newspapers would become a public company.

Because nothing that had been mattered in comparison with what was. For the sixth time he read the report:

'MYSTERY OF NAVAL HERO,' was the headline. And beneath, 'The Admiralty today released the true facts about Lieutenant Jack Dawson, VC and bar, DCM, RN. Committed to prison for spying in 1906, Jack Dawson rejoined the service that he loved as Ordinary Seaman Jack Smith, and rose through the ranks to Sub-Lieutenant, fighting at the Battles of Coronel and the Falklands, as well as Jutland. It was at Jutland that he gained his first Victoria Cross. The second was awarded posthumously after his gallant action in virtually single-handedly sinking a German U-boat, *U76*, off the Western Islands last September.

'Lieutenant Dawson was the son of . . .'

Slowly Bruno crumpled the newspaper in his fist. He wondered if, when he finally reached the other side, Jack Dawson would be there to greet him. Naval hero! All of his life he had dreamed of being a naval hero. Well, to most people he was, after bringing his crippled ship home from Jutland. But that had been Dorf's doing, as much as his.

And now Dorf was dead, killed by Jack Dawson. Bruno had always supposed that one day, if Jack had really survived, they would confront each other, man to man, in the best traditions of chivalry. Instead it had been Dorf. And Dorf was dead. Thus there was nothing, and no one, left. Save himself. And he had been here far too long.

Heinrich served him dinner, and he had a glass of brandy afterwards. By then Becker was waiting for him.

Bruno could now get around the ship very well, even handling ladders with the greatest of ease, despite his crutch, even if he was well aware that the officers accompanying him were always hovering, waiting for him to fall.

Now he and Becker descended into the very bowels of the ship, the double hull beneath the engine room, to survey the charges which had been placed wherever they would cause mortal, and speedy, damage.

'Very good, Becker. Very good,' Bruno said. 'Now, the charges will be set at five minutes to midnight, to explode at midnight exactly. The moment the charges have been set, you will abandon ship, taking all hands into the boats, and rowing as quietly as possible for the shore. When you are challenged, you will surrender. But before you reach the shore the charges will have gone off. However, you will make no attempt to escape

344

in the confusion, or to resist arrest. You must surrender, in an orderly fashion. Is this understood?'

'Yes, Herr Konteradmiral,' Becker said. 'But . . . will not you be in command?'

'It is always possible that something may happen to me,' Bruno said. 'I wish you to understand what is in my mind.'

'Of course, Herr Konteradmiral,' Becker said.

Bruno drank another glass of brandy; food and drink were the only two pleasures remaining to him. By the time he was finished, it was half past eleven.

Heinrich appeared in the bulkhead doorway. 'I have packed your bag, Herr Konteradmiral.'

'And your own, I hope?'

'Yes, Herr Konteradmiral.'

'You have been a good servant to me, Heinrich.'

'Thank you, Herr Konteradmiral.

'I do not know how long it will take for you to be repatriated, but when you are, I wish you to visit Herr Reuger, Managing Editor of my newspaper.'

Heinrich waited.

'He will have something for you, which will make these long years in the Navy worthwhile. Do you understand this, Heinrich?'

'Yes, Herr Konteradmiral.' Heinrich looked puzzled, but his master's instructions were never to be questioned.

'Very good, Heinrich. Now it is time to leave. Take the bags down to the boat, and get on board.'

'Yes, Herr Konteradmiral. Will you not come with me?'

'I have certain things to do, first.'

Heinrich saluted, badly – he had never been a professional sailor – and left with the bags. Bruno picked up the intercom. 'Becker?'

'Yes, Herr Konteradmiral.'

'Fire the charges, and abandon ship.'

'As soon as you are at the boat station, Herr Konteradmiral.'

'I gave you an order, Herr Kapitan,' Bruno snapped. 'Fire the charges now.'

There was a moment's hesitation, as an understanding of what his commanding officer intended penetrated Becker's intelligence – and as, no doubt, so many other cryptic remarks and orders fell into place.

'With respect, Herr Konteradmiral . . .'

'Becker, either carry out my orders now, or place yourself under arrest. And Becker, I am armed. If anyone attempts to come up to the bridge I shall shoot him. Is this understood?'

Becker gulped. 'Yes, Herr Konteradmiral.'

'Thank you, Becker. I wish you to know that it has been a great pleasure serving with you, and I wish you every good fortune in the future.'

Bruno replaced the phone, got up, inserted his crutch into his armpit, and limped to the bridge wing. From there he could look down on the small group of men assembled at the boat station. A minute passed, and then they began to board the boat, and he watched the figure of Becker emerge from the bottom of the superstructure. The Captain got into the boat, and immediately it was swung out and descended into the water.

Bruno looked across the anchorage at the other ships. The night was dark, chosen for that purpose – there was no moon. But here and there he caught a glimpse of an oar flashing. No doubt such telltale signs would also be noticed from the shore, and from the anchor watches on board the Royal Navy ships guarding the Germans . . . But by the time the British understood that something was wrong and took steps to discover what that something was, it would be too late.

He looked down at the boat, now some forty feet from the ship's side. The crew had stopped rowing, and now they all rose in their places, standing to attention, and saluted. Bruno didn't know if they could see him or not, but he saluted in return. Then he went back inside, and descended the internal ladders as rapidly as he could, slipping on one flight and losing his crutch, so that he and it landed at the foot with a bone-jarring crunch.

Panting, he grasped the steel and pulled himself upright, looked at his watch. It was one minute to midnight. Slowly he dragged himself to the next ladder. He reached it on the stroke of midnight.

'Son of gun,' Harry commented, as he sat beside Mary on the bench at the foot of the garden at Silver Streams, and read *The Times*. 'I mean, you have to take off your hat to those guys.'

'They should be imprisoned for contravening the terms of the surrender,' Mary said fiercely.

'And all become martyrs? I reckon they did what any patriotic officers would have done.'

Mary glared at him, and then smiled. 'Yes. Of course you're right. And they have their martyr, anyway.'

'Yeah. I know you hated his guts, but he was quite a guy. Would you believe, that out of all the naval attaches who were on board *Mikasa* at the Battle of Tsushima, I'm the only one left alive?'

'I'm glad there's at least one.'

'I also have the least number of medals. The ones that matter, anyway. Maybe there's a moral in that. But say, here's the good news; I'm being posted home. So you're booked on the *Mauretania*.'

'Oh, Harry!' Her face filled with excitement. 'But . . .'

'It's time you saw the old family home. It's yours, now, you know.'

'Oh, Harry! But how can I possibly leave Ma?'

'Well, as I said, she's welcome to come too.'

'She won't want to leave England. It'd mean she wouldn't see Little Jack every weekend.'

'Well, it seems to me she has a choice.' He pointed to where Giles – on leave after being exonerated of blame for the sinking of K1 – and Lorraine were dismounting from their horses in the paddock. 'She can come to the States and live with her daughter and her son-in-law, and visit England whenever she feels the urge, or she can stay here and live with her son and her two daughters-in-law, and grandson, and visit us whenever she has the urge.' He grinned. 'Or she can do both, for six months of every year.'

'To be able to plan like that, to travel as and when we please, without danger . . .' Mary hugged herself. 'Was it worth it, Harry? All of those lives? All those people we loved? Even those we hated.'

He knew she was thinking of Bruno and Helene.

He squeezed her hands. 'We have to believe that, my dearest girl. We just have to.'